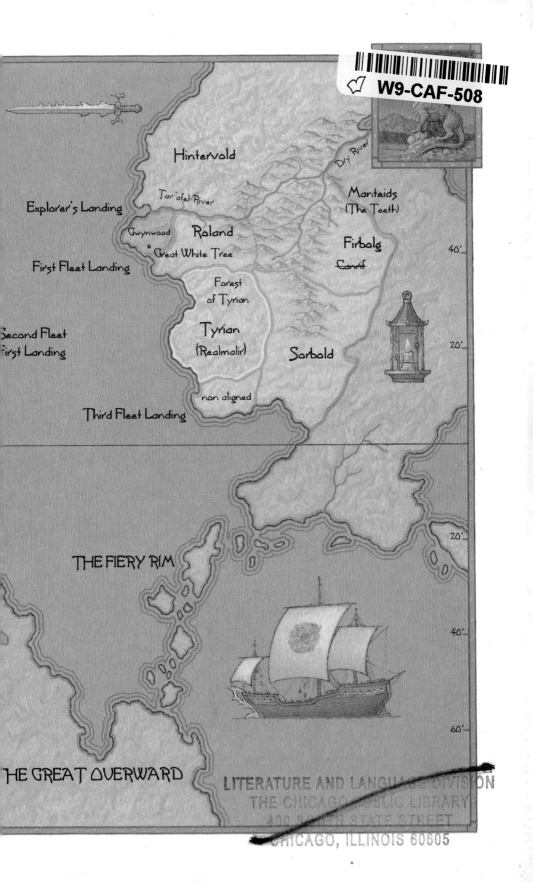

Hintervold

Dry River

Tar'afel River

Manteids
(The Teeth)

Explorer's Landing

Gwynwood   Roland

Firbolg

Great White Tree

Canrif

40°

First Fleet Landing

Forest
of Tyrian

Second Fleet
First Landing

Tyrian
(Realmalir)

Sorbold

20°

non aligned

Third Fleet Landing

THE FIERY RIM

20°

40°

60°

HE GREAT OVERWARD

The Assassin King

The Symphony of Ages Books by Elizabeth Haydon

Rhapsody: Child of Blood

Prophecy: Child of Earth

Destiny: Child of the Sky

Requiem for the Sun

Elegy for a Lost Star

The Assassin King

The Assassin King

BOOK SIX OF
THE SYMPHONY *of* AGES

Elizabeth Haydon

A TOM DOHERTY ASSOCIATES BOOK
New York

THE ASSASSIN KING

Copyright © 2006 by Elizabeth Haydon

Maps and ornaments by Ed Gazsi

A Tor Book
Published by Tom Doherty Associates, LLC
175 Fifth Avenue
New York, NY 10010

www.tor.com

Tor® is a registered trademark of Tom Doherty Associates, LLC.

Library of Congress Cataloging-in-Publication Data

Haydon, Elizabeth.
    The assassin king / Elizabeth Haydon.
        p. cm.
    "A Tom Doherty Associates book."
    ISBN-13: 978-0-765-30565-7
    ISBN-10: 0-765-30565-8
    I. Title.

PS3558.A82896A9 2006
813'.54—dc22

                                    2006025852

First Edition: January 2007

Printed in the United States of America

0 9 8 7 6 5 4 3 2 1

*For Rhiannon
and Brayden,
with love*

ACKNOWLEDGMENTS

I'd like to express my grateful appreciation to my editor, Anna Genoese, for her patience and vision, and to my family, for all their support and love.

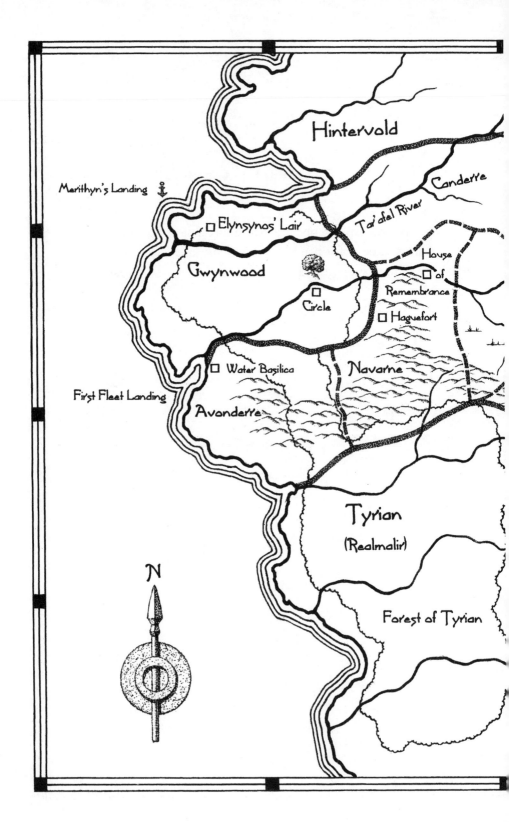

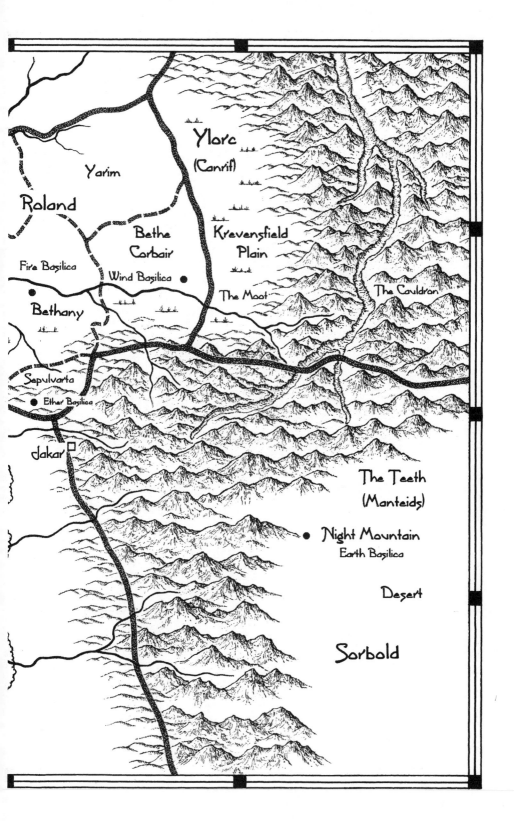

ODE

We are the music-makers,
And we are the dreamers of dreams,
Wandering by lone sea-breakers,
And sitting by desolate streams;
World-losers and world-forsakers,
On whom the pale moon gleams:
Yet we are the movers and shakers
Of the world for ever, it seems.

With wonderful deathless ditties
We build up the world's great cities,
And out of a fabulous story
We fashion an empire's glory:
One man with a dream, at pleasure,
Shall go forth and conquer a crown;
And three with a new song's measure
Can trample an empire down.

We, in the ages lying
In the buried past of the earth,
Built Nineveh with our sighing,
And Babel itself with our mirth;
And o'erthrew them with prophesying
To the old of the new world's worth;
For each age is a dream that is dying,
Or one that is coming to birth.

—Arthur O'Shaughnessy

THE POEM OF SEVEN

Seven Gifts of the Creator,

Seven colors of light,

Seven seas in the wide world,

Seven days in a sennight,

Seven months of fallow,

Seven continents trod, weave

Seven eras of history

In the eye of God.

SONG OF THE SKY LOOM

Oh, our Mother the Earth;
Oh, our Father the Sky,
Your children are we,
With tired backs.
We bring you the gifts you love.

Then weave for us a garment of brightness. . . .
May the warp be the white light of morning,
May the weft be the red light of evening,
May the fringes be the fallen rain,
May the border be the standing rainbow.

Thus weave for us a garment of brightness
That we may walk fittingly where birds sing;
That we may walk fittingly where the grass is green.

Oh, our Mother Earth;

Oh, our Father Sky.

—*Traditional, Tewa*

THE WEAVER'S LAMENT

Time, it is a tapestry

Threads that weave it number three

These be known, from first to last,

Future, Present, and the Past.

Present, Future, weft-thread be

Fleeting in inconstancy

Yet the colors they do add

Serve to make the heart be glad.

Past, the warp-thread that it be,

Sets the path of history

Every moment 'neath the sun

Every battle, lost or won,

Finds its place within the lee

Of Time's enduring memory.

Fate, the weaver of the bands,

Holds these threads within Her hands,

Plaits a rope that in its use

Can be a lifeline, net—or noose.

PART ONE

An Ill Wind

1

On a morning of unsurpassed fineness, the sun rose over an incandescent sea, rippling with light so bright as to be painful in its radiance. The winter wind dancing over the gleaming waves, fresh with the sweet hint of a spring coming far away in the southlands, carried with it the scent of blood.

Rath cursed and lowered his head to his chest, pulling his brown hood farther down over his stinging eyes. He waited for the water beneath his translucent eyelids to clear, then blinked several times and looked up again at the shoreline. The sea was so calm that the edge of the land barely wavered in the distance. Rath clutched the oar in his sinewy hands and put his back into rowing for the beach.

With each stroke, each pull, each screech of wood against the oarlock of his small boat, he canted his list of targets, every one of their names engraved permanently on his memory. *Hrarfa, Fraax, Sistha, Hnaf, Ficken,* he whispered in the odd, buzzlike language of his ancient race, the one form of speech that was inaudible to the wind. Rath was always careful not to put information on the wind, especially the sea wind, where it would blow recklessly about the wide world, to be heard by any ear that knew how to listen. Rath was well aware of the loose tongue of the wind; he had been born of that ephemeral element.

He gritted his teeth as he rowed, mentally cursing the waves over which he traveled. Water had long blocked his Seeking vibration and kept him from his quarry. Each stroke moved him closer to being free of it, but that did little to calm his growing ire. Until he was away from the sea and the cacophony of thick vibrations that it generated, he would be unable to hunt. So he concentrated, as always, on his list.

Hrarfa, Fraax, Sistha, Hnaf, Ficken.

Once through the roster of would-be victims that had been his agenda for as long as he could recall, he silently intoned one last name that had been recently added.

Ysk.

It was not a name in the language of the others, but rather one that had been conferred on its owner by an ignorant species, a demi-human race that barely formed words at all. *Ysk* was the Firbolg word for spittle, for the regurgitation of something foul. That monsters had given some-one such a title could only convey the deepest disgust, contempt that had no limit.

It was perhaps the worst name that Rath had ever heard.

It was also a dead name, a name whose power had been broken more than a millennium before, whose history lay at the bottom of the sea on the other side of the world. A name all but forgotten, indeed, completely erased from the wind and from memory, except for the recollection of Rath and his kind.

It was the last name on his list, but the first one he would actively seek upon landing.

When the beach was finally close enough that rowing was dispropor-tionate effort, Rath climbed out of the boat and left it drifting in the tide. He had sighted his landing carefully so as to be able to come ashore unnoticed in a small, rocky alcove between two fishing villages. His luck was holding; there was no one in sight for as far up and down the beach as he could see.

He turned away from the sea wind with one last glance over his shoulder; the little boat was slowly backing away in a graceless dance, spinning aimlessly in the current. Rath waded to shore, ignoring the pebbles and seaweed that coated the sand beneath his feet. His soles had no nerves in them anyway, the calluses from millennia of walking through fire were almost as thick as a boot would have been.

Once on the beach, he hurried forward until the scrambling froth of the waves was no longer able to reach him, then stopped in the cold, dry sand, pulled back his hood, and tilted his head to the southwest, listening to the wind. He waited for the span of a hundred heartbeats, but no voices akin to his own could be heard; none of his fellow hunters had anything to report, as was the case most of the time.

As it had been for centuries into millennia.

Rath lingered a moment longer, then turned his back to the west, away from the crashing of the waves and the rustling of the foam. He took a breath of the salt wind, inhaling over the four openings of his windpipe, clenched his teeth, and loosed his *kirai,* the Seeking vibration by which his race sought their prey. The buzzing sound came forth from the deepest opening in his throat, a vibration heard only by him.

Then he opened his mouth, allowing the air that was rising from within his lungs to pass over the top opening in his throat, forming words again.

Hrarfa, Fraax, Sistha, Hnaf, Ficken.

One by one he canted the names of the demon spirits he was hunting, feeling the slight variation in tone as he changed from one name to another. If the *kirai* matched any of those names to a vibration it detected in the air, his throat would burn as if with caustic fire; he would taste the beast's blood in his mouth, feel its heartbeat in his own chest. He could lock on to that rhythm and follow it.

But, as always, there was no taste of any of the names on the wind.

Finally, he intoned the last name.

Ysk.

This name, of course, was different. Unlike the others, it was the dead name of a living being, a name once given, in another lifetime, to a man with a soul. However tainted that soul might be by the ravages of time and personal failure, it could never be as acidly evil as the essence of the demonic beings Rath and his fellow demon hunters regularly pursued. And however dead the name might be, Rath had reason to believe its original owner was, in fact, still alive, though his vibrational signature had changed along with his name.

And not long before, he had heard the dead name, spoken aloud, on the nattering wind. He hoped to get a taste of it once more, now that he had crossed the sea and finally come ashore in the place to which he had tracked the name, the place it seemed to have been last spoken.

He inhaled, letting the wind pass over his tongue, then canted the name.

Ysk.

There was a remnant of it still on the wind coming from the southeast, though faint and hollow; perhaps it had been years since it had been voiced. Still, this continent, this place known in old lore as the Wyrmlands, was the place where the name had last been sounded. Rath could taste that much.

Satisfied, he stripped his pack from beneath his cloak, opening it carefully on the sandy ground as the wind whipped off the sea, buffeting the skin of his naked head. He quickly checked his provisions and the minimal tools of his trade, as well as the dagger he wore in a calf sheath. The weapon was little more than a child's knife, meant only for the meanest of self-defense against any beast or man that he might not be able to otherwise avoid. No one who observed him would consider him armed.

Rath carried his deadliest weapons in his head.

Determining his water supply to be sufficient, he quickly repacked his provisions and slung the pack beneath his flowing brown cloak. Then he glanced at the sea one last time; the little boat was no longer in sight, lost in the blazing glare of the rising sun.

A moment later, to any eye other than his own, so was Rath.

2

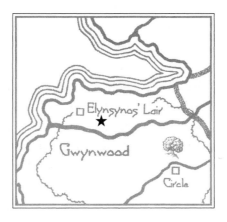

THE FOREST OF GWYNWOOD,
NORTH OF THE TAR'AFEL RIVER

𝒯he same sunlight sparkling on the sea thirty score miles away was illuminating the frosty dew that lingered in the air of the forest, bathing the wood in hoary radiance. Shafts of dusty gold illuminated the bare trunks and limbs of the white trees, making them gleam even more starkly against the neighboring evergreens, patchy with frozen snow.

No winterbird broke the morning stillness with song, no rustling in the branches or undergrowth signaled the presence of any of the forest residents that traditionally braved the cold months or felt the beginnings of Second Thaw that had been evident for a full turn of the moon. This place, always alive with wild music, emitted no sound, not the fluttering of needled boughs, nor the cracking of icy burdens in the diffuse sun. Even the wind itself, a customary singer that rattled the empty branches and whispered through the laden pines when all other noise had abandoned the wood, was still.

Deathly still.

As the sun climbed higher, the frigid moisture of the morning air dispersed somewhat, bringing clarity to the scene, if not warmth or sound. The low-lying fog began to lift, frosty air swirling above the ground that was warming as winter neared its end. And as the air began to grow clearer, the light spilling into the silent glen came to rest upon a gigantic edifice that loomed in between the broken trees and burnt expanses of grass, marking the place where part of the world had died.

At first, while still shrouded in mist, the structure appeared to be nothing more than an outcropping of gray boulders flecked with copper mica, improbably rising up from the soft loam of the greenwood. But as the sun broke through the frosty air, the shape of the stone became clearer, its smoothly sculpted edges revealing draconic attributes—stone spikes that rose over the curled backbone, taloned claws and feet wrapped protectively around itself, a curved tail terminating in a cruel barb. The brightening of the morning revealed, moment by moment, what appeared to be an immense statue of a dragon, crouched in a defensive posture, perfect in detail down to the tiniest scales in its stone hide, streaked with ash, a gaping hole gouged into its side.

The eyes in its weathered face were open. Even the greatest of sculptors in the Known World would have been unable to replicate the depth of sorrow and the peace of resignation in its expression.

The hovering mist swirled but continued to hang, heavy in the cold air, as it had each morning since the new moon.

Then, beneath the mist, a swirl of light appeared, spinning evanescently below the frosty layer of clouds.

Then another. And another.

One by one, from all corners of the greenwood, great serpentine bodies began to appear. Had any human eye been there to witness, it might not have been able to discern them at first. Most of the beings that were gathering had taken ethereal form and, bodiless except for their own will, composed of starlight older than the world was old, they hovered, lighter than the air, in the heavy fog of the glen. Their journeys concluded, their destination achieved, the great wyrms of the world began to solidify into the flesh granted them by their tie to the primordial element of earth.

The power that they brought with them pervaded the air of the wood, making it heavy with ancient life. To have stood among them too close would have been like drowning in a quicksilver avalanche, or being ground to bits by ruby millstones, these primeval wyrms, giant repositories of all of the world's lore, wardens of the earth, who shared an uneasy stewardship marked by traditional wariness, distrust, and territoriality.

The first to arrive was Valecynos, one of the eldest, daughter of the Progenitor of their race and a Guardian of one of the five World Trees, Ashra, that grew within the Fiery Rim half a world away. Always regarded as one of the bravest and rashest of their kind, like the tree of living flame that she guarded, Valecynos remained in a semi-fiery form, her gleaming hide changing from flickering scarlet to burning gold to the darkness of smoke, all within the span of a heartbeat.

She waited for a moment in the fog, her fiery eyes taking in the sight of the stone dragon before her. Then, as the heavy mist began to evaporate in the heat of her presence, she slowly approached, staring at the sight before her as if she were seeing the very end of the world.

Next to come into the glen was Mikanic, the dragon who held sway over much of the expanse of the Great Overward, the southernmost land mass of the earth. His power and dominion were undisputed among his kind, his counsel never ignored, though he seldom offered it and kept to himself beneath the shallow surface in the vast sands of the desert wastelands that comprised the center of his domain. His dry brown hide and multitude of slender spines were a stark contrast to the fleeting colors of the Guardian beside him; in normal practice he would have bowed in greeting to one of the Five Daughters, but the import of the moment was too heavy, the portent too fearsome to call for the observance of protocol.

The ground within the greenwood rumbled as others appeared, having chosen to travel within the earth rather than take to the wind in ethereal form. Sidus, a coal dragon from the lands of darkness beyond the sea, emerged from a yawning fissure in the ground, his quick black eyes glancing about suspiciously. Near him a moment later Witheragh arrived; born to reign deep within the mountains in a place where gold ran in hot rivers, his skin was encrusted with the gemstones that the Nain miners had cut, polished, and offered as tribute to him. He was followed by Salinus, a wyrm whose white hide was streaked with yellow and gray like the vast salt beds where he held dominion. They, like the other great wyrms appearing in the glen, fell silent at what they beheld there.

Finally, Dyansynos, another of the Daughters and the Guardian of Frothta, the tree of living water, came to her sister's side, taking in the horrific sight, as if to share the burden of it with Valecynos. Like all dragons, she had no larynx, no voice box to give sound to her words, but her thoughts were audible to those gathered in the greenwood.

"It is as we feared," she said, her words soft, as they pained her mind to form them. "Llauron has Ended."

As if in agreement, the wind blew through the glade for the first time since sunrise, rattling the branches of the trees, whispering ominously.

The great wyrms continued to stare at the stone dragon in silence. The profound horror of a wyrm giving up its life in such an absolute way had only been experienced one other time in history, and it was a sacrifice of such magnitude that it was only spoken of in the darkest of times, and then only in whispers. To End was more than to die; it was to disperse all of the elemental lore a dragon carried in its blood back into the universe, to forgo any legacy of blood, where the beast's decaying body returned to the earth, leaving veins of precious metal or caches of gemstones, which would one day adorn the crowns of powerful men, be valued and hoarded and fought over, as the dragon had done with its treasure in life. These great beasts, who believed that they were without souls, who acknowledged that the Afterlife held no place for them, longed, as each sentient creature longed, for some vestige of immortality.

To End was to consciously give up any chance of that forever.

More terribly, it left a hole in the shield of power by which the race of dragons protected the Earth. With the loss of each member of the ancient race came the loss of the control, of the stewardship, by which they kept the forces of chaotic destruction that were imprisoned within the very earth from destroying it.

Finally the harsh voice of Sinjaf, the vaporous dragon steward of the great poison swamps and everglades of the eastern island chains, crackled through the silent glen. "Llauron was not wyrm, but wyrmkin," he said curtly, his fear transmitting like a headache to the assemblage. "He was born a man, with dragon's blood in his veins, true, but not really one of us. His loss, while tragic, hardly affects the shield—"

"Llauron served to guard the Great White Tree of earth, just as the Daughters guard the three other remaining trees," interjected Talasynos, a Daughter herself and protector of Eucos, the tree of living air. "From the time he was a child he has tended it, loved it as we Daughters love the World Trees. When my sister Elynsynos gave up her corporeal form to escape her pain, he, as her grandson, took on her stewardship. Had he not, the tree would have been destroyed, as so much of the Wyrmlands were destroyed, in the wars of men. His transformation to dragonkind was complete; he gave up his humanity to join our service. Do not fool yourself, Sinjaf; this loss is as great as it would have been should Elynsynos herself have Ended."

The last of her words echoed hollowly through the glen.

Finally, Mikanic gave voice to what they all were thinking. "Where is Elynsynos?"

The great wyrms focused their eyes, then their other, deeper senses, on the question, seeking her vibrations in this place over which she had held dominion since birth. They scanned the horizon, sought her within the running sap of the trees, beneath the surface of the ground, tasted the air around her for a trace of her ethereal form, listened for any whisper of her on the wind.

Not a single echo of her could be felt.

The horror of the Ending surged within the assemblage into even greater fear.

"Surely she cannot be dead," came the insistent voice of Chao, a sparkling creature from the bright lands of the rising sun; frail and nervous, he was the most evanescent of the kin. "We would have felt it as we did the death of Marisynos, who guarded Sagia, when the Island of Serendair was consumed in cataclysm."

"Perhaps we did feel it," said Sidus darkly. "The reverberations from Llauron's Ending were vast enough to draw all of us here; mayhap Elynsynos's death was masked within them. Clearly her dominion is broken; these lands of hers are without protection, vulnerable. Can you not feel the loss of her magic?"

"There are so many holes in the shield already," murmured Valecynos. "We have lost so many of our kind—look at us. Only a few hundred remain of what was once the greatest of the Firstborn races; how can we guard the Earth with but a few of us? Without a Guardian for the last of the World Trees?"

"We can but concentrate on what is below," said Witheragh, "and leave the rest to the races of man."

"The races of man are the root of the woe!" exclaimed Dyansynos. "You may coexist happily with the Nain, Witheragh, but most of us live in conflict with the other races, maintain an uneasy truce, or avoid them altogether by keeping to the depths, hiding in the bowels of the Earth. It is their folly that invites the Unspoken in; it is their bodies to which the demons crave to cling, being without form themselves. It is through man that the F'dor propagate, through man they accomplish their destructive will."

"Men must fend for themselves now," said Mikanic. "There is naught we can do for them. While Elynsynos was here, she held these lands completely under her dominion, more so than any of the rest of us has managed since the beginning of the world. Her folly, her association with a man of a Firstborn race, led to the downfall of that, to the war that followed. It is foolhardy for us to try to save any of them now. We must do the best we can in holding a fragile world together, to guard against the evil ones in the Vault of the Underworld, and those that walk the upworld. Whatever befalls the races of man is of no consequence. And to that end, we should bless our brother and be gone from this place, back to our own lands, lest we leave them vulnerable."

Amid silent assent, the dragons turned once more toward the stone corpse of one of their own kind.

"What was he doing, when he Ended?" Chao asked nervously. "Why is he crouched, yet his head is erect, his eyes open?"

The dark evergreens rustled loudly as the wind blew through the greenwood again.

"He must have been sheltering something," said Talasynos. "Whatever it was, he must have considered it worth the loss of not only his life, but his legacy, and all of his lore."

"We can return at least some of that to him in blessing," said Valecynos. She closed her incandescent eyes and began to chant without sound, without words, joined a moment later by the others.

Llauron's stone shell was suddenly engulfed in flames, clear, pure elemental fire with no trace of ash or cinder, the kind that burned brightly deep within the heart of the Earth. The streaks of ash that had once marred him now purged by the flames, the chant changed, summoning cold rain from the clear morning sky. Once the body was cleansed, the wyrms altered their chant again, summoning the wind, which dried the droplets of rain as a mother dries the tears of a child. Finally, when the body had been blessed by those three elements, the very earth below it opened gently to receive Llauron, forming a grave deep within the forest he had loved in life.

When all the elements of the natural world had anointed the place where he had Ended, the dragons fell silent. They remained in the green-wood, standing vigil, until the night came, and ether, in the form of starlight, came to rest on the grave. The oldest of the five elements, ether was considered the magic that tied their race to the rest of the universe.

"May it bring you peace, and whatever immortality you can attain, Llauron," intoned Valecynos. *And may whatever you sacrificed yourself for have been worth the price you paid,* she thought.

As the wind picked up again, the immense serpentine bodies loosed their ties to the corporeal flesh of earth. Translucent, gleaming ethere-ally, they caught the wind as gossamer does, or burrowed back within the ground and returned to their lands.

Trembling with fear.

3

DEEP WITHIN THE HINTERVOLD

$\mathcal{A}$t least one of the race of dragons did not attend the blessing of
Llauron's body. Her absence did not mean that she had not witnessed
the results of the Ending, however.

She had been the cause of it.

That Llauron had been her son was only a fragmented awareness for
her; she had lain in a grave of coal ash and soot for almost three years,
blasted from the skies with ethereal fire, and as a result, her memory was
not what it used to be. In fact, she had only a few lingering recollections,
and none of her children inhabited any of them. She had long forgotten
the primal rule of wyrmdom, that no dragon would ever consider killing
another dragon, since the loss of even one made for a terrible hole in the
shield of protection they maintained in the world.

If she had known, she would not have cared.

She knew little more than that she had recently awakened in the
earth, in pain and confusion, and that giving vent to her pain through
destructive wrath eased her agony a little.

She also knew, as she lay in her empty palace of ice and frozen stone, that she was dying.

The dragon Anwyn had only been in wyrm form for a relatively minuscule period of time, a few years out of the millennium and a half that she had lived. She had only assumed the form a few times over her life, always as a means to achieve an evil end, and had been caught unawares by the blast of starfire that had crippled her wing and consigned her to a deathlike state in her black coal grave. She had no idea what had caused her to awaken. She only could recall pieces of memories, images that she often did not understand, and how satisfying hatred felt when it was translated into destruction.

And one clear memory: the lingering hate for a woman with golden hair, the woman who had put her into the prison of her grave.

All of that had receded into the recesses of her mind now as she struggled for breath on the stone floor of her keep in the frozen mountains. Within her chest cavity a piece of metal was embedded, jagged of edge, round, thin, and razor-sharp. It had been cold-fired in its manufacture and made from a type of metal that expanded greatly when it came in contact with heat, but of course she did not know that, either. She only knew that until she had made her way back here, to this place of endless winter, it was tearing at the muscle of her chest, growing bigger as the heat of her body made it expand, slicing nearer and nearer to her three-chambered heart.

Now she was lying as still as she could, trying to keep her mind clear and herself from panicking, struggling through the ruins of her fragmented brain, searching for a memory that could help her.

Healing, she thought desperately, breathing as shallowly as she could, watching her spittle pool on the floor, tainted pink with blood. *I must find healing.*

But in her life, Anwyn had cared little for the healing arts, and so had little idea of where to find them.

Near a window that looked out into the mountains she could hear a humming sound louder than the ever-present north wind howling outside her palace; a moment later she realized that she heard it not in her ears, but in her blood. Slowly she turned her head, wincing in agony, and attempted to focus her gaze on whatever was calling to her.

Atop an altar of heavily carved wood lay a tarnished spyglass.

Like a strike of lightning, realization came to her.

The spyglass had been the tool of her trade for most of her life, an instrumentality that had once belonged to her sailor father, but rather than looking at objects far away at sea, Anwyn had employed it in her capacity as the Seer of the Past. She did not remember any of that, but had a sense that if she could reach the spyglass, it might be able to show her what to do to save herself. So, as she had struggled to bring herself to this place, she now put the last of her energy into dragging her body, enormous of heft and grievously injured, to the altar.

The wind beyond the ice-slicked panes of glass screamed in triumph as the dragon's image, mirrored in the window, came nearer. She could feel her damaged heart beating wildly as she made her way across the floor, leaving a trail of dark blood behind her. With great care she reached a taloned claw up over the wood and felt carefully around where she had sensed the vibration; when she could feel the cool metal beneath her claw she fought against grasping it too eagerly.

With the last of her energy, she slid to the ice-covered windows overlooking the vast chasm below her, lifted the glass to her enormous serpentine eye, and peered through as best she could.

She had forgotten that the spyglass could only show her things from the Past, but that didn't matter. The image that formed as she peered through the lens rang a clear chime in her memory. It was the picture of a place of historic and mysterious healing properties, a desert citadel where hot springs flowed, healing gardens bloomed with herbs to soothe the mind, body, and spirit, where the warmth of the sun coupled with the medicinal attributes of the claylike sand could draw even the deepest infection from the body, or the most damaging memory from the soul, leaving nothing but sweet clarity and peace. That this haven for the suffering had slipped into the sands of the desert before her father had even set foot on this continent fifteen hundred years before, and that she had never even seen the place, let alone experienced its healing power, was also something she did not understand. She only knew that she could see, in the tiny lens of the spyglass, exactly what she was looking for.

The lost city of Kurimah Milani.

Gasping for breath, the dragon began to laugh raggedly.

4

HAGUEFORT, NAVARNE

$\mathcal{B}$y inexplicable happenchance, at the moment Rath came ashore, the man who had once carried the reviled name that the hunter was seeking was within a few score miles. That man was staring in silent contempt at the rosy brown stone edifice of a small keep known as Haguefort, observing a reunion that made him unconsciously desire to expectorate in the same disgust as was conveyed by what used to be his name.

Ysk.

Since the time when that name had been contemptuously conferred upon him, the man had borne several other titles as well. In long-ago days he had been cleansed of Ysk by a wise and highly skilled Namer, a man trained in the science of vibration and its manipulation. The Namer had called him simply the Brother, for Ysk was, he said, brother to all, but akin to none. It was a name that gave him power by which he could have come to be a great healer, but instead he chose the opposite side of the coin, passing his time in the trade of a solitary assassin.

A less-skilled practitioner of that same science had renamed him decades later, and now that he ruled over a mountainous kingdom of Firbolg, the same race of monstrous beings that had long ago given him the title Ysk, he was known by many dreaded and silly appellations: The Glowering Eye, The Earth Swallower, The Merciless, The Night Man. He had narrowly escaped becoming the owner of the most respected traditional title given to chieftains and warlords among the Bolg tribes, which translated roughly as The Supremely Flatulent, by virtue of the fact that he could not be described as such, or by any other title tied to the senses. In the dark caverns and tunnels of Ylorc, he was never seen or heard, and certainly never smelt, unless he wished to be.

Now, at this point in his history, he was known as Achmed the Snake, king of the Firbolg.

The name given to him at birth had vanished from history, and from all but the deepest vaults of his memory. He had only given voice to it once in almost two thousand years, and had spoken it softly, in the depths of the Earth, to the Namer who had given him his current appellation.

He watched that woman now being led up the steps of the rosy brown keep, shaky from recent childbirth and the sting of the late-winter wind, and exhaled deeply. He turned to his Sergeant-Major, an enormous half-breed who had been his constant companion for most of his life.

"No one is watching. If we leave now, they won't know we're missing until we're already home."

The Sergeant-Major shook his head, hiding a smile.

"Nope, sir, 'twouldn't be right," he said, trying to sound serious. "Ol' Ashe asked us to wait 'ere so we could brief 'im on what happened in the forest. We ain't supposed ta talk about it 'til we meet in council to keep the mem'ries fresh." He pointed in the direction of two young people, the Duke and Duchess of Navarne, who were holding a squalling bundle. "But if we're talkin' fresh, Oi say we 'ave a bite ta eat while we're waitin'. Sound good ta you?"

Achmed smiled slightly. "You're suggesting we eat Rhapsody's baby?"

"Yeah. Why not?"

The Firbolg king's smile faded as the guards from the keep arrived to take him to his solitary chamber.

"Because there's not enough to share," he said within plain earshot of the soldiers.

"You're right, as always, sir," Grunthor called out amiably as Achmed was led away. "'Ow about you just let me bite off the 'ead, an' you can 'ave the rest?"

The Firbolg king shook his head. "No," he said without turning around. "It's related to Ashe, so it probably tastes like mutton. You know how much I hate mutton."

The chambermaid who had taken the baby from the children let out a little gasp of horror and scurried away from the two monstrous men. The young duke, his nine-year-old sister, and the keep's guards, long accustomed to the two of them, however, didn't raise an eyebrow.

When the Lord Cymrian had first commanded that all present be ushered to separate rooms and kept in silence until their meeting, most of the others had scowled. Each of the people who would be summoned in what Lord Gwydion had promised would be a short time hence had urgent business to discuss, terrible findings to report, and all were frustrated at the delay.

All, that is, except for Sergeant-Major Grunthor, the giant Bolg commander, who nodded acceptance at the order and quietly followed the nervous human servant to his room. Once the door was closed, the Sergeant quickly surveyed the surroundings and, finding them to be acceptable, set about the task of cleaning his personal arsenal.

In much the same way that some men collected drinking flagons or hunting trophies or concubines, Grunthor collected bladed weapons. He was, in fact, even more enamored of his assortment of blades than most other collectors, as each was the center of an interesting story, a memory of bloody conquest made sweeter in the reflection of steel.

When his schedule allowed him the time, the giant Bolg commander, half Firbolg, half Bengard, and seven and a half feet of muscle beneath skin the color of old bruises, would shrug off the bandolier he always wore across his back and spread the weapons he had chosen to garner out on a table or his bunk, where he would polish them lovingly, often humming a battle cadence, off-key, under his breath as he did. He had taken the time to name each of them, and therefore felt a personal affinity with it, mementoes of the old world where life had been simpler, if not easier.

He was humming to himself now as he unstrapped the massive bandolier, the creak of leather and steel fittings a nice percussive accent to the tune, a pleasantly gory folk song he had learned from his Bengard mother about the pillaging of a desert town.

The first blade he pulled forth was both the longest and shortest weapon he owned, the tip of a polearm he had affectionately named Sal, short for Salutations. Sal was double-sided, a traditional spear point with a hatchet head on one side, missing the wooden shaft. Grunthor held the tip up to the light of the hearth fire in his chamber, enjoying the way it illuminated the long-dried blood in the channeled grooves chiseled into the weapon by time and wear.

"'Allo, lit'le fella," he murmured fondly. "Gotta get ya a new pole soon—sorry to 'ave left it go so long."

The next blade to receive his attention was The Old Bitch, a spiny, serrated short sword named for a hairy-legged harlot he had been fond of in the old world. "Now, now, darlin', no bitin'," he murmured, carefully oiling the viciously sharp edges. "Usta say the same thing ta yer namesake, all them years ago. Course, she didn't have no teeth, unlike yerself."

With infinite care he tended to the needs of each blade, repairing the leather bindings, polishing the steel, speaking in a low and gentle voice as he babied the weapon, almost as if he were speaking to a young child. Had the sight of him sharpening the edges of swords, filing the points of awls, or adjusting the metal scourges of his bullwhip not been so innately threatening, it would have made an amusing tableau to anyone brave or foolish enough to interrupt him.

One by one, each item in his collection was patiently restored to its best possible shape, the Sergeant taking equal satisfaction in the task and the review of the memories. Finally he came to one last weapon, something he had been told by a First Generation Cymrian was called a triatine. It was a triple blade composed of three thin sides, smelted together at the core, each edge razor-sharp. It was clear to Grunthor that in addition to working well as a slashing weapon, one with length and sharpness enough to maintain distance from an opponent, it also could serve to remove a major core of flesh and muscle should it be applied, triangular tip first, with enough force, even more if twisted properly. This was the last weapon to be added to his collection in the old world, one that Achmed had removed from a dead soldier pursuing Rhapsody, and the only weapon he owned that he had never used.

Cleaning and tending to his weapons helped Grunthor organize his thoughts. He had been unable to find a moment in the course of his journey to Haguefort from the forest of Gwynwood in which he could speak to his king and best friend alone. Achmed had been utterly silent all the way home in the carriage that bore them, along with Rhapsody, her husband and newborn son, to this keep of rosy brown stone that was the duchy seat of Navarne. This place had been the first in which the three of them, minus Ashe, had found a true and unencumbered welcome in this new world, the Wyrmlands, this place to which they had run from the other side of Time.

It was very clear to Grunthor that war was brewing. Whether with traditional forces, or those beyond the realm of his experience, or both, he was ready, eager, in fact, to see combat, to test his mettle again, after so long of being out of practice as a field commander. Unlike Rhapsody, who longed for peace when it was unrealistic, and Achmed, who never believed in the possibility of peace, Grunthor found peace to be a nuisance, a time when weapons got rusty or not kept at the ready, when soldiers let their guard down, or trained without fear as an incentive. His mother's Bengard race had long ago accepted the concept of constant war, invented and internal if necessary, as the best possible state of existence, because it meant a heightened sense of awareness, a sense of shared sacrifice.

And, of course, fun.

As he oiled the little short sword he had named Lucy, a crooked grin came over his swarthy face, allowing a meticulously polished tusk to protrude from below his bulbous lip. Lucy was the sword he had given to Rhapsody so that he could teach her, centuries ago, to handle a blade. She had become a credit to him as an instructor, and wielded a historic weapon of her own now, but the image that was still dearest to his heart was of her, shorter than himself by the length of his arm and only possessing a third of his mass, holding back from attacking him with too much force in their earliest training sessions. He could have crushed her like a cricket without dirtying his boot much, but instead he had come to respect her, to appreciate her and her talents, if never really understand her.

His grin faded as he remembered the more recent sight of her, pale and gray from loss of blood and the internal ravages of bearing a wyrmkin child a few days ago, the offspring of her husband, a man who had dragon's blood running in his veins. She and Achmed had emerged from the ossified corpse of her father-in-law, Llauron, a manipulative man Grunthor had never trusted when he was in human form, and whose transformation into the ethereal existence of the dragon state had done nothing to change that opinion. Even Llauron's death, which

Achmed had indicated had saved them both from the rampage of the dragon Anwyn, was, as far as the Sergeant-Major was concerned, not a tragedy. It was the least the old man could do.

Seeing her in the forest, wan and bloodless, as she disappeared into her husband's carriage, from which she did not emerge except to enter the keep of Haguefort, had left him feeling unsettled, a state to which he was not accustomed. With a vicious snap of a leather bandolier binding, Grunthor resolved to make certain he had a moment to assess her condition and speak with her before they parted again.

He was putting away his weapons when a knock came at the door. True to his word, Ashe had kept the waiting brief. Grunthor placed the bandolier over his shoulder and made his way down the hall behind the guards to what he hoped would be a fruitful planning for a massive military adventure.

He found it impossible to repress humming a cheerful tune at the prospect.

*W*hile Grunthor was cleaning his weapons, the Bolg king was instead using his time in wait to observe a small flock of castle swallows, winterbirds that nested year round in the crags and crevices of Haguefort's high walls, and to muse over old losses.

The chirping of the birds seemed brighter in tone as they wafted higher on the wind, their calls to one another tickling the sensitive nerve endings in Achmed's scalp. That in and of itself was not unusual; virtually anything that lived or moved registered its vibrations somewhere in the Bolg king's skin. The web of veins and nerves that scored every inch of his body surface was the major factor in his ability to sense prey when he was hunting, and to be irritated by everything else when he was not.

But what Achmed was noticing as he listened to the birdcalls was that one particular musical interval, a high trill that was repeated every eight heartbeats, seemed to nullify the irritation of all the other birdsong against his skin, drowning the pinpricks in a soothing buzz that actually felt almost pleasurable. He recognized the sensation.

It was the same feeling he experienced most of the time when he was around Rhapsody.

Achmed exhaled slowly. There was the irony; though he was consistently perturbed at the choices the Lady Cymrian had made over the millennium and a half he had known her, as irritating as her openhearted, empty-headed idealism was to him, there was an innate musical vibration about her that soothed the constant torment that life visited upon his every waking and sleeping moment.

As soon as the thought came into his head, the door opened. Rhapsody came into the room; Achmed knew without looking, because the ache in his skin was suddenly abated, quelled by the musical vibration she brought with her wherever she went.

He did not turn even as she came to the window. "Where's the screaming thing?" he asked, watching the swallows fly in formation over the balcony railing, banking on the warm updrafts. "I thought it had been cemented permanently to your breast."

Rhapsody chuckled. "His father has him," she said, coming alongside him to follow his gaze as the birds flew over the keep's tower again and out of sight. "And really, for a newborn, he's very quiet. But perhaps your race is quieter in its infancy, as in all other stages of life. Don't Dhracian babies ever cry when they are hungry or cold? Or do they just communicate their needs silently, the way an entire colony of adults can?"

Achmed shrugged. "I've no idea," he said flatly. "I was raised by Bolg, not Dhracians, if you recall. I have no more knowledge of Dhracian infants than you do."

He finally turned to look at her and winced at what he saw. One of the fairest aspects of her face had always been the color palette; her rosy skin set off the emerald-green of her eyes, framed by golden hair that caught the light in a room. Achmed, who had known her before her transformation from spirited street trollop to serene lady of the Alliance, knew that while some of her famous beauty was instilled in her by the power of the elemental fire she had once absorbed, much of it had been in her all along, even in the bad old days on the long-dead Island of Serendair half a world away.

Now, as he looked at her, he saw a very different woman. Rhapsody's normally sun-kissed skin was pale as porcelain, her eyes a dimmer shade of green, like spring grass instead of the normal verdant hue of a forest in summer. Her glistening hair had lost a little of its shine, and the tips of her fingernails and the whites of her eyes seemed bloodless. She looked tired and spent, a reasonable appearance for someone who had just survived a difficult childbirth and the near-death experience that followed it.

"I thought your husband requested us all to remain silent," he said, turning back to the window.

"He did." Rhapsody came closer and slid her small hand into his. "And I will respect that request after I thank you, once again, for saving my life, and that of my child. We can speak more later, but I cannot let another moment pass without telling you how grateful I am that you are my friend, in spite of whatever hateful things I may have said to you in the past. I hope you will forgive me for them."

Achmed did not look at her, but merely nodded and continued to stare out the window. Rhapsody watched him in silence, but he never met her glance again, just followed the patterns of the swallows on the warm winter wind. Finally, when the silence became heavy, she squeezed his hand and left the room, taking the comforting music of the vibrations she emitted with her, along with what was left of Achmed's modestly good mood.

When he could no longer hear the distant echo of her footsteps on the polished marble floor of the hallway beyond his door, he gave voice to what, in another lifetime, he would have said aloud to her.

"I can feel the very world unraveling."

NEAR THE BORDER OF THE PROVINCES
OF NAVARNE AND BETHANY

The soldiers had been following Velt the fruit monger on the road for a long time before he noticed them.

Velt normally considered himself a fairly observant man, but the late-winter wind had been stinging his eyes most of the day, and the roadways of eastern Navarne were hilly, winding through and around frozen haystacks and the hummocks that sculpted the wide, empty fields of this sparsely populated farmland. He did not really look behind him until he was out on the straight, flat stretch of thoroughfare past the village of Byrony, and by the time he did, he was well beyond any place where he could hide or make an excuse to pause in his journey.

So when he noticed the dark mass approaching in the distance he clicked to his horse and slowed his pace, preparing to move off into the grass if necessary when they passed.

Beads of sweat broke out on his wrinkled forehead that had been cool and dry in the late-morning sun; Velt did not know why, but suddenly he was nervous, more anxious to be home than he had been a moment before.

Calm yourself, idiot, he thought to himself. *You have nothing to fear from the soldiers of Roland. You've done nothing wrong.*

And yet the hair on the back of his neck was still standing on end, as if he were about to be caught smuggling stolen jewels rather than transporting the load of winter apples he had been fortunate to obtain in Kylie's Folly, a farming settlement in southern Bethany.

As the ground beneath his wagon began to tremble, transmitting its vibrations through the buckboard on which he sat, Velt suddenly realized why he was nervous. Merchants had for the last several years been encouraged by the crown to join the routes of the guarded mail caravans that plied the trans-Orlandan thoroughfare, the roadway built in Cymrian times bisecting Roland from the western seacoast to the edge of the Manteids, the mountain range also known as the Teeth, in the east. While it was not illegal to have taken the shortcut Velt had chosen, he suspected he might be in for a dressing down by the approaching soldiers.

He stole a glance over his shoulder and sighed miserably. The blue and silver colors of their regalia were visible now, confirming their allegiance to the Lord Cymrian. Velt willed himself to be calm and prepared for a tongue-lashing.

It was not forthcoming.

The crossbow bolt hit him squarely in the spine between his shoulder blades, just above the rib cage.

At first Velt could not comprehend what had happened; he only knew that as he concentrated on keeping the horses steady he felt the wind go out of him, followed a second later by a numbness in his legs. Then there was nothing, no sensation in his lower body. He tried to turn, tried to twist, but succeeded only in throwing himself off balance and out of the wagon, narrowly missing becoming ensnared in the tack.

In contrast to the loss of feeling in his lower extremities, the fruit monger could feel every pebble in the roadway that was impressed into his face, absorbed the shock, then the nausea as his nose was smashed to the ground below his limp body. He struggled to breathe as the roadway shook, his stunned mind a jumble of questions, but one overriding instinct warning him to remain still and feign death.

He could hear the soldiers approach as well, a great thudding sound that mixed with the terrified pounding of his heart. He kept his eyes closed and tried not to move as the horsemen came nearer. It did not occur to him to beg sanctuary in the name of the Lord Cymrian, or to protest to a regiment that served a peaceable ruler for attacking a fruit merchant who was minding his own business. Velt was too much in shock to wonder anything but why this was happening to him.

He continued to breathe shallowly, inhaling snowy dirt, as the cohort came upon him. Velt prayed that whatever end was about to come would be quick.

By happenchance he had been at the Navarne winter carnival four years before and had survived a grisly assault by the soldiers of Sorbold on that festival, had hidden with his wife and children behind the keep's wall while the carnage ensued over what seemed like hours. When it was over, he had joined those giving aid to the bloody victims lying in the pink snow, and witnessed many long agonies that ended in shuddering death. From that moment on Velt had prayed for a quick end when the time came.

It appeared that time was upon him.

He gritted his teeth as the horses' hooves spattered him with gravel. He waited for them to stop, but the soldiers rode on as if oblivious to him.

Finally, as the thunderous noise began to dim, Velt grew brave and opened one eye a crack. The cohort was almost out of sight, but he could see that the horses were gray mountain horses, rather than the standard bays and chestnuts most often seen in this part of the lowlands, or the roans preferred by the Lirin to the west. Freezing as his body was, Velt's heart was suddenly colder.

The last time he had seen such horses they were under the soldiers of Sorbold who were assaulting the winter carnival.

The extremities of his body were going numb, and Velt's mind was following. As the fog closed in, he looked up at the wagon looming above him.

Could've at least taken the apples, he thought before the darkness took him. *They'll be withered and frozen by the time anyone finds them.*

As will I.

5

HAGUEFORT, NAVARNE

𝒢wydion Navarne was pacing the thick carpet outside the Great Hall, awaiting his turn to be called into the room. That this was his first council since becoming fully invested as duke on his seventeenth birthday a few months before weighed heavily on his mind as he strode up and down upon the heavy fibers woven into a tapestry that told the history of his family. With each step he unconsciously traced the lineage of the tuatha Navarne, from its Cymrian progenitor, a First-Generationer named Hague who had been Lord Gwylliam the Visionary's best friend, to the ascendancy of his own late father, Stephen Navarne, who in his youth had been the best friend of Ashe, the current Lord Cymrian, Gwydion's own namesake, godfather, and guardian. The rich colors of the plaited threads—forest-green and crimson, deep blue, royal purple and gold—told a melancholy story that was fitting in its mood.

Over and over as he walked in circles he silently repeated what he had seen in the harbors and outposts of Sorbold, the great nation of threatening mountains and windswept deserts to the south of Roland, struggling to keep the facts and figures straight in his mind.

Seventy-five three-masted cutters, he thought to himself, running down his list again in anticipation of the discussion that would sooner or later come about. Sixty three-masted schooners, at least four score heavy barges, all in the southwestern port of Ghant, all in the course of one day's time.

All carrying slaves, thousands of them, perhaps the contents of ten or more entire villages, probably bound for the salt mines of Nicosi or the sweltering ironworks of Keltar.

Gwydion had been unable to fully quell the racing of his heart since the moment he had witnessed the unloading of the human cargo a few weeks before. Compassion and outrage at the sight had quickly been joined by fear; a little sleepy harbor town teeming with soldiers and long-shoremen, mountain guards and human chattel, had been enough to convince his companion that the war for which Sorbold was preparing would be greater in scope than anything the Known World had ever seen.

Given that his companion at that moment had been Anborn ap Gwylliam, the Lord Marshal of the first Cymrian empire and perhaps the greatest military mind that had ever existed on the Middle Continent, Gwydion had been quickly and nauseatingly convinced, especially since Anborn had engineered the previous war to be described as such.

The heavy carpet beneath his feet bulged up into a ridge from where he had unconsciously worn a groove. Gwydion smoothed it down with his feet, pushing the bump to the edges, arriving at the fringe at the same moment that the doors to the Great Hall banged open with urgency.

Standing in the door frame was his father's long-trusted chamberlain, Gerald Owen, an elderly Cymrian who had served Gwydion's father and grandfather, and perhaps a few ancestors before him. The old man stepped back in surprise, then opened the door wider for the young duke.

"Finally," Gwydion muttered as he entered the Hall. "I've been waiting a week to talk to him."

"He's aware of that, sir," Gerald Owen said smoothly, closing the door behind him. "The Lord Cymrian needed to see that the Lady Cymrian and the baby were attended to before the meeting. She was in a grave state when she returned."

Gwydion stopped and turned back quickly. "And is she better now?"

he asked anxiously. Rhapsody had adopted him and his sister Melisande four years before as honorary grandchildren, though in many ways she had been more like a second mother. "Will she be missing the council?"

"Yes, and no," came a warm baritone voice from behind him. Gwydion looked over his shoulder to see his godfather standing in the center of the feeder hallway leading into the central meeting place of the keep. Ashe, as the Lord Cymrian was called by his intimates, was a man in possession of the blue eye color most often associated with Cymrian royal lineage, but whose face and body bore the lines of the mixed races of human and Lirin, with draconic vertical pupils scoring his eyes and copper-colored hair that appeared almost metallic in its sheen, signs of the wyrm blood that ran in his veins as well. "She has been tended to, and will be sitting in on the council meeting. We would be sorely lacking in wisdom were she not to attend."

"Agreed," said Gwydion, looking askance at the empty room. "But where is she? To that end, where is everyone? I saw Anborn come in earlier, and Achmed and Grunthor both a moment ago—where did they go?" His eyes fell upon the metal walking machine, abandoned in the corner of the room, a marvel of engineering provided by Anborn's brother, the Sea Mage Edwyn Griffyth, to help the lame Lord Marshal regain the ability to walk upright. "What is going on here, Ashe?"

Outside the enormous windows of the Great Hall an icy wind howled, drowning the silence, buffeting the glass until it rattled.

The Lord Cymrian eyed him seriously, then turned and walked over to a heavy wall tapestry depicting the voyage of the Cymrian fleets from the lost island of Serendair. He drew the drape aside and pressed his hand into the stone of the wall; darkness appeared as a hidden passageway opened.

"Do you remember this place?" he asked.

Gwydion's throat felt suddenly dry. "Yes," he said. "Gerald Owen hid Melly and me there during the slaughter at the Winter Carnival four years ago."

Ashe nodded. "It's not a perfect place to meet in secret, but being underground and away from the wind, and any ears that might be listening, it's the best we can do for now." The vertical pupils of his cerulean blue eyes caught the light from the windows and contracted visibly; Gwydion wondered if the change was from more than the light. "Make haste, Gwydion; we are about to convene the most dire discussion undertaken in the history of the continent."

The young duke nodded and stepped into the dark passageway, followed a moment later by the Lord Cymrian, who closed the doorway as he entered, plunging them both into empty blackness.

A moment later he felt a crackle in the air around him, and the earthen walls of the dark passageway began to glow with a warmth that held no real light, but rather the radiance of heat. The dim illumination gave Gwydion enough vision to make out the rough-hewn stairs that twisted down into the blackness below, where he knew a small room was concealed, little more than a root cellar, behind a rock wall. The Lord Cymrian chuckled.

"Thank you, Aria," he called into the darkness below.

"My pleasure, Sam," came Rhapsody's voice in return. "Mind your step, Gwydion."

"Well, it's good to know that at least she is well enough to make use of her fire lore and to still order me around like a child," Gwydion murmured to his godfather as they slowly descended the stairs into the gloom. "'Sam'—I've never asked you this—why does she call you that, anyway?"

The Lord Cymrian smiled but said nothing, following the turning staircase down into the subterranean repository. Gwydion shuddered involuntarily at the memory of being thirteen in this place, left in charge of his five-year-old sister and a handful of sobbing children he did not know, waiting to hear if any of their parents survived the assault of the soldiers of Sorbold on the winter carnival where they had all been celebrating a few moments before. His father had lived; Gwydion tried to blot out the memory of the sounds that had risen from those whose parents had not been so fortunate.

At the bottom of the stairs in the darkness Rhapsody was waiting for them; Gwydion thought perhaps heat had caught in her golden hair, making it shine even in the lightless gloom, but a moment later recalled that her title as the bearer of Daystar Clarion, the ancient sword of elemental ether and fire, was Iliachenva'ar, translated from the old tongue as meaning one who brought light into a dark place, or from one. His "grandmother" certainly had that ability; seeing her now, even in the gloom after all her months of absence, somehow gave the dank air a sudden freshness of hope.

Or perhaps, rather than Rhapsody herself, it was the presence of the tiny sleeping infant that she cradled in her arms.

Ashe rested his hand on her waist and brushed a kiss on her cheek. "You didn't wish to remain within?" he asked.

"I didn't like the way Achmed and Grunthor were looking at Meridion," she replied mildly, drawing the baby closer. "They kept dropping broad hints about missing breakfast."

Ashe smiled slightly and opened the stone door hidden within the rough granite wall.

An almost blinding light spilled into the dark stairway from the room beyond. Crouched within it around a small wooden table on which a large parchment scroll was lying were the two Firbolg, Achmed and Grunthor; Anborn, looking testy as he usually did; and a Lirin man Gwydion recognized after a moment as Rial, Rhapsody's viceroy in the forest of Tyrian where she reigned as their titular queen. Rial's presence made Gwydion's hands tremble unconsciously; if the Lirin elder statesman had traveled all the way from the sacred forest to the southwest of Roland, the scent of blood in the air must be unmistakable.

"Hurry up and get inside, all of you," Anborn growled.

Ashe stepped aside to allow Rhapsody to enter first; Rial rose and bowed respectfully as she entered, but the other three men remained seated, Anborn because he had no other choice, and the Firbolg because they had no intention of doing otherwise. As she passed into the small hidden room Gwydion leaned discreetly toward Ashe and murmured in his ear.

"How did Anborn get down here without the walking machine or a litter?"

Ashe cleared his throat to cover his reply. "He allowed the only other Kinsman who was able to carry him," he replied under his breath. Gwydion nodded and bowed to Grunthor, knowing that it was to him Ashe referred. The order of the Kinsmen was sacred to soldiers, a brotherhood deeper than that of blood, achieved over a lifetime of soldiering or a great deed of self-sacrifice, chosen by the wind itself. Rhapsody, Grunthor, and Anborn were the only Kinsmen Gwydion knew of in the world, though his "grandmother" had assured him there were others.

The Lord Cymrian pulled the stone door shut behind him. In the light of the lanterns Gwydion caught a better look at his face, and of those around him. In spite of the appearance of calm, there was a tightness about Rhapsody's lips, a floridity to Anborn's face, a tenseness in Ashe's shoulders which belied that calm. Gwydion shuddered; he had believed his own news would be the most painful to share with the council. Clearly he was not alone in bringing bad tidings.

A humming beneath the table caught his attention, and Gwydion looked down. There on the floor was a partial hexagonal ring of swords, laid tip to tip, hilt to hilt. He recognized three of them immediately.

The first was Daystar Clarion. Flames licked up its blade, and after a few seconds Gwydion realized it was the weapon that was providing the light in the room rather than the lanterns. It was crossed with a battered, nameless blade he had seen many times before in the hand of Anborn, a weapon Gwydion had received numerous sparring blows from in the course of his training with the Lord Marshal. Seeing it now, its tip against the historic blade, made him wince from the memory.

Daystar Clarion's hilt abutted that of a Lirin longsword with a redwood handle; Gwydion knew this must be the weapon of Rial, the Lirin viceroy, whose duty was the protection of the forest of Tyrian. Gwydion had seen up close some of the Lirin defenses, and knew that however humble the blade appeared, when wielded in union with the tens of thousands identical to it, this sword was part of one of the greatest and most secret military machines on the continent.

The hilt of Anborn's sword abutted that of another legendary blade, Kirsdarke, the weapon of elemental water that his godfather carried, a bastard sword that was inscribed with gleaming blue runes on the blade and hilt. The sword appeared to be fashioned of silver steel as it lay on the floor, but in the hand of its bearer, known in the ancient tongue as the Kirsdarkenvar, the blade took on the appearance of living water and froth that ran in waves from the tang to the tip. It was crossed with a strange weapon, something Grunthor had once shown him called a triatine, which Gwydion knew from his history lessons had only been used more than a millennium before on the lost island of Serendair and nowhere else in the Known World.

Between Grunthor's weapon and Rial's was an empty space.

Gwydion could feel the eyes of the others in the room on his back.

Unconsciously his hand went to the hilt of the sword in the scabbard at his own side. The import of the space that had been left for his weapon was not lost on him. He had attended many of Ashe's councils before as the heir to the duchy of Navarne, but now he was being included for another reason, as the bearer of an elemental sword. Only five such weapons had ever been forged, and as far as anyone knew, only three now existed.

All of which were present in the room.

Gwydion Navarne glanced nervously over at Achmed, who was watching him, his mismatched eyes intent, his all but lipless mouth twisted in the hint of a smile. Gwydion thought back to the day, not that long ago, when the Bolg king had presented him with the sword.

This is an ancient weapon, the elemental sword of air known as Tysterisk. Though you cannot see its tang or shaft, be well advised that the blade is there, comprised of pure and unforgiving wind. It is as sharp as any forged of metal, and far more deadly. Its strength flows through its bearer; until a short time ago it was in the hands of the creature that took Rhapsody hostage, part man, part demon, now dead, or so it seems at least. In that time it was tainted with the dark fire of the F'dor, but now it has been cleansed in the wind at the top of Grivven Peak, the tallest of the western Teeth. I claimed it after the battle that ended the life of its former bearer, but that was only because I wanted to give it to you myself. Both Ashe and I agree that you should have it—probably the only thing we have ever agreed on, come to think of it.

Anborn coughed impatiently.

Quickly Gwydion drew forth the air sword from its scabbard. Tysterisk, when not being used in combat, appeared as little more than a hilt carved with swirling symbols that seemed to move and dance when in his hand. In the humming presence of the other two elemental weapons the slightest outline of a blade could now be seen. The young duke hastily placed it on the floor, its hilt abutting Grunthor's triatine, its ephemeral blade crossed with Rial's solid one, completing the circle.

Anborn gestured to the chair beside him, and Gwydion took a seat, noting that the swords beneath the table had been arranged with common weapons interposed between each of the elemental ones. He recognized the wisdom of keeping the immense power of those swords separated, but also recalled something else Achmed had told him when the king had presented him with Tysterisk.

I haven't done anything to be worthy of such a weapon, Gwydion had said haltingly.

The Bolg king had snorted with contempt.

That's a fallacy long perpetuated by self-important fools. You cannot be "worthy" of a weapon before you begin to use it. It's in the use of it that your worthiness is assessed. It is an elemental sword—no one is worthy of it. In truth weapons of this kind of ancient power do choose their bearers, and make them, in a way.

Gwydion watched as Rhapsody bent down, still cradling her infant son, and brought her hand to rest over the circle of swords. She was a good example of what the Bolg king had said, Gwydion knew. While he had been told little of Rhapsody's life, one detail she had shared with him was that she was of humble birth, the youngest child of a farming family. Her transformation into the Lady Cymrian, and Lirin queen, might have been attributable to many things, but certainly she would not have become the warrior that she was known to be without the aid of Daystar Clarion.

Perhaps he would have a chance to prove himself more than just a boy duke as well.

His musings were shattered as she began to sing, a soft note from the back of her throat that resonated at the same pitch as the hum of the elemental weapons. Gwydion listened, enchanted, as she began to weave the swords' names, along with words he didn't understand, into her song. Though he knew little of music, and nothing of the Lirin science of Naming, he thought he recognized a change in the musical vibration of each sword, until the three of them, along with Rhapsody's voice, were making a perfect chord.

When the music seemed to be holding steady, Rhapsody took Daystar Clarion by the hilt. As her hand made contact, the fiery blade leapt to life, its flames roaring in brilliant colors that stung Gwydion's eyes. Maintaining her song, she passed the sword over the ring of weapons, as if picking up invisible threads.

A circle of sparkling light appeared, hovering below the table, then expanded as she waved it away to the earthen ceiling of the hidden room, where it remained, pulsating and still ringing with the chord, as she put her weapon back in the hexagonal ring. It continued to hum, softer, back to its original monotonal pitch, as she ceased her wordless song and fell silent. She listened for a moment, then nodded to herself, smiled at her husband, and prepared to be seated.

Ashe held Rhapsody's chair for her as she settled in with the baby, then took his seat at the table. He unrolled the large scroll, revealing a map of the continent that highlighted in green the lands of the Cymrian Alliance, comprised of Tyrian, the southwestern coastal Lirin realm, the six central provinces of Roland, as well as the Firbolg mountains known as the Teeth at the easternmost border. The northwestern forest of Gwynwood and the small city-state of Sepulvarta, both religious strongholds of the continent's two major sects, were depicted in white but dotted in green, indicating their allegiance to the Alliance as well as their independence.

Sepulvarta, sometimes called the City of Reason, was the seat of the Patriarch, the head of the church known generally as the Patrician faith, while Gwynwood was the holy forest of the Filids, nature priests who tended to the Great White Tree of earth. As Lord Cymrian, Ashe was the titular head of both sects, but only ceremonially; he had continued to recognize the independence of both orders upon the formation of the Cymrian Alliance, sponsoring discussions between the two sects that had been adversaries during most of the fourteen centuries since the Cymrian refugees first came to the Wyrmlands.

"Thank you for your forbearance," Ashe said. "I know that each of you brings terrible news, as do I. I have asked you to retain it in silence before sharing it, so that the impact of your words will be as pure and accurate as possible."

His voice resonated inside the hovering circle of light, the sound remaining trapped within it. The Lord Cymrian reached into his pocket, removed a coin minted with his own aspect, and tossed it on the earthen floor outside the protective spinning light. It landed without sound; satisfied, he continued his address.

"We know we are facing war—what is at question is the scale of it, and who is allied against us. Each of us holds a piece of that answer, and it is critical that we have as much of the puzzle as we can know before we put our defenses in place. We must ascertain whether what is coming is a war of conquest, driven by the greed of men, or if it is something far darker, more ancient, which has always loomed in the distance. Rhapsody, Namer that she is, has the power to not only record the words for posterity, but to help derive additional meaning from them once they are laid out for her. She has canted a circle of protection to keep our words secret from any ear that could hear them, hiding us all from any eye that could see within our council chamber. She will now remain silent, concentrating on each of our stories. I will speak first." He turned slightly toward Anborn.

"My father, your brother Llauron, is dead, Uncle," he said softly, his voice emotionless. "Worse, he has Ended, forsaking all of his draconic lore as the Progenitor did, in a final act of protection of Rhapsody and our child, his grandson." He waited, allowing the import of his words to sink in.

Anborn stared at him for the span of seventy heartbeats.

"The shield of the world is compromised," he said finally. "This is grave news indeed."

Gwydion Navarne blinked but said nothing. It never failed to amaze him how passionlessly the members of the royal Cymrian dynasty were able to absorb tidings about the deaths of their family members, especially given the history of a thousand years or more that they shared. It might have caused him to believe that as humans with dragon blood, or wyrmkin, they were incapable of emotion, except that he himself had witnessed their desolation in the loss of others. He had seen firsthand the grief of Ashe when Rhapsody was missing or away, and the agony Anborn underwent following the death of his man-at-arms and friend, Shrike, a lowly soldier. It was a puzzle he not only could not decipher, but one whose very pieces were invisible to him.

Then again, he mused, maybe it was more a matter of the deceptions they had perpetrated on each other over the centuries. Both Ashe and Llauron had been forced, or chosen, to feign their own deaths, to remain hidden from the sight of the living world for years. Perhaps this lack of loss was the price of that.

"Additionally, I was unable to find my great-grandmother, Elynsynos, who would most certainly have been there if she were able," Ashe continued. He looked askance at Rhapsody, whose eyes glistened with tears, but whose face remained stoic otherwise. "My own ability to discern her presence is limited to a range of approximately five miles, but there is such a patent lack of ethereal energy in the air, such a loss of lore from the forest ground, that I fear the worst."

Anborn's face whitened noticeably. Gwydion felt the air in the room become suddenly drier, more caustic.

"Gods," he whispered. "If that be true, then with her death and that of Llauron, the Great White Tree is now unguarded, and the lands that once were her domain—most of the western continent, even unto Tyrian in the south—are no longer under draconic protection." His hand shook slightly as he traced the area. "For all that humans do not even discern that wyrms protect the very ground on which they walk, the loss of both of them will leave a good deal of the Alliance vulnerable, should there be F'dor about."

Ashe nodded, his jaw clenched. Then he turned to Achmed and Grunthor.

"Tell us, please, what you experienced in the forest of Gwynwood. Rhapsody was too ill to talk about it on the way home in the carriage."

The Bolg king's mismatched eyes gleamed in the flickering light. "Well, I suppose if you are counting the number of dragons left in the world and bemoaning the loss of those two, you can gain cheer from this," he said archly. "One we had thought dead is actually alive—your bloody *grandmother*, Ashe."

The Lord Cymrian's face went rigid, and the draconic pupils in his eyes expanded.

"Anwyn?" he asked in a choked voice. "Anwyn is alive?" He looked from the Bolg king to Grunthor, who remained at attention, as he always did in Achmed's presence, then finally to his own wife. "How can that be? The three of you killed her, locked her in a grave of scorched earth within the Moot before the eyes of almost everyone in this room. The sword Daystar Clarion took her from the skies with a flash of starfire that ignited the grass all around for miles—*how can this be?*"

"Bloody dragons," Grunthor muttered. "Once is never enough with 'em; ya gotta kill 'em at least twice, maybe more."

"If anyone should know that it would be you, Ashe," said Achmed. "I've been trying with you for the last four years, and yet here you are."

The air around him bristled, and Gwydion Navarne winced involuntarily. He knew the Bolg king's words were black humor, but there was enough truth in them to set off the dragon in Ashe's blood, and possibly Anborn's as well.

"Careful then, Achmed, lest your reputation as a renowned assassin be seen as mere puffery," Ashe said calmly, smoothing out the map. "Where did you see her?"

The Bolg king lowered the veils that traditionally shielded his hideous face from both the gaze of the world and the vibrations of ordinary life that irritated the sensitive nerve endings and traceries of veins that scored his skin, hallmarks of his Dhracian heritage.

"She chased Rhapsody, your brat, and me through a good deal of the forest outside of Elynsynos's lair," he said. "The last I saw of her was at the place where your father's ossified carcass now stands." Rhapsody glanced at him reproachfully but did not speak, still concentrating on the accounts.

"She was alive when he interposed himself between you, enveloped you?" Ashe asked, his jaw rigid but his eyes clear. "When he Ended, with the three of you inside him?"

The Bolg king exhaled. "She took a shot from my cwellan, a bladed disk of cold-fired rysin-steel that expands jaggedly in heat. I think I hit her in the chest area or midsection—it's hard to tell on a dragon. That disk should continue to expand for a while, ripping into the muscle and sinew, until it finally shatters, whereupon the pieces should make their way to the heart. Those disks are called dragonkillers. Ironic—your own grandfather, her hated husband Gwylliam, was the one who produced the design for the manufacturing process four hundred or so years ago before Anwyn had him assassinated. Seems he was bent on finding a weapon that could rip apart dragons as well." His eyes went to Anborn. "Your parents were charming people. Family dinners in your house must have been joyous."

"Why do you think each of us had a personal food taster?" Anborn replied testily. "Shall we return to the matter at hand?"

"She was after Rhapsody," Achmed said. "She seemed obsessed, and unaware, of everything else around her. She did not threaten me, or call out after anyone else—she screamed Rhapsody's name over and over again, using the wind, the rumbling of the earth, anything she could draw power from, to threaten her."

"Sorry Oi didn't come sooner," Grunthor muttered, his polished tusks protruding from behind bulbous lips. "Oi'd 'ave made 'er scream somethin' else." Rhapsody glanced at him and smiled slightly; the Sergeant smiled in return, understanding the unspoken thanks in her eyes.

"It's difficult to know whether or not she died of those wounds," Ashe said, studying the map. "Like Anborn, and myself, and any other of Elynsynos's descendants, she is not a true dragon but wyrmkin; if she were true wyrm, she would never have been able or willing to try to kill my father, or Meridion. No true wyrm would ever kill another, not even in a dispute over territory, which is their greatest point of contention. She has none of the compunction and none of the collective conscience of her mother's race—and therefore she will stop at nothing to vent her hatred. If she survived your cwellan shot, she will continue to appear randomly, whenever she is least expected, until she gets what she wants—and it appears what she wants is to kill you, Rhapsody."

The Lady Cymrian nodded, still concentrating on the report.

"I suspect that she will ultimately die of the wound," Achmed said. "There is no person to whom she can turn to have the shards removed, so sooner or later they will rend her enough inside to cause her to bleed to death—one of my all-time favorite aspects of those disks. I suspect Rhapsody has little to fear in the long term."

"Whether she does or not, dear as you are to me, m'lady, I fear that's the least of our concerns," Anborn said. "While Anwyn may pose a threat by the sheer chaos of her actions and intent, it is unlikely that she is allied with any of our enemies. If the Bolg king has finished his report, we should move on to what is looming on our borders." Rhapsody nodded again silently, still listening intently.

"Indeed," said Rial; the leathery skin of his face darkened as he spoke. "I came, uninvited, to bring you the winter report, m'lady. The southern and western border watchers have compiled very disturbing information that points to a massive buildup of Sorbold military presence at the outskirts of our lands, particularly of the elite soldiers of their mountain guard. Never have we seen mountain guard along any of our borders; this be disturbing enough, but that news be coupled with an increase of blood sport in the arenas of Jakar, which abuts our southeastern border.

"'Tis true that Sorbold has always allowed the practice of gladiatorial arena fighting, though it was discouraged, at least officially, by the late Dowager Empress. But now that this new emperor, Talquist, be awaiting the end of his regency year, the human traffic through our lands to the arenas has swollen like a river in spring. The crowds making their way to Jakar'sid be enormous and violent, drunk with spirits and bloodlust. The forest fringe has been set alight several times, and the border guards have engaged in the repelling of quite a few raids, seemingly incited without reason, just from the ugliness that is building to the south. Additionally, the guardians of our western coastline have noted a substantial increase in ships sailing north."

"North?" demanded Anborn. "Gwydion and I saw a massing of them in the *south*—speak up, lad, report."

Gwydion cleared his throat. "In the harbor of Ghant, Anborn and I witnessed seventy-five three-masted cutters, sixty three-masted schooners, and at least four score heavy barges arrive and unload in port, all in the course of one day. That rivals the traffic of Port Fallon in Avonderre, the busiest seaport in Roland."

"And dwarfs that of Port Tallono, Tyrian's largest," added Rial.

"Not even Argaut, half a world away, traffics that many ships daily. Only Kesel Tai on the island of Gaematria has greater sea trade than that," said Ashe, indicating the solitary land mass in the midst of the Wide Central Sea to the west. "Or at least they did; the Sea Mages have been limiting their contact with the outside world of late. The ship-building schedule is dramatically behind, the vessels I've ordered are arriving a few weeks late consistently. Has Edwyn Griffyth indicated why to you, Uncle?"

Anborn snorted contemptuously. "As if my brother communicates anything to me, and as if I would be interested in anything he says. Over the centuries the Sea Mages have been less and less interested in commerce with the outside world, preferring to pass their days in the folderol of magical research, invention, and the science of tidal studies, or some such rot. They have been fairly useless for centuries now; they were famously absent in the Great War, and have been even less interested in our plight ever since." His azure eyes gleamed as a thought occurred, and he turned to Achmed. "Except for that idiot ambassador my brother sent with the walking machine last autumn; he seemed quite intent on contacting you."

The Bolg king's forbidding countenance soured even more. "Oh, he did, rest assured," he said. "I let him live in spite of it. That's your fault again, Rhapsody."

The Lady Cymrian kissed her new son's downy blond hair, ignoring him, maintaining her silence.

"The ships were laden with human cargo," Gwydion continued. "Slaves, or would-be slaves, it seemed, captives from entire villages, being transported in wagons like chattel. Men, women, children; the distribution seemed very efficient. They were split up at the docks and dispatched in many different directions."

"So Sorbold has been building up its internal capabilities for war, its army and naval forces, at an extreme rate in less than a year," Ashe said, noting his uncle's rising anger at the discussion of the slavery. "Anborn has always had his suspicions, but how did the speed of this escape our notice? Talquist isn't even emperor yet; he chose to take only the title of regent for a year. All the ambassadorial meetings between the Alliance and the new Sorbold diplomatic mission have been cordial. There have been no hostilities in the time since the death of the Dowager Empress. There have been no raids that I have heard of in Roland, Tyrian, or the Non-aligned States except for the drunken thuggery during times of blood sport you just mentioned, Rial—and certainly none where captives were taken. And had there suddenly been orders for more ships by the crown of Sorbold placed in Manosse or Gaematria, surely the harbormasters and the Sea Mages would have alerted me."

"One would hope so, given that Manosse is one of your late mother's holdings, and Gaematria is a member of the Alliance," agreed Anborn.

"So where are these ships and slaves coming from?"

As the words left Ashe's mouth, he sat up suddenly as if shot by an arrow in the back.

"Gerald Owen is coming down the stairs," he said softly. "I gave specific orders not to be disturbed."

Gwydion Navarne felt an old fear well up inside him, a dusty and atrophied panic left over from the slaughter at the Winter Carnival, causing the saliva in his mouth to taste of metal and cinders. His guardian's dragonsense, set off by the action in the Great Hall above, left a cracking dryness in the dank air.

Ashe rose and strode out of the glittering circle to the hidden door. He opened it and stepped into the dark antechamber beneath the roughhewn staircase.

"What is it, Owen?" he demanded.

The old man's reply was soft.

"A visitor is here to see you, m'lord," he said. "This man knew you were meeting; he instructed me to beg an audience of you—when asked his name, he said merely that you and he had traveled the road as strangers and companions four years ago on the way to the Cymrian Council."

The Lord Cymrian stood silent for a moment, then looked back into the lamplit chamber where his councilors were waiting.

"Perhaps the answers to some of these questions has just arrived," he said. He turned back to Gerald Owen.

"Send him down."

6

The occupants of the hidden room looked at one another in amazement as footfalls could be heard descending the stone steps.

"Is he mad?" Anborn said in a low voice. "It was his bloody demand that this meeting take place in secret; why in the name of every wench I've ever bedded would he be breaking the seal of this place to allow an interloper? Your husband is a fool, Rhapsody."

"Won't get an argument from us on that," Grunthor said.

The Lady Cymrian rose, still weak, and stepped over to the doorway.

From the darkness at the bottom of the staircase a figure emerged, cloaked and hooded. The man came immediately to Ashe and spoke a few soft words in a low tone, then followed him into the hidden chamber. The Lord Cymrian closed the door behind him.

Even beneath the plain broadcloth cloak it was clear that he was tall and wide of shoulder, taller than any of the men present except for Grunthor. He did not bow, but turned in the direction of Rhapsody and the infant for a moment, then reached out a large hand, one sheathed in a lambskin glove, and rested it gently on the baby's head.

Gwydion Navarne watched the odd spectacle unfold in silence.

With the other hand the man reached up and took down his hood, revealing hair streaked gray and silver with age, though there was still enough white-blond hue to it to hint of what it must have looked like in his youth. His beard was long, curled slightly at the ends, and his eyes were clear and blue as the cloudless summer sky, reflecting the flickering light of the lantern.

Constantin, the Patriarch of Sepulvarta.

For a long moment after he knew he should be kneeling, Gwydion remained frozen in place, finally rising long enough to sink to one knee. His father, Stephen Navarne, had been an adherent of the Patrician religion, though he was also a good friend of Llauron the Invoker, the former head of the Filidic order of nature priests, and had been conversant in and respectful of the religious practices of both sects. Stephen's attitude, unique as it was in the polarized world of faith, was unsurprising given both the geography of his duchy and his accepting nature. Navarne was located at the crux of the northern forest of Gwynwood, the eastern border of the neighboring duchy of Avonderre, and the northern fringe of Tyrian, making it the crossroads of the continent's faiths.

So the magnitude of the Patriarch's appearance in his family's home was not lost on Gwydion Navarne. The Patriarch only left the Basilica of the Star, Lianta'ar, in Sepulvarta for occasions of state, such as royal funerals, marriages, or coronations, or in the direst of emergencies.

As far as Gwydion knew, no one royal was being buried, married, or crowned.

The Patriarch's white brows drew together, and gestured impatiently at Gwydion.

"Get up," he said tersely. "It's far too crowded in here to be doing that, and inappropriate for a man who has been invested as duke of an Orlandan province. Rise from your knees and sit down." Gwydion complied, abashed.

"What brings you here at this time, Your Grace?" Ashe asked quickly, offering the Patriarch a chair.

The holy man's body, while elderly, still bore the signs of great strength from his youth; he waved a hand dismissively at the chair.

"I can't remain here long, lest it be discovered that I am gone from Lianta'ar," Constantin replied. "I bring disturbing news—but by the look of things, I am not alone in that."

"Step within the circle, then. Rial, Anborn, and Gwydion were reporting on the preparations Sorbold is making for war," said Ashe, sitting down beside Rhapsody. He ran a hand gently over his son's head. "It would appear that Roland, and perhaps the other members of the Alliance, are the targets of their intended aggression."

"Eventually," the Patriarch agreed, coming within the protective light. "Some will fall before you, others after, if Talquist has his way."

The silence in the room thickened until it was palpable.

"Tell us what you mean, Your Grace," Ashe said finally.

The old man's searing blue eyes caught and held the lanternlight, reflecting and intensifying it.

"The first place Talquist will attack is Sepulvarta. His troops are massing even now on the mountain rims and in the foothills to our south. The holy city-state is the doorstep of Roland and the Middle Continent; Talquist will wipe his feet upon us as he crosses the threshold into your lands. I have no doubt of this."

"The holy city?" Gwydion said, his words slow with shock. "How is that possible? Sorbold is an adherent to the Patrician faith! One of the five elemental basilicas is within their domain. Even in the most ferocious of battles in the Cymrian War, when all else was left in desolation, Sepulvarta was spared. It would be an affront to the All-God—"

"Was it not an affront to the All-God, or the One-God, as the Lirin call Him, when the Third Fleet sacked the holy forest of Gwynwood a thousand years ago? We burned the Outer Circle, and even attacked the Great White Tree," Anborn said bitterly. "I—Elynsynos's own grandson—led those attacks. In war, nothing is held sacred. That Sepulvarta has remained unscathed until now is purely a coincidence—a miracle."

"The Lord Marshal speaks the truth," Constantin affirmed. "War is coming to us first; it has already begun. It is one of three things I have traveled here, in secret, to warn you about, Lord Cymrian. I have also come to tell you that Nielash Mousa, the Blesser of Sorbold and one of my chief benisons, is dead or dying. He has given his life in the defense and protection of Terreanfor, the basilica of Living Stone, in Jierna'sid."

"There was an assault on *Terreanfor*?" Achmed asked as Anborn started to become agitated. "Why would Talquist attack the only one of the five basilicas within his own nation?"

"The attack was not from without, but from within," said the Patriarch. "Terreanfor, being the sacred basilica of elemental earth, is the greatest known repository of Living Stone on the continent. Talquist has been secretly harvesting that precious commodity of the basilica for his own purposes. The man who told me of his treachery witnessed it personally; partook in it, unwillingly. This blessed element, this gift of the Earth-Mother, has been made use of in the unholiest of ways—I suspect the assassination of the Dowager Empress and the Crown Prince Vyshla were the first of these events, but I have no idea how Living Stone could have caused that to happen."

"The Dowager Empress was a withered crone well past her deserved time to live," said Anborn. "And her fat bump of a son could hardly rise from his own chair without assistance. What makes you think their deaths were not of natural causes? It is gravely important that we not attribute to malice that which should rightly be explained otherwise; we will become lost in what threat is real and what is not."

"True," said the Patriarch. "But while I cannot prove their sudden and mutual deaths to be regicide, I do know that Talquist rigged the Weighing on the Scales of Jierna Tal to have himself anointed emperor. All the modesty and the humble choice to remain regent for a year was an act; Talquist has been planning his ascension for a long time." The searing blue eyes narrowed. "I have known this man, and his cruelty, for many years."

The small earthen room fell silent, even to the flickering lantern. Not much was commonly known about the origins of the Patriarch; he had appeared from seemingly nowhere at the first Cymrian Council of the new age, mixed in among the Diaspora of descendants of the exodus from the lost island of Serendair.

Ashe and Rhapsody exchanged a glance with the two Bolg; they all knew his story, but had never revealed it. "You needn't expound further, Your Grace," said Ashe.

The Patriarch shook his head. "If these men are your most trusted councilors, they deserve to know," he said, eyeing Anborn, Rial, and Gwydion. "A war is brewing that has the potential to lay waste to much of the Known World. Any secrets of my past are insignificant now—it is better that all hidden things be known, so that we can hope to stave off at least part of the destruction that is to come. It is as the All-God would want it."

"As you wish," Ashe demurred. "No man here is likely to judge you."

"The Lord Cymrian speaks the truth," said Rial. "All of us are less than perfect in the One-God's eyes. Go on, Your Grace."

"In my youth, I was a slave in the gladiatorial arenas of the borough of Nikkid'sar, in the city-state of Jakar in Sorbold," the elderly man said.

"And while I am an aged man, since that time of my bondage only a few years have gone by in the sight of the world. Being born of demon blood—a misbegotten offspring of the last known F'dor to bedevil this land—I was a brutal killer, knowing no remorse, only bloodlust." He paused as Gwydion, Anborn, and Rial blinked in astonishment. "It was the Lady Cymrian who saved me—and you, Lord Marshal, when you rescued both of us in the process, though you undoubtedly do not recognize me."

"I certainly do not," said Anborn. "And if I had had my way, the gladiator that Rhapsody pulled from the arena in Sorbold would have died by my own hand. Had she not stayed that hand, your tainted soul would be roasting in the Vault of the Underworld now, if you are that wretch, that spawn of the demon."

The Patriarch nodded, no offense visible in his expression. "I am the same man who, four years ago, Rhapsody took behind the Veil of Hoen, to the mystical domain of the Lord and Lady Rowan, that place on the doorstep of death, where the near-dying find healing of one kind or another, either passing through the Gate of Life to the Afterlife, or being restored to health, to return for a greater purpose in the material world." His gaze fell on Ashe. "I believe you know this realm."

The Lord Cymrian smiled slightly. "I do."

"So, having been healed there yourself, you know the weight of the responsibility that comes with that second chance at life. When that which was demon was removed from my blood in that drowsy place of healing between the worlds, I had little left of me; all I had known was violence and murder. So I remained there in study, allowing much of my life to pass in absorbing the healing arts and the wisdom of the Rowans. My excessive longevity—bequeathed to me by the Cymrian mother I never knew—allowed me to spend centuries on that side of the Veil without dying there. When I finally returned to this side, I was old, had lived the equivalent of six hundred years, but only a short time had passed in the eyes of the world. For this reason, no one recognized me. The name of Constantin had been associated only with the young, hale killer of the Sorbold arena. I made no attempt to shield myself, have not altered that by which I was called, but no one has made the association— not even Talquist, who owned me when I was a gladiator."

"It does not surprise me to know that Talquist engaged in the promotion and propagation of bloodsport before he ascended the throne," said Rial. "But how has he come by so much power so quickly, without even being officially crowned?"

The Patriarch looked down at the Ring of Wisdom on his hand; it was a simple ring, with a clear, smooth stone set in a plain platinum setting. Inside the stone, as though internally inscribed, were two symbols on opposite sides of the oval gemstone, resembling the symbols for positive and negative, the signs of balance between Life and Void, the two great constants of the universe.

"Before he rigged the Weighing and stole the throne of Sorbold, Talquist was a merchant," he said quietly. "While the royalty, the nobility, and even the military tend to view the merchant class as lower, inferior, in truth they have always had the greatest base of power, because they control the trade, and the contact with the outside world, of a nation. Talquist has long had access to allies in foreign lands that the Dowager barely maintained diplomatic relations with. He has a fleet of merchant vessels that have been plying the seas for years, keeping abreast of all that is going on in the Known World. I suspect he is an ally of the Magnate of Marincaer and the Baron of Argaut, both of whom also own large shipping concerns on the other side of the Central Sea and the world. He has been trafficking the goods of the mines and linen factories of Sorbold for decades; I suspect he is a far richer and well-connected man than anyone knew. Now that he has the Sorbold navy under his command as well, he rules the sea from the southern tip of Tyrian all the way to Golgarn in the east. And probably beyond."

"But where are the slaves coming from?" Ashe asked. "Merchant ships are not equipped to assault coastal villages, and Sorbold naval vessels are not attacking the coastline of the Alliance. If the Sorbold navy had sailed across the Central Sea to Manosse, or some far-flung land away from the continent, Talquist would be vulnerable at home. This does not make sense—something is missing."

"Agreed," said the Patriarch. "Much is missing—much more than you can even imagine."

Something in the sound of the holy man's voice made Gwydion's blood chill suddenly. The council had been trading information of terrible consequence and unfathomable grief with efficiency and detachment; it was as if in the face of impending invasion and a war that would bring about the deaths of thousands, only the coldest logic could remain. But now, there was something deeper in Constantin's words, something otherworldly. A quick glance told him that the others had heard the ominous warning as well; Rhapsody's eyes were glittering, her face frozen.

"Tell us," said Ashe finally.

The Patriarch's eyes went to each person in attendance. Finally he averted them, as if to keep them from boring through the others.

"Many things are missing, but I will begin with the one closest to your own family. Rhonwyn, your aunt, Lord Marshal, your great-aunt, Lord Cymrian, the Seer of the Present, has been taken from the Abbey of the Sun in Sepulvarta."

The members of the assemblage looked blankly at each other. Rhonwyn, like her two sisters, was a living relic, with the vision of Fate. Though unlike her sisters, Rhonwyn was gentle and frail, most of the population that knew of their existence was too intimidated or frightened to even meet their gazes. A few intrepid souls occasionally worked up the courage to approach them long enough to seek a prophecy, often leaving in terror before it was finished.

"Define 'taken,'" said Ashe quickly.

"Though the abbess did not see it occur, she believes that the Seer was abducted," said the Patriarch. "I left Sepulvarta upon hearing this news, though I had already determined to come to you with other tidings. When the abbess climbed the staircase to the Seer's tower to bring her the morning meal eleven days ago, she was gone. Rhonwyn has not left that abbey in a hundred years, save to attend the Cymrian Council that invested you both, m'lord and lady. She is incapable of it—incapable of independent survival."

Achmed and Rhapsody exchanged a silent glance. Several years prior they had climbed that same staircase together to visit the frail Seer, one of the triplet daughters born to the dragon Elynsynos and Merithyn, the Ancient Seren explorer who had been her lover. The three sisters, known in the language of the Cymrians as the Manteids, had each been born with a surpassing gift of sight, and all were impelled to speak only the truth about what they saw, though what was true was not always the same as what was accurate.

Each of the sisters was thought to be, at least on some level, insane. Anwyn, the Seer of the Past, was the least so—the Past was a more concrete realm than either the evanescent Present or the uncertain Future—and she had been known to connive in the use of her gift of sight, hoarding the knowledge it gave to her and dispensing it in ways to be interpreted as she wished it to be.

Manwyn, the Seer of the Future, was both the most unbalanced and most sought after, because being able to see what had not yet come to pass gave many desperate pilgrims the belief that her aid might help them achieve or prevent what they could not otherwise be able to achieve or prevent. Most left her crumbling temple disappointed or deluded, because the prophecies the madwoman chanted at them often had many interpretations.

Rhonwyn, the most fragile of the sisters, actually had the clearest grip on reality. The difficulty was that it was momentary; as seconds passed, the Present turned into the Past, and she could not recall from moment to moment what had been asked of her, or even what she had said. Few had the patience or the insight to tolerate speaking with her for more than a few minutes, and generally gave up in frustration, leaving her alone and unsought after in her decaying abbey, smiling to herself and staring up with blind eyes that had no irises into the sky above her.

"For a week or more before the Seer disappeared, she had been visited regularly by a priest from the manse of Sorbold within the city of Sepulvarta," the Patriarch continued gravely. "Each day the man would come to the abbey with two acolytes, climb the courtyard stairs, and pose a single question. Then he left, returning at the same time the next day."

"Did the abbess conveniently overhear the question?" Achmed asked.

"After a few of the daily visits, she made it a point to be working in the outer garden beneath Rhonwyn's tower at the time the clergy arrived," said Constantin. "She tells me that the same question was asked on two occasions—the last two days before the Seer disappeared."

"And what was it?" Anborn demanded.

The Patriarch glanced at Rhapsody. "The question the priest asked was this—'Where is the Child of Time?' On the two occasions that she overheard, the Seer was silent, then said only that there was no Child of Time. It would seem that on the last day the priest received a different answer. By my estimate, that would have been on Yule, the Turning Day of the new year." His voice became softer. "When was your son born, m'lady?"

The Lady Cymrian's face went white; Achmed and Ashe exchanged a glance.

"New Year's Day," Ashe said finally, "as the night passed from one day to the next, from one year to the next. But why was a priest of Sorbold seeking this child—our child, if he be this so-called Child of Time?"

"Because his emperor has been searching for that child ceaselessly," said the Patriarch darkly. "I have heard it in his prayers, and in those of the remaining priests of Sorbold." He eyed Gwydion Navarne, the only adherent of his religion in the council. "In our faith, unlike that of the Filidic order of Gwynwood, prayers are not offered directly to the Creator, but through channels, to the pastor of each congregant's local temple, who offers up those prayers and the others of the locality to central abbots, who pass them along to the benison of their area, who present them, in prayer, to me. I offer them to the All-God in supplication through the great spire of Lianta'ar. At each step the worship becomes more powerful, more pure, because it is joined by so many other offerings of praise and thanksgiving. I do not normally discern what is being asked for—it is only my responsibility to add my own entreaties for the All-God's grace and make the offering.

"But, as I told you, Nielash Mousa, the benison of Sorbold, is dead, or dying. And Talquist has killed many of the order, especially those who lived within the manse at Jierna Tal."

"Why?" Ashe asked incredulously.

Constantin's brow blackened. "We'll get to that in a moment," he said darkly. "As a result of this carnage, the prayers of the faithful in Sorbold are now scattered, misdirected. So they come to me directly, and as a result I hear them—and it distracts me from my station. Of late I have heard the same entreaty made over and over to the All-God on behalf of the emperor—and that is to find the Child of Time."

"Again, I ask you, why?" Ashe said, his tone darker. The air grew noticeably drier as the dragon in his blood grew more agitated.

The elderly cleric returned his stare, then sighed, his lined face showing his age for a moment.

"If you are asking me for Talquist's reason, I cannot give you an answer. I hear his prayers, but I cannot see into his heart, black and twisted as I know it to be. But I can surmise a possible motivation—though I pray to the All-God I am wrong."

"Tell us," Anborn commanded impatiently, but Ashe held up a hand to his uncle. He had seen the clouds form in the Patriarch's searing blue eyes, and knew whatever realm he was looking back into was a terrifying one. He glanced at Rhapsody, who was as white as the blanket she cradled.

"Please, Your Grace," he said quietly. "Explain, in whatever way you need to do so."

Constantin remained silent; as he waited in thought, it seemed to Gwydion that the last of the moving air in the room was inhaled and gone. When finally he spoke, his words were soft.

"Over time there have been those who can see beyond the realm of sight, beyond the places where the eye has dominion," he said. "Sometimes that special sight is due to a gift granted at birth, or because of a special heritage. It is an ability that can, under extraordinarily rare circumstances, be learned, if taught by one of great knowledge. Or sometimes it is not an ability to see, but rather the opportunity to transcend the limits of normal sight with an instrumentality that has the power to do so. I do not know which of these methods Talquist might have made use of, but I suspect he has done so, at least once, probably more often. And the place I believe he may have gained an unwarranted glimpse into is that place between the doors of life and death, the Veil of Hoen, of which we were speaking a moment ago.

"The Veil of Hoen, for those of you who have not ventured there, is a place of dreams, the realm of the Lord and Lady Rowan. The Lady is the Keeper of Dreams, the Guardian of Sleep, Yl Breudiwyr. The Lord is the Hand of Mortality, the Peaceful Death, Yl Angaulor. In that place of transition there are many things that are not known in this, the material world. One of those entities is known as the Weaver. Do you know of this being?"

"You mentioned this once to me before, but it is not an entity I have any knowledge of outside of your words," said Ashe.

"The Weaver is one of the manifestations of the element of Time," the Patriarch said seriously. "Those who know the lore of the Gifts of the Creator generally only count five, the worldly elements, fire, water, air, earth, and ether. But there are other elements that exist outside the world. One of them is the element of Time, and Time in pure form manifests itself in many ways. The World Trees—Sagia, the Great White Tree, and the three others that grow at the birthplaces of the elements— are manifestations of Time. As is the Weaver.

"The Weaver appears as a woman, or so it seems, though you can never recall what her face looks like after you see her, no matter how much you study it at the time. She sits in that drowsy, timeless place, before a vast loom, on which the story of Time is woven in colored threads, in patterns, the warp, the weft, the lee.

"The Weaver is the manifestation of Time in history," he continued. "She does not intervene in the course of events, merely records them for posterity. It is a fascinating tapestry that she plaits, intricate in its connectivity. All things, all beings, are threads in the fabric; it is their interconnectivity that weaves what we know as life. Without those ties that the threads have to one another, there is merely void; absence of life."

Ashe nodded. "When you told me of this before, you said that in those ties, there is power—that those ties bind soul to soul, on Earth and in the Afterlife. It is the connection that is made in this life that allows one soul to find another in the next. This is the means by which love lasts throughout Time." His hand covered Rhapsody's, and they exchanged a glance that brought smiles to their faces, in spite of the coming threat.

"I did," said the Patriarch. "But what I did not tell you was what I noticed in the tapestry she was weaving. In this massive record of history there are millions of threads, woven together into the perfect depiction of the tale of Time.

"In one place, however, there is a flaw—a discrepancy that in a tapestry on this side of the Veil would scarcely be noticed, if it was seen at all, an imperfection in thread or technique. But an imperfection in history that has already occurred should not be possible in the Weaver's tapestry; it is only a record of what has gone before, without variability or equivocation. It is almost as if the threads of Time had been taken apart and rewoven there—as if Time itself had been altered in this one place in the Past."

The only sound for a long moment was the crackling of the lantern flame.

"Time—rewoven?" Ashe asked at last. "How can that be? I thought you said the Weaver does not interdict in history, but just records it."

"Aye," said the Patriarch. "And as far as I know, she does not. But the split threads, the imperfections in history, appear only once in all of the tapestry, at least from what I could see—and it seems to have happened in the Third Age of history, at the very beginning of the Seren War—centuries before Gwylliam's coronation, or the Cymrian exodus from Serendair."

Gwydion saw the blood leave the faces around the room, most especially that of his guardians.

"Be there any clues as to how Time was altered?" Rial asked.

Constantin shook his head. "Only a prophecy woven into the threads above the flaw, a riddle of sorts that seemed to precede whatever event would have left history marred."

"Do you remember it?" Anborn asked tersely.

"Indeed," replied the Patriarch. "It was a primary object of my studies while I was beyond the Veil, but I never was able to connect it to anything else in history. It appears to be the last prophecy uttered in pure Time, before whatever change occurred took place."

"Tell us, man, and be quick about it!" Anborn ordered harshly.

The Patriarch shot him a look of displeasure, then turned to the Lady Cymrian, whose face was now pale as milk.

"I speak these words to you as a Lirin Namer, m'lady, in the fervent hope that you might be able to decipher them," he said softly. "To my knowledge they have never been uttered in this world, as they took place in Time before it was changed." He cleared his throat and intoned the words carefully.

"THE PROPHECY OF THE CHILD OF TIME:

Brought forth in blood from fire and air
Sired of earth
A child of two worlds
Born free of the bonds of Time.
Eyes will watch him from upon the earth and within it
And the earth itself will burn beneath him
To the song of screams and the wails of the dying
He shall undo the inevitable
And in so doing
Even he himself shall be undone.
This unnatural child born of an unnatural act
The mother shall die, but the child shall live
Until all that has gone before is wiped away
Like a tear from the eye of Time."

Rhapsody's back went rigid. Her shoulders stiffened and her arms began to shake. Then she looked down at the sleeping child in her arms. Her lips, until that moment firmly pressed together, responding to neither taunt nor tenderness, fell open as the words spilled out of her mouth.

"Dear One-God," she whispered.

7

AT THE BORDER OF THE HINTERVOLD
AND CANDERRE

The wyrm paused at the bitter river, silver with glacial ice, that separated the southeastern edge of her lands from the northern tip of Roland. Her body was trembling from exhaustion and the cold that clung to the Hintervold long into spring. She had fought to drag herself this far, had battled the wind, the loss of blood, and the confusion that continually took her mind whenever she tried to concentrate for more than a few moments on anything other than the woman she wanted to kill.

It seemed to her, poised on the brink of the flowing glacial melt, that she was losing the battle.

The river, for all its rushing rapids, was shallow, the dragon knew. The inner sense that she had been gifted with from birth had allowed her the same ability to assess the world around her in intimate detail that all wyrms possessed, even when she had been in human form, though she did not remember that time. Apparent to her in minute specificity was the temperature of the tumbling water—a hairsbreadth above that of solid ice—the speed at which it was traveling—two and a quarter times as fast as a unsaddled stallion could run—the number of fingerling cetrinfish that slept in the mud of the riverbed—seven hundred thirty-six thousand four hundred eighty-eight—and myriad other pieces of information about the height of the clouds above her, the degree of snowmelt on the riverbank, its width, the trees that surrounded it, all the elements of life that were taking place around her.

The number of facts to process was clouding her mind. The dragon struggled to clear it, focusing all her attention on the river.

The form she had been trapped in, seemingly for the rest of her life, was a cold-blooded one, and so exposure to a great degree of cold might serve to slow her heart to the point of death, she knew. Conversely, the hated thing that was expanding within her, tearing her flesh, causing her agony, was growing from the heat that her body generated, the firegems within her stomach that allowed her to vent her anger in caustic flame were feeding the steel, allowing it to grow.

Anwyn quickly calculated that the river's chill might make it stop, though she knew that the three-chambered heart that beat within her serpentine chest might choose to follow suit.

She decided she had no choice but to take the plunge.

Steeling herself as she had against the pain of her wound, the beast slowly slid into the frigid waters.

Her gnarled feet slipped almost immediately against the slimy rocks at the bottom of the riverbed, causing her bleeding chest to slap the crest of the rapids. The wyrm gasped from the shock, struggling to keep from falling, face first, into the river and being swept away by it. There was something both old and young in the translucent water, the knowledge that it was simultaneously forty thousand years and forty minutes old at the same time, having been glacial ice less than an hour before. In spite of the pain and cold, the beast liked the sense of Past that raced along with the current, like time slipping over her the way water runs down a hole in the ground, returning to where it belongs.

I will *live,* she thought angrily to herself. *No matter how much they seek to destroy me, I will always prevail, because my hatred is stronger.*

The wyrm came to a stop midstream; the water was barely up to the joints in her legs. Once she adjusted to the temperature, she found that the dissolved solids speeding along around her gave her a sense of strength, a tie to the Past, a prehistoric time that only she could see. Even without the spyglass it was coming into focus, a land, far off, of dry desert sands and healing springs, of rocks for basking beneath the moon and temples that lay buried in two millennia of clay beneath the skittering wind.

Kurimah Milani, she thought. It was a place lost to the desert long before her birth, a land that had been beyond Elynsynos's dominion, and thereby she knew almost nothing of it, save for its reputation as a place of almost divine healing that had been swallowed in sand and howling wind five hundred years before her father had set foot on the soil of the Wyrmlands. *A place of the past, truly,* she mused, struggling for purchase, finally abandoning the struggle and allowing her feet to sink into the muddy earth below the riverbed. *As I am a thing of the Past, perhaps it will welcome me.*

The dragon, her feet anchored in the frozen silt of the riverbed, slowly began to make her way east, fighting the current each step of the way.

8

HAGUEFORT, NAVARNE

ℜhapsody, I beg of you, please do not panic," Ashe said quickly. His hands moved under the baby's back, even though the loss of color in his wife's face was scarcely greater than that in his own. "You remember what my father said about prophecies—that they are not always as they seem to be."

He carefully took his son into his arms as his wife leaned back against the earthen walls of the chamber, and attempted to smile down at the infant, but could not close his ears to the memory of the rest of his father's statement. *The value of seeing the Future is often not worth the price of the misdirection,* Llauron had noted. Ashe had found that while the interpretation of prophecies could be misleading, in the end to ignore them was a choice with even more dire consequences.

"I am not panicking," Rhapsody said, her voice steady, though her face was still pale. "But there is no question in my mind that Meridion may well be the child of which this prophecy speaks, though I do not understand why something in the tapestry of the Weaver, from a time where history seems to have been undone, would apply to him. When Jal'asee, the Sea Mages' ambassador from the Gaematria, was here during Gwydion's investiture, he spoke to me of the lore that was growing within me, with the mixing of your blood and mine. He used that same nomenclature—saying that he would be a Child of Time." She inhaled, remembering the mage's words, spoken with the wisdom of the most ancient of all races.

Your child will be blessed, and cursed, with the power of all the elements, Rhapsody. You walked through the fire at the heart of the Earth—do not fear; of course I know this, because you clearly absorbed it. What the rest of the world mistakes for mere beauty, one such as myself, who has seen the primordial elements in their raw form, can recognize them. You and your child were cradled in the arms of the sea during your recent captivity—I know this too, not by seeing it, but because the waves told me of it during my journey here from Gaematria. Your husband is the Kirsdarkenvar, the master of the element, so there is a tie to water in both parents. The earth is in you both as well—you because you have traveled through Her heart, your husband because he is descended of the wyrm Elynsynos, as thus linked to it, as you are both linked to the star Seren. And finally, as the Lirin queen you are a Child of the Sky, a daughter of the air. So your child will have all of the elements nascent within his blood. Do you know what all of those elements add up to?

Tell me, she had whispered.

Time. He will have the power of Time. I hope you will do me the honor of allowing me, when the child is old enough and the occasion permits, to help teach your child how to use it.

"Then, when he was born," she went on, "he, like all dragons, needed a name to be formed, and so I gave him one that harked back to Merithyn and his own father, but ultimately I wove the phrase *Child of Time* into his appellation as well."

Ashe nodded at the memory. His time with his new son had been so brief, but at least Fate had been kind enough to allow him to witness the baby's birth in the cave of the Lost Sea, the lair of his great-grandmother, Elynsynos, where Rhapsody had taken refuge.

Elynsynos, who had long ago forsaken her earthly draconic form for one of ether, had taken the physical shape of a woman, the same form she had assumed to meet Merithyn, his Seren great-grandfather, so that she could assist Krinsel, the Bolg midwife, with the delivery.

As he witnessed the miracle unfold, Ashe's eyes had gone from his wife's face to that of his great-grandmother, who in all the elegance of her regal beauty wore the plainly excited, childlike expression he had often seen her wear in dragon form. He had continued to watch in a mix of fear and awe until he felt Rhapsody's hand clutch his. He closed his eyes now, relishing the memory like a treasure in his own hoard.

Sam?

Yes, Aria? The word was Lirin for *my guiding star,* and it had fitted her role in his life perfectly.

She had reached up falteringly and rested her small hand on his chest.

I need the light of the star within you. Our child is coming.

He had bent closer to her and rested his hand atop hers.

Whatever you need. How can I give it to you?

Open your heart. Welcome your child.

All Ashe could do was nod as Rhapsody began to softly sing the elegy to the lost star, Seren, that she had learned from the Seren Sea Mage. As she sang she wept, listening only to the music radiating from the piece of that same star that had been sewn within the realm of the Rowans within his own chest, the pure, elemental song of the lost star, blended with the music of wind and fire, the lore that resided within her, and the earth and water that had come from his blood.

Come forth, my child. Come into the world, and live.

Ashe felt his throat tighten, remembering how close she had been to death as his son was coming to birth.

Elynsynos had conferred one last time with Krinsel, the Bolg midwife Achmed had brought from Ylorc at Rhapsody's request, then the dragon in Seren form raised her hands in a gesture of supplication and reached into Rhapsody's belly from above, her hands passing through as if they were made only of mist and starlight.

It was, he thought, the most magical thing he had ever witnessed.

Elynsynos then drew back her hands and lifted aloft a tiny glowing light, pulling it gently from his wife's failing body and putting it on her chest, into her hands.

Name him, Pretty, so that he can form.

Ashe had barely heard the words she had spoken over the thundering of his own three-chambered heartbeat.

Rhapsody had reached for him with one hand. When his fingers had entwined with hers, she whispered the Naming intonation.

Welcome, Meridion, Child of Time.

For a moment, nothing remained in her other hand but the glowing light. Then slowly a shape began to form, a tiny head, smaller hands held aloft, then waved about. A soft coo erupted a moment later into a full-blown wail, and suddenly the cave was filled with the ordinary human music of a crying infant.

The most beautiful sound he had ever heard.

"I still believe it is very possible that this prophecy is not even about our child," he said to the assembled group. "There are too many things that do not apply; obviously, and blessedly, Rhapsody did not in fact die, as the mother in the prophecy was proclaimed to do. Furthermore, even though he is unique and unusual in his lore and lineage, Meridion is not an unnatural child." His face colored for a moment. "And he was certainly not born of an unnatural act; he came into the world, had his beginnings, in the same way every other child does."

"I'm not so sure that's true," Achmed said. "Sexual congress with a dragon could possibly be viewed by any number of reasonable minds as an unnatural act. It is certainly not something I want to contemplate on a full stomach."

A flash of heat shot through Ashe, and ugly words spilled forth from his mouth before he could stop them.

"And what, then, would you consider your own conception, Achmed? I shudder to even imagine what coupling would have produced a being that is half Dhracian, one of the most ancient of all the world's races, and half Firbolg, one of the most bastard strains of demi-human monsters ever to scar the face of the earth. You're hardly one to talk about being born of unnatural acts."

Rhapsody regarded him reproachfully as the rest of the council stared at him in silence. The Bolg king said nothing, but the Sergeant-Major glowered at him in a way that added threat to the very air of the tiny hidden room.

"Perhaps it is not Meridion's conception, but rather his actual birth that the prophecy means by *brought forth in blood from fire*," Rhapsody said. "Not even you can deny, Sam, the usual circumstances of his delivery. His birth took almost all the blood in my body, from which I am still weak. And, given what has happened to me over time, it could be assumed that I am the fire from which he was brought forth, and you, as a dragon, are the earth that is his sire. But it seems to me that all of this is irrelevant. If there's any chance whatsoever that the Child of Time Talquist is seeking could be Meridion—or if Talquist thinks he is—then we must do everything we can to protect him, whether or not he is the child of which the prophecy speaks."

"I agree," said Ashe. He exhaled deeply, contemplating what to do next.

"I thought, Rhapsody, that you are supposed to remain silent," said Anborn. "There is still much to report; I do not believe His Grace is finished with his tale, and I am by no means finished with mine. Let's get on with this."

"Indeed," said Constantin, "I have one more thing to relate about the actions of the Emperor Presumptive. Some time ago, two of the priests of Sorbold who lived in the manse proximate to Jierna Tal and to the Earth basilica of Terreanfor escaped the fire that destroyed their manse and all of the abbots, acolytes, and priests that dwelt there. For all that this fire was seen as a tragic accident, these three men witnessed otherwise. Those clergy had first feasted in great opulence within the palace of Jierna Tal, where their food was laced with some sort of drug to lull them into sleep. Those who were in its grip never awoke, a mercy of the sort given the death that awaited them. Others were driven back into the manse with arrow fire by Talquist's guards when they tried to escape the flames."

"Why on earth would he do such a thing?" Gwydion Navarne asked in amazed horror.

"Because of what he had asked them to do earlier in that day," replied Constantin darkly. "These men, before they were renamed and hidden elsewhere, made it to Sepulvarta without Talquist's notice, having escaped the fire in the manse, and came to me, relating what they had witnessed. They reported that Talquist had been harvesting the Living Stone of the basilica of Terreanfor, as I told you earlier. They related the specifics of it, however, a horrifying tale in which a massive stone statue of a soldier had been sliced from its pedestal in a lower vault of the cathedral, brought under cover of darkness to the square of Jierna Tal, and placed in one of the weighing plates of the great Scales of Sorbold, the very same instrumentality that conferred upon both myself and Talquist our offices.

"In the other plate some sort of creature was also placed, a freakish miscreant, a poor pathetic soul of twisted body. Then the Weighing was begun. The priests reported that Talquist placed something in the other weighing plate of the Scales against which it was balanced, along with drops of his own blood.

"And, in an abomination against nature and the All-God, the statue was animated, brought to life of the sort, and made to move under its own power."

"Dear One-God," murmured Rial. "What happened then?"

"Blessedly, the titanic statue ran off into the desert beyond the foothills between Sorbold and Sepulvarta, where it crumbled back into sand," said Constantin. "The sword of Living Stone that it tore from its hand before it ran into the night dissolved into sand as well in the streets of Jierna'sid. This act was an abomination, a despoliation of a holy shrine that alone would justify Talquist's removal from office, and in my view his execution. It was a rape of the cathedral of Terreanfor, a desecration that was unforgivable. But more than that, I have to wonder what the purpose was of this experiment. Fortunately, it was an experiment that failed ultimately, and while we may never know what he was attempting, at least we will not have to suffer the consequences."

"Allow me to assume my traditional role of skunk at the lawn fete," said Anborn. "You are incorrect in your assumption, Your Grace. The statue you mention did not in fact crumble to sand in the godforsaken desert of Sorbold. I witnessed this titan myself a few short weeks ago when I was doing reconnaissance in the streets of Jierna'sid. It was a monstrous thing to behold; it came up the main thoroughfare of the city, lurching as if drunk, though certainly it was more likely a factor of its own unnatural state of being. Everything in its path was destroyed; oxcarts, hay wagons, street booths, and most especially the soldiers of Sorbold, who charged it to no avail. It was a terrible sight to witness; while it was awkward and clumsy, there is no question that it was also invulnerable to standard weapon fire and bent on destruction. When last I saw it, it had crushed over eighty soldiers, had damaged untold numbers of shops and wagons, and was making its way in direct course for the palace itself. Mind you, I had little regret, as it appeared to be heading for the emperor himself, but if he is alive and threatening Sepulvarta, perhaps the statue's intentions were other than what I assumed."

"Perhaps indeed," Achmed noted. "I am not certain what is significant in all of this, except that it shows that Talquist is willing to do whatever it takes to achieve his ends. In that way he is no different from me."

"Well said," retorted Anborn. "Very well, then, m'lady, what say you? Have you analyzed what we have reported and determined anything from the lore of it?"

Ashe rose quickly from his chair. "Forgive me, Uncle," he said, "and the rest of you. Before we go further, I wish to speak to my wife alone for a moment outside this chamber. Please indulge me."

Rhapsody held up her hand.

"Before we do," she said, "I need to ask Achmed something. At the risk of being rude, I'll ask him in Bolgish; I'm sorry for my lack of manners, but time is of the essence." The rest of the men in the circle nodded, and so she turned to the Bolg king as the baby in Ashe's arms began to stir, making soft sounds of hunger.

"If you are willing to tell them what you are undertaking within the mountain," she approximated in the harsh, limited language of the Firbolg, "and why, I will help you achieve your ends that I have refused up until now."

Achmed's eyes, mismatched and closely set so that they appeared to always be sighting down a weapon, gleamed.

"To what degree?" he posited in return. "On your terms, or mine?"

"Up until now I have only shared with you the very basics of what I learned in the translation of the ancient scroll you asked me to undertake," Rhapsody answered. "If you will share with this council your intentions and the knowledge of what you are doing, I will tell you whatever I know and will help you in whatever way I can. I need to be able to tell my husband why I am spending so much of my time on this when war is coming, and I have other responsibilities."

The two Bolg exchanged a glance.

"Done," said the Bolg king.

The Lady Cymrian rose and extended her hands to her husband for the child.

"We will return momentarily," she said to the assembled group. "Meridion needs to nurse; thank you for your forbearance."

"I will have Gerald Owen bring in a small repast so that you can refresh yourselves and eat," said Ashe. *I will not need to do so,* he thought. *What I'm about to do will leave me with no stomach for it anyway.*

9

Anborn could feel war coming on, but that was not unusual.

Anyone who had attended the meeting in the tiny room behind the tapestry could feel the same thing; in fact, not to be able to do so denoted a thickness of skull that would be embarrassing. What Anborn was feeling was not as much the advent of war, but gut sensation of his role in it, or at least what he suspected his role was to be.

And, for the first time in many centuries, he was secretly looking forward to it.

He sat back as far as he could, taking his useless legs and extending them by hand as Gerald Owen and Melisande Navarne made their way into the hidden room with trays of food for those remaining within.

His eyes narrowed as they sighted on the young girl with golden ringlets who was placing a tray down on the table in front of him.

"Who is this?" he demanded gruffly. "I thought this meeting was to be held in secret, and yet here you have brought in an unknown serving wench, quite probably a spy."

The girl's black eyes rolled in fond annoyance. "You are in severe need of a new joke, Lord Marshal," she said, lifting the lid of the tray and handing him a linen napkin. "You know very well that I am Melisande Navarne, seeing as you are my godfather, and have been tossing me around like a ball since I was a baby."

"Ah, and that is why I know you to be an imposter," Anborn said smugly as he laid the napkin across his useless legs. "Melisande Navarne is *still* a baby; she fits in the length of my forearm between my wrist and elbow." He clapped his hand against his arm for emphasis. "You, however, are a big impudent lummox, and could not possibly be that sweet, tiny little girl."

Melisande assumed the position of a servant, her arms behind her back.

"Much as it pains me to remind you that you are *aging,* Lord Marshal—"

"Ow," Grunthor muttered as Rial and Achmed lowered their heads, smiling.

"—I am in fact your goddaughter and the Lady Navarne, second in line to this duchy, I might add. I am nine years old, soon to be ten on the first day of spring, and am more than four times the length of your forearm. Additionally, I can run, ride, shoot an arrow, and wield a dagger; I am expert in horsemanship and routinely curry and tack the entire livery. I get far better reports from the tutors than my brother *ever* did, and am very tired of being left in the nursery when important matters are being discussed. I could be quite valuable to the council, certainly at least as a messenger or maybe a spy." The girl's dark eyes sparkled with a mix of excitement and resentment. "I would like to register my displeasure at being left out of everything, plainly but politely, and say that if Rhapsody had had so stifled an upbringing she would never have grown into the lady, queen, and warrior that she is. I consider this a terrible waste of valuable Cymrian assets."

"I'll waste *your* valuable Cymrian asset, young lady," the Lord Marshal shouted, swinging playfully at her hindquarters. Melisande dodged, as she always did at this point in the game, then hurriedly followed Gerald Owen out of the hidden room.

"Well, that one 'as a mouth on her," said Grunthor approvingly. "If you can't find somethin' for 'er ta do, give 'er ta me—Oi'll make right fine use of 'er."

"Don't tempt me," muttered Gwydion Navarne. "I can have all her possessions packed and on the keep steps in less than fifteen minutes."

"Spoken more like a frustrated older brother than an invested duke," said Anborn curtly. "Mark my words, young Navarne—that girl will make you proud that you are related to her one day."

"Probably," said Gwydion Navarne ruefully. "And it's more likely to take fifteen *days* to get her packed."

$\mathcal{I}$ confess, Rhapsody, it is very disturbing to discover that you are keeping a secret from me with Achmed," Ashe said as they came from behind the tapestry into the Great Hall. "I thought there was nothing that we kept one from another. I have certainly trusted you with all of my secrets, hideous as many of them have been."

Rhapsody squeezed his hand. "I would have told you all that I know about this, Sam, but it is not my secret to tell. Some time back, when you and I were both in the desert of Yarim, when the Bolg were tunneling for water below the fountain of Entudenin, Achmed showed me a thin parchment document from the oldest of times, long before the Cymrian era, perhaps even from the Lost Island itself. It was a schematic of a machine the likes of which I had never seen before that employs the rainbow spectrum of light together with the sound spectrum of the musical scale to generate different sorts of powers—the power of healing, the power of scrying and hiding, and many others I have not yet figured out. He did not leave this information with me, even though I recognized it as being some of the most elemental and basic lore of the world, ancient in its origin, and I warned him to be careful with it, that even the master Namers are only privy to some of that lore.

"When he came to Gwydion's investiture, he brought the document with him yet again. He asked me to translate it, and I took it with me when you brought me to Elynsynos's Lair to visit with her. In that time, I came to understand what it meant, what the lore was, and what the risks of using it were. It almost ended our friendship, as a matter of fact. After Meridion's birth, I told Achmed I never wished to see him again, because he was so insistent on having the translation in spite of my warnings. But upon reflection, and after we had a heart-to-heart talk when we were trapped within the protection of Llauron's body, I came to understand what it is that he really wishes to do. He has had some experience with this instrumentality before, in the old land, and he feels that if we are in fact going to be battling forces that precede history, we must have weapons whose origin and power preceded it as well."

"There is wisdom in that," Ashe acknowledged.

"In addition, while the instrumentality as Gwylliam and Anwyn utilized it threatened to wake the Sleeping Child, the wyrm that sleeps at the center of the earth, Achmed seems to have discovered a way to power it, not from fire or from the Earth's lore, as they did, but rather to utilize the light of the sun and the stars to do so, which should make it much safer to use, even though it still must be done judiciously. It should also be more powerful—each of the elements has greater power in the order it was created, so ether supersedes all, followed by fire, water, wind, and earth sequentially. Using ether to power our Lightcatcher should make it both immense in its effect and as safe as it can possibly be as well. If we can use it to guard the Earthchild and secure the mountains, scry to find the enemy and defeat them, it will have been worth the risk and the damage our friendship has sustained because of it."

"I do not doubt your wisdom, Aria," Ashe said, taking her hand in both of his. "It is perhaps petty, especially given all that we are to each other, but there is something that galls me about Achmed requiring secrecy of you that keeps us apart, even the smallest of ways. I guess it's an immature resentment; chalk it up to the possessiveness of dragon blood."

Rhapsody kissed his hand. "There are no more secrets between us," she said, "though there are some that only we know. There is a secret that you and I keep, alone, one to the other, and always have."

Ashe smiled ruefully. "Really?" he asked. "It seems to me that there are none between you and both of the Firbolg. You've known them far longer and in far different circumstances than we have known each other, even if we did meet first in time."

"Yes, but only you know that, and only you know my real name," she said. "I have only spoken it once in this world, and it was in the wedding ceremony we held in secret. Only in the grotto of Elysian can the reverberations of that name be found, and even the greatest of Namers would have trouble doing so. And they still do not know that we met first on the other side of Time; only we share the memory of that sweet night, something that has comforted me, and no doubt you, often over the intervening time. So, you are in fact the guardian of my lost lore, and of my heart. You are my past, and my future. And that will ever be."

Ashe sighed. "If only I could be your Present," he said.

The baby in his arms let out a squeal of hunger, and they both laughed.

"I think someone is in line ahead of you," Rhapsody said. "And while you can roar with the best of your kind, he still wins for sheer volume and pitch." She put the fussing baby to the breast, gently caressing his golden curls.

Ashe exhaled solemnly.

"Aria, I am going to ask you to do something that I would rather die than see you do."

Rhapsody looked up in surprise. "Then don't," she said simply. "If you feel that way about it—"

"We have no choice," Ashe interrupted. "You must leave here, with Meridion, tonight. If we hadn't accepted the mantle of leadership, it would be one thing; I could spirit you and the baby away, take you across the sea or hide you in the holy forest of Gwynwood near the Great White Tree, and you would both be as safe as it would be possible for me to make you. But we have committed our trust and our fealty to a nation, to an Alliance, and now that war is looming, we cannot go back on our vows, even for the purpose of remaining together. At the same time, the rest of the world can be damned if it means that either you or our son is in danger; that is the one thing I cannot bear. I will not be able to remain sane should anything happen to either of you. *The Rampage of the Wyrm* may have been a fictitious manuscript according to Elynsynos, but I feel deep within me an undeniable belief that it would come to pass should I lose you. I have already set the forest alight more than once when I believed you were lost to me. Just the knowledge that there are entities out there, scrying for Meridion, makes the wyrm within my blood ascendant, longing for vengeance and destruction.

"While I believe that Highmeadow has the strongest of fortifications possible, to keep you here when there are eyes watching, looking for our son, would be folly and selfish, not to mention unwise. There really is only one place that both of you will be safe as the world begins to cave in."

"What are you saying, Sam?" Rhapsody asked, her voice shaking.

Ashe lowered his head. "With your permission, I want to petition Achmed to take you into his care. You and the baby should leave with him and Grunthor tonight, before the light breaks, and travel off the road, probably through Canderre and Yarim rather than Bethany, and possibly through the northeastern corner of Bethe Corbair, where there is nothing but desert, no landmarks or fortifications where you could be found by one who has the power to scry from a distance." He exhaled deeply. "I cannot tell you how much I wish to vomit at this very moment. Nonetheless, I believe we need to move in all due haste. If the Bolg can agree, and I have no reason to believe that they will not, and if you are willing, and feel that you are able to make the journey, as soon as this council ends I will set about making provisions so that you can leave before First-light."

Rhapsody leaned back against the wall as the child nursed.

"What a beautiful love song," she mused.

"Pardon?"

"What you just said to me were perhaps the most beautiful words of love I have ever heard," she said, smiling sadly. "I well know how much you hate this idea, how much it galls you to the very soul, how difficult it was for you to propose it. It will be similarly difficult for me to grant your request. But, as I don't have a better idea, I fear you are right, and to do anything else were to insufficiently safeguard our greatest treasure." She looked down at the baby, now drowsing at the breast.

"You will do it then?" Ashe asked, his expression a mixture of relief and dread.

Rhapsody closed her blouse and swaddled the child again.

"I will, for him," she said. "I will go to Ylorc and help Achmed with his infernal Lightcatcher, in the hope that it may both protect the mountains and help turn the tide to end the war more quickly. But I tell you this, Sam: when Meridion is weaned, and safe, I will return to the front. I am the Iliachenva'ar; I have no business bearing a sword of elemental fire in hiding. It would be an insult to Oelendra and the training she gave me to stand by for the sake of my own safety when others are dying."

"I would expect nothing less," Ashe said. Rhapsody smiled at him. "And should you receive word that something has befallen me, let Anborn prosecute the war until you are ready to assume command."

Rhapsody's smile faded. "Come; we should be returning," she said. She rose and gave Ashe her hand again, and together they headed back to the small, dark room beyond a hidden door.

He stopped one last time at the window just before the tapestry, in a pool of light from the nearby windows, and sat down on a bench beneath it. Rhapsody sat down slowly as well.

"You have not told me of Llauron's death," he said quietly. "Did my father suffer in the end? I know you will tell me the truth, sworn to it as you are, being a Namer, but do not spare me the blow of the words as my wife. Just tell me."

"He did not, in my estimation," Rhapsody said gently. "He stepped between Anwyn and me, with Meridion in my arms, and surrounded us with his ethereal essence—and then he was gone, his body a shell of elemental earth, a mist lingering within it. There was no pain, no hurt your grandmother could have inflicted on him, though I suppose there was regret in the last knowledge of her being willing to take his life, after all he had done and sacrificed for her throughout history. You saw the expression in his eyes, Sam; it was peace, and resignation—he knew he had saved his grandchild from certain death. I think, if nothing else, that will bring him to the door of the Lord and Lady Rowan, and to life everlasting."

Rhapsody watched for the hint of water in his cerulean blue eyes, eyes scored strangely and beautifully by draconic vertical pupils, but there was no such sign, an absence that betrayed an even deeper sorrow, one beyond tears.

"I don't know what possessed me to be so cruel to him the last time we saw each other," Ashe said. "He was so excited about Meridion, so desirous to make amends so that he might be part of his grandchild's life. And I spurned him, turned him away, told him he would never gain what he wanted. I don't know what possessed me."

She took his hand.

"The same thing that possesses me to leave all that I know, all that I love," she said simply, without sentiment. "The duty—and the desire—to keep our son safe at any price." Her small calloused fingertip caressed his palm. "Llauron understood that as well, more than anyone I have ever known. He Ended, protecting his grandchild. Only once more in all of history has such a sacrifice been made. When he is older, Meridion will know how much Llauron must have loved him to make it. And, though I can't be certain, it seems as if he may have passed some of his lore along to Meridion—I thought I beheld a mist hovering in the prison of Llauron's body that the baby breathed in."

Ashe continued to stare out the window of the keep at the silver trees glistening black with the onset of Second Thaw.

"It's nice to think so, anyway," he said at last, rising from the bench and pulling her up with him. "Come, let us go back and finalize what we have decided. Then we can have Meridion's Naming ceremony before you leave. At least one happy memory should come from this day."

He pulled aside the tapestry and led her carefully down the stairs to the secret entrance, then opened the door to the hidden room, where the rest of the group meeting in secret was finishing their repast.

They returned to their places at the table. Ashe placed the sleeping baby back in Rhapsody's arms.

"Thank you for your patience," Ashe said. "The decisions we have come to are dire ones, and will be difficult on each of us to enact. Each requires sacrifice that in many cases is almost too great to be borne—but that is the way of leadership."

"Alas," said Anborn.

"First, I wish to officially ask the Firbolg king a boon." Ashe looked at Achmed.

"You're asking me for a favor?" Achmed said incredulously. "If it is the commitment of troops, the answer is no. The Firbolg army has already come to the aid of Roland once, at the Great Moot. Under the circumstances, I'm going to need every soldier I have."

"I couldn't agree more," said Ashe archly. "My request is this: take my wife and son tonight, under cover of darkness, and travel off the road, over the desert to Ylorc, where I ask you to keep them hidden and safe within the Teeth. Something hunts our son; knowing this, I cannot rest, nor can I prosecute this war correctly until I am certain that he is as safe as it is possible to make him, as well as his mother. Since Rhapsody has agreed to assist you with the building and development of your Lightcatcher, she may as well have the protection of the mountains to hide her and the baby. Do you agree?"

Achmed and Grunthor exchanged a glance. Then the Bolg king's mismatched eyes returned to Ashe.

"Ylorc was Rhapsody's first home on the continent," he said. "She has title to a small duchy there. She's always welcome in the Teeth."

"Yeah, and the Bolg will be glad ta see the baby, too," Grunthor said, chuckling.

"First recipe I see with his name on it, I will light a whole tribe of them on fire," Rhapsody said.

"I now ask the Lady Cymrian to assess what she has heard from each of us, and tell us what she thinks," said Ashe.

The Lady Cymrian exhaled.

"It sounds to me like the war that is coming is more a war arising from men's greed than from the demonic desire for destruction," she said. "But that matters little. Chaos and anarchy are magnets for the F'dor; sooner or later there will be a power beyond these days, from the old times, that we will be facing. For that reason, the Lightcatcher is a wise investment.

"I would also guess from what I have heard that there are more allies involved on Talquist's side than we know about. For all that Sorbold was a more or less solitary nation under Leitha, the Emperor Presumptive is a former merchant. He no doubt has friends and trading partners all around the world. We must discover quickly which ones beyond our borders he has recruited to aid him in his attempt at conquest of the Middle Continent."

"I would guess the Hintervold," Anborn said.

"Perhaps, though the Hintervold is dependent on Roland for foodstuffs, and Sorbold cannot easily provide that," Rhapsody said. "It will be interesting to turn over as many rocks as possible and discover what crawls out."

She turned to Rial, her loyal viceroy. "This is my final command to you, my friend: go back to Tyrian and serve, as you did before my crowning, as her Lord Protector. Safeguard the forest for now; we do not need to involve the Lirin at this point, though you must instruct the woods guards and the Lirin border guards to prevent any troops that would pass from Sorbold to Roland from doing so, even at the cost of a martial challenge. And Rial—go to the palace at Tomingorllo, where the diadem rests in its case. Make the attempt to pick it up, as I once did. Perhaps it is time for the crown of stars to change heads; I will be too far away to act as titular queen for a long while. The Lirin deserve better."

"The crown, and the Lirin, have already made their choices, m'lady," Rial said.

"Even a diadem of ethereal diamonds has the right to revisit a decision every now and them," Rhapsody said, smiling at her confidant. "We must be ready for what is to come; while this may be only an upworld war to begin with, I suspect it will not remain such."

"Rhapsody is correct," Ashe went on. "While the footprints of those that once dwelt within the Vault of the Underworld are not discernible here, the bloodshed and violence that is to come is a bait for the demonic, a temptation that may draw them in. So we must be prepared to repel not only the forces driven by greed and the desire for conquest, but be ready to grapple with darker forces, evil from the First Age that can only be destroyed by lore from the same time. For this reason, I wish to pronounce the decisions of this makeshift council, comprised of members of different factions of the Alliance and the church, in the presence of a Lirin Namer, that history will record our actions as defensive, and undertaken for the sake of safeguarding the Middle Continent, and its people, against the threat of invasion by those who would conquer the earth, and those that dwell beneath it."

"Do so, then, nephew," said Anborn. "I am happy not to be in your place this day; you will not know how painful this moment really is until years from now, when the pages of history are written about it. Believe me when I tell you this."

The Lord Cymrian's voice was steady, kingly. "Very well—this is my decision, made in concert and with consent of all present, pending their assent," he said. "Anborn has always been best in the command of men. If you will agree, Uncle, to take up the mantle you cast aside centuries ago, and again serve as Lord Marshal to the forces of the Alliance, it would put the best leader in the field. You also have personal friendships among some of our more tentative allies—the Nain, the Icemen of the Hintervold, the Blesser of the Nonaligned States—all of these at one time or another were brothers-in-arms of yours. Though there is no need to drag any of those allies into this war if they are not needed, it would be good to know that we can count on their loyalty if they are—loyalty either to the Alliance or its military commander."

"As you wish, nephew," Anborn said. His voice was quiet and circumspect, with none of the condescending tone in which he generally spoke, especially about things martial.

"It therefore falls to me to hold the land itself," Ashe went on. "The draconic part will guard the Tree and serve to sustain the shield of the world. That which is man, the Lord Cymrian, must fight to protect the people who dwell upon that land. In the name of Llauron, my father, and that of Elynsynos, my great-grandmother, I will do both. I will call the Council of Dukes at once, and take over command of all of the provincial armies, putting them under Anborn's direct command."

"Tristan Steward will not like that," Gwydion Navarne said. "I believe he has expected to be given that post as Lord Regent."

"He will think otherwise when he sees the scope and scale of what we are up against," said Ashe. "But we do not have time to wait for the gathering of the provincial forces, if what you suspect is coming is nigh, Your Grace. Anborn should accompany you back to Sepulvarta immediately, taking with you all of the forces you can muster from the outposts and garrisons in southeastern Navarne and southern Bethany. I will draft up articles of command that will give you authority to conscript any military forces you can reach; there should be almost ten thousand along that route, give or take however many are in the process of guarding mail caravans."

The Patriarch nodded. "That seems wise. I would hope that you would not leave Roland vulnerable to aid Sepulvarta; that would be a fool's errand."

"Indeed," said Ashe. "Anborn, will ten thousand be sufficient for your rescue of the holy city?"

"More than enough to break a siege, if one has begun," said Anborn. "But I have to tell you, Nephew, that I suspect they will not be of the caliber needed to do so. I have been warning you for three years, since you took on this bloody lordship, that war was coming, and that preparations needed to be made."

"And I heeded you," Ashe said patiently. "You may be pleasantly surprised, Uncle."

"I am *never* pleasantly surprised," the Lord Marshal muttered. "The very concept of surprise is an innately unpleasant one."

"I will conduct the strategic aspects of the war—the defense of the Middle Continent and the rest of the Alliance—from the fortress at Highmeadow. I will send ships immediately to our allies in Manosse and Gaematria across the Wide Central Sea, to alert them to what is happening; Talquist has the naval advantage, but with their assistance, we can even the field.

"I will also heed the wisdom of my wife, much as I fear my own repercussions of our decision," Ashe went on. "I will entrust her, and our son, to Achmed, king of the Firbolg, who is not only our ally but her dear friend, for the purpose of safeguarding her and Meridion from whatever evil seeks him. Rhapsody has agreed to go to Ylorc with Achmed, and to aid him in the development and utilization of the instrumentality he calls the Lightcatcher, a remaking of Gwylliam's Lightforge designed and built by the Nain before the Cymrian War, for the purpose of protecting the lore it uses. The Bolg king reaffirms his commitment to the Alliance, though makes no promises of troop involvement, and asserts that the use of the instrumentality will be for the defense of the said Alliance, if and when possible. Have I characterized your position correctly, Achmed?"

The Bolg king snorted. "For the purposes of history, certainly. History means nothing to me; I have yet to see an example of it that I have believed."

"Perhaps this will be the first, then," Ashe said mildly. "Rhapsody, Lirin queen and Lady Cymrian, has asked Rial, Viceroy of Tyrian, to expand his role to Lord Protector and to see if the diadem in Tomingorllo assesses him to be worthy of the kingship in her stead. She reiterates her primary fealty to Tyrian, second only to that of the Alliance as a whole." The Lady Cymrian exhaled and nodded her agreement.

"I cannot tell you how sad this makes me, m'lady," Rial said. "I remember fondly the day you picked up that diadem, made from the shattered pieces of the Purity Diamond, destroyed by Anwyn in a pact with the demon against her husband. It came to life in your hands, a symbol of the unity you would bring to the Lirin kingdoms—and the Cymrian Alliance. To think that you may have to give it up to protect both of those entities now is tragic."

Rhapsody shook her head. "I'm giving up nothing, Rial. In my heart I will always be a daughter of Tyrian, whether I wear the diadem or a kerchief on my head. I only wish I could have brought about an era of peace to that united kingdom, rather than having to take up arms to defend it once again. At least this time the Lirin have Anborn fighting on their side, and not against them. That alone is worth the loss of the crown."

"What is to come will change us all in ways we cannot even contemplate now," said Ashe. "But know this—it will surely come to pass. We cannot avoid it, but at least we are united in our determination to stand together against it. In this way, the second Cymrian era could not be more different from the first."

Anborn nodded. "And we will prevail. In this way, it could not be more different, either."

"Glad as I am to have you with us, Lord Marshal, even you cannot hold back the raging ocean; its will cannot be stopped," Rial said somberly. "The best you can do is build a seawall and keep patching it. With any luck the storm will pass before it gives way."

"I'd rather think of a way to drain the sea," Anborn muttered. "But, as I can't, sandbag duty it is."

"Yes," said the Patriarch, rising with the others as the council meeting came to an end. "But on that day when you discover such a way to drain the sea, I am with you, bucket in hand."

As he ambulated noisily down the corridor leading away from the Great Hall, with its many porticos and side hallways, Anborn reached effortlessly behind the drape of an alcove where a small stone statue of Merithyn the Explorer was displayed and grasped a handful of gold ringlets, dragging their owner's head out from behind the heavy velvet swath. A high-pitched gasp echoed up the Grand Staircase to the floors above.

"Ah, yes, you *do* make a fine little spy, don't you now, m'lady?" he said with exaggerated courtesy, smiling at the shock in the glittering black eyes. "But apparently your assets are not as valuable as you thought. Keep working at it, though." He released her curls and patted her head affectionately, then made his way down the rest of the hallway, the clunking metallic sound of his walking machine reverberating through the whole of the quiet keep.

The girl remained in shock, still watching him, until the echoes faded into silence again. Then she hurried back to the buttery in the dimness of night, the light from the great lamps seeming to cause her shadow to lengthen, her hair to darken and fade into the gloom.

10

$\mathcal{T}$he wind off the sea was strong in the fading winter's ebb, growing as the advent of spring approached. The gusts of the prevailing winds were steady enough to carry weather for miles inland, the vapor from the warming ocean blanketing the coastal towns and forests like a dream from which the land struggled to wake, winding its misty way eastward.

Rath cursed as yet more icy water whipped around his head, drizzling down his neck. The ability to step between gusts of wind, letting the updrafts carry him great distances and sparing his feet the walking, was a great advantage of his race and profession, but it was not without cost. The arc along which he traveled in this way was an invisible wave of sound, oftentimes inaudible to the human ear, borne on the wind and anchored on each end at two points in the physical world. Rath had been upworld long enough to be able to recognize the beginnings and endings of such waves, and therefore more often than not was able to manipulate the wind to his benefit, as if opening a door at one end of the gust unto the other end, saving time in his travels and passing unnoticed across the wide spaces of the world.

Occasionally, however, the wind was temperamental, refusing to be ridden the way a rogue horse or a jackass might. When this occurred, Rath found himself far off his planned course. Sometimes a fair wind turned foul when he was wrapped within its arms, following what had been a clear, strong wave, only to dump him unceremoniously short of the mark in a swamp or midden, or even in the middle of a pond. Whatever weather the wind was carrying was also unpredictable in its path, and as a result he would sometimes find himself bathing in sleet, being pelted on all sides by hail, or drenched in rain even though it had been a fine, dry gust into which he had originally stepped.

In short, walking the wind was a necessary evil. But it was the only way one of his race, and his mission, could traverse the world quickly enough to follow the fragment of a fading heartbeat, the whisper of a demonic name.

The gust subsided at the end of the wave of sound, and Rath stumbled out of the wind into the solidity of the world again.

He pulled his hood farther forward over his face and looked around him.

The place he had landed on the rogue gust was vaguely familiar, but Rath could not be certain if that was because he had walked this place before, long ago, or if every small, putrid farming settlement in a backward forested area was indistinguishable from another. Either way, he had appeared in a place that was as sleepy and nondescript as it was possible to be.

A dense copse of trees and holly bushes loomed behind him, and Rath quickly stepped within it; he did not see the villagers about, but his sensitive skin registered vibrations that indicated humans were somewhere nearby, oblivious to his presence, most likely, but able to see him should he be out in plain sight.

Once safely out of view, he began to cant his litany.

Hrarfa, Fraax, Sistha, Hnaf, Ficken.

He tasted the wind for each name, concentrated until his throat went dry and his skin burned, but there was, as usual, nothing to be found. He listened for the *kirai*s of his fellow hunters, and there too he found only silence or neutral reports; the searching songs of those like him had not discerned any new threads or heartbeats, any new clues to the whereabouts of the F'dor that those hunters pursued.

As it had been for most of history.

Rath exhaled slowly as the link to the minds of his fellow hunters dissolved. He prepared to move on, but there was a sour sensation in his mouth, a taste of something evil, or perhaps just something *wrong,* remaining behind where a moment before there had been nothing but the ambient air. Wickedness, evil, hate, they were so palpable that they often left behind traces of acid floating on the wind. Rath's heart began to beat slightly faster, but his inner senses were not enflamed yet; he had experienced this sort of thing many times over the millennia, a misdirection or false lead that would put him off his trail.

F'dor, after all, were not the only entities in the world capable of terrible malevolence.

Rath had no time for other such entities. His mission, bred in his blood and older than most of the Earth was old, blotted out all else.

He inhaled deeply through his nose once more, his sensitive sinuses the last bastion of detection, only to find that whatever had been on the wind had vanished into it, if it had ever really existed in the first place.

Rath turned his attention away from the distraction and cleared his mind again. Once more he loosed his *kirai,* this time calling the name of the living man he sought.

Ysk.

Once again, the slight tinge echoed back to him, distant, but still clear enough to be discerned. Rath tried to hold on to the vibration, but it, too, eluded him.

Then, a moment later, he realized why.

It was coming from a different direction than when he had first discerned it.

The signal he had picked up when he first landed originated in the southeast. He had been following the prevailing winds in that general direction in the hope that he might catch a stronger vibration. Rath had guessed that the name had been sounded in what other hunters who had trod this continent more recently than he had described as the Bolglands, where Canrif, the royal seat of the Cymrian Empire, had once stood. But now, somewhat clearer and cleaner, it was echoing to the northeast, and not very far away.

Rath inhaled deeply, expelling all the wind from his lungs. His target had moved and, moreover, the dead name had been sounded again recently, making a new vibration for him to follow.

He closed his eyes and raised his hand to the wind, opening his mouth slightly, fishing about for a new gust of a strong northeasterly breeze to get him closer to his target.

A jolt of shock ricocheted through him as he was struck violently from behind, the blow driving the air from his lungs as his chin and teeth smashed into the snowy ground.

Caught unaware in the midst of his concentration, Rath gasped, inhaling the blood that had begun to pour from his sensitive sinus cavities. In shock, he dimly heard the sounds of raucous laughter, the grunts and scuffling as he was flipped onto his back in the snow and roughly gone over, his legs and abdomen battered with what felt like heavy sticks.

After a few seconds his mind cleared, and he could think again. He sensed that he was in the grip of four brigands or, more likely, drunken ne'er-do-wells by the reek of them. Two of them were slapping wooden tools, rakes or hoes it seemed, against him to keep him supine, while a third searched his robe pockets and the fourth rifled his pack, unimpressed by the sounds of disappointment that he uttered. Rath lay still, feigning stupor and collecting himself, until the one rummaging through his clothes discovered his knife. The man yanked it from the calf sheath and held it high amid the buffoonish laughter of the others.

"Well, lookee 'ere, boys!" the bandit crowed. "He's got a lit'le blade! Right sweet it is, too—can probably terrify an *apple* with it!"

"Ya know what they say about men wi' lit'le blades, Abner—"

"Yeah, poor fellow, got no shoes neither, damn him. He's a baldy, too, no hair. A right sorry sort."

The laughter grew more uproarious. "Good job, Percy—ya picked someone ta rob who got less'n *we* got! What's the odds of that?"

One of the brigands tossed his hoe on the ground and snatched the knife angrily.

"He'll have even less in a minute," he said tersely. He shoved the first man out of the way and grabbed for Rath's robe below the waist.

With a speed born of the wind Rath seized the robber's wrist and clenched it in the viselike grip of his race. With grim satisfaction he ground the bones against each other, feeling them pop from the joints. The man gasped raggedly, then began to wail in pain, a hideous noise that scratched against Rath's skin.

He tilted the man's arm at an impossible angle and with the man's own hand dragged the small knife across his throat, slashing through the veins and cartilage to the bone.

The three other brigands froze, even as the pulsing blood from the neck of their comrade showered them in gore.

Rath rose from the ground, kicked aside the body sprawled in the pink snow, snatched up his pack, and quickly searched the wind for a favorable updraft. He opened his mouth and let loose a strange hum, the call that summoned any wayward breeze that might be gusting through.

In answer, a southeasterly breeze filled his ears, drowning out the animal-like sounds of terror from the remaining robbers. Rath pulled up his hood, preparing to depart, and lowered his gaze to take in the sight. He cursed inwardly, annoyed with himself for having been caught unaware by such pathetic specimens of humankind.

One of the men's faces melted from the rictus of horror before his eyes into a mien of black fury. He scrambled to his knees and lunged wildly at Rath, encouraged after a few seconds by his bewailing fellows.

"Get 'im, Abner! *Get* the bloody bast—"

Rath's eyes narrowed in his angular face. He changed the character of the vibration he had used to call the wind into a discordant drone, intensifying the modulation and increasing the frequency, punctuating it with harsh clicks from his epiglottis.

The two men who remained crouched on the ground shrieked in pain and grabbed their heads as their temples throbbed, the veins threatening to burst. Rath reached down and seized the man who had charged him by the back of the neck in his iron grip, then stepped into the open door of the wind.

The updraft was a strong one, its trajectory high. Rath allowed it to carry him and his struggling passenger aloft till it was at its apex twenty feet from the ground, then released his grip, dropping Abner headfirst onto his fellows with a thud that resounded like the crushing of a melon. The pink snow beneath them splashed red.

Not at all an unattractive picture when viewed from above, thought Rath as he traveled down the long wave of the gust, moving quickly across the ground where the air temperature was colder. He closed his eyes and allowed the wind to carry him northward, toward the east, where upon landing he would once again seek the man with the dead name.

Ysk.

His closest prey.

11

HAGUEFORT, NAVARNE

$\mathcal{A}$s soon as the council dispersed, both the lord and lady went to the chamberlain of Haguefort.

Gerald Owen was an older Cymrian, and had been in the service of the family Navarne for several generations. He set a great store by efficiency and proper etiquette, and took great pride in the meticulous running of his staff. He was in the process of getting the Lady Navarne ready for bed when the Lord and Lady appeared in the hallway.

"Owen?" Ashe called as the two of them approached.

Gerald Owen turned in surprise. "Yes, m'lord?"

Ashe pulled the elderly chamberlain aside. "Pack Melisande's belongings, and enough of your own for a brief journey." He looked over to the young Lady Navarne, whose face was growing pale at his words. Rhapsody put her arm around the little girl's shoulder. "You will take her to the Circle at Gwynwood, where you are to entrust her to Gavin, the Invoker of the Filids. Then return to Haguefort and gather the staff; direct them to begin packing in a written missive before you leave. They will be relocating to the stronghold at Highmeadow when you return."

"Yes, m'lord," said the elderly chamberlain smoothly, but his hands were shaking. "When do you wish the Lady Navarne to leave?"

Ashe glanced at Rhapsody. "Before dawn," he said, then turned and left the room. Gerald Owen bowed quickly to Rhapsody and followed him.

"You're—you're sending me away to Gwynwood—alone?" Melisande stammered.

Rhapsody knelt down and turned the trembling little girl to face her.

"Shh," she whispered. "Yes. Don't be frightened. I have a mission for you."

Melisande's black eyes, glazed an instant before in building terror, blinked, and in the next second were sparkling with interest.

"A mission? A real mission?"

"Yes," said Rhapsody seriously. "Wait a moment, and I'll tell you about it."

She closed her eyes and reached out both hands to Melisande, who took them excitedly. Then she began to chant softly, words in an ancient language taught to her more than a thousand years before by her mentor in the art of Singing, a science known to her mother's people, the Liringlas, called Skysingers in the common language.

The air in the room was suddenly drier as the water within it was stripped, and a thin circle of mist formed around the two of them, glittering like sunlight on morning dew. A moment later the words Rhapsody was speaking began to echo outside of the mist in staggered intervals, building one upon the other until the room beyond was filled with a quiet cacophony. Melisande had witnessed this phenomenon before; Rhapsody often called such a circle of masking noise into being whenever the two of them were whispering, giggling, and sharing secret thoughts to protect their words from imaginary eavesdroppers. In the back of her mind, she knew innately that those days were about to come to an end.

When she was satisfied that their words had been sufficiently occluded, Rhapsody opened her eyes and looked down at the Lady Navarne.

"I need you to do something for me that I can entrust to no one in this world other than you, Melly," she said, her voice soft but solemn.

The words rang with a clarity that Melisande recognized as the Naming ability of True-Speaking; she straightened her shoulders to be ready for the gravity of what was to come.

"This night I will send a messenger bird to Gavin asking him do as you direct him when you arrive. I can only entrust this request to you in spoken word, because if something should happen to the message, it would be disastrous." Melisande, orphaned by such disasters, nodded soberly, understanding the full implication of the Lady Cymrian's words.

"Once you arrive at the Circle, ask Gavin to take you, along with a full contingent of his top foresters and his most accomplished healer, to the greenwood north-northeast of the Tar'afel River, where the holly grows thickest. These are sacred lands, and I can give you no map, for fear of what might become of it. Gavin will know where this is. Tell him to have his foresters fan out at that point, keeping to a distance of half a league each, and form a barrier that extends northwest all the way to the sea, setting whatever snares and traps they need to protect that barrier. They are to remain there, allowing no living soul to enter. They should comb the woods for a lost Firbolg midwife named Krinsel, and should they come upon her, they are to accord her both respect and safe passage back to the guarded caravan, which will accompany her to Ylorc. Are you keeping up with this so far?"

"Yes," said Melisande. She repeated the directions perfectly, and the Lady Cymrian's emerald eyes sparkled with approval.

"Gavin himself is to take you from this point onward. A sweet-water creek flows south into the Tar'afel; follow it northward until you come to Mirror Lake—you will know this body of water because its name describes it perfectly. At the lake you are to leave Gavin and travel on alone. He is to wait for you there for no more than three days. If you have not returned by then, direct him to return to the Circle." She paused, and Melisande repeated the directions again flawlessly, her face calm and expressionless. "Walk around the lake to the far side. There you will see a small hillside, and in it, hidden from all other vantage points, is a cave. Its entrance is approximately twenty feet high, and on the cave wall outside the opening is an inscription—*Cyme we inne frid, fram the grip of deap to lif inne dis smylte land.*"

Melisande's small face lit with excitement.

"Elynsynos! You are sending me to *Elynsynos?!*"

"Shhhh," cautioned Rhapsody, though she couldn't suppress a smile at the reaction. "Yes."

"I remember those words from my history lessons," Melisande said. "*'Cyme we inne frid, fram the grip of deaþ to lif inne dis smylte land*— Come we in peace to life in this fair land.' That's the inscription Merithyn the Explorer carved on her cave, the birthplace of the Cymrian people—and how we came to be called by that name."

"You must walk respectfully as you approach her lair," Rhapsody said, import in her words. "Tread softly, walk slowly, and pause every few steps to listen. If you feel warm air flowing from the cave, or hear the leaves of the trees begin to rustle noticeably, stop and ask permission to enter."

"I will," Melisande promised, her face shining.

Rhapsody crouched down and ran her hands up the young girl's arms.

"As much as I pray that this will come to pass, I regret to tell you that I think that you may hear nothing," she said, the pale golden skin of her fair face growing rosy. "It is my fear, Melisande, that you will find her dead, or injured, or not there at all. If you find her dead, return to Gavin and report what you have found. If she is injured, but can still speak, ask her what she wants you to do. If she cannot, again, go to Gavin, but return with the healer to the cave, and stay with her while they attend to her wounds.

"But if she is missing, when you report to Gavin, tell him to seal the cave. There is great treasure there, much of it not readily recognizable. If that lair is plundered, it would mean even greater woe to the continent than it will have already experienced with her loss. And take nothing, Melisande—not even a pebble. To do so would be a desecration."

"I understand."

Rhapsody stood straight again, her hand still on the young girl's cheek. "I know you do," she said, pride shining in her eyes. "Understand this as well—if through your efforts Elynsynos is found and restored to health, you will be doing this continent one of the greatest services that has ever been done it. And even if it is too late—" She swallowed, her mouth suddenly dry. "Even if it is, you will be safeguarding more than I can possibly explain."

"I'm ready," said Melisande.

Rhapsody smiled, and bent and kissed her adopted granddaughter.

"We wouldn't be sending you if we didn't believe it," she said. She waved her hand dismissively in the direction of the circle of mist, and the babbling voices ceased; the glittering circle broke and shattered, its water droplets descending slowly to the floor like falling sparks from a campfire.

"When my mission is done, where will I go then?" the Lady Navarne asked anxiously as Gerald Owen reappeared in the room, hovering politely in the doorway.

Rhapsody considered, then put her arm around the girl and walked with her to the door.

"I suspect Ashe will want you at Highmeadow," she said as they went to meet the chamberlain. "In the four years it has taken to build, it has the strongest defenses, and the most intelligent construction, of anything I've seen on the continent, even exceeding those of Tyrian, which are brilliant. There is nowhere on the continent where you will be safer."

Melisande kissed her grandmother on the cheek as they parted ways in the hall.

"It sounds to me like that is not saying much."

The Lady Cymrian sighed.

"Alas, sworn as I am to the truth, I cannot disagree. I love you, Melisande. Travel well."

The chamberlain and the young girl watched her walk away in a rustle of brocade. Her golden hair caught the lanternlight as she passed the sconces in the hall, seeming to capture it and take it with her, leaving the corridor dimmer when she was gone.

12

$\mathcal{G}$wydion Navarne and Anborn were deep in the process of mapping out the garrison of the Alliance army in relation to their proximity to known Sorbold outposts before the roaring fire when a knock came at the door of the study. Without awaiting a response it opened and Rhapsody came into the room, her face set in a calm mien but her skin wan and bloodless, either from weakness or from worry.

Anborn looked up in annoyance.

"What do you want?"

"I've come to say goodbye."

The Lord Marshal took off his spectacles and laid them down on the map.

"No," he said shortly. "That will not do. I'm busy—go away."

"But I'm leaving in a few moments," Rhapsody said, nonplussed. They had often had such exchanges; she had long been accustomed to Anborn's gruff manner, and knew that it masked something deeper, most likely a fear for her safety, and very possibly that of the continent. "The very least you can do is pause long enough to say goodbye as well."

"Are you deaf? No. I will not."

Rhapsody turned to Gwydion Navarne, who looked uncomfortable.

"Excuse us for a moment, Gwydion," she said. "I think Ashe might need your assistance in the preparations anyway—we depart as soon as the horses are provisioned and ready."

The young duke nodded and left the room.

Rhapsody came over to Anborn's chair and stared down at him. His hair was still black as night save for the streaks of silver that had grown slightly wider in the four years since she had met him; his upper body was still muscular and strong, but he had the air of an aged man, much more than the time would warrant. *He has grown old before my eyes,* Rhapsody thought. "All right," she said briskly, "we're alone now. What is this nonsense?"

Anborn exhaled wearily. "Aside from the few cherished opportunities I had to actually *kiss* you goodbye when we were pledged to marry, do you ever recall me saying that word to you?"

Color flooded into the Lady Cymrian's face. Anborn's reference was to a time she still regarded with awkward memory, confusing days during which she had asked him to be a loveless consort to her as Lirin queen. The Lord Marshal had been good-natured about it, as well as in releasing her from her pledge when he discovered that she and his nephew were in love, but this was the first time he had teased her about their near-miss at matrimony.

"No," she said haltingly.

"And I don't intend to do so now. We both have work to do which will take us from this place; you are merely leaving first. So do it; be done with it. Go. I have no desire to mark this parting with such a word. Unless, of course, you wish to kiss me first—that does tend to take some of the sting out of it." He winced as her eyes began to glisten, then shook his head. "Forgive me, m'lady, I'm being coarse and unpleasant, and you don't deserve it. It is not you from whom I should have withheld a goodbye, but rather someone else much like you, very long ago." He watched her press her lips together to forestall the question that had risen to them, and almost chuckled. "Thank you for not asking. I will tell you the story some day, when we are sitting at ease, playing with my great-nephew."

Rhapsody smiled slightly, putting her hand to her cheek, now pale again. "Agreed," she said, "but only if you wish."

Anborn sighed. "There is little that I wish anymore, Rhapsody. I've lived too long, seen too much, to bother wishing for anything. This cursed lengthy life span, bequeathed to me either by whatever my father did to cheat time, or my mother's dragon blood, has given me a sour outlook. This is the way of stupid longevity. It insures cynicism, because it guarantees that unlike the rest of oblivious humanity, the all-but-immortal realize that they will never really know peace. You, being similarly cursed, just haven't figured it out yet. When one lives long enough, he learns that there is no such thing as peace, just longer and shorter intervals between wars. Life becomes an endless and often arduous series of goodbyes, laced with dread, unless you can learn to expect never to see anyone you care for again. I have learned this lesson in the ugliest ways imaginable, Rhapsody. So I will bid you farewell, wish you safe journey and Godspeed, express my hope, and expectation, that you and your child will be safe among the Firbolg, and that your undertakings will prove fruitful to the war effort. But I will not say goodbye to you."

The Lady Cymrian smiled, her wan face taking on more color for a moment. "Very well, then." She reached into the leather bag and pulled out a large conch shell, turning it over in her small hands; Anborn watched her absently caress the horned crown with the calloused tips of long slender fingers that had hardened in uncounted years of playing stringed instruments, not unlike the hard pads on his own digits, ossified from centuries of plucking bowstrings. *Odd,* he mused as she took his hand in her own and turned it upright, then placed the shell in the scarred palm and gently bent his broken-knuckled fingers around it. *I suppose we each make music in our own way, she for the purpose of lifting hearts, me for the purpose of piercing them with arrows.*

Rhapsody saw the look of wry amusement pass over his face and smiled.

"Long ago, back on the Island, when I was first learning to be a Storysinger, I knew a barkeep named Barney." She chuckled. "Did you know all barkeeps in Serendair were named Barney? Every one?"

Anborn studied the shell. "No. Why?"

"The legend had it that a barkeep named Barney had witnessed something he should not have in the course of his rum-serving duties, and the dangerous man whose name was mentioned in what he had heard sent an assassin from a faraway town to find and kill the barkeep. So this Barney left his little town in the dead of night, made his way to Easton, the largest port city in Serendair, and found a job in another tavern, along with putative safety. A year or more went by, but the assassin was patient, and eventually discovered that Barney was now living in Easton, so he made his way to that city, intent on completing his contract.

"Word of the killer's approach arrived quickly—bartenders hear everything first—news that an assassin was coming, looking for a man he had never seen, who was working in a place with a great many taverns, inns, and pubs. Upon his arrival, the assassin went to the first pub he found, a place with two men working the bar. He asked if Barney was about. 'Indeed,' came the reply, according to legend. 'Which one ya lookin' fer?' Not only were both men in that establishment named Barney, but in each such place the city over, every man serving ale or spirits from behind a tableboard was invariably called by the same name. Bartenders take care of their own; they work in a business that requires them to hear much and say very little. So when they heard the plight of one of their fellows, they underwent Renaming as a group, to a man, so that henceforth they would be even more anonymous, even more safe from the retribution of nefarious men and assassins. Unless the hired killer was willing to take the life of each man serving spirits in the entirety of the city, he would never find the one his employer sought to have killed. So he gave up and never returned, because even an assassin has standards—and a need for ale once in a while."

Anborn, who had chuckled at the tale, allowed the humor to leave his eyes as they met hers.

"Was that assassin Achmed?" he asked quietly.

Rhapsody's face went slack. She released the shell and the Lord Marshal's hand, and turned away toward the window of the room.

"I don't know," she said after a moment, her back to Anborn. Silhouetted against the setting sun, she seemed even more thin and wraithlike than he had noted upon seeing her after her ordeal. "I didn't know him in those days. I would doubt it, however. My understanding is that Achmed rarely, if ever, missed a shot or lost the trail of prey." The last words fell awkwardly from her mouth; she shut it abruptly and pulled at the drape, letting more of the fading light enter the room. *And he would have had no compunction about killing every Barney in the town if he had to. Achmed can pour his own ale.*

"Do you ever stop to think your loyalty to him is misplaced?" Anborn asked, his voice uncharacteristically gentle. "Don't get me wrong, my dear; I am in no position to condemn any man for the sins of his past. It just appears to me that you are risking much of what you love for someone whose entire view of the world is anathema to everything you profess to believe."

The Lady Cymrian remained silent for the span of seventy heartbeats.

"I always thought you liked him," she said after a moment.

Anborn drew himself up taller, then sighed dispiritedly.

"I do—but that doesn't change the validity of my concern for you. You'll notice I have asked you the same about my nephew and, in fact, myself. You are a woman that treasures things none of us truly care for—and to that end, in trying to see good in us which does not exist, you may undo yourself. And your child."

Rhapsody returned to him and sat by his side. "I was telling you the story of Barney," she went on as if she had not heard him. "*My* Barney—the one I knew in Easton. He was a little old proprietor of an inn called the Hat and Feathers. Had a wife named Dee and a generous heart. He was also the first person I ever spoke the True Name of—or, more precisely, I wrote it down when I was learning to graph musical script. I told him to have a troubadour play it for him one day, if one should come along. And apparently one did; he played Barney the song of his own name, though neither of them knew what it was. Barney found it to be a catchy tune, and so he hummed it to himself every day, while washing glasses and serving ale." Her eyes grew brighter. "He still does, as far as I know." She averted her eyes as Anborn's gaze grew suddenly sharp.

"Say what you mean," the Lord Marshal commanded.

"I mean that all those centuries ago in the Third Age of history, a man learned to sing his True Name to himself, day into night, for each of the days of his life forward. His beloved wife grew old and died; war came to the Island, and went, taking a generation with it. Centuries of rebuilding passed, until Gwylliam's vision of the Cataclysm was revealed, and when the Cymrians made an exodus to this place, Barney went with them. He lived through the whole thing, Anborn—the exodus, the journey, the building and undoing of the Cymrian empire, the war, the years of silent misery—and to this day, he quietly tends bar in a small fishing village on the western coast, looking exactly like the same man who I kissed on the cheek and walked away from two thousand years ago. The song of his name has seemed to have sustained him; each time he hums the melody, it remakes him, in a sense, to what he was on the day he learned it."

She tapped the shell in his hand.

"Grunthor gave me this a few years ago, when we first came to this place. A thoughtful gift; he believed it might help with the nightmares that had been plaguing me since girlhood, thought I might be comforted by the sound of the sea. And he was right, though I think perhaps it was more the kindness that consoled me than the roaring of the waves." Her smile brightened even as the look in her eyes grew serious. "In that time I have kept it carefully as a reminder of what it was that allowed me to survive all that had befallen me—not my wits, if I have any, or my strength, minimal as it is, but the love of those dear to me. I give it to you now, and in it I have sung the song of your True Name, Anborn ap Gwylliam, son of Anwyn." She squeezed his hand.

The Lord Marshal sighed. "I am not in need of your comfort, m'lady," he said as pleasantly as he could. "I am in need of focus and concentration—war is looming. The last thing I wish to be distracted by is foolish consolation."

"I know," Rhapsody said. "It is not for consolation that I am giving it to you, but for healing." Her voice became softer, as if the words caused her pain. "It was I that caused you to be lame, when you caught me from the sky as I fell from Anwyn's grasp at the battle after the Cymrian Council." She waved him into silence as he attempted to speak. "It is because of me that you have lost the freedom you once had, the freedom you told me you valued above all other things. I have tried many times to heal those injuries, to make you whole again, but my knowledge, my abilities, are not strong enough."

The Lord Marshal squeezed her hand. "Your abilities were sufficient to keep me from death, to return me to health, if not vitality—"

"It is not enough," Rhapsody interrupted. "If you are to lead the forces of the Middle Continent again in a war that is perhaps directed by malicious greed and a desire for conquest, or perhaps something darker, something demonic, you will need to be as hale and able as it is possible for you to be. And what I have come to understand since Meridion's birth, since my time in Elynsynos's Lair, is that I have been going about this in the wrong way. I could heal you, Anborn, save you from death, but I cannot remake you to what you were, because only *you* can do that. Only you know the man you were, and are, what you have seen and done. Only you own the memories of everything that has happened to you in the course of a very long lifetime. Good and bad, those memories are what make you whole—and I believe only you can embrace them enough to allow them to restore what you were."

The large hands that encircled her small ones trembled slightly. Anborn looked down at where their hands were joined.

"I don't know that I want that man back," he said tonelessly. "I've done many terrible things in my life, Rhapsody, things you may know of, many more that you don't. Perhaps, in the course of prosecuting the war that is to come, I will do them again, or worse. If the cost of purging those things from my soul was the loss of my legs, then so be it."

Rhapsody inhaled. "It was not," she said, her voice ringing with a Namer's truth. "You cannot purge anything that has happened to you, as if it were an impurity of steel to be smelted away in a forge fire. All that has gone before has made you what you are, like notes in a symphony. Whole or lame, you are who you are. *Ryle hira,* as the Lirin say. Life is what it is. Forgive yourself." She released his hands and pushed the shell against his chest. "At least try to be as whole as you can, if not for yourself, then for the men you lead. And for me."

The Lord Marshal's rigid face relaxed a little.

"You are very infused with admiration for yourself, and your place in my esteem," he said jokingly. "All right—what must I do?"

"Hold the shell to your ear, perhaps before you lie down to sleep, perhaps when you wake. Listen to the music within it; it may take you a while to even hear the song in the crashing of the waves. Hum it, or sing it if you can hear the words, though that is not an easy thing to do unless you are trained as a Singer. Just try, please—try to remember who you were and blend that in with who you are. I don't know if it will make any difference, but we are about to be parted, one from the other, for what we both know will be a long time, if not forever. I beg you, Anborn, do this one last thing for me. If not for me, do it to add one more healthy body to the fight for the survival of the Middle Continent, and perhaps the world."

Their eyes met sharply, and for an instant they both recalled another discussion years before, the meeting in which she had asked him to consider being her consort.

Let us not mince words, General. We both know that war is coming; it draws closer with every passing moment. And while you have seen war first-hand, I have seen the adversary—or at least one of them. We will need everything we have, everything, to merely survive its awakening, let alone defeat it. I will waste neither the blood nor the time of the Lirin fending off a martial challenge over something so stupid as my betrothal. A marriage of convenience is an insignificant price to pay to keep Tyrian safe and at peace for as long as possible. We will need every living soul when the time comes.

"I will," the Lord Marshal promised finally. "Even as I split the ears of the men encamped near me with the horror of my singing voice, for you I will make the attempt, Rhapsody. I will try to imagine you as I do, singing to my great-nephew, and perhaps that will ease my sense of ridiculousness. But, in return, you must promise to let go the silly burden you have carried of the responsibility for my laming. My rescue of you was foretold in prophecy centuries before I ever laid eyes on you, and if I learned nothing else from my cursed mother, may maggots eat her eyes, it was that you cannot fight Fate." His blue eyes twinkled in the growing darkness. "Of course, if I see Fate coming, I intend to make a good tussle of it anyway."

A knock sounded as the door opened, and Ashe's shadow appeared in the doorway.

"The preparations are under way, and should be completed shortly, Aria," he said. "The quartermaster intends to have the horses tacked and ready to leave in a quarter hour." He eyed Anborn for a moment, then extended his hand to his wife.

Rhapsody rose and came to him, taking his hand. "Who has the baby?"

"Grunthor."

"Do you think that was wise? Did you feed him first?"

"The baby?"

"That wasn't who *I* meant." Rhapsody turned one last time and smiled at the Lord Marshal. "Good fortune in all that you will be undertaking," she said. "And remember your promise."

Anborn swiped an impatient hand at her.

"Go," he said curtly.

Rhapsody watched him for a moment longer, then let go of Ashe's hand, came back to where the Lord Marshal sat, and stood before him. She bent down slightly and pressed her lips to his, allowing her hands to rest on his wide shoulders, taking her time, breathing in his breath. Then she returned to her astonished husband and left the room without looking back.

Anborn waited until the heavy door had closed solidly behind them, their footsteps fading away in the hallway beyond. When at last he could no longer hear any trace of sound, he picked up his spectacles and returned to his work.

"Goodbye," he said softly to the map on the desk in front of him.

13

$\mathcal{I}$'m not even going to ask what just happened," Ashe muttered as they walked down the hallway with the same sense of controlled urgency that had been in place since the meeting. "That was not a sight I had hoped to keep in my eyes as we are about to be parted in the advent of war. Please be certain that you do not do that to Achmed where I can see—I'll be unable to take nourishment for weeks."

Rhapsody was lost in thought and didn't hear him.

"Who did Anborn neglect to kiss goodbye that never came home?" she asked when they finally reached the door to their chambers.

Ashe looked blank, then took the handle and opened the door.

"I've no idea," he said, gesturing for her to enter first. "Anborn has lived a long time, and through some terrible days. I imagine he has lost many people he has cared for, though no one special comes to mind except perhaps Shrike, and I don't expect they did much kissing."

Rhapsody went to the candelabra on the table near the bed and touched the wicks, sparking them into flame.

"His wife, perhaps?"

Her husband closed the door. "I would doubt that. Estelle was a fairly horrid woman, and when she died a decade or so ago my father told me Anborn was more relieved than anything else. I was in hiding then, so I don't really know much about what has gone on in Anborn's life. He has an oft-stated fondness for tavern wenches and serving girls; I don't think it's impossible that he may have lost one or more that he cared for."

Rhapsody shook her head and came into his arms.

"I don't think that's the answer, though you are probably right that it was not Estelle." She thought back to a frozen glade at the forest's edge in Tyrian, on the night Constantin had made reference to in the council meeting, when the Lord Marshal had come in answer to her Kinsmen's call on the wind to find her and the then-gladiator lost and freezing to death. Anborn had rescued them both, had taken her, frost-bitten and all but naked, into a hidden shack that had served as a way station for him, where he tossed her a soft wool tunic of fern-green, long of sleeve, pointed at the wrist, to cover herself.

This doesn't look like it would fit you too well, Anborn. To whom does it belong?

It belonged to my wife. She won't mind you wearing it—she's been dead eleven years now. It looks far better on you, by the way.

I'm very sorry.

No need to be. We didn't like each other very much. We didn't live together, and I rarely saw her.

But you must have loved her once.

No. For such an intellectually gifted woman, Rhapsody, you can be charmingly naive. '

Then why did you marry?

She wasn't an unattractive woman. Her family was an old one, and she was principled; if she ever cuckolded me, I never knew it, and I believe I would have. I was loyal to her as well, until she died.

The honest cynicism had stung her.

That's all? Why bother? she had asked him.

A fair question, to be sure. I'm afraid I don't have an answer for you.

Did you have children?

No. I'm sorry to disillusion you, Rhapsody. You obviously know what my family is, and so know that we don't have the most romantic history. From the very beginning, sex and mating in our family has been about power and control, and it has remained thus. And I can't foresee a time when that will change—dragon blood is pervasive, you know.

The brutality of the observation had not been lost on her.

Ashe pulled her closer. "In these last moments before we part, forgive me if I say that I couldn't care less about whoever Anborn kissed or did not kiss—except that it was quite disturbing to witness it being *you*."

She shook her head to clear it of the memory and smiled up at her husband.

"We only have a few fleeting moments—either the quartermaster will declare the provisions and mounts ready, or the baby will wake, screaming, in Grunthor's arms, and we will need to rescue them both. Perhaps we should forget about Anborn for the present and just be alone together, while I am still here."

"Agreed," the Lord Cymrian said. Without another word he swept his wife from her feet and laid her carefully down on their marriage bed, then lay down beside her. He took her small face in his hands and stared down at it, as if to commit to memory every feature again, as he had done each night into each day that they had been together for the last four years, the vertical pupils in his eyes shrinking in the candlelight, the cerulean blue irises gleaming with an intensity surpassing that of an ordinary man.

It was the dragon within his blood that was assessing her now, Rhapsody knew, a nature both alien and familiar to her that obsessed over each thing or being that it considered to be treasure. She could feel her skin prickle beneath the vibration of his inner sense as it memorized the length of each of her eyelashes, the number of breaths she took, the beating rhythm of her heart. She could feel his anxiety rise and knew that he also perceived how weak she still was from childbirth, how much blood she had lost, how fragile her health had become. The dragon Elynsynos, to whose lair Ashe had originally guided her during a sweet spring long ago, had provided most of the insight she had into this side of the man whose soul she shared.

Wyrms are not avaricious—we do not desire much, Pretty, only what we believe is rightfully ours. We are each part of a shield that protects the entirety of the world, and yet we do not wish to own everything in that world. That which is part of our hoard, our treasure, is not our prisoner; we guard it jealously, but only because we love it with everything that is in us. What humans see as possessiveness, dragons believe to be the purest form of love. This is true whether the treasure is a single coin, a living being, or a whole nation of people.

Independent as her own temperament was, she had come to understand that element of his nature, all the while knowing that he battled it, grappled with it, struggled against it every day, endeavoring to keep from letting the draconic side of himself frighten or subsume her. As she looked back into his eyes now, she could see straight to his soul, and within her own she felt an overwhelming sense of impending loss; she had learned to treasure him in the same way.

Ashe saw the tears glinting in her eyes, perceived the lump in her throat, and slid his fingers deeper into her hair, cupping her head and covering her mouth with his. Time became suspended as they shared a breath, the musical rhythm of inhalation and release that was the song of their joined lives.

When their lips separated he saw that her wan face was wet with the tears she had fought so long to hold in check; his dragon sense had registered her weeping, but the sight of it always squeezed his heart more than he was prepared to withstand. There was something within him that perceived her as even more beautiful in tears than when she was smiling, and the thought disturbed him greatly. He pulled her closer as she buried her face in his shoulder, secretly glad to be rid of the sight.

"A quarter hour, no more," she murmured. "Why does it always seem that we are limited in our time together? We are barely in each other's presence more than the span of a few heartbeats before we are once again parted. And how can you withstand losing our child again? I am afraid, Sam—genuinely afraid that this will be more than you, man or dragon, will be able to withstand. I know I would not be able to bear it were it you that was leaving, taking him with you."

The Lord Cymrian exhaled slowly; he had been contemplating, with dread, the same thing.

"I will hold on to the few scraps of comfort that remain—the knowledge that, with what is to come, you and Meridion will be safe. I will continue to remind myself, as the dragon grows impatient and angry, that I have never deserved you or the happiness you have brought me from the start." He put his hand over her mouth to quell the protest that threatened to spill out. "For all that I know you love me, Rhapsody, you really don't know how much I love you; the inadequacy of my tongue prevents me from putting it into words. Each wrong I've done you, each error I've made, each time I have allowed pain to touch you, digs a deeper hole of regret that has, like all other vessels within me, filled up yet again with more longing to be with you. Sometimes I think that if ever I were to hurt you, even inadvertently, that the breath would turn to ice within me. To do anything other than to commit you to Achmed and Grunthor's protection and get you both as far from the coming hostilities as possible would be to risk that hurt—and that is what, more than anything, I would be unable to bear. So, for the sake of the One-God, do not endanger yourself or our child, I beg you—the knowledge that you are safe as the world begins to fray and come apart is the only thing that keeps me from following my father into the ether—or perhaps to an Ending not unlike his."

Rhapsody went rigid. "Gods, don't even say something like that aloud," she choked, but in his eyes she could see the veracity of his words, and knew that he was not exaggerating.

Ashe smiled, and ran his calloused hand through her shining hair.

"Oh, and one other thing—I still have to make good on the promise I made you long ago: that when all of this is past, and others come forward to take over the burden of leadership, on that day, and not one day more, I will take you to the forest of your choice, to the glen of your choice, and build for you the goat hut you have long desired, where we can live simply, raise our children, and forget that the world exists beyond our hedgerow."

Rhapsody relaxed beneath the warmth of his smile, though the understanding unspoken between them of what might be a fatal outcome for either or both of them was clear.

"Done," she said.

A polite knock came at the chamber door.

"Ready, m'lord," came the quartermaster's muffled voice.

The lord and lady rose quickly from the bed and headed, as if of one mind, to each of their dressing rooms, returning a moment later, holding objects in their hands.

Ashe extended his arms first, in which he held a battered cloak, gray on the outside with a blue interior. A shadow of mist, like fog hovering above a lake in morning, seeped out from between the folds.

Rhapsody smiled. This was the cloak of mist that had hidden him from sight and other forms of detection all the years he had been in hiding, walking the world mostly unseen and unnoticed by those around him. It was in this garment she had first beheld him, at least on this side of Time, in the course of a botched pickpocketing that had caused uproar in the streets; the memory of the scuffle that had ensued was both bittersweet and comic. The mist had been imbued into the cloak by Ashe's command over the element of water, as bearer of the sword Kirsdarke; he had worn it so long that the mist remained, clinging to the fabric, shielding the wearer from prying eyes and scrying.

"Take this with you, Aria," he said briskly. "It's more than large enough to hide both you and the baby; if the prophecy was right and there are eyes watching him, this should blind them, at least while he is within it. Try to keep him within its folds at least until you reach Canrif, and perhaps beyond."

Rhapsody nodded and took the cloak. "I will, thank you, Sam." She extended her hand in turn, her fist closed, and held it over his. She opened her hand, and into his palm fell a pearl, luminescent and shining as the glowing moon. In it was contained the memory of their first wedding, a ceremony of their own making conducted without witness in the grotto of Elysian, her hidden underground home within the Bolglands. It was a memory that only they had shared, in a place where she had always felt safe. "And you keep this, to remind you of happy times, and better times to come when this is over."

He squeezed the pearl and nodded in return.

"You know the dreams will return," he said.

"Yes."

Ashe regarded her sadly. On the night they had met in their youth, on the other side of Time, she had told him of her disturbing dreams. When they had come to know each other again on this side of Time, those prophetic, prescient dreams had evolved into night terrors, causing her to thrash about violently in her sleep, even as they sometimes provided a key to what would come to pass in the Future, or what had happened in the Past. He, dragon that he was, had the ability to chase her nightmares away, had been able to provide a protective vibration that kept the nightmares that had once tortured her at bay while she slept. Over the years he had finally seen her at rest, at peace in his arms. "Who will keep you from the nightmares now, Aria?" he asked softly.

"The nightmares are the least of it, especially if they help foretell what may come," she said. "I suppose the answer is that *you* still will, Sam. In a way, the sacrifice you are making—we are all making—may be the only chance we have of keeping from being consumed by far more terrifying nightmares that do not go away upon waking."

Her hand came to rest lovingly on the side of his check. "But I will come to you in dreams, if I can," she said softly.

"You are ever there, Aria."

She shook her head. "No, I mean that I will try to visit you, to be with you in a way that is more than dream, but less than the flesh. Being alone with Elynsynos for months, studying ancient texts of primal lore, I have come to understand much more about how Namer magic works than I ever knew before. And one thing I may be able to do is visit from time to time, in a way where we are both aware. Especially after Achmed has finished his project."

Ashe kissed her, then opened the door.

"Either way, you are ever there."

Both of their backs suddenly straightened, as if shot with an arrow.

"Meridion is crying," they said to each other in unison.

Ashe stood back to allow Rhapsody out the door first. As they hurried together down the hall, he looked down at his wife.

"There is no possible way you could have heard that," he said fondly. "You must be developing a dragon sense of your own. I must be rubbing off on you."

Rhapsody snorted and doubled her speed, beating him to the stairs by four strides.

"Hardly. Every new mother is a bit of a dragon."

Ashe watched her descend the stairs two at a time.

"Hmmm. *That* explains the ferocious mood swings."

The quartermaster had readied and provisioned four horses, two light riding, two heavier war horses. One of the war horses was of enormous size, and packed with very little weight; Grunthor examined it and nodded in approval. The other of the two heavy horses and one of the light riding horses bore most of the equipment and supplies for their long journey.

The other light riding horse had been equipped with an extra long saddle.

"I think at least at first you should consider riding with Achmed," Ashe told Rhapsody gravely. "Your ordeal in the forest of Gwynwood, Meridion's birth, and the long journey back here have taken their toll on you, Aria. I am not certain that in the current state of your health you can withstand the rigors of the swift ride, especially holding the baby swathed in the mist cloak. Therefore, I think wisdom dictates that you and Achmed share a saddle, at least for the first portion of the trip. I will rest easier knowing that you are unlikely to fall from the horse."

Rhapsody smiled and kissed him.

"You will always be in my thoughts, as I know we will be in yours," she said. "Each night before I go to sleep, I will try and visit you in your dreams. Remember the songs I sing to you when we are together and know that I will be singing to you even while we're apart, and to Meridion; keep that picture in your mind, and we will never be far away from you."

Ashe smiled sadly in return.

"Now I can count every one of your eyelashes, and each beat of your heart. I know how you are breathing, and how you shape the currents of air where you stand, how they change as you move. Once you are outside a range of five miles, it will be as if you are lost to me forever," he said. "Just keep yourself and our son safe, my love. Knowing that you are doing so is the only chance that I have to hang on to sanity."

Rhapsody embraced him, knowing that he spoke the truth.

Piece o' news Oi thought you might want to know, sir," Grunthor said quietly as Rhapsody and Ashe were saying their final goodbyes. "While you were away, ol' Ashe's grandma, that bloody dragon, Anwyn, made 'er way to the Bolglands and tried to get in. No worries, sir; we repelled 'er easily enough."

"How did you manage that?" Achmed asked incredulously. "I have the only weapon in the whole of the Bolglands capable of piercing dragon hide, and it was with me. What did you do to drive her off?"

"We backed up the sewage cistern and blasted 'er out of the tunnels with the *hrekin,*" Grunthor replied. "About an 'undred thousan' gallons of the former contents of Bolg arses; seemed an appropriate enough weapon. Besides, dragons are extra sensitive to all the senses, if I recall correctly. Stunned 'er, it did. Left an 'eck of a mess as well, which we thought about cleaning up before you got 'ome, but decided instead it made a lovely battlement. So we just sort a shaped it into a barricade and left it to stink up the place right nicely. Don't expect she'll be comin' back anytime soon."

"And you neglected to mention this at the council of war?" Achmed said, amused.

"Yes, sir," Grunthor said. "If 'e 'ad known that the dragon had already broached the Bolglands, there was a possibility 'er 'usband would not let her go. And in my judgment, sir, dragon or no, she's safer with us anyway."

"Agreed," Achmed said, mounting his horse. "It should be interesting to see her reaction to your new barricade; Rhapsody considers cleanliness to be a sacrament. Let's be on our way as soon as he can tear his lips off her and the squalling brat."

14

The cohort of the Second Mountain Guard of Sorbold came to a halt at the place where the road leading north into the province of Canderre crossed with the forested trader's route heading east from the wooded lands of Navarne to the capital city of Bethany.

The wind was cold, but the sky clear; darkness and the absence of travelers in winter had covered their journey from their southern homeland with but minimal exception. Each stray merchant or farmer had been easily dispensed with, with no major outcry or notice in the sparsely settled area, just as they had planned.

Now, as they approached the keep and the surrounding walled village that was Haguefort, the commander gave quiet orders to more surreptitiously travel the forest road, to cling to the fringe of the woods for cover, in single and dual file, to keep from attracting notice of any of the patrols that were most likely stationed throughout the area, guarding the home of Gwydion of Manosse, the Lord Cymrian.

And his family.

The commander silently signaled to the troops, and they followed him quietly into the woods, their surefooted mounts all but silent along the forest trail.

They had gone the better part of a league when the sound of horse approaching could be heard in the woods to the north.

Quickly, the commander signaled to two of the scouts and dismounted. They followed him, sliding down from the saddle silently while the rest of the cohort quietly came to a stop deeper into the fringe.

The commander and the scouts crossed the forest road and crept through the underbrush, dry and dead from the snow that still gripped this part of the continent, so different from their homeland of dry and arid mountains. They passed through the forest easily, having been trained to do so at great expense, and stopped within a thick copse of evergreens to wait.

Beyond the stand of trees at the edge of their sight was a forest path, a meager route where farmers traveled to avoid the main road and to harvest the fruits of the forest, wood for hearths, berries and wild herbs, and game. The sound of a small number of horse at full canter could be heard in the west; the three soldiers sank lower to the ground, waiting.

After a few moments the horses and riders came into sight. There were four beasts, two light riding horse and two heavy draft, with what appeared to be two riders atop one each of the light and heavy, the others carrying supplies. The man atop the heavy horse was enormously tall and broad; the beast was breathing noisily as it ran.

The travelers did not tarry; they traversed the forest path, gaining speed as the woods grew thinner, and disappeared into the distance.

The commander rose quickly.

"Take the third wave, and follow them," he said to the first scout. "It may be nothing, but my instinct says they should not be allowed to slip past. Bring back their horses if you can; they will aid in the journey back."

The scout nodded, and all three men made their way quickly back to the main forest road.

The cohort divided itself up quickly and quietly, the third wave taking to the north in pursuit of the riders, the second doubling back southwest to serve as a far flank, the remainder heading quietly west.

To Haguefort.

15

The small carriage was outfitted and ready at the western gate shortly after the two Firbolg and the Lady Cymrian had departed by the northern one.

Gerald Owen coughed as the dropping temperature stung the inside of his lungs. He looked up into the cold night sky from the courtyard, illuminated only by a single hooded lantern, at the stars spreading out beyond the canopy of trees that were the beginning of the wooded lands to the west of Haguefort, through which they would be riding, eventually melding north into the holy forest of Gwynwood and the Circle, their destination. For all that bitter cold had returned, the sky itself was clear and the wind gentle; it seemed that they would have favorable enough weather to make good time.

He conferred quietly with the drivers and their two escorts, then signaled to the window of the keep.

A few moments later the buttery door opened quietly, and the two Navarne children appeared, both clad in dark shirts, trousers, and gray cloaks that blended into the night. Gwydion Navarne closed the buttery door quietly, then took his sister's hand and led her through the herb garden and across the cobbled courtyard to the tree-lined area where the coach was waiting.

"Oh, good, they've used the roans yoked in a doubletree," Melisande whispered. "Should be a fast ride."

"Is everything ready, Gerald?" the young duke asked nervously, loosing Melisande's hand and passing the bag carrying the last of her supplies to the coachman. Melisande snagged the waterskin from his hand and attached it to her belt.

"Everything, m'lord," the chamberlain replied. "The Lady Cymrian sent word by winterbird to Gavin at the Circle, so he will be expecting us, no doubt. I'll see to it that Lady Melisande is delivered promptly and safely."

Gwydion nodded, trying not to vomit. Melly had been too little to remember the last time they had seen their mother, but the memory was as clear to him as if it had happened yesterday instead of nine years before. He had been eight years old at the time, a quiet lad of books with a deep love of the woods that his mother shared. She had also shared his propensity for shyness, unlike his father and sister, whose natures were abundantly social and warmly cordial. He missed her still, the scent of lavender or lemon in her hair, the gentleness of her hands as she smoothed the covers around him at night, the way the corners of her mouth crinkled when she smiled—the memories always made the hollow space in his stomach ache when he let them come back.

Worst of all was the last one, of she and her sister, his aunt who he barely remembered, climbing into just such a carriage, on their way to the city to buy Melisande some shoes in which to learn to walk. They were laughing, her black eyes, so like Melly's, were sparkling, and she had held his face in her hands, had kissed him on the cheek and forehead and whispered in his ear, words he could still recall in the very tone of her voice.

Be a good little man. Help your father. Remember that I love you.

He had endeavored to fulfill all of those requests. Most of the time it wasn't difficult.

"I know you will," he said rotely to the chamberlain.

Melisande, who rightfully fancied herself an excellent groom, had already made a check of the horses' bindings, to the quiet amusement of the coachmen, and was standing at the door of the carriage.

"Enough," she said impatiently. "Time to go."

Gwydion exhaled deeply and went to the door. He put his hands on her shoulders.

"Listen to Gerald," he said seriously. "And don't take any silly risks." He saw her eyes narrow, and suddenly remembered how it felt to be underestimated because of age. He quickly reached into his boot and pulled out a small knife in a sheath. "Here," he said more pleasantly. "You know how to use this better than I do—it was Father's."

Melisande's expression of annoyance melted into one of delight.

"Thank you," she said eagerly, taking the knife and turning it over in her hands. She hugged her brother quickly, then reached for the door. Gwydion forestalled her, opening it for her and lowering the step. She climbed up, then leaned over and kissed him on the cheek.

"Don't do anything stupid," she said, her black eyes dancing. "And don't have too much fun without me."

"Same to you," Gwydion replied. "On both counts." Melisande grinned, her golden curls bobbing within her hood, then stepped into the darkness of the coach. Gerald climbed in behind her.

"Don't worry, m'lord. I'll see to her safety."

Melisande leaned out the carriage window. "I'll see to my own safety. Make certain you see to yours."

Gwydion nodded, shut the door, feeling like the world was coming to an end.

Again.

He stood in the darkness of the courtyard, watching until the carriage was swallowed into the dark branches of the trees and the night.

Melisande Navarne had never been in the woods to the northwest of her home.

She had been to Tyrian once, to the wedding of Rhapsody and Ashe, and had once been allowed to go with her father to the province of Canderre, northeast of Navarne, to visit distant cousins. She had begged him to take her east to Yarim as well, because the exotic desert clime enchanted her imagination, and she longed to see the place her mother's family and her own black eyes had come from, but Stephen Navarne had always ruled it too distant, and the times too dangerous, to risk. *One day, when you are older, and the world is better, we will go, Melly, you and I,* he had said. One of the saddest lessons of Melisande's young life was the knowledge that even though one day she might indeed see Yarim, the only one of the circumstances in her father's promise that would come to pass was that she would be older.

On occasion she had also traveled to the southwest, most especially to the coastal province of Avonderre, where her family attended religious observances at the great seaside basilica of Abbat Mythlinis, the cathedral dedicated to the element of water. It was a place that she had both a fascination with and a fear of.

Melisande sat back in the dark against the smooth fabric of the seat, listening to Gerald Owen snore, and closed her eyes, thinking about the basilica. She remembered the first time she saw it, on the Naming Day of someone's child she didn't remember, and had been afraid to go inside. It was one of her earliest memories, from when she was no more than four years old. The basilica had been built at the water's edge and fashioned to resemble one of the great broken ships of the First Cymrian Fleet, the vessels in which her ancestors had come to this continent, fleeing the coming cataclysm on the homeland, the Island of Serendair, on the other side of the world. Being young, she had not realized that the representation of an enormous shipwreck had been intentional; she had believed they were entering the cadaver of a real ship, sundered on the sand, and the thought had disturbed her greatly.

Once inside, she was even more certain that she was right. The immense entrance doors, fashioned from planks of varying lengths with a jagged notched pattern at the top, appeared to depict a vast hole torn in what would have been the keel of the ship, with a crazily angled spire that was supposed to represent the ship's mast. Great fractured timbers, the bones of ships lost in the passage, were set within the dark stone walls, making the interior resemble the skeleton of a giant beast, lying on its back, its spine the long aisle that led up forward, the timbers ancient ribs reaching brokenly up into the darkness above.

If looking up had terrified her, looking to the sides was even worse. A line of thick translucent glass blocks had been inlaid in the walls at about the height of her shoulders. The churning sea was diffusely visible through them, bathing the interior of the basilica, and the faces of the people gathered therein, with a green-blue glow.

Instead of feeling the power of the All-God, or appreciating the celebration of the birth of a new child, she had instead panicked and screamed until her mortified father had removed her from the basilica.

Now she was on her way to the Circle, to a place her father had respected but felt was unsafe to bring her. Beyond that, she was charged with traveling to the lair of a beast that was, in her time, the matriarchal wyrm of the entire continent, a being about whom the history books were full of dire tales, from the abandonment of her triplet daughters to the rampage that left the western half of the Middle Continent in cinders. Rhapsody had called the stories lies, had loved the dragon and in fact had gone to stay with her during her pregnancy, trying to learn everything she could about the care and delivery of a child with dragon blood. She trusted the dragon; Melisande trusted her adopted grandmother implicitly, but still wondered if there wasn't at least a grain of truth in the old stories.

Whatever else she was, Melisande was blessed with an intrepid spirit and a curious nature. Being the younger child of a noble line, with little expectation of ever sitting in the duchy seat of her father's line that her brother now occupied, she had been allowed to explore what she wished, to study subjects and skills normally reserved for boys, and to question the ways of the world. So when she was asked to embark on the mission she was now undertaking, she knew she should be nervous.

Instead she was merely excited.

She was dozing, wrapped in light dreams of the basilica of water and the dragon's lair of the lost sea, when the first bolt hit as her carriage came under attack.

Gerald Owen was shocked awake by the impact.
"Driver—*driver!*"

"We're under attack," came the muffled reply. "Stay down."

The elderly chamberlain's eyes opened wide; Melisande took his hand, and together they moved clumsily to the floor of the coach as it picked up speed, the vibration from horses' hooves thundering through the shell.

From the roof of the carriage they heard a light thump and the sound of a crossbow firing in return.

"The footman is an expert in the crossbow," Owen said to the girl, trying to keep his voice from shaking. "The Lord—made certain of it. He should be able to repel anything that might give chase." Melisande nodded and smiled encouragingly.

Several more *thuds* slammed into the back of the carriage, behind where their backs had been a moment before. The lady shuddered at the sight of four bolt tips sticking through the upholstered fabric.

Outside the carriage they could hear the noise of pursuit and evasion, shouted commands and cursing. The carriage rattled and shook from side to side as rocks and ruts in the road were made into more serious obstacles by speed.

"Don't—don't worry, m'lady," Gerald Owen stammered.

"I'm not," replied the girl. "But you are standing on my hand."

"Apologies," the chamberlain mumbled, quickly moving his foot.

Missiles screamed by beyond the window in the carriage door. The sound of a bolt hitting its mark echoed from above, a crossbow firing in return, and the carriage rocked wildly from side to side, spilling the contents of the seats to the floor and sending the two passengers sprawling. With a horrific thump and another violent shake, the carriage lurched violently as it ran over something large in the road; Melisande shuddered. By the sound and direction of it, it seemed to be the driver.

Her theory was born out a moment later as the carriage began swerving unevenly in the roadway. Shouts from above could be heard, answered by others behind.

"I—I don't think the door is locked," Melisande said, watching it flap open and closed.

Gerald Owen struggled to his knees and crawled over to the door, reaching to lock it. Just as he sat back, a rider appeared at the left side of the carriage, visible only in minute flashes through the velvet drape, and slammed his hand against the carriage door, then reached through the curtain at the window. The thunder of a horse could be heard next to them.

"Go away!" Melisande shouted. "Just go away! Leave me alone!"

"M'lady, shhhhh," Gerald Owen cautioned, reaching for her.

The hand came through the window again, farther this time, a rough, calloused hand with sword blisters on the palms. It grasped wildly, then pulled back again.

Melisande dodged as it came within a hairsbreadth of her. She struggled toward the right side, but the careening coach was veering between ruts in the road, the horses unbalanced by whatever was occurring in the combat.

The arm lunged in once more, this time grazing her cheek before seizing a handful of her hair and dragging her back toward the window. The Lady Navarne gasped aloud.

Gerald Owen lunged awkwardly for her, grabbing her legs and pulling her back, but the hand did not let go, only wrapped her hair around it like a rope, and yanked again.

Fury replaced the panic in the black eyes. Melisande pulled the knife Gwydion had given her from her boot and, with an artful arc, swung at the arm, missing.

Another yank, and her head grazed the window curtains.

Melisande, her back now against the bottom of the door, slashed above her head, hitting her mark and dragging the knife shallowly across the wrist of the arm that had held her fast an instant before.

The arm retracted quickly amid cursing in a tongue she didn't recognize, then shot through the window once again, bleeding slightly and reaching around in wild swings through the carriage.

Then it grabbed the door handle and began to twist it.

The child steeled herself, waited until the hand was fully engaged around the knob, then took a deep breath and, without so much as a blink, buried the blade to the hilt in the back of the man's hand below the knuckles.

A scream of pain, followed by gagging, rent the air outside the carriage window.

Melisande grabbed for the knife, still embedded in the hand, and dragged the hilt downward, slashing open flesh and muscle and covering herself and Gerald Owen in pulsing blood.

"I said *leave me alone!*" she screamed. "I'll cut your bloody *fingers* off if you touch me again!"

The carriage shuddered violently as horse and rider impacted the side. Then it lurched up in the air with another sickening thud, a scream trailing away behind it, and smashed down in the forest roadway, rocking sickeningly before falling with a jolt onto its right side, all of the contents shaken loose and landing on top of the stunned passengers.

Woozily, Melisande struggled to right herself. She was aware of the sounds of strife outside the carriage still, but her attention was turned at the moment to Gerald Owen, who was lying in a heap at the bottom of the carriage, a gash over one eye.

"Gerald—"

"Go, child," the elderly chamberlain whispered. "Get away from—here if you can."

The little girl looked around wildly, then reached above her head and pushed the door open. She climbed up slowly, using the door for cover, and looked around.

A gray mountain horse was standing across the forest road, its tack tangled and saddle bindings broken, but otherwise uninjured. Farther back in the roadway behind them a crumpled body lay in a twisted heap, marks from the wheels of the carriage scoring it. The hand was extended lifelessly on the ground, slashed open in a pool of blood. The body of her coachman lay off to the side of the road farther back.

Farther away still she could see the two soldiers in her escort engaged in combat on horseback with four men in similar uniform; she could only distinguish between them by the color of their mounts. Melisande shuddered; shock was threatening to close in on her. She hoisted herself up by her arms out of the toppled carriage and looked behind her.

The footman with the crossbow was lying on the ground in front of the carriage, pinned beneath the broken doubletree, moaning incoherently. Before him one of the horses was pinned as well, the other dancing nervously in its hitchings. Melisande went cold; she glanced around and, seeing no one else, crept over the collapsed coach to the footman.

She tried to lift the doubletree off him, but it was too heavy. He was gray in the face, sweat pouring from him, but he did manage to meet her eyes.

"Fly, m'lady," he said. Then he shuddered and fell unconscious.

Practicality descended. Melisande contemplated taking the mountain horse but discarded the thought, realizing she had no knowledge of the animal and that it was ill-suited to taking on forest paths. When she believed the soldiers were too engaged to see her, she hurried to the roans, and with small nimble fingers and speed born of much practice, she unbuckled the one standing and mounted it, pulling herself up easily. It was a horse she knew well; it recognized her and did not bolt.

She kicked the horse and leaned forward over its neck as it started, then broke into a fast trot, a faster canter, and finally a smooth gallop down the forest road.

She kept up the gallop for the better part of half a league, then slowed to a trot again. The forest road was dwindling to little more than a footpath, and the night sky was giving way to the gray of predawn. By the time the clouds grew rosy she had left the road altogether, traveling north, as best as she could figure, spurred on by panic and an inner call to flight born of the horror she had witnessed.

When the sun finally crested the horizon, filling the frosty woods with diffuse light, making the trees shine silver and white in its radiance, Melisande finally came to a halt. She listened, but heard nothing behind her except the sounds of the forest, of ice creaking on the boughs of trees, the rustle of the pine needles in the morning wind, and the calls of winterbirds that were just beginning to wake.

She had absolutely no idea where she was, except utterly lost.

Finally able to breathe, she dismounted and looked around, then the sensations that had shut down in her fight for survival came roaring back. Even through her boots and heavy woolen stockings her feet were chilled; she was shivering with cold and trembling with fear, and hungry, but without any supplies or provisions except the waterskin at her side and the knife in her boot.

She looked around at the endless greenwood, realizing she was not even sure where the path was now. *The Circle should be north of here*, she reasoned, *or perhaps west*. Her chin quivered, but she willed it to stop. Then she straightened her back, took hold of the horse's bridle, and started off toward the north.

She had gone a thousand paces when grief overwhelmed her. Melisande sat down on the rough ground beneath a towering shag bark hickory tree and began to sob as if her heart would break.

After a few moments, calm restored, she stood up, got back on the horse, and started off into the forest in search of the Circle and Gavin.

16

AT THE EDGE OF THE KREVENSFIELD PLAIN

*W*hile those who dwelt in the upworld would not consider the sort of sleep that Dhracians experienced real slumber, it was for their race the closest equivalent, a time of cessation of thought and activity, a drowsiness that allowed their bodies to rest and recharge, as every other living thing did, a panacea of revitalization required of all creatures with a beating heart. Even the near immortality bequeathed to them being sons of the wind, born at the beginning of history, did not spare them the need for rest.

Rath closed his eyes as he contemplated this, lulled by the thundering of the wind around him as he took shelter in the lee of a grassy hillock. While the primal elemental power of their race and those like it, known as the Firstborn in the nomenclature of the human world, exempted them from many of the limitations that those races that came later were hobbled by, there was something inescapable in the need for rest, even as they traveled the upworld in endless pursuit of their prey. He wondered sometimes idly if death or damnation would be preferable to the endless vigilance required of him and his fellows, the obsessive, interminable need that drowned out all other reason for life, the blood-lust for the destruction of the demons of fire known as the F'dor.

Certainly it would be easier.

But preferable or not, easier or not, it didn't matter.

It was inescapable.

As he drifted off into the state of relaxation, Rath was haunted by what passed for dreams, the same sorts of images and memories that filled his mind each night when the last of his *kirai* had been expended, when he no longer tasted the wind actively for traces of the F'dor stench, when his duty was delayed for a few brief hours while the rest of the world slept. Like those others of his race, he had trod one time or another each of the seven continents, crossed each of the seven seas, had traveled almost every footpath, every byway, had wandered through parts of the world seen only by the birds and inhabited only by mountain goats, all in the endless search for what had escaped, and still eluded them. It was an unforgiving hunt, an endless quest, and all the centuries that had passed had served to leave little memory of anything good.

Rath rolled to one side in his slumber. In spite of all the visions his eyes had beheld of the world, there was still within his memory a clear recollection of another place that he had not seen in thousands of years. As his breathing deepened and slowed, he visited that place yet again as he had each night since leaving it.

From the recesses of his mind came forth thoughts of a time in the world long before humans had spawned and propagated the planet, when but five races held sway, his own being one of them.

His mother race, what men called the Kith, believed the stories of the creation of the world told to them by one of the only other races that had preceded them on it, the Seren. The Seren Singers told of the birth of the Earth as a piece of the star that broke off from its mother and sailed across the universe, coming to rest in orbit around that blazing entity that had given it life. The rock had continued to burn, the Seren said, with flames of worldly fire, the first element unique to the Earth. Finally, when it seemed that the flames would consume the new planet, they receded and sank into the core of the new world, where they continued to burn, hot and pure. The new planet was said then to be covered with the element of water, and the living sea spread to all corners of the globe, teeming with the beginnings of life.

It was then that the awareness of his race began. The legend said that the wind rose from the stirrings of the sea, blowing back the waves to reveal finally the land, the last of the elemental lores. From this wind came the beings known as the Kith; Rath remembered clearly the tales told him in darkness of what the world had been like at that time, when the sons of the wind were free to walk the world unfettered, unencumbered by any duties, sworn or unsworn. They were a harsh race, uninterested in alliance or commonality with the beings that emerged from each of those other elements—the tall, thin golden creatures that were said to have been born of the element of starlight, ether, known as the Seren; the elusive, membranous beings known as the Mythlin whose skin was porous, their flesh almost gelatinous, as they spread across the seas from which they had sprung; the Wyrmril, or dragons in the tongue of man, serpentine beasts that chose a form other than the model that had been provided by the Creator, who jealously guarded the Earth from which they had been formed, nascent with the traces of each of the other elements that had touched it. The Kith, more than any of the other races, were loners, happiest when free to roam about the wide world in the arms of the wind.

But that had been before Rath's time.

Long before he had been born, there had been an intense battle in which four of the primordial races had become uneasy allies, banding together for the purpose of sparing the world from the destruction of the first of the worldly elements to be born, the destructive and all-consuming element of fire. For while fire had had a natural beginning, some forms of it had become tainted and perverted very early in the life of the world, serving not the power of Creation, but rather that of destruction, of Void, the antithesis of life. The beings that had sprung from fire, and had twisted its purposes to destruction, were the ephemeral spirits known as the F'dor, the race he and his brother hunters now sought.

As always, Rath's breathing became labored as the cycle of his memory recounted the image of the Vault in which the F'dor had been sealed away within the depths of the earth by the four races of the Alliance. It had been outside of that very vault where he had been born and come to awareness, the child of two Dhracian parents, the tribe of Kith that pledge to serve as the jailers of the F'dor, standing endless vigil at the doors of the Vault of the Underworld. Rath and those of his tribe were even more harsh, more emotionless than the rest of his kin, largely owing to the bleakness of the earth and passageways in the darkness in which they dwelt. To be Dhracian was to be born into a form of endless agony, a perversion of nature, a child of the wind locked away from all vestiges of air or freedom, instead doomed by the promise of generations before to stand guard in endless darkness trapped in the earth for all eternity.

Or least it would have been that way, had it not been for the intervention of the Sleeping Child.

Rath's heartbeat began to race, as it did each time he slept, each time he dreamt of the day in his memory when the falling star crashed to earth, exploding the dome of the Vault. It was a cataclysm that defied words, a shattering of the tunnels and hallway in and around the prison of Living Stone that contained the most destructive force the universe had ever given birth to, in screams of agony from the jailers and ecstasy from the captives as they roared forth, into the world, dispersing like milkweed down on the wind. Rath had been young then, but he still remembered the taste of salt water in his mouth, the burning in his nose as the sea roared in, the terror of his fellow Dhracians as they drowned within it, not at the imminence of their own deaths, but in the knowledge that the world they had served to guard was no longer safe.

His mother had been one such to die.

He was still haunted by the sound of the laughter, thundering in his ears, burning his eardrums, and, even worse, the diminution of it as the voices drifted away, falling silent as the demons dissipated into the world.

As one of the surviving jailers, he had partaken with grim glee in battling the remaining demons back into the Vault, had helped in the rush to seal that Vault again, containing them within the earth once more. It gave him some satisfaction to remember the howls of fury, the harsh voices disappearing into their tomb of Living Stone, but he had had enough of a glimpse of the inside to know that it was only a temporary containment. Those that had escaped had a single purpose outside of the destruction of all that lived.

To free those that had not been lucky enough to make it out the first time.

The sleeping Dhracian twitched, remembering in his dreams the glimpse he had of Bloodthorn, a tree not unlike the ones that grew in each of the places where Time began, but brutal and twisted, a perverse abomination, not plant as much as living entity, with branches and limbs of writing thorns lashing out like the tentacles of the sea creature seeking prey. It had impaled and swallowed a number of his surviving kin before the Vault was resealed; Rath's soul still pounded in pain recalling the sounds of their screams.

His father had been one of them.

He woke with a start, as he often did, bathed in sweat that quickly dried in the cool breath of the wind. The dream was gone, as was his repose, but it served to remind him of why the Hunt was necessary, of why the needles that ran in his veins were an essential measure to safeguard the world from that which would see it in flames again, as it had once been at the beginning of creation. It was a grim reminder, but an indispensable one, and it gave him the ability to go on living one more day, to continue in his pursuit of that which hid from the wind itself, formless and ephemeral, and purely destructive.

And any living being that would aid those evil entities, knowingly or unknowingly.

Hrarfa, Fraax, Sistha, Hnaf, Ficken.

As usual, his *kirai* yielded nothing.

Rath tried again.

Ysk.

The salty taste returned to his mouth, an echo of common blood.

Rath rose, shook the dust of the road from his garments, and followed the sound once again.

IN THE FIELDS OF CANDERRE

$\mathcal{A}$chmed dragged his mount to a stop, twisting his face away from the back and shoulders of the woman who rode on the horse before him, swathed in a cloak of mist from which a foul stench was emanating.

"*Hrekin,*" he said sourly. "Rhapsody, for the sake of everything that is holy, or unholy even, what is that repulsive smell?"

"Oi think ya got it right the first time, sir," said Grunthor merrily. "Children is one of them things what tastes better than it smells."

Rhapsody chuckled. "If you even lick your lips within an arm's length of him, I'll cauterize your intestines with Daystar Clarion—don't think I won't, you child-eating lout," she replied.

Achmed exhaled loudly in annoyance. "When I offered to let you ride with me, it was because your husband was concerned you would fall off on your own in your weakened state," he said, turning to keep his nose from the area of stench. "You did not warn me that your child would make a fine catapult shell—better than rotting garbage or dead fish."

"Do you want to stop so that I can change him?" Rhapsody asked, opening the folds of her cloak, sending Achmed writhing away again, covering his sensitive sinuses. The tiny child was sleeping deeply, his black lashes a fringe on the rosy face barely visible in the light of the moon. "I know he smells bad, but it might be best if we just let sleeping children lie."

The Three fell silent and exchanged a glance. Rhapsody's comment had inadvertently served to remind them of the direness of their situation.

Long ago a poem had proclaimed a prophecy of three sleeping children, each one known indiscriminately as the Sleeping Child.

> The Sleeping Child, the youngest born,
> Lives on in dreams, though Death has come
> To write her name within his tome
> And no one yet has thought to mourn.
>
> The middle child, who sleeping lies,
> 'Twixt watersky and shifting sands,
> Sits silent, holding patient hands
> Until the day she can arise.
>
> The eldest child rests deep within
> The ever-silent vault of earth,
> Unborn as yet, but with its birth
> The end of Time Itself begins.

The first child in the prophecy was sheltered within Achmed's kingdom in the mountains, an Earthchild, a being made of Living Stone, left over from when the world was born. For all he knew she might even be the last of this race, which the dragons fashioned out of elemental earth, considering them their progeny. The ribs of her body were made of the same Living Stone that comprised the Vault of the Underworld, the prison that held the demons in check, and would thereby act as a key to it were she to fall into the hands of the F'dor.

And they know she was there.

The second child mentioned in the prophecy was the star that fell into the sea on the other side of the world, the same star that shattered the Vault. That burning star, which slept beneath the ocean waves for thousands of years, rose and consumed the Island of Serendair in fiery cataclysm fourteen centuries before.

And for all the destruction that ensued, for all the lives that were taken, the middle child brought about far less damage than the other two could.

The third Sleeping Child of the poem, the eldest born, they had seen with their own eyes in their journey along the Axis Mundi, the root of the World Trees that tied them together along the center line of the Earth. It was a wyrm of immense proportion, comprising nearly one-sixth of the world's mass, sleeping in the cold dark wastes below the Earth's mantle.

Waiting for the day the F'dor would call it by name and awaken it.

Whereupon it would consume the earth.

"You have to change him now," Achmed said as the horses danced in place. "The odor is burning the skin off the inside of my eyelids."

In the distance a flicker of movement caught his eye. Had he not twisted to get away from the stench of the child, he never would have seen it, but there it was again, the subtle indication that they were being followed on horseback.

Grunthor had seen it, too. He clicked to the other horses that he was leading, the two light riding serving as pack horses, and began to trot away again toward the east.

With a speed born of years of experience, Achmed silently vaulted off his horse's back, surprising Rhapsody and causing her to sway in the saddle.

"Keep going," he said softly to Grunthor. "I'll take care of these." He waited until the horses had gotten a slight head start, then found a low clump of leafless ramble off to the side a way where he took cover.

After a few moments he could feel the sound and vibration of approaching hooves in the ground. A moment beyond that, the handful of soldiers in Ashe's regalia appeared behind them, traveling quickly and quietly, following closely but making no effort to catch up.

There was something about the way they sat in the saddle that caught Achmed's notice. He had seen Anborn training the retinue of the Lord and Lady Cymrian, and knew that his trainees were prone to sit forward and up, the position that would best prevent them from getting quickly off, and most protect their viscera. But those coming down the road were sitting high in the saddle, in total contradiction to what he knew the Alliance soldiers' training to be.

And they were riding the gray mountain horses of Sorbold.

The Bolg king crouched down and swore silently. There was a time when he would have felt them coming from a quarter mile away, and felt their very heartbeats in his skin, and could return fire accurately at that distance as well. But his blood gift, the ability granted him early in life as the first of his race born on the Island of Serendair, the first of Time's birthplaces, had deserted him when he left the Island, disappearing through the root of Sagia, the tree of elemental starlight. When he arrived in this place, fourteen centuries later, his ability to unerringly follow the heartbeats of every living creature on the Island had vanished, leaving him, somewhat ironically, only able to do so still with those who themselves had come from there.

Still, his skills were keen, his talents well honed.

Achmed silently loaded three whisper-thin circular blades onto the arm of his cwellan, the weapon he had designed for himself a lifetime before.

He set the recoil and waited.

When the cohort had passed him without notice, he loosed the recoil arm into the backs and necks of the men on horseback, slicing through the seams of their armor. He reloaded and fired again and again, even before the first body hit the ground.

In the distance he could hear the horses, now riderless, coming to a confused stop.

Achmed trotted after them, stepping over the bodies, and quickly searched their supply packs. As he suspected, there was nothing to identify them as anything other than soldiers of Roland. He rifled their provisions, then turned the horses loose, finally checking the bodies also for marks of other identification.

In the distance he saw Grunthor and Rhapsody reining to a halt and turning back. He started across the field to catch up with them again, bothered most by the fact that what alerted him to the presence of his stalkers had been an odious signal from a newborn, rather than his own sensitive network of nerves and blood vessels.

"I'm getting too old for this *hrekin*," he muttered.

When they were encamped that night, the baby fed, changed, and asleep for the evening, along with the two Firbolg, Rhapsody pulled a small flute from her pack, a simple reed instrument that she always brought with her when traveling. While Meridion dozed in her lap, shielded as always by the cloak of mist, she began a simple melody she had often played for Ashe before the fire in their days together.

The clouds of the inky black sky sailed quietly overhead on the night breeze, unhurried. She imagined she was tying the notes of the song to them, sending them like a missive of love across the sky, hoping that her husband was standing beneath the same firmament, watching the same stars.

As she played, she was at first unaware of the tears on her cheeks.

Loss, deep and strangling, roared up within her, choking her, making her song sour and thin. Rhapsody lowered her chin to her chest, remembering their days of journeying together, neither trusting the other, and yet comfortable in each other's presence, falling slowly and inextricably in love all the while.

She could not believe that once again they were parted.

She cleared her throat, savagely brushed the tears from her face, then began the song again in earnest, weaving into it the musical pattern of his name. When the melody was complete, she sang softly behind it as it hovered in the air.

Gwydion ap Llauron ap Gwylliam tuatha d'Anwynen o Manosse, I miss you, she intoned, directing the long waves of sound into the wind, attached by an invisible thread to his name. *I love you—remember me.*

Then she curled up with their child, kissed him, and fell into a sleep of disturbing dreams.

$\int$ar away, in the keep of Haguefort, her husband was standing on the balcony of the library, watching the eastern sky.

The wind rustled through his hair, carrying with it a warmth that had not yet come to the winter-wrapped land. There was a song in that wind, a song he had heard long ago, when Rhapsody had summoned him to the grotto Elysian, to reunite him with a lost piece of his soul she had recovered.

He could hear her voice in his memory.

Gwydion ap Llauron ap Gwylliam tuatha d'Anwynen o Manosse, I miss you.

Ashe smiled.

"I miss you, too, Emily," he said, knowing that she would not hear him in return. "But I will see you tonight in my dreams. May yours be sweet."

I love you—remember me.

"As if I could forget." The Lord Cymrian stood for a long time under the starry sky, but no more of the message was forthcoming.

Finally he sighed, and went to bed, wrapped in warm memories of a girl in a grassy meadow on the other side of Time.

17

THE FOREST EDGE OF NAVARNE
AND GWYNWOOD

Melisande had been traveling for the better part of a day when she began to suspect she was going in circles.

She had been traveling for the better part of two when she began to suspect she was being followed.

Melisande heard the trickling of water in the distance and urged the horse forward, knowing it was thirsty. Under a tree was a spring-fed pond, partially frozen, that she thought they had paused at the day before; she swallowed her despair and dismounted, leading the horse to the water, then refilled her waterskin while it drank.

Out of the corner of her eye she thought she saw movement, a little more than a stone's throw away to the north, though when she looked more carefully she beheld nothing but the snowy forest, the evergreens with branches bowed heavy with icy burdens, the bramble and under-growth frosted with recent snow.

Melisande stood erect. She stared harder into the greenwood, but still saw nothing. Still, she drew her knife from the boot sheath and held it out threateningly.

"Show yourself," she demanded of the trees and hillocks.

Nothing but the wind answered her.

She waited for a long moment, then, feeling foolish, she took a drink from the pond. Fighting the pangs of hunger and desperation, she turned to mount and be on her way again.

Standing behind her in a thicket of saplings was a man, a farmer or huntsman by the look of him. He was human, middle-aged and bearded, his expression somber, his face and clothing unremarkable. He wore a brown broadcloth cloak of modest quality and deerskin boots; had he not stepped slightly out of the thicket, she would never have seen him, so plain and colorless were his garments. A long tapering basket of woven reeds and a quiver of arrows were strapped to his back, and he carried a bow, but no other weapon was visible. He said nothing, but watched her with dark eyes that seemed keen and a touch intimidating.

Melisande drew her dagger again quickly.

"Stay back," she said, in a voice she had hoped would sound threatening.

The stranger did not move.

Melisande took hold of the bridle. "Remain still," she said.

The man complied, saying nothing.

The girl turned and prepared to mount, then looked at the knife in her grip. She shifted it to the right hand, then reconsidered; should the man attack her, she would be at a disadvantage, as her left hand was dominant. The stranger just watched her as she cogitated. Finally, she stuck the knife between her teeth like a pirate and climbed into the saddle.

The man just continued to watch her.

Melisande took the knife from her mouth and pulled back on the reins. As she prepared to depart, the stranger finally spoke. His voice was gravelly, as if from disuse.

"Are you injured?"

I certainly wouldn't tell you if I were, Melisande thought. "No," she said, "but you will be if you try to interfere with me."

The man shrugged. "You are lost."

"I am also the Lady Melisande Navarne, and there are by now any number of armed soldiers looking for me," Melisande said, struggling to maintain a brave front. "So be on your way, and I will be on mine."

The man folded his hands.

"And where are you going, Lady Melisande Navarne? I can offer directions. Unless you prefer to continue wandering aimlessly in the forest in winter." The man swallowed, as if so many words at one time had been uncomfortable to produce.

Melisande inhaled. She wanted to be able to trust him, but having just experienced the kindness of strangers in the woods, she was afraid to let him get too close to her.

"I am on my way to the Circle, to see Gavin the Invoker," she said at last.

The man's eyebrows drew together. "You are going the wrong way. The Circle is west; you've been heading south."

Melisande sighed miserably.

"I could take you there," the man said.

The horse danced in place. Melisande shifted on its back, her leg muscles sore and cramping. "Why should I trust you?" she asked, secretly hoping he would provide her a reason to do so.

The man turned to go. "Come if you wish. Remain if you wish. If you're right, your soldiers will find you eventually." He began walking away through the underbrush.

"Have—have you ever been there?" she called after him.

"Where?"

"The Circle? Have you gone there before?"

The stranger stopped and considered. "On occasion. Though not often." Then he turned away again and disappeared between two stands of trees.

Melisande hesitated, then, seeing no alternative, urged the horse forward, keeping her distance from the brown figure that blended disturbingly into the woods around them.

After several hours, Melisande began to wonder if the stranger was trying to lose her even more deeply in the forest.

In spite of being on foot while she was riding, the man moved through the greenwood at a much greater speed than she could.

Her stomach growled and cramped; she had had nothing to eat since supper the night before she left, and was weak with hunger. When the man finally stopped for the night, she worked up her courage and addressed him as politely as she could.

"Have you any—food you could spare?"

The stranger turned around and regarded her sharply. Then after a moment he took the reed basket off of his back, fished around inside it, and took out a packet wrapped in cloth. He tore back the wrapping to reveal a small husk of hard-baked black bread, then came forward and offered it to her. Melisande drew her knife quickly.

"You eat some first," she said, brandishing the blade.

The man nodded. He took the husk and bit the end off it, chewing and swallowing. He took another bite, and a third, finally popping the last of the husk into his mouth. Then he turned around and headed back off into the forest, leaving the crestfallen girl behind him.

Melisande exhaled sadly, then kicked the horse and followed him. *Well, that was stupid,* she chided herself. *Perhaps he has the right idea—I'll just remain quiet from now on.*

They continued walking in silence, with no sound except for the winter wind and the noise of the horse's hooves. As they traveled, Melisande noticed that the forest was changing. At first it seemed brighter, or that there was more snow on the branches and boughs of the trees, but eventually she realized that more of the trees themselves were of white or pale bark—alders, birches, silver maples. She knew from her studies that the prefix *gwyn* meant *white,* but until she had seen the place she didn't realize why it had been so named.

There were also many places where the ground beneath the blanket of snow was black and scorched, where trees showed signs of fire damage. In these places new saplings and scrub were shooting up; the baby trees stood straight against the winter wind, making a place for themselves where disaster had taken their forebears. Melisande felt a kinship with them; the same had been true of her and Gwydion.

Finally, after the sun had begun to set, they came to a large cleared place in the deep forest that appeared to be a woodland village. Throughout the area were many cottages and huts, some of stone and others of earth with turf roofs, or the wattle and dab walls. In addition there were several very large buildings made of wood, with heavy doors and conical thatched roofs. Smoke rose placidly from the hearths of the buildings.

Above the doors of the huts and cottages were brightly colored hex signs of painted or inlaid wood or enamel in complex and beautiful patterns. Most of the dwellings had gardens or kraals in the side or back-yards that had been put to bed for the winter, but doubtless would be uncovered in spring as a source of food for the residents of the houses, which had been whitewashed or faced with stone as ornamentation.

The man had chosen to avoid the main pathways that led through the forest village, but Melisande could see, in spite of the cold, people milling about in robes of wool, some dyed with indigo or goldenrod or engilder leaves to bring forth hues of blue or yellow or green. Others had been soaked in butternut shells or heather, producing tones more earthy, shades of dismal brown and somber gray. These men and women were carrying baskets and tools, and by the descriptions she had heard from her father and Rhapsody, she assumed that they were some of the Filids, the nature priests who worshipped in what they considered a sacred forest and tended to the Great White Tree, the last of the places where Time itself was said to have begun.

In addition to the robed clergy were armed men, carrying bows, spears, axes and other weaponry of foresters and scouts, and attired in leather armor. Melisande recognized the clothing of the stranger as being similar to these foresters, and realized that he was probably one like them, or one of them. It made her relax a little; if he served Gavin, or knew him, he was unlikely to do her harm.

Just before the sun disappeared below the horizon, they came to a vast meadow in the forest. Towering there, its trunk whiter than the snow, with great ivory branches that spread like immense fingers to the twilight sky, was the Great White Tree. Its pale bark glimmered in the last rays of the setting sun, its sheer size made Melisande pull her mount to a stop and stare at it. It was more than fifty feet across at the base, and the first of its giant limbs was easily more than one hundred feet from the ground, leading up to more branches that formed an expansive canopy that reached out over the other trees of the forest, as if sheltering them from the sky.

Around its base, set back a hundred yards from where its great roots pierced the earth, had been planted a ring of trees, each one of a different species. Farther back, low stone walls lined winter gardens that were decorated with ribbons and sprays of greenery, undoubtedly in celebration of the coming spring. Melisande sat atop her horse, staring at the overwhelming beauty that had been described to her, but not sufficiently for her to understand until now.

How long she remained there, lost in thought, she was not certain; it was almost as if she had fallen asleep sitting up from the exhaustion and the ordeal, and the beauty of what she was witnessing. A voice below her shook her from her reverie.

"Child? Can I help you?"

Melisande looked down. The man was gone.

A woman was standing next to the horse, clad in an indigo-colored robe with a cowl at the neck. She was slender and dark of hair, with slight streaks of silver running through it, and her face and body had many of the same racial features that Rhapsody's had. *She must be Lirin,* Melisande noted; she had seen Lirin before, but rarely, and each time she encountered them she thought of her father, who had had a fondness for the race.

"Ehm, yes," she said, struggling to blink away her exhaustion. "I am here to see Gavin the Invoker."

The woman's eyes widened, and she smiled. "Really? And who are you, child?"

Remembering how pompous and silly she had sounded when she first met the man, and how unimpressed he had been, she tried to keep her voice and words more humble.

"My name is Melisande," she said.

"Well, Melisande, you appear to be very tired. Here, come down and I will see to your needs. My name is Elara."

The Lady Navarne shook her head. "No, thank you. I really must see Gavin—I've come a very long way to see him, and he's expecting me."

The woman exhaled. "I don't even know if he's here," she said, looking uncomfortable. "I believe he is gone, actually. But I will send word that you've arrived. Do come down; you look like you are ready to fall from the horse."

Gratefully Melisande dismounted; she stumbled upon touching the ground, faint from hunger, her legs weak. The nature priest put an arm around her and led her to a large building with a conical roof near the outside edge of the winter gardens, from which men and women robed in the colors of the earth were entering and exiting.

Elara held open the oddly carved door on which the hex sign displayed above it had been painstakingly rendered in wood and gestured for the child to go in before her. Melisande complied, her head pounding.

Inside the wooden building, warmed by a huge hearth on which a fire was roaring, were many long, low tables with short-legged chairs, around which nature priests were sitting, eating, and talking. The room resolved into silence as Elara led her to such a table and bade her sit; then the conversations resumed quietly.

"Wait here, and I will get you something to eat," the priest said.

"Please, I must see Gavin," she blurted, panic rising within her. "Please. You don't understand; I have to see him."

Elara squeezed her shoulder. "Eat something first," she said. "I will send word to his house; if he is here, and wants to see you, he will send for you."

"Thank you," Melisande said, struggling to keep from crying. She set her teeth and nodded her thanks as the priest brought her a cup of warm spiced cider and a plate of dense dark bread and hard cheese, then spoke softly to a man in a brown robe without a cowl, who stared at her for a moment, then left the building.

Elara motioned her to sit again. "How did you come to be here?"

"A man found me in the forest," the little girl said between sips of the warm cider. "He didn't say much, but when I told him I needed to see Gavin, he knew where the tree was and brought me here."

"Probably one of the escort foresters," Elara said. "They do tend to be rather taciturn and quiet; it's their job to walk the forest and give aid as needed. So why do you need to see Gavin, Melisande?"

A sensation began in the girl's abdomen not unlike the feeling she occasionally got when ill, before her stomach rushed into her mouth. She tried to keep the tears back, but they cascaded past her defenses and began pouring from her eyes. "We were attacked. The coachmen are dead, the soldiers too, maybe," the little girl said, hiccoughing. "And maybe—Ger—Gerald. I was sent—to see—Gavin—and—"

The nature priest's face took on a look of alarm. She put her arm around Melisande again.

"Sent by whom, Melisande? Who would send a child to the Invoker of the Filids? Do you understand what it is you are asking? Gavin is the leader of an entire faith of more than three million adherents. It would be like presenting yourself at the basilica in Sepulvarta and asking to see the Patriarch, or going up to the palace and demanding to speak with the Lord and Lady Cymrian."

The little girl put her head down on her arms. "Well, the Lord and Lady Cymrian sent me to him in the first place," she said miserably. "So I didn't think it would be this difficult."

"The—what?" Elara lapsed into speechlessness. She pushed the cider and bread closer, and watched in silence as Melisande ate and drank.

The carved door to the building opened again, and the man in the brown robe returned, his eyes wide. He nodded to Elara. The Filidic priest looked down at the little girl and smiled.

"Well, your request is about to be fulfilled. Come; I'll take you to Gavin."

18

The two Filidic priests waited until Melisande had finished the cheese and cider. She stuffed the bread in the pocket of her cape, gaining smiles from both of them, and then was led back out to the winter garden, past many more people in robes tending the sleeping beds and hardy shrubs, all the way to the circle of trees surrounding the Great White Tree.

The sun had gone beyond the horizon, leaving nothing but inky black clouds in a remnant of blue at the edge of the world. The moon was just rising, hanging low in the sky and spilling cold light across the meadow. A pathway from the building to the circle of trees was lit with lanterns hanging from wooden posts, all the way to the other side of the meadow.

The closer they got to the gigantic tree, the warmer Melisande felt. There was something entrancing about it that reached down into her heart. Rhapsody had told her of her time in this odd place of natural magic, of the foresters like the man who led her to the Circle, who plied the woodland trails, escorting pilgrims to sites sacred to those who followed the faith practices of the Filids, of the vast herbal gardens where medicines and herbs used in rituals were carefully tended; of the healers who could cure the wounds and illnesses of both men and animals, and especially of the Tree, which she said sang an ancient song that was indescribable in its beauty. Melisande did not hear the song, but still could feel its power.

She tried to remember what the Lady Cymrian had said about Gavin himself. Rhapsody had studied with him, had wandered a good deal of the forest in his presence, and seemed fond of him, but had said little more about him, mostly because it seemed that no one knew him very well, even the foresters who he trained. He had been the Chief Forester when Rhapsody met him, and was chosen to take over as Invoker when Ashe's father, Llauron, had given up his human body to take on dragon form. All of this was very jumbled in Melisande's mind; she had been very small when it all took place, and so seemed like little more than a fairy tale to her—a fairy tale in which she knew the players.

As they crossed the dark meadow she began to see what she thought were signs of recent fire again. Many of the trees in the circle around the Great White Tree were newly planted or had been badly burned, including the great copse of ancient trees, vastly tall and broad, in and around which the house they were heading toward was built.

Unlike the house that Llauron had lived in, which she had seen drawings of in her father's museum, this was little more than a large cabin, with a high hip roof and walls of fragrant cedar. Llauron's house had been built by his father, Gwylliam the Visionary, and set within the trees and built around them at many odd angles, with sections placed high in the forest canopy and a tower in the center that was tall enough to look above it, and surrounded by many beautiful and cozy gardens. She had been fascinated by the drawings of it, and her father had described to her the great inventions that Gwylliam had installed to allow fragile plants to grow inside glass rooms in winter, tubes through which people spoke to people in other rooms, and a tower aviary in which the messenger birds lived in beautiful bamboo cages intricately designed to match the destination buildings to which they were trained to carry their missives. He and Ashe had spent many happy hours there as boys; the memory of his face, recalling those times, stung even as the surroundings entranced her.

By contrast, the new house was clean of line and simple, barely larger than the carriage house at Haguefort, which was itself a small keep. The windows were round with carved shutters, with simple boxes affixed beneath them, wrapped for winter's sleep. The house was all on one level except for a small lookout tower with an enclosed stairway that reached high above the forest canopy. Two lampposts flanked the cabin, the flame within them glowing brightly, if not warmly.

The only remarkable thing about the place was the door. In the lantern shadows it appeared to be marred by soot but unburned, it was arched, made of wood that Melisande did not recognize, and scarred by salt. The minuscule remnants of an image were barely visible, flaked leaves of gilding still able to be seen, evoking a mythical beast, a dragon or griffin of some sort.

A great stone wall, lined with sleeping gardens, led up a pathway to the heavy wooden door, which was guarded by foresters.

"This is where Gavin lives," Elara said. She walked up to the guardians and spoke to them in a tongue Melisande did not understand, to which they replied in kind. Elara nodded and turned back to the little girl.

"Gavin is at the Tree," she said. She nodded back across the meadow, where a number of Filids and foresters were milling about, some tending the guardian circle of trees, some conferring, others in ritual prayer. "Come."

Melisande followed her back up the path and beyond the circle of guardian trees, to a spot beneath an enormous white limb glimmering in the light of the ascendant moon.

Several bearded men in simple green and brown clothing were talking quietly among themselves. The one with his back to her gestured off toward the north, and the rest of them bowed and left. The remaining man stood for a moment, as if listening to something only he could hear, then turned and looked down into her face.

It was the forester who had brought her to the Circle.

"Gavin, this is the girl we told you of," said Elara. "Her name is Melisande."

The forester nodded, then hid a smile at the look of thunderous shock on the young girl's face. "Hello, Lady Melisande Navarne."

"*You* are Gavin?" Melisande exploded.

"I am."

"Why didn't you tell me?"

The somber man looked even more directly at her. "You didn't ask," he said. "You merely told me who *you* were." He signaled to Elara, and the Filidic priest bowed to him, smiled at Melisande, and withdrew, gesturing to the others within the circle to follow her.

Gavin waited until they were alone beneath the Great White Tree, then returned his attention to the girl. "In the future, I respectfully suggest you consider asking the names of those in your presence, and being less forthcoming with your own, m'lady. A brave spirit can't always overcome a foolish head."

Melisande's face flushed hot in the light of the lanterns. The Invoker saw her embarrassment, and gestured for her to walk closer to the Great White Tree with him.

"We are now outside of the wind, and within the protection of the Tree," he said when they came to a stop beneath its outstretched limbs overhead. "This is the safest place in the forest to speak, without fear of being overheard, Tell me, then, Lady Melisande Navarne, why did the Lady Cymrian send you to me?" His dark eyes twinkled. "Aside from your rare brave spirit and even rarer ability for survival for one your age."

Melisande took a deep breath, concentrating and trying to remember Rhapsody's words exactly as she had spoken them.

"The Lady Cymrian bids me ask you to take me, along with a full contingent of your top foresters and your most accomplished healer, to the greenwood north-northeast of the Tar'afel River, where the holly grows thickest. She said that you will know where this is." The Invoker nodded thoughtfully. "I am to ask you to have your foresters fan out at that point, keeping to a distance of half a league each, and form a barrier that extends northwest all the way to the sea, setting whatever snares and traps they need to protect that barrier. They are to remain there, allowing no living soul to enter."

The Invoker inhaled, watching her sharply, his eyes gleaming intensely in the dark.

"When this is accomplished, she asks that you yourself take me from this point onward. A sweet-water creek flows south into the Tar'afel; we are to follow it northward until we come to Mirror Lake."

The Invoker shook his head. "Those are sacred lands, where I have never trod. That is the realm of the dragon Elynsynos. I know of no such lake."

"She said that we will know this body of water because its name describes it perfectly. At the lake I am to leave you and travel on alone. She asks you to wait for me there for no more than three days. If I have not returned by then, you are to return to the Circle and go about your business."

"Leaving you to whatever fate you have met?" the Invoker demanded.

Melisande exhaled. "I suppose so, yes."

"And you agreed to this, Lady Melisande Navarne?"

The little girl squared her shoulders and drew herself up to her full height, which reached its summit at a little above the man's waist.

"I did. And I fully understand the implications."

"And is that all? You merely need me to provide escort into the forbidden lands and to abandon you to Fate there?"

"No," Melisande said quickly, remembering the rest of her instructions. "Within that time I expect to return to you with one of two requests—either to come back with me along with the healer, or with the intention of sealing the dragon's cave."

The Invoker stood suddenly straighter.

"What has happened to Elynsynos?" he asked, stricken.

"I don't know," Melisande said plainly. "But Rhapsody fears the worst."

"This is dire news indeed," said the Invoker, turning away toward the silver trunk of the Great White Tree. He was silent for some time, then turned back to the little girl.

"If you are willing to undertake such a task, it would be my honor to escort you in it," he said finally. "I have but two last questions for you, Lady Melisande Navarne."

"Yes?"

"How old are you?"

"Nine," the little girl replied. "But I'll be ten on the first day of spring, which is very soon."

The Invoker nodded. "And how old do you feel today?"

Melisande's brows drew together in confusion, then in thought.

"Much older than that," she said. "At least twelve."

"Very good," the Invoker said.

"And may I ask you something now?"

"Indeed."

"How did you come to find me in the forest? Do you know if my chamberlain and soldiers are alive?"

The Invoker smiled. It was an unusual expression, one that he did not seem to wear very often.

"The second question first: your chamberlain is indeed alive, and two of your soldiers. They were found by my woods guides and returned under escort to Haguefort.

"As for how I came upon you—the woods told me there was a brave young woman who had fought off attackers and was lost within them. I came to find you, for such a person cannot be left to the vagaries of misfortune and fate. And so I will again, Lady Melisande Navarne. Take heed and believe this—no matter what comes to pass, I will come for you."

PART TWO

The Eye of a Building Storm

19

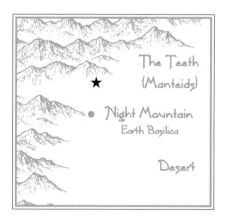

The Teeth
(Manteids)

★

● Night Mountain
Earth Basilica

Desert

THE PALACE OF JIERNA TAL,
JIERNA'SID, SORBOLD

Dangerous as it would be to admit it, Talquist hated seers.

As he paced the heavy carpet that adorned the marble floors of the imperial palace, he muttered extravagant curses under his breath, vile but amusing obscenities he had learned from the sailors during his days in the Mercantile, where his first fortune had been made. For all that the power of the crown was heady, in secret Talquist missed those days, wandering the wide world with little more than sand in his pockets and a scheme in his head. He missed the sight of ships coming into port flying colors from around the world, the smell of burlap sacks bulging with spices and seeds, the sounds of laughter in dark taverns and the groans of longshoremen off-loading goods into the night in misty rain. In particular he missed the sea, for the sea had always been good to him, had given him everything of value he owned.

Most especially, it had given him the power he now sought to expand to the water's edge on the other side of the Known World.

The regent emperor paused as he passed the enormous looking glass in his bedchamber. An ordinary man stared back at him, heavyset and muscular of body, swarthy of skin, dark of complexion, hair, and eye. A man no different in appearance than any other man in this realm of endless sun, sand, and mountains except that he was bejeweled in gold and clad in robes of finest linen, the product for which Sorbold was best known in the trading world. An ordinary man on the outside, perhaps.

But within that ordinary man, Talquist mused, was a vision that was anything but ordinary.

For all that he was a visionary, however, Talquist was not a seer. The regent emperor began to pace again, his breath coming out in grunts of building frustration. He had been planning for a long time, biding his time, acting his part, putting all the pieces in place as meticulously as the artisans of Keltar who carved intricate representations of the world in gemstones smaller than a thumbnail. But while he could envision his dreams, and knew how to position his resources to achieve them, his sight failed at that point. He could not monitor whether or not it was coming to fruition.

At least not yet.

All of that is about to change, he reminded himself.

His calm restored somewhat, Talquist turned and walked back up the winding stone staircase at the southwestern corner of his bedchamber to the tower room at its top.

Every corner of his chambers had such a parapet, the three others each housing crossbowmen of superior skill, as did the wide central balcony on the main level. The balcony and two of the towers stared west, into the red sunset, over the mountains that ringed the capital city of Jierna'sid, to the grassy steppes and the wide Krevensfield Plain beyond, all the way to the sea, a thousand miles away. The other two towers faced the southeast and northeast, where the lookouts scanned the mountains at their back in the glare of the rising sun.

But only this one bore the signs of fresh mortar and brick, recent repairs to what had been a gargantuan hole.

As Talquist reached the top step, he asked himself if by not having archers he was wasting space in this tower that would leave him vulnerable, but discarded the thought a moment later in the recollection of the forty thousand troops quartered in this city alone, all of whom had naught but his continued safety and security foremost in mind.

The room at the top of the stairs was small and spare, with no decoration except a map of the continent adhered to the wall. The southern and western walls were open to the wind to facilitate bow shots and other defensive projectiles; the corners of the map flapped in the stiff breeze. The opening looked out on the courtyard on the western side and a chasm on the southern one.

In a small cane rocking chair facing out the western tower window a woman was sitting with her back to him, her head tilted toward the sun, her eyes closed in the glow of its radiance on her face.

Talquist inhaled slowly, attempting to measure his breathing, so that he would remain calm. He stepped onto the stone floor and slowly came up behind her.

The woman did not move or seem to notice.

"Good day, Rhonwyn," he said as pleasantly as he could.

The woman did not open her eyes, but her smooth forehead wrinkled into furrows at the sound of his voice.

Talquist inhaled more deeply this time. This was the fourth attempt this day he had made to communicate with the Seer of the Present, and each time had been angered more than the last. Her mythic status as one of the three Seers of Time and, more importantly, his acute need of her unique abilities demanded a patience of him that he normally did not possess.

"Good day, Rhonwyn," he repeated.

This time the woman opened her eyes and turned slowly in her chair to face him. Despite her age her face was smooth in the bloom of youth, her hair red-gold at the crown of her head, but as it tapered down in a long braid bound in leather thongs it passed into dimmer stages, darkening and turning gray until it reached the snow-white tip.

Her eyes, blank scleras without irises, reflected distorted images of himself back to him.

"No," Rhonwyn said. "I think not."

Acid filled the back of Talquist's mouth; while the woman's tone was fragile and dreamlike, nevertheless, the words stung of insult. He swallowed his sour rage and came to her side, looking out the window at the distant courtyard below.

Jierna Tal was one of the modern architectural marvels of the world, a smooth stone palace perched on jagged crags above an almost bottomless chasm, rising in clean angles skyward to unseen heights, its corners finished in spiraling minarets and bell towers that occasionally were shrouded in low-hanging clouds. The tremendous distance from the cobblestones of the streets to the top of the towers served frequently as a metaphor to remind Talquist how far he had risen from the gutter to his now-exalted position. Just past the courtyard the chasm, part of the palace's defenses, descended another thousand feet as if to accentuate the point.

A long shadow lay across the courtyard, twisting occasionally and glinting in the amber light of the sun. Talquist glanced to the city square on a hill above the palace.

Towering there in the afternoon haze was another reminder of how far he had come, and to what he owed his elevation. The great Scales loomed high above Jierna Tal, an immense and ancient artifact brought from the old world by the Cymrian refugees whose descendants now held power in the Middle Continent. Gigantic beams balanced two plates of burnished gold wide enough for a cart and oxen to rest within; Talquist smiled. He himself had stood in one of those weighing plates and had been lifted aloft, to the stunned response of the crowd below, who, after recovering, had declared him Emperor Presumptive.

He had modestly insisted, in the wake of the untimely deaths of the previous monarch and her heir, that a suitable waiting period of a year pass before his coronation, and instead chose to become regent of Sorbold, stewarding the power that in the spring would officially be his.

He did not wait to make use of that power in unofficial capacities.

Now the dusty streets of Jierna'sid, once little more than a pathetic market of beggars and sheeted tents, workmen, animal traffic, and greasy pit fires for roasting goat meat, had been transformed into a tidy place of military patrols and marching cadences, expanded linen factories and tradesmen whose sole clientele was the army and the crown. Jierna Tal, long out of place in its dingy surroundings, had been transformed as he had been transformed, into the royal center of a growing city blooming in the desert heat, growing strong in the blessed rays of the endless sun for which Sorbold was known.

It was only the beginning.

Talquist looked back at the ancient Seer. Rhonwyn's slender hands held a battered metal compass, an instrument said to have been used by her Seren father fourteen centuries before to find his way to the Wyrmlands from the Lost Island of Serendair. Her ability to know the truth of the Present was a birthright gained from the elemental power of Merithyn the Explorer and her dragon mother, Elynsynos. Talquist, a descendant of the indigenous humans that had lived at the outskirts of the Wyrmlands for time uncounted before the Cymrians came with their odd powers and their ridiculous longevity, was not impressed.

But even if the power of the Cymrians did not impress him, their longevity—a seeming resistance to all of the ravages of time—was something he craved above all else.

Given the length and intensity of his list of cravings, that *was* impressive.

He had heard once, long ago and in passing, that the spark which lit the fire of the Great War that ended the Illuminaria, Gwylliam the Visionary's great era of empire building and enlightenment, was a family argument about succession. It was well known in the lore of the sea that Edwyn Griffyth, Gwylliam's eldest son, had spurned his birthright and gone off to live evermore in Gaematria, the mystical realm of the Sea Mages, so Talquist surmised that Gwylliam had been denied the heir he wanted to his throne, a dynasty that would live on after him, even though he was thought to be immortal.

Talquist wanted no dynasty. He needed no heirs.

He wanted to live forever.

He came over to the fragile woman and crouched down beside her.

"Come now, Grandmother," he said, his merchant's voice as smooth as Canderian silk, "look beyond the fog and fragments of dreams that cloud your eyes, and tell me—has the raiding party been successful?"

The mirrors in the Seer's eyes reflected his face, her expression blank.

Inwardly Talquist cursed. He had still not learned how to speak easily to her in the correct structure she needed to grasp his questions. Rhonwyn could only see the Present, and what he had asked required knowledge of the Past. He swallowed and tried again.

"The raiding party of the Second Mountain Guard of Sorbold—is the Child of Time in their possession?"

The ancient woman shook her head.

Talquist exhaled. "Where is the raiding party now?"

The Seer's fleeting grip on the moment prior faded from her face before his eyes. "What raiding party?"

He struggled to keep the seething anger out of his voice. "The raiding party of the Second Mountain Guard of Sorbold—where is it at this moment?"

Rhonwyn ran her fingers, shaking with age, over the nautical instrument in her hands.

"Forty-six, forty-eight North, two, twenty East," she intoned.

Talquist consulted the map on the wall. Those coordinates positioned his covert soldiers, disguised in the uniforms of common Roland cavalry, in the sparsely populated forest lands of eastern Navarne, less than a day's journey from their intended target: a small keep in the western duchy of Navarne.

Haguefort.

"And the Child of Time?" Talquist pressed. "It is well?"

The Seer blinked, then closed her eyes again, basking in the reflected light of the sky.

The regent clutched his hands into fists so tight that his neatly trimmed fingernails threatened to puncture the skin of his palms. It was all he could do to keep from seizing the compass and driving one of its sharp legs through the ancient Seer's heart. He willed himself to be patient, as he always had to during these interviews.

"Is the Child of Time in Haguefort well? Answer me."

Rhonwyn opened her eyes and looked at him while her hands manipulated the battered instrument.

"I see no Child of Time in Haguefort."

"What are you babbling about? A fortnight ago, your answer to my question 'where is the Child of Time?' was 'in the forest of Gwynwood.' Every day since then you have been giving me positions leading it back, unmistakably, to Haguefort. Yesterday, your very answer to my question was 'Haguefort.' If it's not there, where is it?"

The woman's mouth quivered, but she said nothing.

Black rage exploded behind Talquist's eyes. His hand, unstayed by any rational thought, shot out and gripped the ancient Seer by the throat. Intellectually he knew the sacrilege he was committing, but his intellect was entirely overwhelmed by his frustration.

The brittle bones of her ancient neck crackled in his clenched hands. The Seer gasped, her lips quivering with shock. The regent emperor loosed his grip, panting, and stepped away from the fragile woman.

"Now, again, Rhonwyn," he said through gritted teeth, "where is the Child of Time? *Where is it?*"

Purple bruises appeared on the skinfolds below Rhonwyn's chin, then quickly disappeared. She idly ran her hands over her neck, her face contorted with fear, which faded a moment later into the Past, replaced by serenity once more.

"I see no Child of Time on the face of the Earth," she said blithely. Then she leaned back in her chair and began to rock slowly again, her eyes closed in the warmth of the sun.

Talquist swallowed, and tried one more time.

"You said the Child was with the Lord and Lady Cymrian each time I have asked you its whereabouts since its birth," he said softly. "Is it still with them?"

"Is what still with whom?" The Seer's face was blank, her tone without comprehension.

A bitter taste filled Talquist's mouth; after the span of a few heartbeats he realized it was the grist from his own clenched teeth. The dust of his molars was a foul reminder of the night he had stood before Rhonwyn's sister Manwyn, the Seer of the Future, and had done a version of this same irritating dance, seething in silent frustration while the madwoman cackled and swung on her platform over a dark pit in her decaying temple in Yarim, tossing insane predictions into the incense-heavy air. Finally he had lost his patience and raised his crossbow, pointing it at her heart.

Tell me, hag—or I will put an end to your ramblings. Answer my question—what must I do to achieve immortality? Who has the knowledge of how to live forever?

The woman stopped as if frozen. Her mirrored eyes fixed upon him, and her thin mouth crooked into a half smile. She looked through the battered sextant that her explorer father had bequeathed to her at the stars glowing in the dark dome of her temple, then returned her blind gaze to him once again.

You will not kill me, Emperor, she had said. *The future holds no picture of my blood on your hands, though they will be red with that of countless others.* Manwyn had laid down on her belly then, inching toward him on her suspended platform. *If immortality is what you seek, you must find the Child of Time.* She cackled, as if to herself. *It sleeps now within the belly of its mother, but soon it will come out into the light and air of the world. And Time itself will have no dominion over it.*

Talquist swallowed the bitter grit, remembering how the breath had gone out of him as he lowered the bow.

How will I learn immortality from this Child of Time? he had asked, his voice wavering.

The Seer had sat bolt upright, as if suddenly struck. Her hands went to her mouth, trembling. Then she stretched out a shaking hand, and pointed at him accusingly.

Murderer, she whispered, the golden skin of her face paling visibly in the dim light of the candles. *Murderer. Murderer.*

Her voice rose to an even more insane pitch. *Murderer!* she began to shriek, until the word became a scream. *Murderer, murderer!*

He had left her rotting temple then, the madwoman's howls ringing in his ears. His spies reported that the guards of the Seer's temple had shut the great cedar door into her chambers to the pilgrims who came seeking prophecies; rumor held that Manwyn had continued to scream nothing but the word *murderer* from that day on, night into day into night again.

Talquist inhaled deeply, then bent down beside Rhonwyn once more.

"One last time for today," he said softly, his voice deathly calm, though his stomach was boiling. "Tell me the exact whereabouts of the Child of Time."

The Seer turned to face him and slowly opened her eyes. Talquist reared back in shock; each of the mirrored scleras contained, for the first time in his notice, a clear blue iris, its dark pupil contracting in the light of the setting afternoon sun.

The Seer looked at him thoughtfully.

"Right before you, I suppose," she said steadily. "My sisters and I were often called by that name—children of Time." She broke her gaze away and looked out the window at the mountains beyond. "I remember, Anwyn," she said quietly.

Fury roared through Talquist so quickly that he did not even notice she had spoken in the past tense. He seized the back of her chair to steady himself and leaned close enough for his lips to brush her auburn hair where it faded to gray.

"I'm not certain you can fathom, in your blithering state, what risks I have taken on your supposedly infallible word, what sacrifices I have made, m'lady," he said acidly. "I sent soldiers into Roland ere I was ready to begin the assault, tipped my hand before I was ready. The Patriarch no doubt has learned of your disappearance by now, perhaps even your great-nephew, the Lord Cymrian, knows as well. The element of surprise is an arrow already off the string and away—this is *your* doing, Rhonwyn, as if you had given the order yourself."

"Manwyn, the Present will be veiled," the Seer whispered, staring into the sun. "No more will you see me when you search the skies of the Future—farewell, sister."

Something black broke within the Emperor Presumptive. He seized the brittle woman by the back of her neck and arm and, without thinking twice, hurled the ancient prophetess out the window of the parapet, past the courtyard and into the chasm below.

Her scream followed her down by a split second, frightening the roosting swallows that had perched in the hollows of the castle's stone, sending them fluttering skyward in a great white and gray rush.

Talquist rose to his feet shakily, his control returning, and stood at the window, staring down into the all-but-bottomless crevasse. He looked for any sign of the mythic woman, listened for any sound that portended the survival of one of the three daughters of Fate, but heard nothing save the whine of the wind racing through the canyon, bringing dust in great scattering swirls to the stones of the courtyard. He contemplated the loss to the lore of the world that he had just delivered.

"I had always heard that Time flies," he said. "Oh, well."

Boot steps thundered up the steps. Talquist turned idly to see his chamber guards, followed a moment later by his puffing chamberlain, appear at the top of the stairs.

"Are—are you all right, m'lord?" the chamberlain inquired between breaths.

"Never better," Talquist said. He looked out the window into the depths of the chasm once more.

"The commander of the imperial army is awaiting your pleasure in your antechamber, m'lord. He says you summoned him, but that I was not to disturb you if you were not ready for him."

"Send him in."

The chamberlain hesitated. "Are you certain, m'lord? He is happy to wait if his presence is an imposition. Commander Fhremus doesn't wish to interrupt your work."

Talquist smiled. "Not at all," he said as he headed for the stairs. "He's interrupting nothing; I was just killing Time."

Far across the continent, on the other side of the Krevensfield Plain, deep within her moldering temple of splashing fountains and decaying tapestries, the Seer of the Future ceased wailing.

For more than five months she had been keening without ceasing, howling away in her insanity. The pilgrims who occasionally had sought her advice had long stopped coming to her great carved door; no gold coins had been dropped in the offering box. Even the guards had left, being unable to bear the nightmarish sound any longer.

Now, with the murder she had foreseen accomplished, her sister's very existence forgotten, the clouds within her mind dissipated. Manwyn sat slowly up on the swinging platform above the deep well in her temple; her gaze returned to the heavens painted on the dome above her.

And softly began to sing to herself a song of madness once again.

20

HAGUEFORT, NAVARNE

Che commander of the raiding party of the Second Mountain
Guard reined his horse quietly to a halt, signaling for the other soldiers
to fall in behind him. The remainder of the cohort took shelter along the
far side of the great wall that encircled Haguefort, the only sound the occasional snorting of the animals in the cold air. The commander nodded
to Mardel, one of his spryer lieutenants, to dismount and draw near for
instructions.

The young soldier complied, tossing his reins to another, and came
forward.

The commander leaned over and spoke softly.

"Slip over the wall and open the gate for us. We will ride the wall
where it is unguarded and then cross to the far entrance. Take your time.
You know the rest."

Mardel nodded, saluted, and jogged silently to the wall. Upon approaching it he could see that the commander had chosen an opportune

spot; although the wall had guard towers every twenty feet or so, this side appeared to be largely unguarded.

He waited in the shadows, nonetheless, until he was satisfied that no one atop the wall could see him. After a few moments, when no sign of a guard appeared at all, he quickly crossed to the wall and felt around for handholds.

Atop the wall were metal spikes, but Mardel had been trained for just such a purpose. He scaled the wall quickly, then slid between two of the spikes with ease, then crouched low and dropped down to the ground within, rolling to absorb the shock of the twelve-foot fall, ending up on his feet.

He glanced around and saw nothing but thick shadows within the walled field. He clung to the wall, staying low in case there was anyone on the keep balcony in the distance, but the lights of the small castle were low; probably the entire house had retired for the evening.

It only took a few moments to traverse most of the inner field. Mardel could hear soft sounds without, noises that would not have been detected had he not known that the remainder of the cohort was traveling at approximately the same speed outside the ramparts. His heart pounded with excitement as he passed a low two-story building that their reconnaissance had described as the Cymrian Museum that the keep's previous lord, a famous historian, had maintained.

The gate was almost within reach. Mardel glanced one last time at the balconies and windows in the distance and, seeing no one on or near them, made for the gate.

A ringing sound, followed by a hum, rent the air, followed a split second later by pulsing waves of blue light.

Mardel turned around slowly.

Behind him in the shadows, almost within arm's reach, was the dark figure of a man silhouetted by the blazing light of the sword in his hand. That sword had a blade that ran in blue ripples from tang to tip, waves of what appeared to be water flowing hypnotically down the shaft, appearing to fall away into nothingness.

The shadow was crowned with hair of shiny red-gold, metallic in its sheen like burnished copper. That, and two blazing blue eyes in the middle of the face, was the only part of the man not cloaked in darkness.

"Oh, let me guess—you were sent in to open the gate, am I right?"

The voice issuing forth from the shadow sounded almost bored, as if annoyance was too great an expenditure of effort.

Mardel stood stock still.

Before his eyes, the tip of the watery blue sword was at his neck.

"Again, you were sent to open the gate? Answer, or I will cut your throat."

"Yes," whispered Mardel.

The dark figure lowered the weapon.

"There's a much closer one near the main entrance. Would have saved you a lot of running."

Mardel swallowed but said nothing. Of the entire cohort of the Second Mountain Guard, he was the least experienced, though he had been in military service to the crown almost half his short life. While he had partaken in bloody raids and served in some unsavory situations, he had never been surprised on a raid before, especially by someone who blended into the darkness without detection.

"How many?" The man sheathed his blade, dousing the light and returning the inner field to shadow again.

"Fifty men," Mardel lied.

The hidden man snorted. "Only fifty?" He rolled his eyes, the blue irises gleaming in the white scleras, and gestured toward the wall with utter contempt. "Open the gate."

A metallic clanking could be heard in the near distance behind the man.

"Want assistance?" a curt voice called.

The first man shook his head, the light of the keep's bonfire catching the red-gold of his hair.

"Only if you are bored, Uncle. This fellow claims to be opening the gate for fifty men, though it's actually twenty-seven."

An even ruder snort issued forth from the near distance.

"Only fifty? Open the gate and let them in. I should be done moving my bowels by then."

The blue eyes sighted on Mardel again.

"You are dressed in the colors of my regiment," the shadowy man said slowly, his tone less bored and more threatening. "You imbeciles have broached my lands, lands that stand under a flag of peace, disguised in my regalia, and come to my home in the night, threatening my family, and you only claim to have brought *fifty* men? I am insulted."

Sensing the futility of effort and the danger of waiting, Mardel drew his sword.

Before he could level it the glowing blue blade had seemed to leap forth from its scabbard and dragged itself in one clean slash across his throat. Mardel fell to the ground, bleeding his life onto the snowy grass.

Ashe sheathed his sword and strode to the gate. He took hold of the ropes of the portcullis and raised it slowly in the dark.

"Come," he whispered in the tongue of Sorbold. "The house is asleep."

The commander heard and nodded assent, signaled to the remains of the cohort, which quietly rode through the gate. The gate was shut quickly behind them.

Even before the cohort had had a chance to regroup, the blue glowing sword was slashing the bindings of the two closest saddles, as the shadow wielding it pummeled the falling riders with the hilt.

A shriek ripped past them and three more riders fell, pierced by crossbow bolts that came out of the darkness.

"Did you get a chance to examine the Bolg king's weapon?" Anborn's voice called over the sounds of the horse chaos as he fired off another round of bolts, felling three more soldiers.

"I've seen it before," Ashe replied, crossing blades briefly with one of the cohort before dragging him from his saddle and slashing his throat in a blaze of blue and white rippling light. "Why?"

"Nice recoil," Anborn commented, firing again. "Do you need any further assistance? I think I may have left my hot toddy in the library, and it's probably getting cold."

"No, by all means," Ashe said as he dodged out of the way of two of the horsemen's picks. "I'll join you for one in a moment, once I've taken care of this. I saved one to talk to—you can help interrogate later, over brandy, if you'd like." His last word was punctuated by the thrust of his sword through a Sorbold chest.

Gwydion Navarne, watching in the recesses, just shook his head as his namesake dispatched the rest of the soldiers, then took hold of the unconscious man he had incapacitated early on and dragged him back to the keep in the dark. He turned himself and followed Ashe's shadow in the flickering light of Haguefort's lanterns.

21

The Teeth
(Manteids)

★

● Night Mountain
Earth Basilica

Desert

*G*ood day, Fhremus," the regent said as the doors closed behind a tall man in the military regalia of the Dark Earth, the dynastic line of the empress who ruled before Talquist. The regent emperor winced involuntarily at the sight of the dead empress's crest, as he always did, needing to remind himself that he had chosen to keep the military uniforms of Leitha and the dynasty of the Dark Earth until spring, when he would be finally invested as emperor. Nonetheless, like other choices he had made in the name of appearing humble, the image of a golden sun bisected by a sword always caused him to flinch in anger.

Especially given the symbol he had chosen for his own.

That same sun, rising rampant between the shorelines of two seas.

The soldier, whose bearing was still youthful in spite of his many years in command, bowed respectfully.

"M'lord."

Talquist gestured at the heavily carved table of dark wood near the doors of the balcony.

"Sit."

The soldier bowed again and complied, but once at the table he stole a glance at the regent as if assessing his health. Talquist noticed, but said nothing, instead making his way casually to a similarly carved sideboard where an impressive array of glassware and decanters of the finest potent libations from around the world was displayed.

"Would you care for something to drink, Fhremus?" Talquist asked, pouring himself a splash of Canderian brandy in a low crystal glass.

"Thank you, no, m'lord," the commander answered rotely. "My attention to your safety forbids me to compromise my senses in your presence."

Talquist chuckled darkly. "Nonsense," he said humorously. "My safety is assured, not only by a retinue of palace guards, but by measures you cannot even imagine. So, go ahead, Fhremus, fortify yourself. I expect you may need it."

The suggestion had become a command.

Fhremus rose from the table and came to the sideboard, where he selected a single malt from Argaut, a nation in the southern hemisphere far across the Central Sea, and poured himself a few fingers of it. Then he followed Talquist back to the table again.

"Excellent choice," said the regent, watching Fhremus over the rim of his own glass. "Argaut has many excellent distilleries. I hope you enjoy it."

"Thank you, m'lord."

Talquist leaned closer.

"Yes, Fhremus, I am alive and whole, in spite of any rumors to the contrary."

The commander smiled nervously. "I am glad to see that, m'lord."

The regent settled down more comfortably in his chair. "I have always admired your devotion to the nation and the crown, Fhremus," he said, inhaling the bouquet of the brandy. "I was greatly impressed at your wisdom during the Colloquium following the empress's death in insisting that the empire remain united, especially in the face of the lobbying by the counts of the larger provinces to disband both the empire and the army. I will never forget what you said at that meeting, that 'the might of the Sorbold army comes from two factors—commonality of purpose and love of our native land.'" The soldier nodded and sipped his drink.

"That wisdom is about to be proven more than anyone could have envisioned," said Talquist seriously. "I want you to speak freely to me, Fhremus, without fear of reprisal, not soldier to emperor, but Sorbold to Sorbold. What is most common between you and I is a deep love of our nation. That nation is under dire threat, a threat that must be met with force, swiftly and overwhelmingly. If we delay or do nothing, we will lose any advantage that our terrain and military might would have given us in what will be a battle for our very survival."

The supreme commander blinked. "Threat? What threat?" He stared at the regent. "I just reviewed all the reports of the field commanders from every one of the twenty-seven city-states, and there has been no hostile activity reported in three months—none since the empress's death, in fact. It would seem that the Alliance is concentrating on farming and securing the trade routes, with a minimum of military buildup. Roland appears peaceful, and there have been no sightings of Bolg outside the mountains of Ylorc. And, of course, the Lirin of Tyrian are keeping to themselves, as always. We are at peace."

"So it might seem," agreed Talquist, taking another sip and straining it through his back teeth. "But you forget, Fhremus, that prior to being chosen as emperor by the Scales, I was hierarch of the Western Mercantile, and so my information comes not only from within the continent, but from outside it."

"And there are indications that we are under threat of invasion?" The soldier's demeanor changed subtlely; his muscles tensed and his spine straightened, while his eyes took on a gleam in the light of the afternoon sun spilling into the room from the balcony.

"If left unchecked, it will lead to that," said Talquist. "But consider the geography of the continent. You have to look at this land as the Creator fashioned it, rather than as it was divided by man, the result of the Cymrian War four hundred years ago, and then perhaps you can see what the Creator intended for it.

"Sorbold is the foundation of the entire continent in the south, granted divine protection by the Creator in the form of forbidding mountains and implacable deserts, a vast expanse of territory and a large population that is tempered in the sun, strong and relentless and proud. Our willingness for centuries to maintain our military and our defensive infrastructure has given us the upper hand from a tactical standpoint. Even our inland seacoast is protected, for the most part, by the land mass that surrounds it. We have outposts at the water's edge from the Non-aligned States to the Skeleton Coast, outposts that incoming ships must pass in order to land in port. So we are a formidable, almost unassailable opponent under normal circumstances."

The commander nodded; the regent had just provided the same assessment he would have himself, and it was a case for limited worry.

"The Middle Continent in the west, comprised of Tyrian, Roland, and Gwynwood, is the breadbasket of this part of the world," Talquist continued. "Its geography of wide plains, forests, and fields gives it some natural defense, but few places from which to launch an offensive strike. Only the forested realm of Tyrian is close enough to one of our city-states to mass an invasion without detection. And the Firbolg king on our border to the east shares the same defensive mountains that guard our north—he could mass an army of invasion, but without support from Roland we would likely be able to repel it easily."

Again Fhremus nodded, and again he made silent note of his assessment.

"To the north lies the Hintervold, and it, as you know, is an icy wasteland only inhabitable in part, and only in part of the year. It is a treasure trove of skins and ore and gold, of peat for fuel, with a short but intense growing season that produces a small harvest of vegetables of massive size, but cannot feed itself through its own agriculture. Without the food Roland provides to it, the Hintervold would be even more barren than it already is. In short, this continent was meant to be *one* empire, ruled and defended by the south, fed by the middle, with pelts harvested and gold mined from the north to feed the trade stream. Alas, the wars of our ancestors have left us divided."

"But allied, at least," said Fhremus.

Talquist's face lost some of its pleasant aspect. "We are friends to the Cymrian Alliance, but not a part of it," he said shortly, his tone causing the hairs on Fhremus's neck to stand up. "We are also friends of the Hintervold and of Golgarn, on the Bolg king's southeastern border, but no official alliance exists between Sorbold and those nations, either. That is about to change."

Fhremus sat forward in shock. "We are about to enter into a treaty with the Hintervold and Golgarn?" he asked incredulously. "Those three nations ring the Middle Continent on all sides. Won't that be seen as a threat by the Alliance?"

The regent smiled humorously. "It might, if they knew about it. But what I am telling you, Fhremus, is that our generous friendship and trading practices have lulled the Alliance into believing that we are vulnerable. They believe, as the Creator did, that this continent should be united as one empire. The only difference is that they believe *they* should be in control of it."

All the sound suddenly left the room save for that of the warm wind at the balcony.

"And while they know they are no match for us militarily and strategically," Talquist continued after a moment, "the Alliance has moved ahead with acquiring weapons that they feel will give them enough advantage to start a war."

"What sort of weapons?" asked Fhremus nervously. He put down the glass; the alcohol was irritating his throat, rather than soothing it. Everything the man who would shortly be emperor was telling him was counterintuitive to what his instincts said, but he knew the look in Talquist's eye, and therefore knew better than to question the knowledge of someone with a spy in every doorway the world over.

Talquist pulled his chair closer.

"Bear this in mind, Fhremus," he said, swirling the remains of his brandy in the glass, then putting it down on the table. "The man who leads that Alliance has more than one sort of power. Gwydion of Manosse is the grandson of Gwylliam the Visionary, the man who carved one of the most advanced nations in history from solid *rock*. His uncle is Edwyn Griffyth, the high Sea Mage of Gaematria, Gwylliam's son, probably the best inventor in the Known World. As a result, he has at his disposal some of the most ingenious mechanical designs ever developed. He is allied with Achmed, the Firbolg king, whose unique and impressively deadly weapons we have already seen hints of through subterfuge, since the king refuses to sell them to us. Why do you think that might be? Why would the Bolg king trade arms to the Alliance, but not to Sorbold?"

Talquist watched Fhremus silently absorb the implication, then went to his desk and returned with a large piece of parchment that he laid in front of the commander. On it was a detailed sketch of a heavy machine fashioned in metal, with footpads that interlocked with gears and upright supports.

"One of our spies at the docks of Avonderre sent this quite a few months back. It was being off-loaded at Port Fallon, in from Gaematria and bound, by cart, to Haguefort, where the Lord Cymrian currently resides."

"What is it?" Fhremus asked, studying the schematic.

Talquist was watching him intently. "It's a walking machine, apparently," he said, picking up his glass and inhaling the aroma, then setting it down again.

Fhremus nodded. "Perhaps for Anborn, the Lord Marshal of the Great War," he said. "He is lame—and Edwyn Griffyth is his brother. No doubt Anborn's brother is seeking to help him recover the use of his legs, or at least some mobility."

"No doubt," Talquist agreed. "But why do you suppose that the Lord Cymrian ordered the supplies to build five hundred thousand of them?" Fhremus looked up from the parchment. "Do you imagine that there are a half million cripples in Roland?"

"Five hundred *thousand*?"

Talquist smiled grimly. "I've seen some of the manifests of the ships arriving every day from Manosse and Gaematria. If this is revealed in the few I've seen, imagine what else he is importing, and to what end?" He watched Fhremus carefully, looking to see if his own lie had been detected, but the soldier was not observing him.

The commander tossed the parchment sheet into the center of the table.

"I can't imagine, but I hardly think that machines to allow lame men to walk need give the army of Sorbold cause for alarm."

"On their own, you are correct," said Talquist patiently. "But think more broadly, Fhremus. Consider with whom the Lord Cymrian is allied, and what you know of his activities. Not long ago, the entire top of one of the inner peaks of the Teeth exploded—all of the Western Command felt the reverberations. A *mountain peak,* Fhremus—it was not a volcano, no lava flow was reported. Do you have any idea of the power required to blow a mountain peak into shards?"

Fhremus didn't, but he understood the implication.

"The Bolg king is developing powerful explosives," he said, "and so are we. I don't understand what that has to do with the mechanical walkers for the lame, m'lord."

Talquist's smile became cruel. "It disturbs me that the commander of the entire nation's army cannot put pieces together better than that,

Fhremus. Think back for a moment; you returned to Jierna'sid at great haste not in response to my summons, but because of what you had heard in the streets—is that not so?"

The commander's face went rigid.

"That's all right, Fhremus—if I were you, and had been informed that the regent emperor had been the target of a titanic stone assassin, a statue twice as tall as a man that moved under its own power, and had destroyed half a brigade as it waded through them on its way into Jierna Tal, I would have come in all due haste as well. I assume you have seen the carnage firsthand; although the streets had been cleansed of the human litter by the time you arrived, you must have seen the shattered carts, the broken gates, yes?" He gestured to the newly repaired wall in the staircase leading up to the southwestern parapet.

"Yes," said the commander.

"Touched as I am by your concern for my well-being, I am happy to assure you that not a hair on my head was harmed. Would that I could say the same for the eighty-eight troops and uncounted bystanders."

"How—"

The regent raised a hand, and the soldier lapsed into silence. "I thought by now you knew that my ascension to emperor was foreordained by the Creator," Talquist said haughtily. "The Scales themselves anointed me; I am divinely protected, as I believe I mentioned to you before." His dark eyes took on a wicked gleam. "There are many things you do not yet know about me, Fhremus—and many more which you do not realize I know about *you*. But trust in this—Sorbold, the land we both love, is in more capable hands than you realized."

"Indeed, m'lord," murmured Fhremus. He took another swallow of the single malt.

Talquist's eyes narrowed slightly. "Come," he ordered. "I will show you what our enemy is capable of, both in power and intent—and what we are preparing to do about it."

He rose, turned, and strode to the inner reaches of his chamber. The commander leapt to his feet and followed him, leaving his glass on the ornately carved table, where the dregs caught the light of the waning sun in the bottom like a stain of drying blood.

22

$\mathcal{I}$t did not particularly surprise Fhremus to learn that the recesses of the Emperor Presumptive's chambers held a series of vaults and tunnels; the dynasty of the Dark Earth and the dynasty of the Forbidden Mountains before them, the rulers of Sorbold for more than seven centuries, had built into Jierna Tal as many mysteries and escape routes as they had fashioned into the empire itself. He had occasionally been allowed entrée into such hidden places in the time of the Empress Leitha, but had not been shown this series, in what had once been her bedchamber.

He kept his face expressionless as the layers of drapery and tapestry were pulled aside, revealing each time a thicker, more metal-bound door, each with a subsequently more complex and difficult system of locks. Whatever the regent emperor had locked away in his chambers must have been either of great value or great danger, he reasoned, something that had apparently only been shown to a select few. He was not certain whether to feel honored or threatened.

When he entered the vault behind the final door, he decided he needed to embrace both impressions.

Fhremus had heard enough from his troops to recognize what it was that he was seeing; still, it took him a moment to make the connection between the tales of horror that had been told to him and what he was witnessing within the emperor's own chambers.

Talquist set his glass down on a side table, drew back a heavy velvet drape, and revealed an alcove in the corner of the room.

There within, standing on its own, was an immense statue of multicolored stone, veins of purple and vermilion and green running through what looked like wet clay drying at the edges to the color of sand. It was a statue of a soldier, of primitive garb and manufacture, one of its hands roughly hewn as if a tool or weapon of some sort had been torn from its palm in the course of its curing. Its facial features and hair were similarly roughly carved, and it was crowned with an armored helm that Fhremus recognized as in the style of the ancient indigenous peoples of the continent that inhabited Sorbold in the time before written history, before the Cymrian era of the Illuminaria, when most of the accounts and chronicles of the world had begun to be written down, inscribed on great scrolls and kept in libraries.

The statue was perhaps ten feet at the apex, its arms and legs muscular and thick in the crudeness of its carving, with none of the features of human limbs save for knees and elbows. Its eyes were hollow, absent of pupils, and it stared at the ceiling, its hands at its sides.

Fhremus had had such a statue described to him, not long before, in the breathless voices of his own soldiers. They had each told him tales of such a mammoth titan lumbering down the main thoroughfare of Jierna'sid, murder in its intent, as it waded through a throng of defending soldiers, crushing them like wheat beneath its feet. It had dashed wagons and horse carts, broken through gates and barricades, until it made its way into the palace of Jierna Tal itself.

He had come back to the palace in all due haste at the reports, hoping to find the emperor alive, believing the possibility of him to be uninjured slim. Instead, he discovered the damage to Jierna Tal to be minimal, mended in most places, including the corner of the emperor's own chambers, and the emperor in excellent health, with no apparent injury, none the worse for wear. Upon beholding Talquist for the first time since he heard the reports, he began to wonder if they had been the product of hallucinations.

Until this moment.

"That's not, er, the statue—"

"Yes, indeed," said Talquist smoothly. "It is, in fact, the titan of animated stone that just a sennight ago burst forth into the streets of the city, crushing soldiers and destroying everything in its path. A beautiful thing, is it not?"

"If you say so, m'lord," said Fhremus, not knowing what else to say in response.

The Emperor Presumptive chuckled. "You have to at least admire the handiwork of our enemies, Fhremus, even if you don't appreciate their intentions. I have to admit when I saw it from the balcony I was sore distressed, not knowing what forces of nature could have come together to allow such a thing to exist. But in my time as a merchant I have seen many oddities, many strange things in many lands, and more than anything else I have seen weapons in all shapes and sizes—poisons that you would never believe to be toxic, hidden in the softest of silk, blades so unobtrusive that you would not even notice them before you bled to death, traps so ingenious that even the most vigilant of guards would not see them before plunging to his death or being crushed beneath a block of immense stone—so there is very little that surprises me anymore, Fhremus. Thank the Creator that I'm in His favor, that as His anointed one I'm under His protection. Otherwise Sorbold would be leaderless again, as we so recently were after the death of our beloved empress and the crown prince. Who knows—perhaps you would once more be at another Colloquium with the counts of the major provinces again looking to disband the empire and absorb the smaller lands into their own."

"Indeed, m'lord," Fhremus murmured.

"So how do you suppose this giant stone assassin came to be animated?" the emperor asked.

"Really, I've no idea."

"Then allow me to educate you in the lore of our enemies," said Talquist tartly. "We are not up against mere men, Fhremus, men like ourselves who have only our wits, our brawn, and our blood to defend the land we love. We're up against an alliance led by men of insidious power, heirs to the throne of Gwylliam and Anwyn, with the blood of the Cymrians in their veins, and the powers which that evil race possessed. These are not mere mortals, Fhremus—time seems to take no toll on them, have no dominion over them. Many of the dynasty of Gwylliam are still alive, more than a thousand years after that cursed despot set foot on our shores, in the wake of the tidal wave he brought with him, and began systematically butchering our people on the path to what would eventually become his stronghold in the mountains now called the Teeth. In addition, the Patriarch himself is in league with the Lord Cymrian. This Patriarch, so recently installed, is an apostate, following a long line of those who perverted our religion, the holy and pure worship of the Creator that our ancestors practiced, and instead call him by other unholy names, the All-God, the One-God. In the Patriarch's hands and the hands of his benisons are all of the elemental basilicas, and the primal lore of living earth, wind, fire, water, and starlight housed there. And his ally, Gwydion of Manosse, the Lord Cymrian, is in league with Tyrian, the Bolglands, the Nain, Manosse, Gaematria, and in control of all the armies of the Middle Continent. How can one fight against such foes?"

"We are ready to do so, m'lord," said Fhremus.

"No, you are not," replied Talquist darkly. "You underestimate our enemies, and the powers they have at their disposal. Observe."

He stepped before the statue and raised his hand.

"Awake, Faron," he commanded.

Within the sightless eyes of the statue two blue irises appeared, milky at first, then taking on an expression of threat. Fhremus stepped back involuntarily.

"Move the table," Talquist commanded, pointing to a thick sideboard of heavily carved wood weighing as much as three men.

The statue stared at him for a moment, then at the commander menacingly. Then it stretched as if sore, flexed its arms, and walked to the sideboard, which it seized and threw across the room into the wall, where it crashed, one of its legs broken.

Talquist turned to the shaken commander and smiled.

"This, Fhremus, is the handiwork of our enemies. What in stasis would be no more than a stone statue is in fact a living machine, animated by only the Creator knows what sort of Cymrian spell or magic. Blessedly, I have turned him to my will, and now he follows my commands. What would have been my assassin will now be the standard bearer of your army. Had I been any less than what I am, any less blest by the Creator Himself, I would be in my grave, and Sorbold would very likely be at war."

"Sorbold will be at war anyway, m'lord," said Fhremus. "Gwydion of Manosse cannot be allowed to send assassins after our Emperor Presumptive, and let that go unanswered. Revenge must be extracted for this, lest he feel emboldened to try again."

"So now perhaps you can see one—and only one—of the reasons we must move now, rather than waiting to be attacked," Talquist said, picking up his glass and finishing the contents. "The piece you are overlooking is that Gwydion of Manosse is not merely the lord of the Middle

Continent, and a man with massive ancestral holdings in Manosse and Gaematria, but he is the descendant of a bloody *dragon*. Between the mythic power of his ancestry from Serendair, which all the Cymrians have to one degree or another, the bedeviled lore of the Sea Mages, who have studied the tides and currents of the seven seas for so long that it is said they can control them, his grandfather's knowledge of machinery and invention, and whatever magic the dragon bequeathed him, is it really so hard for you to imagine that the Lord Cymrian, who has found a way to animate solid *stone,* has also discovered a way to make incendiary, unmanned machines capable of walking over borders, and perhaps even through mountains, with the ability to explode and wreak havoc on our cities, our outposts, and our holy sites?"

"What then are we to do, m'lord?" Fhremus asked.

"We will begin with the Patriarch," Talquist replied, secretly pleased that the commander had bought the lie so easily. "We will take Sepulvarta first; truly that should be the northernmost point of our border anyway. That land is in the foothills of the Manteids, and once we own it, there is only the wide Krevensfield Plain to the north beyond, which is indefensible. It is where we will begin to take back what is ours."

"The holy city?" Fhremus asked nervously. "You plan to make war on the All-God's capital?"

"He is called the Creator," Talquist replied, an edge of steel in his voice. "It is the Cymrians who've chosen to name him the 'All-God;' what sort of foolish name is *that*? We are about to right centuries of wrongs here; our task is a holy one." He sighed morosely. "No one wants war less than I do, Fhremus. I am a merchant by background; I had hoped that my reign would be a time of peace and prosperity, that our goods would reach new markets around the world. War disrupts trade; there is nothing I want less than that. Unlike the Cymrian rulers of the Alliance—not just Gwydion of Manosse, but his Lirin wife, and the Bolg king, who knows how long *he* will live—I am a mere mortal, Fhremus. I will live a human's life; even Leitha, with her extraordinary longevity, lived a mere ninety-one years. Time has no sway over the progeny of a dragon, nor those who came from the cursed Island of Serendair. Our grandchildren will be dust in their graves while these tyrants are still in the bloom of youth! Our time is limited; we must make the most of what little we have. We owe it to the Creator."

A nagging bell rang softly in the back of Fhremus's mind. He tried to remember if he had ever seen the Emperor Presumptive at any of the services held in the local abbotry or any of the chapels that served the soldiers who were quartered in Jierna'sid, and decided he had not. The commander himself took every opportunity to be blessed by the local priests, as did most members of the imperial army. But, he reasoned, that was not unexpected; undoubtedly the Emperor Presumptive had his own chapels and houses of worship within the palace.

None of that mattered anyway.

"I stand ready to receive your command, m'lord," he said finally.

"Come with me, then, Fhremus," Talquist said, a pleased look on his face. "And I will show you how one defends a nation."

23

Fhremus had, over his many years in the army, smelled many horrific odors. The caustic smoke of the steel fires in the smithy, the repulsive reek from latrines and offal piles that were the result of any large
encampment of soldiers, and the stench of corpses moldering beneath
the blazing Sorbold sun were all familiar to his nose; he had become almost inured to them.

None of them could have possibly prepared him for what assaulted
his nostrils in the tunnels beneath Jierna Tal.

As he followed Talquist down the cavernous passageway, his instincts, honed by years in battle, were on fire, the gut-deep sense of danger that served to warn every soldier of an adversary or threat looming
ahead of him in the dark. Having seen the regent emperor's new standard bearer, who followed silently behind them, all but indiscernible in
spite of his stone frame and massive size, Fhremus could only imagine
what awaited him at the bottom of the tunnel.

The smell of decay that permeated the very stone of the walls was
like breathing in death, even through the dense weave of the linen scarf.

As they descended, the darkness became more and more impenetrable
and the tunnel wider. The small lantern in Talquist's hand did not serve to
dispel even the gloom that weighed on their shoulders, but instead provided little more than a hoary ball of cold light that gleamed hesitantly
into the blackness directly ahead of them, then was swallowed in shadow.
In a way, Fhremus was grateful. He could not see what lurked on the cave
walls at the edge of his vision, but more than once caught sight out of the

corner of his eye of what appeared to be skittering movement across the dank surface. He steeled his will and concentrated on keeping the regent within his limited sight.

The farther they walked, the danker the air in the tunnel became, until Fhremus had beads of water dripping from his helm and eyebrows. His skin was clammy with more than trepidation; moisture beaded on his oiled jerkin and ran down off the front of it, splashing in thin rivulets on his boots.

"This place was at one time the sewer of Jierna'sid," Talquist said. His voice, muffled by the scarf and the mist, echoed against the distant walls and was swallowed in much the same way as the light had been. "Then the dynasty of the Dark Earth, Leitha and her forbears, built the great aqueduct system, abandoning this place." Fhremus remained silent, his eyes futilely scanning for the walls that had receded into the dark.

Then, in the distance, he began to hear a strange sound, like the harsh whistling of wind over the desert, punctuated a moment later by a deep hum that fluctuated below it. The noise was constant, growing in volume as they grew closer. Though he did not recognize the sound, it chilled him deep within, even as it scratched mercilessly at his eardrums.

"We are almost to the giant cistern," Talquist said, his voice suddenly soft. "Follow closely, Fhremus, and do not lose your footing. 'Twould be tragic."

Fhremus glanced over his shoulder. He thought he could make out the dimmest shadow of the titan's outline, but when he looked again he saw nothing but darkness. Nervously he turned back again.

Talquist had come to a stop at the edge of what appeared to be a massive circular canyon, a hole of vast proportions that had once contained all the runoff of the mountains, a water volume similar to that of a river in flood. Fhremus stopped behind him, fighting nausea from the stench that had become acidic, stripping the lining from the inside of his nose and resonating up into his sinuses.

Below the canyon's rim the noise had grown to a deafening pitch, a screaming whine below which a growing bass note was rising, thudding like war drums.

Talquist held the light over the rim, then beckoned him closer.

"Come," he said softly, a tone of reverence in his voice. "Look."

Fhremus swallowed silently and approached the edge. As he did, something small and hard grazed his face; instinctively he brushed it away, like a fly, and peered down into the darkness.

For a moment it seemed as if he was standing above the funnel of a tornado at night. In the inky blackness below, air seemed to swirl with the ferocity of a whirlwind, screaming as it passed. The movement was as vast as the greatest desert dust storm Fhremus had ever seen, towering walls of sand that had torn up and buried entire villages. But unlike a storm, the motion was chaotic, sporadic, with millions of flashes that had no course, just speed and sound.

The regent emperor was watching his face closely. His smile widened, and he held the lantern up over the swirling chasm of stench, screeching, and sickening motion.

In just the faintest ray of light, Fhremus could see what was spiraling in the cistern.

"Dear All-God," he whispered, feeling bile rise in the back of his throat and burn. "Are those—?"

"Plague locusts." Talquist finished the question for him. "This is a young swarm, nymphs, hoppers mostly. No fledglings yet—the vast majority of the eggs won't even hatch until the first week of spring. They haven't grown wings—yet."

The dank, putrid air of the place churned in Fhremus's lungs. The first two words the regent had just spoken were considered a profanity in this realm of endless sun and little water, where crops were scratched from the unforgiving earth in the southern temperate region of the country but almost nonexistent in the northern mountains and steppes. The dryness of the land had been both bane and blessing; while the soil yielded little in the way of foodstuffs, the pestilence of unstoppable swarms had been minimal, because the vermin needed water in which to breed.

Like the swill at the bottom of the abandoned sewer.

Even so, despite not having been seen in this region in Fhremus's lifetime, the history of locust plagues was devastating enough to have left long scars on the memories of the population. The misery and starvation that the hordes of ravenous insects left in their wake was so terrifying to the Sorbolds, as well as the people of the Middle Continent, that the appearance of a single grasshopper could cause widespread panic that led to many fields being unnecessarily burned.

Fhremus bent down and retrieved the carcass of the one that had struck him in flight. How anyone could mistake a simple grasshopper for one of these creatures was beyond him—the angular head, the saw-toothed mandibles, the sharp, knifelike wings, were the hallmarks of a creature that harbored evil in its midst.

He swallowed his rising gorge.

"I don't understand, m'lord."

Talquist had been watching him closely, and nodded.

"Come then, Fhremus, and I will show you more." He turned and walked away into the darkness. The imperial commander tossed the carcass into the black pit and followed him quickly, casting a last look over his shoulder as if to confirm that he was awake.

The air in the tunnel around him grew even heavier with rotten moisture the farther they traveled. The stone giant followed them, moving as silently as death, or at least it appeared so, as the screaming hum of the cistern had been replaced by a deep, clicking thrum, pounding and pulsing in Fhremus's ears and echoing the rough corridor walls around them. They passed what appeared to be old feeder tunnels of the sewer system, many of them occluded or entirely blocked with the rubble of centuries, until finally they came to a foul-smelling pond of sorts, the water foisted with green waste, possibly plant life, though Fhremus could not believe it possible that anything natural could grow in such a place.

The regent emperor strode confidently into the water, wading slowly but purposefully out until the slime covered his boots halfway up the leg. Then he turned and gestured to Fhremus to follow him. The soldier complied, coming alongside Talquist when he finally stopped, gazing into the gloom ahead of him. The titan remained at the water's edge, motionless.

Talquist's eyes were burning bright in the radiance of the cold lantern. He pointed into the darkness ahead.

"There, Fhremus, see the answer the All-God has provided to our need for protection against those who would threaten our land."

He held the lantern aloft.

Fhremus squinted to see past the light. Ahead of them in the muck lay the massive body of what appeared to be a serpent, a dragon or horned snake, perhaps; it was impossible to tell, as it had been largely devoured, consumed in thousands of tiny bites. As he stared harder, he could see that the carcass was comprised of what appeared to be striated stone, like the titan waiting on the bank behind them, its glassy eyes smooth except for the gouges that had been dug in them. A tail, missing large sections, coiled behind it, while broken remains of wings could be seen, stripped to the stone cartilage. The statue of the beast appeared to be sprouting grass or grain of some sort, like an earthen sculpture left in a field to go fallow.

And all above and around it hovered screaming locusts, most the size of his hand or bigger, feeding avariciously on the grain, and on the carcass itself.

But, unlike the nymphs and hoppers in the cistern swarm, they seemed to be actually *flying*.

Talquist turned to the giant. "Faron, if you please, bring us one."

The titan looked down at the green ooze for a moment, then waded into the water. Fhremus involuntarily held his breath as the giant walked by him, causing a wake to rise up the sides of his boots in its passing. It continued, undeterred by the onslaught of swarming creatures until it came to the feeding ground, where it reached out with an almost sickening speed and grasped one of the insects. A sickening crack echoed through the cavern; Fhremus winced in spite of himself. Then the titan waded back to where the merchant emperor stood.

"Put out your hand, Fhremus," said Talquist softly.

The commander inhaled, then complied.

The giant stared down at him, its milky blue eyes gleaming in the light of the lantern. It dropped the locust into his hand, then returned to shore.

"Look at it," whispered Talquist, awe in his voice.

Swallowing his disgust, Fhremus moved the locust's body closer to the light. His eyes widened in surprise. Like the smaller insect that had impacted him on the rim of the cistern, this creature was sharp and angular, with razor-like mandibles and legs. But its appearance was very different from the smaller one; this creature had a serpentine tail, its wings were large and webbed, its eyes scored with a vertical pupil, and its jaws more serpentine than insectoid.

Almost draconic.

"Have you ever been in Terreanfor?" Talquist asked, running a gloved finger almost tenderly over the broken body.

"One time only, for the funeral of the empress and her son," said Fhremus.

"Then perhaps you have seen the marvelous statuary there. In the eternal darkness that shelters the Living Stone of the cathedral stands an entire menagerie of life-sized statues, trees as high as the towering ceiling beneath which graze antelope and tirabouri, gazelle, elephants and lions, all rendered in utter perfection—have you seen these?"

"Yes, m'lord."

"They are a sight to behold, are they not, Fhremus? Perfect down to the last detail, with no feature overlooked. The sculptors that rendered them must have been artisans of incomparable skill, would you not say?"

"Undoubtedly, m'lord," Fhremus said, struggling to keep his voice patient and respectful.

The Emperor Presumptive. "Undoubtedly, yes, Fhremus, because what you don't understand is that the *Earth itself* carved those statues. Our forebears, the indigenous people of this land that were living here long before the accursed Cymrians came, with their inventions, their disease, and their wars, understood the role the Living Stone plays in immortality. They buried specimens of each beast, each flower, each tree, within the sacred ground of Terreanfor, and from that sacred ground earthen statues grew—with the exact properties and the beasts and plants entombed within it." He caressed the insect's wings. *And soldiers, many of whom were giants, like the one I harvested to make Faron,* he thought.

Fhremus inhaled silently.

"Those properties survived the creatures' deaths in more than one way, Fhremus," Talquist continued. "More than just becoming statues, those beasts retained what was unique about them; there is strength of gargantuan proportions in the elephants still, a swiftness and quickness of eye in the prey animals, even as they stand, frozen, forever. Even the flowers have retained a modicum of their scent—when they had bloomed and died millennia uncounted before. A form of true immortality, to be certain."

Fhremus maintained his silence, struggling to quell the questions in his mind. Chief among them was the extent of the emperor's knowledge; Terreanfor, before it was recently sealed by an earthquake, had been closed to any but the priests of the manse in Jierna'sid, and only the highest ranking among them had gone inside to maintain the cathedral. How Talquist had become so aware of the place's history and contents was unclear to him, but he quelled any suspicious thought by reminding himself, as he always did, that the All-God had chosen the emperor, and as a soldier it was his duty to support that emperor's vision and carry out that emperor's commands, lest his reluctance be seen as doubting the wisdom of the All-God.

"This wyrm, at one time, was such a being, now a statue formed by Living Stone. In its lifetime, the beast had the same sensibilities, the same powers, as the rest of its species—including the ability of flight. These locusts have been feeding on grain that sprouted from the back of the wyrm—and thereby have absorbed some of its life, its properties, including that ability. They are little half-breeds, little mutant-spawn now—I call them iacxsis, as that is what I believe this lizard-wyrm was called—with their own voracious appetites and the power to travel long distances in the air. Touch it, Fhremus—take off your glove and feel its hide." He chuckled at the shock on the soldier's face as he complied. "Because they have been feeding on Living Stone, they are hard, even more armored than the sturdy carapace of their insect side or the scales of a wyrm would make them. And their shriek is a hundred times the sound of the fledgling swarm; music to my ears."

"Forgive me, but why is all this a *benefit,* m'lord?" Fhremus asked, the words all but exploding from him. "The presence of these creatures, in our land, portends disaster, does it not? The ones that are found in nature bring with them famine, pestilence, starvation, and death—why are you happy to see them in an even more formidable form?"

Talquist chuckled. "You will be happy to see them such as well, Fhremus—when you see the adults. Come."

He waded back out of the slimy water, shook off his boots, and led the commander up another tunnel where the dankness of the air and the horrific hum began to dissipate. The stone titan followed, still making no sound.

They finally came into light and air that smelled as if it might be near the mountain's surface. At the end of this tunnel was a wide stone doorway, and Talquist stopped before it, almost unable to contain himself.

"Do you remember some months back I asked you to lend me some of your slighter soldiers, recruits that had shown strength of lung and a tolerance of the high reaches of our mountains?"

"Yes, m'lord. I hope they have been serving you well."

The regent emperor smiled broadly and stepped to the side of the doorway. "Have a look."

Steeling himself, Fhremus stepped into the doorway.

At first the sight that greeted the imperial commander left him puzzled, unable to grasp what he was seeing. At the far end of the room was an opening, like the mouth of a cave. The opening overlooked the vast chasm that scored the earth beside Jierna Tal, its far fissures and crags shadowy in the approach of night. Closer in was a series of animal pens, like those that might stable horses, numbering in the scores. Soldiers walked the aisles between the pens, conferring with each other, going in and out of the paddocks at will.

He looked back to the opening above the chasm. His mouth dropped open as a shadow passed horizontally before it, then disappeared again into the dusk.

"Dear All-God," he murmured.

"Dear Creator," Talquist corrected patiently. "I understand it will take a while for you to adjust; do not worry. They train here, away from the eyes of the city, as the sun is going down. It's best, at first, to keep this a secret, so that we maintain the element of surprise. Don't you agree?"

Fhremus watched a moment more, rapt, then turned to the Emperor Presumptive.

"Yes," he said.

Talquist smiled broadly and led the commander farther up the tunnel back into his chambers.

"So you understand what a boon this is for Sorbold in her fight against invasion?"

"Yes, m'lord."

"I take it you approve, then, Fhremus, of the defensive steps I have taken to ensure our beloved nation's survival against the aggression that is being mounted by the Alliance?"

Fhremus thought for a moment. "It is not my place to approve or disapprove of your commands, m'lord," he said seriously. "The Scales adjudged you to be the next emperor of our mother country; I am grateful that you saw the wisdom in keeping Sorbold a single empire, rather than dissolving it, as the counts wished to. I am a soldier; I do as my emperor commands."

"Whether or not you approve?" The question hovered in the air, thick as the mist.

Fhremus inhaled deeply through the sodden linen scarf, pulled it from his face, then exhaled slowly.

"Yes," he said.

Talquist's eyes sparkled black in the thin light.

"Excellent," he said. "But on a serious note, Fhremus, it's imperative that your men, and the families they left behind, understand the threat we all face. What is that saying you military men have about the initiative for going to war?"

"The defender fights with the strength of ten conquerors."

"Yes," Talquist said smoothly. "That's it."

"They will understand, m'lord," Fhremus said. "And they will fight to their last breath to ensure your dominion."

Talquist smiled broadly.

"Another form of music to my ears. You may go, Fhremus, but return on the morrow; we have plans to make."

The soldier bowed unsteadily. "Yes, m'lord." He bent over the regent emperor's hand in salute, then left the room, his boot steps echoing down the corner stairway.

When the sound died away, Talquist turned to the stone titan that had emerged from within his deeper chambers.

"I believe he will do well, at least in the first wave, Faron," he said idly. "Past that, we may have to make some changes. Do you agree?"

The stone titan watched the Emperor Presumptive for a moment, then returned to the inner chamber and came back a moment later with an object in his giant hand.

It was an oval scale, tattered finely at the edges and irregularly oblong, scored with many fine lines. In his hand it appeared gray with a slightly blue tinge, but when the light caught it a prism of color danced across its razor-thin surface. Carved into its convex side was the image of an eye, clear and unobstructed by clouds, as the image on the concave side was.

The titan held the scale in his hand, gazing out of the balcony window. A moment later he turned to the Emperor Presumptive and nodded mutely.

Talquist broke into a wide smile.

"Good," he said. "Very good."

He stood and watched as dusk faded to night, the stars twinkling bright in the vast sky overarching Jierna'sid.

24

HAGUEFORT, NAVARNE

Ashe had hoped that in the course of the preparations for war, in all of the noise and hubbub of getting ready for the arrival of the Council of Dukes, and the chaos that was ensuing as the household of Haguefort made ready to move a good piece of itself to the fortification at Highmeadow, he would be able to retain his sanity as long as possible. Distraction was good, he reasoned, and with any luck the aching absence he felt for his wife and child the moment they had left his sphere of influence, had stepped outside the comforting boundaries of his dragon sense, would be filled up by the clamor and infighting, the thousands of details and decisions to be made, and a host of other diversions that would keep the dragon in his blood busy.

It had only taken a few moments, long enough for the sound of the horses' hooves to die away into the night. Then within his consciousness he felt rather than heard a deep caterwaul, the keening of a beast that had had something stolen from its hoard. Even deeper within, he could feel the tearing of his soul, in the fairly recently mended place where it had been sewn back together again when he was reunited with Rhapsody.

When the first night without her fell, Ashe took comfort in sitting before the fire that reminded him of his wife and looking back over the haze of time to a different world, a place where he had been happy. It was a time before the War, before the Cataclysm, even before the two Bolg who saw Rhapsody as belonging originally to them, and viewed him as an interloper by virtue of his marriage to her.

When he closed his eyes, he could still see her as she had been then, on the night before her fourteenth birthday, dressed in a simple velvet gown, her breast adorned by a corsage of simple flowers her father had given her. She had been thin then and slight, with long straight hair that hung down her back like a silken wave. Ashe smiled, remembering his first sight of her, crouched behind a row of barrels in the dark outside the foreharvest dance, an event where the people of her human father's farming community had held a marriage lottery, the traditional selection of marriage for the young people of their village.

How he had come to be in that place he still did not know, even millennia later. He had been but fourteen himself, an awkward adolescent boy walking to town on a fine morning on the other side of Time, almost fifteen hundred years after Rhapsody's birth. What had transpired was still unclear; the wind had been fresh, the morning birds had been in full song, the day had been beautiful. A day like any other day.

And then, the world had shifted.

Ashe could almost still recall the exact sensation of nausea and weakness that swept over him as he was plucked from the place he had been and deposited in the afternoon sun in a farmer's pasture in the village of Merryfield, a simple farming town in the center of the Wide Meadows, in the eastern lands of the Island of Serendair. Raised in the presence of magic and beings with ancient powers, he had recovered his composure fairly quickly, and managed to discover approximately where he was in time, if not how he had come to be there.

All of this had led him to the foreharvest dance, and to the side of the girl hiding in an alleyway, wistfully listening to the music as it played within the lighted grange hall, resisting every attempt to marry her off in the traditional ceremonies. He had fallen in love with her from the moment he'd seen her, not just because she was fair and because all the chemicals of his young body had begun to hum with life upon beholding her, but because there was something so ethical, so independent and intelligent in her resistance to being used as chattel that he could not help but respect her, even without having been introduced.

Eventually he'd worked up his courage enough to tap her on the shoulder, to ask her to dance in the light reflecting from the hall, to walk with her to her family's fields where the willow tree she had loved stood guard over a valley stream. Ashe closed his eyes more tightly, listening to the music of the water in his head. The extravagant capability of detail bequeathed to him by his dragon nature allowed him a heightened sense of memory; in many ways it was like reliving that night again, feeling the coolness of the breeze, sensing the brightness of the stars, physically recalling the way her hair smelled like morning, the glow in her eyes that sparkled brighter as she talked about things that excited her, unrealistic dreams of escaping the marriage lottery and traveling the world, seeing the ocean that her grandfather had plied as a sailor, something that she longed for but never had done. And above all, he remembered the way she talked about her dreams, of stars falling from the sky into her hands, holding them fast until one day she could hold no longer, and instead they dropped through her open palms into the meadow stream, glimmering up at her, beyond her reach in the depths.

He had resolved in that moment to fulfill those dreams for her, to marry her, with her excited consent, and to take her from the farmlands off to see the world. His reason for that was twofold. Whether or not he could ever get back his own time was of little interest to him; rather, he had determined that whatever force had brought him over the waves of time to be by her side had placed him in the time before the Cataclysm, just as the war that would tear the Island of Serendair asunder was beginning to erupt. If for no other reason, they had to go away in haste, lest his newly-found soulmate become nothing more than one more victim in two of history's greatest tragedies.

She had called him Sam, the common appellation by which unknown young men were addressed in her town. He had never been given the chance to tell her his real one; it was an endearment she still used. Her voice resounded clear in his memory.

Sam?

Yes?

Do you think we might see the ocean? Someday, I mean.

He had promised her they would, had promised to take her wherever she wished to go, but before they could put their plans in place he was torn back to his own time by whatever unseen hands had placed him there to begin with.

Ashe winced in the flickering heat of the flames. The hollow pain of loss was with him still, even after four years of having her back, even having joined their souls together again.

Even knowing that she loved him eternally.

Even sharing a child with her, a son he loved beyond measure and had barely been given a chance to know. That loss was one he consciously struggled not to think about, because his draconic nature was unpredictable enough, and suffering enough, that he could not risk it.

In the back of his mind a tune was playing. It was a song that Rhapsody had often sung to him on their evenings alone together, a tale of a wanderer that her seafaring grandfather had taught her when she was a child. When she had met up with him again in the new world, he had been solitary, in pain and alone, just such a wanderer, so it had reminded her of him, and of the tree they had fallen in love beneath. Ashe pictured her before him, her harp or concertina in hand, singing the melodious tune in the voice that haunted his dreams.

> I was born beneath this willow,
> Where my sire the earth did farm
> Had the green grass as my pillow
> The east wind as a blanket warm.
>
> But *away! away!* called the wind from the west
> And in answer I did run
> Seeking glory and adventure
> Promised by the rising sun.
>
> I found love beneath this willow,
> As true a love as life could hold,
> Pledged my heart and swore my fealty
> Sealed with a kiss and a band of gold.
>
> But *to arms! to arms!* called the wind from the west
> In faithful answer I did run
> Marching forth for king and country
> In battles 'neath the midday sun.

Oft I dreamt of that fair willow
As the seven seas I plied
And the girl who I left waiting
Longing to be at her side.

But *about! about!* called the wind from the west
As once again my ship did run
Down the coast, about the wide world
Flying sails in the setting sun.

Now I lie beneath the willow
Now at last no more to roam,
My bride and earth so tightly hold me
In their arms I'm finally home.

While *away! away!* calls the wind from the west
Beyond the grave my spirit, free
Will chase the sun into the morning
Beyond the sky, beyond the sea.

His dragon sense roared to life at the presence of a tickling sensation. He opened his eyes.

His wife was sitting before the fire, her song finished, smiling warmly at him. His heightened senses could feel the physical presence of her in the room, a bending of the currents of air around a form that was heavy, real, unlike the dreams and fantasies in which she was nothing more than a picture in his head, a phantasm that vanished with the morning light. There was heft to this vision, a realness that never had been there before. Her scent, the simple odor of vanilla and soap, sweet meadow flowers and wood smoke, filled his nostrils, causing the blood to pound in his head, and his hands shake.

Rhapsody smiled, her green eyes sparkling, backlit by the fire.

Ashe sat straighter in his chair. There was no question she was real, no figment of his imagination or dragon sense playing tricks of the mind on him; the energy of her life force rippled over him like waves in the sea.

Rhapsody, he whispered, almost afraid to shatter what was either a miraculous moment or an illusion of a slipping mind. *You're here.*

Her smile grew brighter in the firelight. *Yes. I'm here.*

Ashe rose slowly from his chair and walked carefully toward the hearth. Rhapsody rose in return, and extended her arms to him in welcome.

He quickened his step, all but running to her, and scooped her up in his arms, drawing her near, pressing his face in the hollow of her neck and inhaling the scent of her skin, burying his lips in her hair, reveling in the solidity, the realness of her, no phantom of his mind, but flesh and blood and the warmth of a beating heart within her chest, thundering against his own.

A shocked gasp rent the air.

Like the slap of an ice-cold wave, the noise rebounded off of Ashe's forehead. He loosed his grasp and took a step back, his frazzled mind trying to gauge what was wrong.

Standing before him in the shadows of the firelight, trembling like a leaf in a high autumn wind, was a young chambermaid whose name he did not remember. She was dark of hair and eye, taller than Rhapsody by half a head, and shaped nothing like her. Her face had gone white with shock, and flushed red in a combination of horror and embarrassment.

Much like Ashe's own.

Made worse by the knowledge that this was not the first time it had happened.

The tea tray she was holding a moment before clattered to the floor, the plate bearing his supper bounced on the carpet before the hearth.

Ashe felt his face freeze in a mask of shock.

"I—I—"

The chambermaid's mouth was similarly open.

"M'lord," she whispered. "No. Please."

Ashe struggled to place the woman, remembering distantly that she had come to Haguefort from Bethany with several other servants in the company of Tristan Steward, the Lord Regent of Roland, as a gift during Rhapsody's confinement. Ashe thought perhaps the other two women were nursemaids of some sort, but this one was a servant of insignificant rank, a chambermaid, who now stood, terror in her eyes, shaking visibly.

"I—I am so very sorry," he murmured, running his hand through his coppery hair, suddenly wet with sweat. "I—I am not feeling well. Please forgive me."

The young woman bent quickly, as did Ashe, fumbling to gather the dishes and food that now littered the floor.

"My fault, m'lord," she whispered nervously.

"No," said Ashe, "no, not at all. I, as I said, am very sorry."

He quickly turned and bolted from the room and out of the keep, into the cold night, seeking clarity.

The chambermaid gathered the dishes, calming quickly, and carried them back down to the kitchen again. She stopped as she passed the window of the library, long enough to see him hurry into the courtyard and come to rest with his head against a lamppost, the candlelight catching the metallic sheen of his hair, making it glow like embers in the night.

25

Ashe's head was buzzing the next morning as if from the after-effects of potent libation. After the first few hours of the headache, he began to rue refraining from imbibing the night before, knowing that even a hangover could not have caused his skull to throb more than the arrival of the dukes of Roland did.

He stood on the balcony, in his hand a cup of strong plantain tea with medicinal properties that his wife had often used to bring him out of the hard repose of dragon slumber, trying to focus his eyes on each carriage as it made its way up the well-traveled road that ran east–west in front of the Haguefort's gates. Archers stood in the recently rebuilt guard towers, providing cover for the carriages, while the Lord Cymrian mused whether or not to give the signal to open fire on some of the occupants as they emerged from the bowels of the coaches.

The first of the dukes to arrive would never have drawn his fire, he noted, as Cedric Canderre stepped, with the assistance of his footman, out of his coach. In his own state of loss, Ashe felt tremendous empathy for the elderly duke, a gentleman and friend who had always lived hospitably and with grace, and while not the most admirable of husbands, had always been a loving and devoted father. To have witnessed the death of his only son and heir presumptive, Andrew, on these very grounds at the winter carnival that had taken the lives of so many could only be a soul-ripping reminder of that loss.

Ashe took a sip of the bad-tasting tea and winced. Had he been less distracted, he would have arranged for the meeting to take place at

Highmeadow, whose halls and defenses were all but complete, and into which they would be moving any day. While the creature comforts had not yet been established in the new fortress, it was certainly furnished enough to have spared Cedric Canderre the pain he was undoubtedly undergoing as he slowly made his way up Haguefort's cobbled entranceway. *Alas,* he thought, *such diplomatic considerations are a thing of the past; it's all I can do to keep my mind clear enough of rage to focus on the meeting at all.*

At the opening of the gate Gwydion Navarne was standing, his hands behind his back. Ashe watched, gratified, as the newly invested young duke greeted Cedric Canderre warmly and took his arm, leading him into the keep. *How like his father he looks,* Ashe thought as Gwydion held the door. *Perhaps there will still be hospitality within these walls, even in Rhapsody's absence, after all.* The thought and the sight cheered him a little; in the contentious discussions they were about to undertake, he was glad to have his namesake beside him, even if the new duke's opinions were often discounted by the others because of his youth and inexperience.

Behind the carriage of the Duke of Canderre hovered two more, one directly on the road, the other jockeying to hold the position of last arrival behind it. The first carriage bore the livery of Yarim, the dry red land to the east of Cedric Canderre's lush and fertile province. The second was emblazoned with the colors of Bethany, Roland's capital and central province. Ashe took another deep draught of tea and willed his head to stop pounding.

Ihrman Karsrick, the Duke of Yarim, waited for a long moment before opening his door and descending the stairs of his coach. He glanced in obvious annoyance at the carriage behind him, which had arrived more than a quarter hour ahead of him, then strode angrily up the walkway, his displeasure evident by the set of his shoulders and jaw.

The Lord Cymrian sighed.

The carriage from Bethany continued to linger at the road's edge for almost an hour more while the coaches of Quentin Baldassarre and Martin Ivenstrand, the dukes of Bethe Corbair and Avonderre, arrived. Ivenstrand's carriage, unlike the others, had come from the east, where Avonderre bordered Navarne on one side and the sea on the other. The duke of Avonderre alighted, looked about, then made his way quickly inside, pausing as the carriage from Bethe Corbair pulled up to the gate. He walked back to wait for Quentin Baldasarre to emerge, then accompanied him up the walkway, conferring as they came.

Finally, when the horse and livery of the four other dukes that had come from a distance had discharged their contents and had made their ways to the stable, the carriage bearing the Lord Regent, Tristan Steward, Duke of Bethany, pulled slowly and deliberately up to Haguefort's gate.

Ashe choked back the bile that had risen in his throat. As much as he had struggled against his deep dislike of Tristan Steward in general since they had been young men, there was an arrogance to the Lord Regent's gait that made the irritable dragon within his blood rise, enflamed. *We are about to be fighting for the very survival of the continent, and this pusillanimous ass is jockeying for position so that he can make an entrance,* he thought bitterly. *Clearly, the Alliance has as much of a threat within it as against it.*

He swallowed the last of the herbal tea, feeling no fortification from it whatsoever, then turned away from the fresh air of the balcony and made his way to the meeting rooms where he knew the bright morning would give way to an endless day of dire plans, petty infighting, and, with any luck, a united army to defend the Middle Continent from the blood that was about to be spilled across it.

Gerald Owen's kitchen was an orderly place, where cooks and wait staff of longtime employ moved efficiently through the day, preparing meals for as few as Haguefort's regular occupants or as many as an entire province with very little disruption. It had long been so; Stephen Navarne, in his lifetime, had made it his business as duke to host many festivals and parties, Naming ceremonies and diplomatic gatherings, as had his father before him, culminating each year in the winter carnival, a combination of religious summit, cultural ritual, and folk celebration that accommodated the western third of Roland and many foreign visitors. Very little could disturb the smoothly running machine that comprised the chamberlain's kitchen and buttery staff.

Tristan Steward, the Lord Regent of Roland, was one of the rare exceptions.

The elderly chamberlain's face had darkened to an unhealthy shade of dusky red after the third ring of the serving bell. He slapped a tea towel down on the wide stone kneading surface before the bread ovens, causing three of the cooks to scatter to different sides of the hot room as the bells jingled more insistently. Then Gerald Owen turned to the slim young chambermaid whom the Lord Regent had brought to Haguefort some months back, along with a donated wet nurse and nanny, and gestured impatiently at her. He could not recall her name, and tried to suppress his irritation, reminding himself that she and the others probably had suffered more than enough during their employ in Bethany.

"You—girl—take the tea tray to his lordship, and make certain there is a modicum of rum to be had with it, or he'll send you back for it. You used to be in his employ, so you know to stay out of his way, lest he strike you. But if that should happen, if he should even attempt it, report it to me immediately; the Lord Cymrian will address it. I've had too many house servants abused, and Lord Gwydion refuses to tolerate it."

"Yes, sir." The young woman picked up the silver tray and headed for the stairs, the vacant look of affected timidity replaced a moment later with a smile.

$\mathcal{F}$or the third time that night, a servant knocked on Tristan Steward's door bearing libations in response to his summons.

This was the first time, however, that the Lord Roland's response was not fully surly, but only annoyed, his irritation eased, perhaps, by the after-supper cordial followed by the half-decanter of brandy he had received on the two previous occasions.

"About time you got here," he murmured grumpily as the slim, dark-haired chambermaid glided into the room with a silver tray, which she set down on the table near the fireplace. "What code do I have to use with your idiot chamberlain to assure that I get *you* when I call, and not some blithering idiot or bewhiskered sot?"

The young woman smiled as she turned back to the Lord Roland.

"Perhaps you should order the tea *first* next time," she said, no hint of deference in her voice. "If you insist on calling for spirits, the wine steward and the sommelier are going to be the ones sent from the buttery to attend to your needs. Lowly chambermaids deliver tea, not brandy."

"But I like brandy," said Tristan playfully, setting down his empty glass and making his way across the room to her. "And I have needs other than those that can be met with a beverage. As you well know, Portia."

The young woman's black eyes sparkled with amusement as her former master slid his hands into her hair, gripping the long, glossy strands with an intensity belied by his lazy tone.

"Ah, so you missed me, did you?" she said, not flinching as Tristan pulled her closer, interlacing his fingers behind the base of her skull, allowing himself to become entwined in the dark waves of thick, rough silk. "I wondered if you would, given how quick you were to part with me, foisting me off on Lord Gwydion like an unwanted set of tea towels."

Tristan Steward blinked at the accusatory tone in her smoky voice.

"I did no such thing," he said reproachfully, twisting his hands in her mane. "It was agony to part with you, Portia; my loins have been aching since the day I left you in this place four months ago. Your mission here is of unsurpassed importance to me, to *us*—and had it not been, I never would have allowed you away from me for a moment."

The chambermaid reached up behind her neck and roughly pulled his hands from her.

"Alas for you, and your aching loins, in the course of doing what you asked, I have come to understand how much you have misled me," she said curtly, turning away from Tristan Steward and beginning to unload the items from the tea tray.

The Lord Roland blanched, the shock interrupting the desire that had been building within him since he heard her light knock on the door, leaving him tingling and nauseated. "What—what do you mean?" he stammered. "I have never been anything but truthful with you, Portia, foolishly candid, in fact. I have shared with you more secrets than I care to count for fear it would make me realize even more than I already do what a foolhardy idiot I have been."

The chambermaid turned back to him, tucking the tray beneath her arms like a shield over her belly, and regarded him coldly.

"What secrets would those be?" she asked, her throaty voice taking on a hint of acid. "Your profound distaste for your wife? That's no secret—everyone in Roland knows it, just as they know your weakness for trollops and bedwenches, and are well aware of the parade of them that appears each time Lady Madeleine leaves Bethany to visit her family in Canderre. It's an open joke, Tristan; it would be a truly miraculous happenchance if Madeleine herself doesn't know it. And I certainly don't blame you—she is a beast of legendary proportion. But it's not exactly flattering to be just the latest in a string of nameless whores whom you use to satisfy your lust and vent your frustration. If you're expecting me to feel grateful, I don't."

"You are hardly a nameless whore to me, Portia," Tristan said smoothly. "You have heard me intone your name repeatedly, in many different places, all the time with a combination of respect and pleasure. And you have never seemed belittled or degraded by our carnal romps. I respect, in fact, admire, your lack of shame, your imagination, your insolence, your vigor, your fire, your contempt for polite sensibilities. You are not my toy; you are very important to me, and I have entrusted you with some of the most crucial of my secrets. You should be honored, not offended."

The chambermaid's stare intensified. "Honored? Oh. Perhaps you refer to sharing me with your brother, the saintly benison of Canderre-Yarim—is that what you mean? Should I feel honored to have been entrusted with the secret of our trysts, both with and without your participation? Do you think Blesser's lack of the celibacy required by his office might have something to do with the problems you have had in Bethany? Perhaps the All-God is not amused by watching one of his holiest servants using my naked body as a table for his supper, or playing lascivious games of fox and hounds, or knobbing me as you—"

Tristan clapped his hand over her mouth and glanced over his shoulder, then locked his gaze on to hers. The flames of the fire were dancing in her black eyes, causing their expression to alternate between amusement and cruelty in turns.

"Lower your voice," he commanded quietly. "Walls of keeps have ears—you should know that."

"The only ears this keep's walls have are my own," Portia retorted. "I have done exactly as you asked, have pressed my ear to every wall, have stood on the eave of every doorway, in the hope of collecting the unspecified information you sought to bring down the man you profess to hate—"

"I do not hate Gwydion," Tristan interrupted hastily. "I never said that—I only resent his elevation to Lord Cymrian over me." Anger began to build in his blue eyes, now also reflecting the flames of the fireplace. "I served in that position, without any of the power or the acknowledgment, for twenty years while he was in hiding, pretending to be dead. I'm the one who held Roland together, who kept the Middle Continent from falling into chaos and war. It was I who defended this very keep during the assault of the Sorbolds during the winter carnival four years ago. You are too young to remember—you did not even live in Roland then, I believe. But I gave everything to this land when it was fragmented, protected it when it was vulnerable. And for all the stewardship I put forth, for all my efforts, I was constantly refused the throne, then eventually cast aside in Gwydion's wake, given a pity regency, stripped of that which is rightfully mine. I trusted you to help me gain it back—and to in turn share it with me. How is it that this offends you?"

Portia's eyes narrowed to gleaming slits, but her mouth crooked into a smile at the corners.

"You're a liar," she said, but there was fire in her voice that caused the knots in Tristan's abdomen to loosen. "Your command that I seduce the Lord Cymrian while his wife was bloated with pregnancy had nothing to do with your desire for the lordship. And you well know it."

"Of—of course it did," Tristan stammered.

"Liar," Portia said again; time her voice was filled with sexual teasing. "I do not doubt you crave the lordship; everyone knows that as well. It's another of your pathetically obvious secrets. When I first came to Roland, I heard it within a few hours of being here. But that's not why you commanded me to seduce him. You wanted to disrupt his marriage because you are obsessed with his wife—and you want her for your own."

"Don't be ridiculous," Tristan said, but the heat in Portia's voice and smile were causing his defenses to give way; he had experienced the sensation before, and it was one of risky relief, something he rarely felt in his tortured existence. He took the tray from Portia's hands and dropped it to the carpeted floor.

"I am not the one who is being ridiculous here," Portia said, stepping closer. "Nor am I blind to your deception of me. You said that I might be able to use my seductive skills on Lord Gwydion, and in turn have him confide secrets to me that would be useful to you in your bid to replace him on the Cymrian throne. But you knew that would never happen; his wife owns every corner of his soul, and he hers. She has only been in this keep for a few moments in all the time I have been here, and that is apparent even in those few moments. Additionally, he cares little, or nothing, for the power of the lordship; he views it, somewhat distastefully, as an unavoidable duty, and longs for the day when someone else—someone *qualified*—will take it over." She reached out a hand and caressed Tristan's face to soften the sting of her words. "I don't know why you didn't just confide the truth to me from the beginning—it would have been so much easier to help you if I had known."

"H—how?" Tristan asked. The heat of his blood was rising, flushing him with warmth, making him painfully tumescent.

The chambermaid's smile widened. She turned away from the roaring fire and walked over to the tall windows that led out to the small balcony, stopping to admire her reflection in the glass.

"Unlike the situation between you and the Beast, neither the lord nor the lady has the desire to stray—and so that betrayal can only be accomplished through deception," she said lazily, chuckling at the distortion of her face in the wavy panes. "And deception of either or both of them will be a challenge. One cannot easily deceive two people who have special connections to the truth. The Lord Cymrian has dragon's blood in his veins, and so his awareness is heightened far beyond the bounds of normal perception. And the word about the keep is that the Lady Cymrian is a Skysinger, a Namer, in fact, and so she has a racial and professional devotion to the truth, which makes her perception of falsehood even keener." She idly stroked the heavy velvet curtain that dressed the window.

"So, then, how will you accomplish this deception?" Tristan asked, his head growing light from lack of blood.

Portia turned to face him again, her eyes dancing with wicked light.

"I won't," she said briskly. "They will accomplish it for me in the only way it can be accomplished—they will deceive themselves. It will be easier, now that she's gone from this place again. The stupid intensity of their love for each other will be their undoing, and when that happens, it will be shattered forever. How melodramatic. But it's true. And when it happens, the world will grow brighter for all of us." She slid her hands into the opening of Tristan's shirt at the neck, then followed with her mouth.

"Tell—tell me how," Tristan said, his voice faltering as the heat of her breath warmed his skin, followed by the delicious press of teeth against his clavicle.

Portia's hot mouth made its way slowly up his neck to the earlobe.

"You are just going to have to trust me, m'lord," she said teasingly. "You must be able to tell that I've been at this sort of thing for a long time. You've been the beneficiary of enough of my talents to be aware of it."

"Yes, yes I have," Tristan murmured weakly. "Did you lock the door?"

With a screeching rip, Portia tore apart his shirt, her eyes gleaming with excitement.

"Of course not," she said, her voice growing husky. "The risk of being caught is what drives the excitement higher—isn't that what you've always told me when pushing me into alcoves and behind sofas in your own keep?" With impatient fingers, she began to roughly unlace the stays of his trousers. "Now, I can assure you the kitchen staff is entirely sick of you, and will do everything they can to avoid coming within your beck and call. And the other members of the Council of Dukes have had as much of you as they can stand already today, I have no doubt. So there is little chance of being disturbed." Her grin grew brighter as her task was accomplished; she took the Lord Roland firmly in hand, then ran her teeth over his chin just below his lips.

"But," she continued, feeling the breath go utterly out of him, "if you like I can stop now, and go to the door, check the corridor, and see if anyone's coming—"

"No," Tristan gasped hoarsely. "No."

Portia chuckled. "Suit yourself," she said, lowering his trousers to the floor and following their descent with her mouth.

To keep from passing out, Tristan counted the breaths before the succor he was painfully anticipating was at last upon him. When Portia finally indulged him, after a teasing delay, he felt his muscles go slack, and his body crumpled to the floor beneath her. Unlike their last coupling, which had occurred on this very floor the night he had left her here four months before, this time it was he who was naked and utterly vulnerable, while Portia remained almost fully garbed, in complete control of the situation.

He was helpless to stop it, totally unable to reverse positions, to regain his standing as the master of a submissive servant.

And even if he had been able, he knew he would never have any desire to do so.

Instead, he surrendered himself to her ministrations, breathlessly allowing her to put him through his paces like an obedient mount. Even as she climbed atop him, gripping him, riding him savagely, he felt the sweet consolation of abandon, the helpless freedom that comes when a tormented soul abdicates any remaining control over its own destiny.

And one more sensation, a seeping entanglement making its way through his heart like the trickling of a stream or the tendrils of a vine, a soul-deep need for the release that her hot flesh drew from him the way a poultice draws forth the toxin of infection, healing him, burning away the prison of his unhappy life, tying him gleefully to this young servant-mistress in a way that he knew would be impossible to disentangle without pain. The feeling left him weak with gratitude.

And when, after many false attempts to summit the jagged mountain peak that was Portia, brought again and again to the brink of ecstasy, only to be held in torturous delay, she finally released him, letting all the poison and disappointment that had taken root in his soul pour forth from him in a heated rush of physical and spiritual delight, Tristan managed to focus his clouded vision for a moment on her face, staring down intently at him with the leaping fire behind it. It was not the rigid mask of pleasure, open-lipped and gasping, that his own aspect had assumed, but rather a studied expression of interest. In that instant, before the surge and the wild remnants of bucking and thrusting transported him back to hedonistic oblivion, Tristan Steward had the impression that she was looking for something deeper in him than he possessed.

The thought did not linger past that moment.

Later, as they lay, disengaged, side by side before the crackling heat of the fire, the Lord Roland took the hand of the chambermaid and kissed it gratefully, happy to feel connected still, even after the moments of passion had passed, to a spirit so unlike that of his despised wife, so unlike his own indolent nature.

"When I am with you, at last I feel brave, Portia," he said quietly. "I feel as if perhaps the world is not passing by without me."

The young woman stretched lazily before the fire, her glowing skin dewy with sweat.

"Glad to be of service, m'lord," she answered, running her fingers idly through his damp auburn curls. "Your satisfaction is the greatest joy to one of my lowly station."

"I'm so sorry that I made you feel less than you are," Tristan continued, his strength waning as exhaustion began to set in. "I apologize for making you feel like a nameless whore—you are so much more to me than that."

Portia lifted herself up onto her elbow and chuckled. "There is where you are wrong, m'lord. I had no objection to you thinking of me as a whore—I am a whore, indeed, one of the most shameless variety. But I am not nameless. I treasure my name; as a lowly chambermaid, I've had to hide it for a long time, keep it demurely unspoken; even that smarmy chamberlain barely addresses me by anything but 'you, girl.' But by the time my work is done, the powerful will speak my name, and tremble." Her eyes sparkled. "Beginning with you, m'lord."

Drowsily Tristan Steward rolled closer and kissed her ear. "Portia," he whispered softly. "I am trembling, Portia."

The woman only smiled, backlit by the roaring fire. She waited until the Lord Roland was all but asleep, then rose up on her palms and placed her lips next to his ear and whispered her name into it as he fell into slumber.

Had he been more awake, he would only have heard the sound of the crackling flames.

26

On the deepest part of that same night, the Lord Roland lay naked on the floor before the dying fire coals, shivering and alone. His exhausted dreams were plagued by an overwhelming sense of loss, of wandering in dark caverns without a light. He was sinking into despair in his slumber when he felt the touch of a soft blanket draped over him, the caress of a gentle hand with pleasantly calloused fingertips across his brow. His body, cold from the loss of both Portia's warmth and that of the fire, discerned the presence of a delicious heat beside him.

Tristan Steward blinked, and rolled onto his back.

In the darkness a woman was kneeling beside him, her long golden tresses catching the remaining glimpses of light from the fading coals. Tristan could barely distinguish her form from the shadows that surrounded her, but the curve of her small face, the shape of her large, dark green eyes was known to him in every waking moment. The familiar scent of vanilla and spiced soap, meadow flowers and sandalwood filled his nostrils, driving away the hollow odor of loneliness and fire ash that had lingered there a moment before.

"Rhapsody?" he whispered, his mind still foggy from drink, his body still spent from sexual fury.

She smiled at him, the warmth of kindness that held no trace of pity in her eyes.

"You seemed cold," she said, tucking the blanket more snugly around him. "I hate for anyone to be cold in my house."

Tristan struggled to focus in the dim light. "You—you're here? Are you a dream?"

She chuckled, then rose and went to the fireplace, her heavy brocade dressing gown rustling musically in his ears as she passed his head. The coals gleamed as she approached; it was a phenomena Tristan had witnessed in her presence many times, as if the last vestiges of the fire were greeting her in homage. She moved the screen aside, took hold of two logs and set them carefully into the ashes, her hands seemingly inured to the fire's sting.

The hearth fire caught immediately, the flames leaping in welcome, spilling flashes of brightness around the dark room, dispelling many of the shadows. Tristan watched her, transfixed, as she returned to his side and sank to the floor beside him once more.

"Not a dream, no," she said softly. "As a Namer, I can feel the silent call of those in despair, and can transcend the limits of space and time to come if the need is great enough." She brushed the shock of red-brown curls from his forehead again. "You must be in very great pain to summon me from so far away. Don't be sad, Tristan—you have so much in your life to be grateful for."

"I know," Tristan said, struggling to wake more fully. "I know, Rhapsody, I am blessed, but—" His words failed, his voice faltered under the weight of his selfish need, his obsession.

"But what?"

He raised himself up on his elbows, looking up into the perfection of her face.

"It's not enough," he said finally. "It's not enough."

The smile left her eyes and her lips, replaced by an expression of thoughtful sadness.

"What would be enough, then, Tristan?"

All the barriers he had built to keep his need in check, to remain socially acceptable, to keep from driving her away, buckled in the face of what might be his only chance to tell her.

"You," he whispered. "You—I need you. From that first meeting when you came to me, long ago, to sue for the Bolg's protection, when I dismissed you, drove you from my presence, I have felt a chasm inside me. I curse myself for being so blind, so foolish—"

"Stop," she said, placing her small, warm hand against his lips.

"There is no need for regret between us. All of that has come and gone, and yet here I remain."

"I need you," Tristan said again; the words thudded stupidly, flat against his eardrums.

"And I am here."

"Not like this," he insisted, taking her hand and pressing it to his lips again, then resting it against his cheek. The warmth, the solidity of it gladdened him; until that moment he was still unsure as to whether or not she was merely a dream, a figment of his drunken imagination. "I want to love you, Rhapsody."

She exhaled sharply, pulling her hand away.

"We are married to other people," she said flatly. "We have children with other people."

"I know, I know," said Tristan Steward. The exhaustion and the late hour made his head light, his words echo stupidly in his brain.

"Then you know that what you are asking for can never be," she said, but her words carried no sting, no accusation.

The beauty of her face, the warmth of her body in the otherwise cold room, even the gentleness of her words of rejection were more than Tristan's twisted heart and fuzzy mind could bear. He began to weep, painful tears slipping in quick rivers of self-pity and inestimable loss. The sincerity of his agony must have been apparent to her, because her eyes opened wide in concern again, and she quickly reached out her hand, resting it against his rough cheek once more.

"Stop now," she said softly. "Stop, please. There is no need. Stop."

Tristan lowered his head to his chest, no longer able to look at her. Even without seeing her he could feel her consternation growing, but he was unable to pull himself together enough to reset the situation to an unbroken form.

Her remaining hand came to rest on his other cheek. "Please, please don't be sad," she said. "I came all this way to comfort you, Tristan, not to cause you pain."

"Comfort me, then," Tristan blurted. "Comfort me, Rhapsody."

For perhaps the only time in his life, Tristan was able to make his mind and body function spontaneously enough on the spur of the moment to take the initiative he needed. He reached out and pulled her into his arms, ignoring the startled look on her face, pressing her body feverishly against his.

He was prepared for the sharp blow across his face, prepared for her to pull violently away, but instead she froze, her emerald-green eyes glistening with an emotion he could not identify. At first he thought it might be fear, but there was no trace of that; rather, it was an intense look of confusion melded with sympathy and, though perhaps only in his imagination, a tinge of longing.

He decided to believe that was what it was.

He abandoned words, and throwing all caution, all decorum, to the winds, he kissed her, covering completely her spicy red mouth with his own, almost as if to steal any objections along with her breath.

When all the waiting, all the long-held fantasy melts away, and the moment that a man has wished for in vain for years suddenly arrives, the weight of time shifts, Tristan discovered. The blood was hammering in his ears in time with his racing heart, drowning out all but its thudding tattoo. Time slowed; dimly he could hear her voice beyond the pounding whenever his mouth moved from her own, his name the only word he could make out, but whether it was being repeated in passion or in resistance he could not be certain.

The rich fabric of the brocade dressing gown whispered in his shaking hands. Beneath the gown her skin was bare, and warm in his palms as he sought her. Like a freezing man discovering a blazing bonfire, he drew nearer, pressing, insisting, and found no resistance, no barrier, only acceptance, only welcome.

How many heartbeats their actual coupling lasted, Tristan was not able to gauge; he only knew that time was suspended in the bliss of finally attaining that which he had come to believe was unattainable. As her arms and legs wrapped around him, her hands cradled his face lovingly, the Lord Roland began to weep, hot, painful tears of disbelief and jubilation in at last having his desire, and his love, returned by the woman who had stolen his soul on the day he met her.

Finally, when he could sustain the act no longer, he pulled her even closer and buried his face gratefully in the waves of her flaxen hair. He kissed her neck, then whispered into her ear, damp with the dew of sweat from the fire and their passion.

"This night, no one is cold in your house."

He could feel her smile against his neck.

She pulled back and lay in the crook of his arm, smiling up at him, the light of the fire dancing in her eyes.

"Are you comforted, Tristan?"

The Lord Roland sighed happily. "Immensely." He leaned up on his elbow, listening past the door. Upon hearing nothing in the hall beyond, he brushed a tangled strand from her face. "And know that I will treasure this night forever—" His words faltered, but he pressed ahead, unwilling to lose the opportunity. "And all those nights to come."

The firelight dimmed in her emerald eyes.

"Nights to come?"

"Yes," Tristan Steward blurted. "Now that we've—now that you and I have—" His words slowed as her face changed, her expression becoming guarded before his eyes. "But you need not fear Gwydion finding out, Rhapsody. We will be careful hence. I would never disclose to him, even in the most accidental of circumstances, what we have done."

She exhaled sharply. "Tell him whatever you want," she said tersely. "He won't believe you anyway."

Tristan blinked as if he had been slapped. Until that moment, he had not realized that he expected her gratitude in return for his discretion. "No, no, I would never compromise you—I love you—I don't want to ruin anything that you value. Just knowing that you care for me—" His words faltered at the blank expression on her face. "You—do care for me, Rhapsody? You must, to have, to have come to me like this—"

"Of course I care for you, Tristan," she said, shifting uncomfortably in his arms.

Tristan felt his fading hope return. "Then we can continue to meet clandestinely?" he asked. His grip on her tightened unconsciously as she squirmed more noticeably, as if trying to break free.

"Of course we can—oh, bugger it, enough. This is making me ill. Get off me, I can't breathe."

With an almost violent shove, she pushed out of his arms and rose to a stand, turning away from him and straightening her dressing gown as she did.

To Tristan's utter shock, as she stood, her body and shadow lengthened, taking on height and width that it had not had a moment before. In the fading light of the fire her hair seemed to darken, her face to elongate, and when she turned around, her eyes sparkled with a wicked black light.

The Lord Roland felt all the breath leave his body.

After two attempts that produced no sound and sour spittle, he finally got his mouth to form the word.

"Portia?"

The chambermaid laughed merrily. She continued to stand, looking down amusedly on his astonishment, until his mouth finally closed.

"Isn't self-deception a remarkably powerful entity?" she asked playfully. "I told you, m'lord, I've been at this a long time." She turned and headed for the door, then stopped for a moment.

"You should get up from the floor, Tristan," she said. "Your position there does not befit the position you will soon attain."

Then she left the room without a backward glance.

27

THE KINGDOM OF THE NAIN

ℱaedryth, king of Nain and Lord of the Distant Mountains, stared ruefully into the darkness beyond the gleaming throne in the center of his Great Hall hidden deep within the cavernous earth. Though the seat of power had been his, undisputed, for nearly a thousand years, it never ceased to give him pause whenever he beheld it.

A single slab of crystal purer than the flawless diamonds adorning his crown, the throne was a rough-hewn chair shaped from the living rock, growing seamlessly from the cavern floor, reaching in jagged and uneven slabs skyward to the dark vault of the Great Hall above. The Nain who had lived in this place before Faedryth, despite being the greatest miners, architects, and road builders the continent had ever known, had left the miraculous formation almost untouched, preferring to merely polish it and tolerate some discomfort of their monarchs' hindquarters rather than insult the earth that had given birth to such an awe-inspiring wonder by altering it in any way. Accordingly, they had also deemed it appropriate to outfit the Great Hall with only the barest of torchlight, so as not to presume to externally illuminate the giant pure gem that glowed with a light of its own.

The Nain king glanced around the empty, cavernous room, and returned to his musings. He recalled the first time he had ever seen this place, led here under a flag of truce by the guards of Vormvald, the Nain king who had reigned over these lands when Faedryth came, more or less as a refugee. Vormvald, then in the hundred and twelfth year of his reign, had graciously taken in Faedryth and his followers, thousands of Nain from the other side of the world where Faedryth had once been their king. At the time they were both men in their middle years, but unlike Vormvald and his subjects, Faedryth and his followers had been granted an enduring and uncanny youth, a dubious blessing of near immortality, conferred somewhere in the course of their flight from their doomed homeland. This dubious blessing had already caused several of their number to take their own lives.

But Vormvald did not know that. The appearance of thirty thousand of his kind, under the banner of a seemingly humble and cooperative leader like Faedryth, had been seen as welcome reinforcement of the military, mining, and construction brigades of the Distant Mountains. He made Faedryth's people, survivors of the destroyed Island of Serendair, at home in his lands, appointed Faedryth his viceroy, allowed the newcomers autonomy under their king, and set about, with the former king's help, transforming his own kingdom, achieving even greater visions of magnificent architecture and invention. The production of the mines doubled, the artisanship and artistry of the forge and smelting fires became legendary, and the kingdom, now united, continued its self-sufficient progress hidden a thousand miles away from any of the other races of man.

The influence of the Cymrian Nain, as Faedryth's followers were known in the Distant Kingdom, was immediately apparent. Their ingenuity with the hinge and pulley, in the forging of weapons with which Vormvald was not familiar, their ability to move earth and sculpt the stone of tunnels and mines, quickly became part of the societal fabric of the Distant Mountains. The old Nain king was delighted with the accomplishments that were wrought, the cities that were built, the works of art that were fashioned, the inventions that were realized. All the while, as each new era of advancement came and went, replaced by another, greater era, Vormvald's eyes began to dim, his hand to weaken, his beard to gray into the whiteness of mountain snow.

But not Faedryth. He remained as youthful as on the day he had arrived in Vormvald's court. He had been a partner in vision, in labor, in the rule of the United Kingdom of Nain, and when Vormvald finally failed in his fourth century of life, passing from the world as each man passes to the next one, Faedryth became the kingdom's undisputed ruler. Vormvald's heirs squawked for a generation or two, but in the end Time erased his dynastic line, and their claim to the throne, and eventually their mortal memories, as easily as the jeweler's cloth polishes out a scratch in an otherwise flawless gem.

Now the crystal throne was Faedryth's. It had been for a millennium and yet, somehow, there was still a newness to it, and an uneasiness, a vague sense of intimidation each time he placed himself on the horizontal plane in the rock that served as the seat. He had become accustomed to its deep power, the pressure and flow, the sheer might that radiated from the depth of the earth through the giant glowing crystal, an authority sanctioned by the very mountains over which he ruled. Faedryth could feel bloods he had not been born to, as if he could feel the breathing of the earth, and that power was now his power. Nonetheless, Faedryth had never taken the throne for granted. Great and vain as he was, the mighty immortal leader of a deep nation of hidden men, smiths and builders, miners and jewelers, and an army numbering almost half a million, in spite of all the riches at his disposal, recognized that there were still a few things greater than himself.

One of those things might be within the black ivory box he now held in his hands.

A soft cough behind him stirred Faedryth from his reverie. Thotan, his minister of mines and his only nonmilitary earl, hovered at the edge of the fireshadows, respectful in his silence. Polite comportment was unusual for a Nain lord; most Nain spoke little unless they were in their cups, but even so did not give much concern to how they were perceived by others. Thotan was different, being the administrator of the merchants, the upworld Nain who took the wares from their mines across the seas to the kingdoms of men and sold them, allowing the rest of the kingdom its peace and solitude in the silent earth. His job required uncharacteristic forbearance and civility; Thotan had been waiting patiently beyond the gilded doors of the throne room since the king had summoned him more than an hour before. Faedryth exhaled, then nodded to him, almost reluctantly.

Thotan turned on his heel and hurried from the room.

The box in Faedryth's hands felt smooth against his calloused palms, and cold. He continued to stare at it, lost in thought, until Thotan returned with Therion, Faedryth's aide-de-camp, followed by fourteen of his most highly trusted corpsmen, each in the silver fittings and banded black leather of Faedryth's personal regiment, in pairs. In their arms they carried something wrapped in linen, heavy, bulky and regular of shape. From the expressions of measured concentration on their faces, it was clear that their cargo was both fragile and precious beyond reckoning.

Faedryth watched in grim silence as the corpsmen gently set their burdens down around the base of the crystal throne and carefully unbound the silk ropes that secured their wrappings. The flickering torchlight flashed ruby-red suddenly as it came to rest on the first of the objects, a large, smoothly honed piece of colored glass with a thickness the width of Faedryth's hand. The piece had a perfectly curved edge on the outside, an arc of a circle a little more than a seventh of the circumference, and tapered like a wide pie wedge to a smaller, similar arc, which Therion's corpsmen were busily fitting into place at the base of Faedryth's throne.

"Careful, you oxen," the king muttered under his breath; he clutched the black ivory box more tightly as the second and third pieces were simultaneously unwrapped, revealing similar pieces of glass the colors of orange fire opal and yellow citrine. A moment later an emerald piece emerged from its bindings, deep and green as the ocean most Nain would pass their lives without seeing. As it was carefully fitted into place, a large gleaming piece of sky-blue, like a topaz of clearest coloration, and a deep indigo arc emerged, not as wide as the others, for its place in the spectrum was smaller than the six core colors. Until the dim torchlight fell upon it, the smaller piece seemed almost black, but in the flicker of illumination the rich sapphire hue glowed quietly, unobtrusively, becoming part of the darkness when the light moved on.

Finally, with the greatest of care, the last piece was removed from its linen wrappings. The violet arc was perhaps the most beautiful of all; there was something achingly clear about the amethyst hue, something fresh, like the beginning of a new day after a dark night, the clearing of a smoke-filled sky when battle was done. As it came forth, the scent of the room changed, the thick staleness of stagnant mountain air giving way to a fresh breeze that stung the king's eyes, making them water at the edges in melancholy memory. The corpsmen, affected similarly, sat back on their heels, almost reverently. The last piece remained, out of place for the moment, awaiting Faedryth's order.

The Nain king looked down at the box in his hands again. The tip of his beard, resplendent gold that curled into platinum at the ends like the hair of his head, brushed the black ivory lid. There was irony there, in the contact of dead hair with the box; black ivory was the rarest of all stones, harvested from the deadest parts of the earth, not from living animals as traditional ivory was. The places from which it was mined were spots of utter desolation, where magic had died, or the earth had been scorched beyond repair, devoid of its unique power to heal itself, unlike after wild-fire or flood, where new life sprang up from the ashes or mud. Black ivory was the physical embodiment of an emptiness beyond death—of Void, the utter absence of life—and therefore anything that was hidden within a box fashioned of it was surrounded by total vibrational darkness, invisible to every form of sight, even the most powerful of scrying.

Even holding such a box made Faedryth's soul itch.

Knowing what was inside it, or rather, not knowing, made it burn.

"Is my daughter here?" he demanded tersely.

"Verily," Thotan replied. "And each surviving generation of your line as well."

Faedryth snorted. "Send in my daughter," he said, beginning to pace the dark floor. "The rest are too old." Thotan nodded; like Faedryth, he was a First Generation Cymrian, one of the more than one hundred thousand original refugees from the Lost Island of Serendair, and thereby seemingly immortal as well. Also like Faedryth, he had seen that immortality eke slowly from his own family, so that while he himself maintained the same vigor of youth he had possessed on the day four-teen hundred years before when he set foot on the ship that bore him away to safety, his children had aged as if they were of his parents' gen-eration, his grandchildren more so, until his more distant progeny had grown old and died, while he continued on, as if frozen in Time.

The gilded door opened again, and Gyllian entered the room. Like her father she had wheat-colored hair, but whereas his was tipped with the beginnings of silver, all of hers save the faintest of golden strands had been given over to the metallic color. She bore her age well in spite of it, and strode directly to her father's side, the lines of her face deep-ened into creases of silent concern.

Faedryth reached out his hand and brought it to rest on the side of her face for a moment; to touch one so aged and wise in such a fatherly way had always seemed strange to him in his eternal youth, but in the few moments of tenderness he allowed himself, the object was always Gyllian.

"The Lightforge has been made ready," he said quietly, words he had spoken to her on several occasions before. "Are you, in the event you need be?"

His daughter nodded, still silent.

Faedryth inhaled deeply. "Very well, then. Stand at the door. Tell the yeoman to make ready." He nodded to Thotan; the minister of mines bowed quickly and left the chamber, followed by Therion and the corpsmen. The Nain king allowed his hand to linger on his daughter's age-withered cheek one moment longer, then let it fall to his side.

"All right," he said brusquely to the ghosts and memories that lingered, invisible, in the air around him. "Let us do this."

"Do you want to wait to speak with Garson one last time?" Gyllian asked, her mien calm and expressionless, as always. The Nain princess had forged her reputation in the battles of the Great Cymrian War, and had been cured in the smoke of those battles like leather, molded and shaped in their endless campfires into a woman with steel in her spine. That notwithstanding, she was measured and deliberate in her counsel, always seeking to exhaust other means before opening doors that, once opened, might not be able to be closed again.

A small, sarcastic bark escaped Faedryth's lips.

"You want to see me heave yet another Orb of State into the wall?" he asked, his eyes twinkling fondly above a darker expression. "There are still shards from the last one scattered on the far floor."

Gyllian's expression did not change. "If that is the price of appropriate consideration, it is a small one," she said evenly. "Before you resort to using the Lightforge, I would see you shatter a hundred Orbs, until you are certain of what you undertake." The stoic expression in her eyes softened into one of concern. "The risks are far too grave not to. And besides, I know it feeds your ego to know that you can still heave and shatter a sphere of annealed glass the way a mere youth of a hundred winters can."

Faedryth chuckled. "All right, then, Gyllian, if you wish it, summon Garson." The princess nodded slightly and returned to the doorway, leaving the Nain king alone in the flickering darkness with his thoughts.

And the black ivory box.

Faedryth was afraid to hold it and, at the same time, afraid to set it down. He had been bedeviled by the contents ever since they had been unearthed from the deepest of the crystal mines almost half a year's time before, was nervous in their presence, fearful that this odd magic might be the final straw to tip the scales of his sanity. While the Lightforge might assist him in knowing, finally, what they were, expending its power was something Faedryth considered only under the rarest, and gravest, of circumstances, knowing the risk to himself, and the world, that came in the process.

The door of the Great Hall opened again, admitting Garson ben Sardonyx and the royal yeoman, wearing a miner's helm with a dark visor, bearing his enormous crossbow across his back and carrying a heavy stand. Faedryth swallowed, his mouth suddenly dry, and gestured impatiently to Garson, who doubled his pace until he was standing in front of the king. The blue-yellow tapetum in the back of his eyes, the physical attribute that allowed all Nain to see in the blackness of their underground dwellings, caught the torchlight and gleamed, making him appear like a feral animal approaching in the dark.

"Tell me again what the Bolg king said during your visit to him," Faedryth demanded as Gyllian returned to his side. "Recount each detail—there may have been something we missed on the previous reports."

Garson's broad shoulders and chest expanded as he inhaled deeply. He ran a hand over his magnificent beard, brown at the chin, tapering to a silver middle and curling into white at the tips; Garson was Faedryth's official upworld ambassador, the only Nain of the Deep Kingdom to speak in diplomacy with men of other races, and had been trained since childhood in perfection of memory. His brows furrowed, but patiently he began to recount the conversation he had already related on three other occasions since returning from his state visit to the Bolglands.

"King Achmed was annoyed from the beginning at my presence, of course," Garson said. "I gave him your message—that you knew he was attempting to reconstruct the Lightforge of Gwylliam and Anwyn in the mountains of his realm, and that you had bade me to tell him that he must not."

Faedryth nodded. "And?"

"He told me I was a brave man with too much time on my hands to have traveled all the way from our lands to dare to instruct him in such a manner."

"Pompous fool," muttered Faedryth. "Go on."

"I told him you had commanded me thus, and he said that he was puzzled, then. He said he knew of no Lightforge, and yet you had risked his ire, which you knew to be considerable, by sending me to barge into his rooms in the middle of the night to issue him an order regarding it. He stated that even he, who places less stock in diplomacy and matters of etiquette than anyone he knew, found that offensive."

"No doubt," said Faedryth dryly. "And he then denied knowing of the Lightforge?"

"Yes. I suggested that perhaps he did not call it by the same name, but that I suspected he knew to what I was referring. I told him that the Light-forge was an instrumentality that the Nain built for Lord Gwylliam the Visionary eleven centuries ago, a machine formed of metal and colored glass embedded into a mountain peak, which manipulated light to various ends. It was destroyed in the Great War, as it should have been, because it tapped power that was unstable, unpredictable. I told him that it poses a great threat not only to his allies and enemies, but to his own kingdom as well. I told him that he was attempting to rebuild something that he did not fully understand, that his foolishness would lead to his destruction, and very possibly that of those around him. I reminded him that he had already seen the effects of this; the tainted glass from his first attempt still littered the countryside around Ylorc. I repeated that this is folly of un-speakable rashness, and that you, Your Majesty, commanded that he cease at once, for the good of the Alliance, and for his own as well."

Gyllian sighed. "You expected a different answer than the one you got, Father? Did you really think the king of the Firbolg would listen sympathetically to a demand phrased thus?"

"I should have asked you to craft the missive," muttered Faedryth, beginning to pace again. "But the Bolg king has always been a plainspo-ken man. I thought that by speaking plainly I was sending him a message he would respect; obviously I was wrong. Then what did he say?"

"He asked me casually how I knew this, citing the distance of our kingdom and our isolation from the world of man. When I told him that you made it a point to monitor events that might have a dangerous im-pact on the world, he called me a liar, then said that he knew we had one of our own, and were using it to spy on his lands."

Faedryth exhaled dismally.

"A reasonable guess," Gyllian said. "He was half right."

"He then demanded I leave his lands and deliver this message to you," Garson went on. "He said, and I quote, 'Return to your king and tell him this from me: I once had respect for him and the way he conducts his reign; he has as low an opinion of the Cymrians as I do, and is a reticent member of the Alliance, just as I am. He keeps to himself within his mountains, as do I. But if he continues to spy into my lands, or send emissaries who tell me what to do, when my own version of your so-called Lightforge is operational, I will be testing out its offensive capabilities on distant targets. I will leave it to you to guess which ones.'"

The air seemed to go out of the vast cavern.

"When I said that I doubted very much he wished for me to convey that message to you, he said, 'Doubt it not, Garson. Now leave.'"

Faedryth wheeled and stared at Gyllian.

"Do you still believe that there is another option?" he demanded.

The princess came slowly to her father's side and gently kissed his cheek.

"No," she said simply. Then she bowed slightly and left the room, casting a glance at the yeoman but not looking back at Faedryth.

"Prepare, and be quick about it," Faedryth commanded the yeoman. The man nodded and quickly began to assemble the stand, setting the crossbow atop it, aimed at the crystal throne.

"Stand ready," he said to Garson.

"I am, m'lord," Garson replied stiffly. "We will be making use of the blue spectrum?"

Faedryth exhaled again. The blue power of the spectrum was the only one with which he was at all familiar; while he did not know the words in the ancient tongue that had been used by Gwylliam, he thought he recalled that they had translated to Cloud Caller or Cloud Chaser. He did know that the strength of elemental blue was in scrying, seeing across vast distances, to hidden places or, when reversed, to hide from eyes that might be similarly seeking him.

He had only made use of one other color on one other occasion; when the Molten River of magma that perennially flowed on the border of his lands went dormant two centuries before, his sage advised him to use the orange power of the spectrum, Firestarter, to summon the lava back from beneath its dome of ash. Had the river not served as a protective wall between his kingdom and the lands of a neighboring wyrm, and had its liquid fire not been critical to the survival of the Deep Kingdom in winter, he would never have attempted it. The resulting explosion and destruction had convinced him never to do so again.

He nodded curtly at Garson, trying to block the image of that devastation from his mind.

Without another word he went to the gleaming crystal outcropping, stepping carefully through the opening in the otherwise fitted pieces of colored glass that formed a spectral circle at the base of his throne, and sat slowly down on the seat ledge. He stared at the box in his hands a moment longer, then looked up to see Garson, his official witness of state, watching the king unflinchingly behind the yeoman, whose crossbow sight was trained on his heart.

"Close the circle," Faedryth commanded. His voice was deep and resonant, containing none of the uncertainty it had held a moment before.

Garson moved quickly to the center of the vast, dark hall and knelt at the foot of the king. Faedryth blessed him impatiently; Garson rose and stepped out of the circle of colored glass, then carefully took hold of the last piece, the one fired in the color of the purest of amethyst, and gently moved it into place, the final piece of the circular puzzle.

As the king watched his upworld ambassador adjusting the violet arc, he thought suddenly of Garson's great-grandfather, Gar ben Sardonyx, who had helped him fire that very piece in the annealing oven centuries ago. He tried to close his mind to the flood of memories, but it was impossible; the power of the throne, though still sleeping, was alive, opening long closed places in his mind, heedless of the wards or locks he might place in its way.

The memories it brought back were painful ones, pockets of acid in the recesses of his brain. He had been the original builder of the first Lightforge, the one in the Bolg king's now-broken tower, had constructed it at the command of his lord and friend, Gwylliam the Visionary, only to see its power misused, its mission corrupted by that very lord and friend in the course of a long, bloody, and pointless war. Faedryth had turned his back on Gwylliam and those who had followed him then, had tossed his sword into the king's Moot in disgust and quit the place, returning to the Distant Mountains and his Deep Kingdom, and had remained there until recently summoned again by the Lady Cymrian, asking the Nain to rejoin the Alliance for the good of the continent. Against his better wishes he had agreed; now, as he sat within one of the wonders of the world above a source of its primeval power, he wondered if he had made a terrible mistake.

As Garson maneuvered the piece into place now, Faedryth thought dryly of how he had condemned Gwylliam's thirst for power, had left all the plans and glass color keys behind him, disavowing all that he had done in the building of the Visionary's great empire, only to find himself, deep within his cavernous realm, thinking endlessly about the rainbow of glass that channeled the very power of life.

The thoughts that had at first plagued him in those days long ago had come to haunt him; like demonic whispers in his ears, the memory of colored glass spoke to him in his dreams, reminding him that their knowledge was fleeting, evanescent, that he would need to hurry if he was to re-form the instrumentality. Even he had needed a detailed schematic when building Gwylliam's original Lightforge, a set of drawings drafted by the greatest of Cymrian Namers that was impossible to commit to memory, which he had consulted every day in the course of the project, staring at them each morning as if he had never seen them before, he, the builder of one of the greatest mountain cities in the world, the man with a ferocious memory who had taken the Visionary's prescient ideas and brought them to reality.

Now he couldn't remember from day to day what was on the drawings.

Because he had left behind in the library of Canrif the fired bricks of colored glass keyed to the exact hue on the spectrum necessary to make the instrumentality work, he had no tool with which to compare any future firings. The only thing that saved him was the memory that each of the glass pieces in the dome of Gurgus Peak had been the same color of the light spectrum that was reflected in different gemstones in their purest state.

And his kingdom had no shortage of pure gemstones for reference.

So he had reproduced the glass spectrum in a simple circle, while the voices in his head had screamed cacophonously at each step of the way, with the pouring, the annealing, the cooling, the engineering of the crystal throne, urging him onward, only to fall into a complete, almost smug silence when the Lightforge was finally finished.

So now he had one of his own, albeit a much smaller one that was only assembled on extremely rare occasions, only a handful of times over the past four centuries. The only thing he feared more than using it was the thought of losing the power altogether.

The deep, melodic voice of the Earth itself hummed around him, rousing him from his musings. The circle was complete.

"Open the vent," Faedryth commanded through gritted teeth.

The yeoman lowered the visor of his helm to shield his eyes.

Garson grasped the lever that was masked by the lower stalagmites of the crystal throne, and pulled it toward himself until it aligned with registrations of the blue arc. He then fell back, shielding his eyes, as a concealed slab of stone below the throne moved aside into the rock below, revealing the light of the flame-well over which the crystal had formed, a direct vent to the fire that burned, thousands of miles below, past the crust and mantle of the Earth, in the very heart of the world. Even with his hands before his eyes, the light was blinding.

The pulsing flames from deep within the Earth sent flashes of hot blue light spinning through the Great Hall, illuminating the distant ceiling, dancing off the stalactites, spitting and hissing in time with the fire below the giant crystal, making it glow like a star hidden in the darkness. The radiance engulfed the crystal throne and the Nain king upon it, turning them both the color of a cloudless sky on a summer's day in the upworld, a color so pure and clear that it stung the back of Garson's eyes through the shield of his fingers.

Breathing shallowly and willing his racing heart to slow, Faedryth, translucent in the grip of the Lightforge's power, opened the black ivory box.

At first he saw nothing, and panic tickled the outer edge of his consciousness. The contents of the box had been brittle, almost vaporous when they were first discovered, and in the dazzling blue luminosity of the crystal throne, lit from below by the very fire of the Earth's core, they clung to the shadows, all but invisible.

Faedryth tilted the box until the contents caught the roaring light. As if it were a living entity, that light growled into the corners of the box, seeking its contents and catching them, illuminating them, giving them color and shape.

At first they emerged from hiding as little more than an evanescent glow, dusty and changing, second by second, like summer sunlight filtering through a window. The Nain king gingerly reached inside the box and lifted one of the scraps into the blue radiance that was pulsating around him.

Draped across his finger was a fragment of what looked like clear parchment, though it was filmy and inconstant and yellowed with age. It seemed to be a made thing, part translucence of gem, part gossamer. Faedryth had never seen its like, not in sixteen centuries of life, nor on either of two continents, nor had any of the advisors to whom he had apprehensively shown it.

The place where it had been found—the deepest reaches of the crystal mines, where the diamond-like formations believed to have been brought to the Earth from the stars in the form of meteorites lay beneath immeasurable tons of age-old granite—was in and of itself a miracle of recovery; it had taken thousands of years for the Nain to broach that mine. That anything had survived the pressure and cold of the crystal bed was improbable at the very best; but here, now, between his fingers was a scrap of delicate material, fragile and changing with each breath he drew. Faedryth disliked the concept of magic, distrusted most of those who used it, who manipulated words or songs or vibrations to alter the world, but even a skeptic and unbeliever as curmudgeonly as he could not help but be awed, and terrified, in its presence.

It was, as far as he could tell, like nothing that existed anywhere in the Known World.

And for that reason, he had to know what it was.

"All the way," he muttered.

Garson, the blinding blue light leaking in behind his closed eyelids, felt for the lever again and pulled with all his might.

The double metal disk below the throne that Faedryth's smiths had sawed through the base of the immense crystal to install four hundred years before ground into place again, focusing all the light from the flame-well through the center of the blue arc, turning the crystal, the king, and the room beyond an even more intense, pure, and imperceptible hue of blue, a holy, elemental color at the very center of the spectrum.

The crystal formation sang with a primal vibration, the clearest of notes, inaudible to Garson or the yeoman, but Faedryth could hear it in his soul, felt it ring through his blood, opening his eyes, not only in the darkness of his throne room, but beyond it, to the world around him, across the plains to the horizons, to the very edge of the sea.

Faedryth gripped the throne, knowing what came next.

The yeoman, who knew what might, sighted his crossbow on the king's heart.

Suddenly Faedryth was engulfed with sight of a capacity beyond anything imaginable by a human; it was as if all the world, in every bit of its detail and magnitude, was apparent to him instantaneously. Like being swallowed by a tidal wave, he was suddenly drowning in information, exposed to every flock of sparrows' migration pattern, every racing front of every storm, the number of shafts of wheat bowing before the sun, the heartbeats of the world, assaulting him from every side.

His mind raced at the speed of a flashing sunbeam, shooting crazily skyward like an arrow off the string, then plummeting suddenly down into the earth, where the passageways sculpted by his own subjects scored the crust like tunnels in an anthill. It swept briskly over troves of treasure, of volcanic lava flowing in the Molten River, dark shafts of endless anthracitic night, speeding beneath the roots of trees and the burrows of forest beasts, until it burst through the Earth's crust again, absorbing all there was to see, all there was to know.

Seeing *everything*.

In that instant, the Nain king realized he was seeing as a dragon sees, with wyrmsight that transcends all physical limits.

And it terrified him, as it always did.

With great effort Faedryth tore his mind's eye away from the racing vision by dragging his head down and staring at the piece of fragile parchment in his hand. He knew there was an image on it, an image he had only glimpsed when the brittle piece of solid-yet-ever-changing magical parchment was first brought to him. At that moment, he could sense that there were colored lights in some form of spectral arrangement, some source of power, light as bright as that from the flame-well beneath him, which he had assumed to be the rebuilt Lightforge of Gurgus Peak. In addition, he had felt something then, just a brief sensation of being aware of another person's thoughts, and it had seemed to him that the Bolg king was present in those thoughts. For a man who eschewed magic lore and vibrational study, whose joy was engineering, mining, the smelting of iron and the building of tunnels, the sensation of reading another's mind, especially when the thinker was unknown and most likely long dead, was particularly unsettling.

With immense difficulty he kept his vision fixed away from the avalanche of images swirling before him and held the fragment up in the clear blue light before his eyes.

The image he had seen once before, at the time nothing more than a hazy smudge, refined instantly into a crisp clarity that was painful in its sharpness. Despite being utterly clear, the picture still made almost no sense to Faedryth, whose eyes throbbed, threatening to burst.

It was as if he was standing himself in the place where the image had been captured, a familiar dark hall that could have been within his own mountain. Faedryth sensed, by the thinness and striations of the stone, that it was within a peak. At the end of the tunnel an arm's length away was an opening, past which there appeared to be a laboratory of some sort, within a large clear sphere suspended in the open darkness of the upworld sky. The colored illuminations he had seen and mistaken for the Bolg king's Lightforge were in fact gleaming lights inside the dome, set in uniform lines into panels that encircled the transparent room. Beneath the panels was a table of sorts, with a doorway in the horizontal surface from behind which light as bright as the flame-well leaked.

Beyond the clear walls of the sphere he could see the world down below, burning at the horizon, as fire crept over the edges, spreading among the continents he recognized from maps of the Earth.

As bewildering and horrifying as these images were, they paled in comparison to what stood between him and the glass sphere.

Hovering in the air before him was a being, a man of sorts, with the characteristics of several different races and all the aspects of youth except for his eyes, blue eyes, deep as the sea, scored with vertical pupils. Those eyes held the wisdom of the ages, and pain that matched it.

His skin was translucent, motile, altering with each current of air that passed by or through it. The man glowed with the same light as the crystal throne, especially his hair, curls of brilliant gold that seemed almost afire. And despite his knowing eyes, and the calmness of his expression, his clenched jaw betrayed a quiver of nervousness. He stared at Faedryth, as if looking at him for the last time. His mouth moved, and words formed; Faedryth did not hear them in his ears, but rather internally, as if they were resonating in his own throat.

Will I die?

Faedryth felt his burning eyes sting with tears he had no connection to, felt his throat and chest tighten in sorrow he did not understand. He heard his own voice then, speaking as if detached from him; he heard himself cough, then form words that rang with awkward comfort.

Can one experience death if one is not really alive? You, like the rest of the world, have nothing to lose.

The translucent being in front of him nodded, then turned away. Faedryth was suddenly gripped with a sense of sadness and loss that shredded his soul; in his mind he felt himself reach for the lad, only to watch the image fade into darkness.

Then, as if underscoring that he was reliving someone else's memory, he was surrounded with another notion, the impression of the Bolg king he had picked up from the first sight of the parchment scraps, and was left with one last thought, which he heard in the voice of the translucent young man.

Forgive me. In my place, I think you would have done the same. Given the choice, I think you would have wanted it that way, too.

He did not know why, but Faedryth was certain that the strange youth was speaking to the Assassin King.

Overwhelmed and without even the slightest clue of the meaning in what he was perceiving, Faedryth's mind threatened to snap. And worse, deep beneath him, channeling up through the living rock of the crystal throne, he felt a different vibration, atonal and physical and slight, almost imperceptible.

As if the very earth was shrugging, dormant parts of it stirring to life.

Terror consumed him as the speeding vision returned, because this time it was as if he was seeing in darkness into his own lands, his point of sight very far away but growing rapidly closer.

Looking for him with the same clarity he just experienced.

In that moment, the Nain king understood what he had done.

He was seeing as a dragon sees because the sight he had called upon, had tapped with the elemental power of color, *was* dragon sight.

The inner sight of a blind wyrm long asleep in the very bowels of the Earth.

The eldest Sleeping Child, said to comprise a good deal of the Earth's mass. Witheragh, the dragon that had whispered the secret to him, had warned him of a prophecy that one day the Sleeping Child would wake.

And would be famished with hunger after its long sleep that commenced at the beginning of the world.

And he, Faedryth, was nudging it from its slumber, directing its vision into his own kingdom.

A hollow scream tore from Faedryth's throat, a war cry that had gone up from his lungs many times in his life. With the last of his strength he pitched himself from the crystal throne, feeling it strip years from his life as he broke through the column of elemental blue light, tumbling roughly to the floor, bruising himself against the crystal stalagmites. His falling body dislodged the pieces of colored glass, breaking the circle and extinguishing the blue light; leaving only the pulsating dance of the radiance from the flame-well spattering off the ceiling high above.

As Garson pushed the lever with all his might, shutting the vent once more, and the yeoman lowered the crossbow sight, Gyllian hurried to her father. Faedryth was facedown on the stone floor; she turned him over gently and winced, seeing the new whiteness in his beard, the new wrinkles in his brow that had not been there a few moments before. It was as it always was, and yet the strong-willed princess never could become entirely accustomed to the sight of her father, so clear of eye and mind, staring wildly, blankly above him into the dancing fire shadows, panicked by the return of darkness when the vent was closed again.

"What did you see?" she asked gently, stroking his hair and sliding her age-crinkled hand into his.

Faedryth continued to stare, agitated, his eyes glazed, breathing shallowly on the floor of his throne room. Finally, when his eyes finally met Gyllian's, they contained a desperation she had never seen before, not in the horrors of battle, or the nearness of defeat, not on the banks of the swollen river of fire that he had caused to return from its sleep, swallowing mining towns and miners with it. He clutched her hand, trying to form words, but only managing to resemble a fish gasping for the breath of water.

"The Assassin King," he whispered when he finally could generate sound. "We have to stop him."

28

NORTHEASTERN YARIM, AT THE FOOT OF THE MOUNTAINS

No one living, nor anyone dead, had ever known, or at least recorded, the story of how the lost city of Kurimah Milani had come to be built.

Or by whom.

Jutting proudly from the multicolored sands of the westernmost part of the borderlands between Yarim and the upper Bolglands, where the desert clay faded into steppes, then the piedmont, then mountains, Kurimah Milani was old when the oldest tales of history were written. Its minarets and heavy stone walls glistened with a sandy patina that was said to have turned iridescent in the sun, giving some of the merchants who first came upon it the impression that it was an illusion, a mirage at the edge of the vast, empty desert of red clay that stretched for miles at the base of the manganese mountains along the Erim Rus, the Blood River.

The legendary city was said to have been located on the Lucretoria, the ancient merchant road along which trade in silks and seeds, spices, textiles, salt, jewels, and ore was known to have traveled. It was not known how long the indigenous population of the continent had been traversing that primitive road, but by the time the Cymrians arrived in what was now the province of Yarim, the Lucretoria had all but crumbled back into the red clay and the sand, and Kurimah Milani existed in nothing more than legend.

The myth was alive enough still, however, to spawn the occasional pilgrimage, small caravans of the sick and infirm for whom all other options had been exhausted, desperately combing the empty desert for even the smallest sign of the renowned healing springs, the fabled sunbeds in which the suffering could bask, like desert lizards, absorbing the red rays of a healing sun, the fountains of crystalline water that poured forth from the hands of gentle-eyed statues, said to be able to purge the most insistent of disease, or the great gemstone that had been rumored to clear mental deformities or illnesses of the mind with a mere touch.

All they found was the wind and stinging red sand.

Sometimes hope is the only thing that keeps a legend alive. The earthquake that took Kurimah Milani into the depths of the desert centuries before the Cymrians came swept all trace of it from human sight, but even that enormous temblor could not erase the deeper sense that somewhere, lost in the monotonous, endless landscape of cold red clay and scrubby vegetation, was a place where miracles still lurked, dormant for centuries, but nonetheless waiting to be found by the patient, the intrepid, or the desperate. Hope kept that sense alive, even when all other searching was exhausted.

Sometimes, however, there is more than hope.

Sometimes there is reason.

The dragon could hear the music long before she knew what she had found.

Exhaustion owned her now; she no longer had the strength to be a slave to hatred. She had long passed the point of return, her mind fading into the numbness that precedes death. Deep within the ground, her dragon sense could no longer discern any minutiae in the world around her, but rather it was monitoring her fading life, counting the beats of her three-chambered heart as it strained to pump the blood welling within her.

And so, when her darkening mind heard the first notes of the ancient song echoing through the earth, she could not tell whether the sound was from the outside world, or whether it was just the noise of her own death approaching.

After a mile or more of crawling toward it, her thoughts began to clear, her mind to focus, and the beast realized that the tone was modulating in a consistent fashion, following a musical pattern that was soothing to her fractured mind and desiccating body. She could feel her blood-starved tissues rehydrating slightly, humming with a renewed vitality. Her heartbeat strengthened, her sight brightened where it had gone dim.

The dragon stopped and lay still for a moment, listening.

The earth through which she was traveling seemed to recede, leaving her tattered skin buzzing pleasantly. The music reached deep into her torn flesh and revitalized it, giving her just enough strength to gather herself and continue her journey, her dragon sense, now awake again, following the song in the ground like a beacon.

$\mathcal{T}$he louder the vibration echoed through the earth, the more confident the dragon felt. There was a sense of revitalization, rejuvenation, in each mile she traveled, stripping away the despair and fear, encouraging her even as the blood continued to flow from her, even as her heart began to fail.

Perhaps I am entering the Afterlife, she mused as she crawled, though she had little remembrance what the Afterlife was.

She was unaware of the disruption of earth she was causing in her journey. As always, when she traveled at a depth of less than a mile, the strata of earth erupted, leaving fissures in her wake, uprooting what few specimens of scrub vegetation remained in the lifeless desert, uncovering long-dead skeletons of men and animals and carts that had been long lost in the shifting sands.

The music filled her ears now, humming in her skin beneath the scales of her hide. It filled her mind with dreams that bled over into her eyes, and so as she traveled, following the sound, the sight into the Past that was her birthright began to take over. What was visible to her eyes was the dry and lifeless clay that the desert had become in the Present, but the second sight within her envisioned something entirely different, a younger, newer land where desert flowers still bloomed, where low-growing trees offered shade to the native animals of the wasteland and the caravans of humans and dromedaries that plied the Lucretoria, passing by Kurimah Milani in great splashes of the color and noise of commerce.

She was seeing the place not as it lay buried before her, but as it once had been, two millennia before.

Looming before her was a glistening sight, shining in the rays of the setting sun. Minarets towered high toward the clouds, a musical welcome ringing from their domed towers. Beyond the entrance gates clear water from fountains leapt and splashed, catching the sunset's rays and falling into lapis lazuli pools, carrying the warm colors with it.

The dragon's damaged heart leapt in excitement. The concept of mirage was completely beyond her ability to conceive, the understanding that she was still within the earth completely gone from her awareness. In her mind she could see all around her the glistening walls of the healing city as she passed through the great gated aqueduct, where streams of crystal water rained down on all those who entered. She closed her eyes as she passed beneath the memory of the medicinal waterfall, feeling the coolness of the spray as it showered her skin, easing her pain, cooling the fire within her.

Insanity must cause the arms to grow, for nothing is out of reach of the madman, a sage once said within her hearing. Had her fragmented mind seen the darkness of the tunnels that, in reality, loomed around her, if it could grasp that the healing spray was nothing more than showers of grit and sand falling upon her, it might have kept her from discovering what treasure still actually remained beneath the blowing sand and red desert clay.

Water, the beast thought as she burrowed past the broken towers buried in twenty centuries of sand, past the wreckage of stone walls and shattered statuary, leaving a trail of dark blood in her wake. Nothing but the song of the place was sustaining her now; her body, more shell than flesh, hummed with the vibration of this place of ancient healing, but even the power of the memory of Kurimah Milani could not replace the life's blood that was leaking from her sundered heart. *There is water here, I know it.*

And she was right. Even though the infamous water gardens had been utterly destroyed in the temblor, and while the copious healing pools and mineral baths filled to overflowing by hot springs running down from the mountains in the distance had been consumed at the same moment of cataclysm, deep beneath the surface sand there was still the remnants of a stream that trickled through the buried vaults that had once been public baths.

In her confusion the dragon had come upon one of the central fountains of the city, a deep, long cavern that had, in its heyday, run the length of a vast interior courtyard surrounded by columns of gleaming marble encrusted with mother-of-pearl from mollusk shells culled from the Erim Rus. Her inner vision led her immediately to the stream, which she saw as a deep pool in which splashing spray danced skyward in time to the fluctuating music of the place. Greedily she drank from it, following its source in search of more water.

A vibration surrounded her suddenly, humming in a tone very different from the one she had been following, irritating her eyes and parts of her skin, but she shook it off. At the headwaters of the stream her mouth and eyes were suddenly filled with sunlight, golden and thick enough to be palpable.

The wyrm gasped in delight. The amber nectar was sweet on her tongue and soothing to the caustic burning of her throat that had been plaguing her since her injury. She drank in more of the thickened sunlight, swallowed it in desperate gulps, feeling its sustenance fill her, strengthen her, cooling the fire in her belly, bringing her peace.

She rolled onto her back in the stream and exhaled slowly, then fell into dreamless, healing sleep.

29

THE HOLY CITADEL OF SEPULVARTA, THE CITY OF REASON

$\mathcal{B}$efore leaving Sepulvarta in secret to meet with the Lord and Lady Cymrian, the Patriarch had ordered the city sealed.

Being the central location of all holy orders within the Patrician faith, as well as a place of pilgrimage to those of other practices, even as far back as the polytheistic religions of the continent that preceded the Cymrian era, Sepulvarta had a long reputation of religious tolerance and free access. The road that led from the trans-Orlandan thoroughfare south to the city, known as the Pilgrim's Road, was always teeming with human and animal traffic, pilgrims and clergy, tradesmen and merchants, all making their way for their own reasons to the independent city-state. On normal days it might take as little as an hour to traverse the road and enter the city; on holy days, or days of heavy import at the time of festivals or famine, the wait could be the better part of a full turn of the sun. On rare occasions visitors to Sepulvarta could pass more than a few nights, sleeping in the street or at one of the many hostels and inns that lined the roadway, waiting to be allowed entrance through the one gate in the enormous wall that circled the entire city.

Sealing the city was a precaution that was not unheard of. Occasionally the flow of visitors to the sacred spots and shrines overwhelmed the places of hospitality within the city's walls. With the inns and wayhouses full, the taverns and pubs gained more guests and patrons than they could accommodate, leading to long lines for food and ale, ugly dispositions and threats, and often violence, all of which was deemed unacceptable for a holy city. The previous Patriarchs, rather than removing the hospitality, as had been done in the oldest days, chose to keep the ale and remove the patrons, at least temporarily, until the holy days were over and the flow of traffic returned to normal.

So when the city was ordered sealed, no one thought the better of it.

As it turned out, it was the one thing that prevented its immediate destruction and that of the farming settlements around it.

Sepulvarta had the worst of both lands that it bordered. North of mountainous Sorbold, south of the wide-open plains of Roland, it was a city perched on a small hill on the edge of the low piedmont and in the midst of the flattest part of the Krevensfield Plain, which served to make it easily visible to travelers and all but indefensible. Fortunately, as the holy See of both nations, there had never been any reason for it to mount a defense. Even in the seven hundred years of the Cymrian War, as the Krevensfield Plain burned with atrocities and the mountains rang with horrific battle, the holy city remained untouched, though, as Anborn had informed the Council, that had merely been by coincidence. By the time his army had taken the farming settlements in the region, it had been far easier to quarter the soldiers in places of plentiful food where they were dispersed, rather than making a headquarters in an obvious place that was just asking to be laid siege. So Sepulvarta remained intact, unspoiled and untainted by the horror that took place all around it.

Anborn's assertions of its lack of strategic value for quartering troops notwithstanding, many citizens of Sepulvarta chose to attribute their good fortune and safekeeping to the beneficence of the All-God and the protection of the Spire. The Spire was a tower with a base that took up an entire city block, reaching a thousand feet in the air to the very top, where it was crowned with a single piece of elemental ether, said to be a fragment of the star Seren that once shone over the Lost

Island of Serendair half a world away. That single piece of star illuminated the city by day as well as night, blessing it with light even in the fiercest of rainstorms, or on the cloudiest of days. Pilgrims approaching the city could make out its radiance for almost a week before reaching it, guided not only by the light of the beacon but by the power emanating from it.

The Spire reached to the clouds above the great basilica that was the cornerstone of the city of Sepulvarta, the cathedral dedicated to the element of ether known as Lianta'ar. Each of the five primordial elements, sometimes called the Paints of the Creator, had a basilica dedicated to it, but Lianta'ar, which was believed to mean in the old language of the Cymrians *Lord All-God, Light of the World,* was by far the grandest, as well as being the youngest. It was the seat of the Patriarch, the leader of the faith, as well as the place where the yearly rituals that protected all adherents to that faith were celebrated. The prayers of the faithful were eventually channeled to this place, and offered to the Creator through the Spire, as close as one could conceivably get to placing one's request directly at the feet of God.

The fourteen-foot-thick wall that surrounded the city was more for pomp and circumstance, as well as for decoration, than for realistic protection. Being unscathed had led the elite soldiers of Sepulvarta to become primarily ceremonial as well. Their uniforms were no longer the armor of men that had to do battle, but rather grand colorful regalia which displayed the many liturgical symbols and colors of the Patriarchy. They checked the visitors coming in and out of the city, maintained a watch on the wall and a guard at the manse of the Patriarch the changing of which was one of the most sought-after spectacles by pilgrims to the city, the defenses in place were woefully inadequate to withstand anything more than an initial assault.

They had never had to be more than that.

The captain of the city's guard, a man named Fynn, was wandering the wall, checking on the archery mounts and enjoying the breeze that was heavy with hints of spring when he happened to gaze off to the south, where the mountains of Sorbold blackened the horizon in the distance.

He blinked in astonishment.

What had always seemed to be a fairly distant horizon appeared to have moved noticeably closer.

After a moment it became clear that it was steadily moving closer still.

The captain cleared his eyes and looked again.

Spread out across the dry plain to the south an army battle line was approaching in columns, clad in the regalia and flying the colors of the emperor of Sorbold—mounted cavalry, infantry, and great cavalcades of wagons bearing ballistae, catapults, and other weapons of siege. At quick count, the captain thought there might be as many as five divisions of several thousand men each, all moving forward across the steppes to the plain, relentlessly but with no particular hurry.

There was no mistaking their destination.

Had he been more battle-hardened, more accustomed to the need for readiness in war, the captain might have gained a few seconds in his response. Those extra seconds would ultimately have made no measurable difference in outcome.

When he finally overcame his shock, he ran to the nearest guard tower, the one to the left of the gate, which unlike the portcullises preferred by other cities was comprised of two enormous wooden doors in which the holy symbols of all five elements had been carved, crowned with the silver six-pointed star of the Patriarch. The gatekeeper was sleeping, his attention unneeded with the city sealed. Fynn shook him violently awake.

"Ring the alarm! *Ring the alarm,* damn you! Look!"

The gatekeeper shot to his feet and almost fell from the wall. He lurched out of the shelter of the tower and began ringing the call to arms. The clanging bell sounded harshly over the city, which was accustomed to the musical ringing of hourly prayer bells from the towers of assorted houses of worship and the great carillon of the basilica, which played hymns and calls to prayer with the rising and setting of the sun each day.

In spite of the city being sealed, there was always morning traffic within the city walls and without, as merchants plied the streets, women went from shop to shop, tent to tent in search of foodstuffs and goods they needed, children ran about, and members of religious orders passed from one sacred place to another. The tinny shout of the warning bells brought that traffic to a standstill, that muted noise of ordinary life faded into shocked silence.

"Get to your houses!" the captain of the guard shouted from atop the wall.

The people in the street below stared up at him, not moving.

"Go, you mindless *sheep*," Fynn snarled down at them. He turned to the gate guard.

"Send a runner to the manse to alert the abbot and the Patriarch. Get all of the archers up here, and have everyone else go through the streets. Tell the people—er, tell them—" He fumbled into silence.

"What shall I tell them, sir?"

The captain inhaled, trying to remember his training. "I don't know, tell them to begin storing water in vessels, that's it—and send two riders out of the gate and down the entranceway to tell the merchants and innkeepers to get inside the city walls immediately—and whatever pilgrims are milling about out there. Hurry; we have to seal the gate when they get within range."

"What is happening, sir?" the young soldier asked, his eyes glazed with fright. "Why is the Sorbold army marching on the holy city?"

"I've no idea—but that's irrelevant. I only know that we are not prepared to withstand a siege." Fynn looked over the wall again and went pale. "Get word to the manse above all else—perhaps the Patriarch will know what to do, or he can send a message for help from other quarters. *Make haste*. And pray."

The gate guard saluted and climbed down the ladder to the streets below, pushing aside a gawking throng as he made his way through them to the guard barracks.

The captain of the guard turned back to the south. The army was advancing unhurriedly, but now they were near enough for him to hear the war toms echoing off the mountains as they came. There was something terrifying about the sound of those drums, deep and slow in rhythm but relentless and insistent.

The stone on the wall began to rumble slightly as the ground began to pick up the vibrations from the approaching horses and wagon wheels.

He continued to stare at the coming army until the archers he had summoned mustered around and below him. He looked up and shook off the shock that was beginning to numb the edges of his mind, making him feel wooly and thick-headed.

"Get into position, and prepare to train your arrows on anyone attempting to breech the wall or the gate," he directed. "Aim at the closest first, and keep firing into the same target until he dies. If they bring a battering ram—and they will need to if they think they are going to force open that gate—keep firing at the men bearing it first; as long as they don't get the gate open, you can keep the rest of the army out." The archers, largely inexperienced in conflict, nodded, trembling.

Fynn shouted down to one of the footguards. "You—get to the smithy, tell them we are in need of whatever coals or hot pitch they can locate. Use the braziers from the temples and the basilica if need be, use incense, anything, but *get something up here* that can repel an assault on the gate." The guard ran off.

With the wall fortified as best as it could be, the captain climbed down the ladder and into the streets just as the basilica bells stopped ringing the musical hour and began tolling an alarm. The sound rang out over the entire city, emanating from the base of the Spire itself, and carrying an authority with it that no other signal had.

At this the population panicked. The mighty gate was dragged open for the last time, and a sea of humanity and animal carts rushed in, stampeding the people already in the streets. The gate tenders tried to push the gates closed again but the throng was too great; they trampled anyone or anything in their way in their desperate rush to gain shelter against the army that now was in sight even from beneath the barricade.

"Get inside the basilica—take shelter there," the captain of the guard shouted, but his words were drowned in the cacophony of the multitude pressing into Sepulvarta.

"Get me a spyglass," he said to one of the soldiers attempting to gain control of the crowd and failing. The soldier saluted and ran off, returning many minutes later, his regalia torn by contact with the crowd. He handed the instrument to the captain, who climbed the battlement again, extended the spyglass, and looked into the distance.

The insignia of the column at the lead appeared to be that of the Mountain Guard of Jierna'sid, the emperor's own regiment. They were clad in banded mail and helm, with heavy crossbows and scimitars standard issue. The spring sun as it rose glinted off their armor and helms, reflecting the light back in blinding waves. The captain's stomach cramped.

At the head of the column a soldier was walking, the army in step with him. The captain adjusted the spyglass, as it was distorting his vision of the leader. He looked again, and realized, to his horror, that in fact the glass was reading true.

The man at the head of the column appeared to be almost a giant, standing easily ten feet tall. He had a flat aspect; in fact, for as little definition there was to his face, he might as well have been made of stone. His movements were awkward and lumbering, his face primitive, but his pace was sure. That soldier seemed almost oblivious of the columns marching behind him; his face was a mask, his expression unchanging.

He was also immensely tall, almost twice the size of the other soldiers, who were following in his train as if he were a hero of renown, or a demi-god.

For all that Sepulvarta was a place of religious oddities, strange ceremonies, and even the occasional miraculous happening, the captain of the guard felt that what he was witnessing was so absurd that he must be dreaming. In the thousand years or so since its founding, the city of Sepulvarta had never seen aggression, primarily because it was understood to be the All-God's city; the thought that anyone would attack a holy seat was almost too bizarre to comprehend, especially adherents to that faith, as the Sorbolds were.

Yet the columns were advancing.

A line of stragglers remained outside the wall, watching the approaching army with a mixture of trepidation and fascination.

"Get those idiots inside the gate!" He grabbed one of the archers. "Aim at the feet of one of them and let fly. They'll move, or they'll be left outside." He turned to the gate tenders. "Prepare to close the gates!"

The call went down the wall as the archer took aim, then fired into the crowd. His arrow wobbled off the string and sliced through the leg of a peasant woman gawking at the approaching army.

Pandemonium ensued.

With a crushing swell, the remaining crowd beyond the wall surged forward, pushing everyone, including women and small children, into a wedge. Screaming, the phalanx of people outside the city swarmed those lingering inside the gates who were waiting for the narrow inner streets to clear. The captain of the guard watched in numb dismay as blood began to flow, children were trampled, violence broke out among the former pilgrims turned refugees.

"Get to the basilica—take shelter there," he repeatedly shouted, the noise of the mayhem drowning him out.

A soldier farther down the wall was signaling frantically to him. Fynn could see that behind the soldier a tall, thin man with a fringe of gray hair in later middle age was standing, clad in robes of the basilica, his arms wrapped tightly around his abdomen in fear. He hurried along the wall, stepping carefully around the archery posts that were going to be the equivalent of tossing a single bucket of water on a brushfire once the army arrived.

When he reached the soldier, he recognized the older man as Gregory, the sexton of Lianta'ar, one of the Patriarch's closest advisors.

"What's—what's going on?" the cleric demanded. "There must be a mistake."

"That's entirely possible, Your Grace," the young captain said, "but they appear to be coming with an intent that makes action necessary." He gave the signal to the gate tenders, and the enormous wooden doors were pushed shut with much noise and great effort, then sealed against the coming army.

Fynn turned to the sexton again.

"What does the Patriarch instruct us to do?" he asked nervously. "Does he have orders for us? We have never had to repel an attack before, Your Grace. We need guidance."

The sexton's face went slack.

"Er, no, His Grace, the Patriarch, has not issued any specific orders," he said haltingly. "I believe he trusts in you, and in the men, to keep the holy city safe."

"Your Grace—"

"That's all, Captain. I have to get to the aviary—it may be necessary to send a winged messenger to the Alliance requesting help."

The captain of the guard smiled in relief.

"That would be a boon, Your Grace."

The sexton nodded. "Carry on." He made his way down the wall and into the sea of refugees.

Fynn returned to his spyglass.

The army of Sorbold was growing nearer, following their gigantic standard bearer. The rumbling now was audible, caught between the mountains to the south and the hill on which the city was situated, it echoed ever more threateningly as the columns approached. Fynn and the rest of the city's guard settled in to wait.

All through the morning and into the afternoon the army approached, never stopping, just relentlessly marching onward to the steady tempo of the war toms. Finally, as the sun was set high in the welkin of the sky, burning red with the brilliance of a spring afternoon, they came within unaided sight.

Fynn had been counting all day. By his reckoning there were five divisions, each consisting of ten thousand soldiers and supply troops. The giant at their lead did not seem to speak or give orders; the army merely followed him across the open steppes.

Strangely, the heavy ballistae, catapults, and other siege weapons were relegated to the rear of the ranks. Fynn thought that odd; from what he remembered of his training, generally those weapons were kept in the mid ranks of an advancing army, to make their setup quick while protecting them from the initial wave of repulsion.

In addition, there were dozens of enormous carts with flat sides, on which wide, low tents had been erected. Fynn could not see what was inside those tents, but the sight of them made his intestines threaten to turn to water.

"Any word from the Patriarch?" he asked the soldiers milling the streets below the wall. The men shook their heads nervously. Fynn sighed. "All right, then, we wait. We can do little else. Make certain the population is in shelter as much as possible." His words rang hollow.

Suddenly the great war toms ceased.

All around the holy city the noise of the approach slowed, the creaking of wagon wheels, the groaning of wood, the tromping of boots and the squeaking of armor, the muted clopping of heavy horse, the rattle of weapons still sheathed, all fell to a quieter level.

A single officer on horseback with two aides-de-camp broke off from the ranks to the right of the giant and headed for the gate. One of the aides-de-camp had a hooded falcon on his arm. They stopped outside of bow range. The officer rode slightly forward while the aide loosed the leather jesses that bound the falcon's feet.

"I am Fhremus, commander of the imperial army of Sorbold," he announced, his voice carrying on the wind with expertise born of a long command. "Harm the bird, and it will be considered an attack upon the whole of the army." He nodded to the aide, and the man let slip the falcon.

"Where's the sexton?" Fynn demanded from atop the wall.

The soldiers, massing beyond the gates, parted, and the cleric was brought forth.

The bird took wing and rose to a pitch that would crest the wall. It warbled gracefully, then went into a rapid stoop, dropping an oilcloth scroll over the wall, and banked, returning effortlessly to its handler.

The message was rapidly retrieved and handed to Gregory. The sexton broke the seal with trembling hands and read the message, which was graphed in the common tongue of the continent, as well as the sacred script of the Patrician faith.

> *Constantin, the Patriarch of Sepulvarta, is a heretic who has committed an atrocity against the Creator, the people of Sorbold, and the Empire of the Sun. Open the gate, send him out, and we will spare the city.*

Gregory stared at the oilcloth, then tossed it to the ground angrily.

"Sacrilege!" he fumed. "Sacrilege and blasphemy." He turned to Fynn. "This is an untenable demand that cannot even be repeated, let alone considered—hold the gate, Captain, keep the wall as long as you can." He glanced up at the Spire, the shining star atop it gleaming in the fading light. "May the All-God defend us."

He made his way back to the manse, knowing, unlike anyone else in the city, that at least one of the reasons that the demand would not be met was that the Patriarch was already gone.

$\mathcal{H}$ow long shall we wait, Commander?" Minus, one of Fhremus's aides-de-camp, asked as the falcon returned to Trevnor, the other.

"We will give them an hour," Fhremus said. "That seems sporting."

He glanced over his shoulder at the titan. Faron, as the emperor had called him, stood silent and unmoving, his arms at his sides, looking for all the world the statue that he once was. *Perhaps he remembers this place, where the Patriarch imbued him with unnatural and unholy life,* Fhremus thought, disgusted at the thought. He had no idea what feeling the statue was capable of, if any, but it would not have surprised him if it were ready to exact vengeance of its own.

When the hour passed, with nothing but the constant ringing of the alarm bells of the basilica as a reply, Fhremus turned to Minus.

"Time's up," he said. "Prepare the iacxsis."

He turned west and watched the sun as it continued its downward path toward night, burning hotly over the wide Krevensfield Plain.

30

KREVENSFIELD PLAIN, NORTH OF SEPULVARTA

℃he hastily assembled support force had stopped at each garrison and town along the trans-Orlandan thoroughfare. From western Navarne through southern Bethany, Anborn and Constantin had presented Ashe's articles of command at each of the way stations of the guarded mail caravan and each outpost of Alliance reserve, and come away with whatever meager offerings in men and supplies there were to be had.

In spite of the region being sparsely populated, and contrary to the Lord Marshal's dark assessment of the preparations Ashe had made for war, he and the Patriarch discovered ready caches of willing soldiers, highly trained and able to depart within minutes. They had been routinely escorting travelers and merchant wares across the continent for more than four years, and knew every side route and alternate pathway from Bethe Corbair and Canrif all the way to the seaport of Port Fallon in Avonderre. Additionally, they had made standard use of the system of avian messengers that Llauron had begun and Rhapsody had established, and so by the time they came to the next successive encampment, they were pleased to discover all available men-at-arms saddled and awaiting them. The soldiers fell in easily, and took over the tasks of maintaining what few heavy weapons the Lord Marshal had brought, as well as the wagon on which the walking machine was being transported.

By the time they had reached the last of the outposts they had assembled a small but eager force of slightly less than ten thousand men, mostly career soldiers but occasionally joined by farmers and merchants who had trained alongside them. Anborn was astonished to discover in some of the later garrisons that volunteers had streamed into the surrounding farms and villages just for the honor of getting to ride with the renowned Lord Marshal of the Cymrian War who was coming to the rescue of the holy city.

"Next time we'll tell them we're after wenches in the whorehouses of Evermere," he said to the Patriarch. "We'll get thirty thousand." The holy man smiled within the hood of his peasant's cloak.

In the small farming village of Brindlesgate, the last stop before the southerly road to Sepulvarta, a clutch of young boys of eleven summers or fewer were waiting atop a mule, a nag, and on foot, metal pots on their heads and hoes in their hands. The soldiers quartered in the barracks nearest the village had shooed them off repeatedly, but the youths kept returning, waiting for their chance to join the mayhem. Finally they caught the notice of the Lord Marshal, who ordered the force to wait in the roadway and rode up before them, reining his horse to a stop.

"What have we here? More recruits?"

Five young faces stared back at him, mouths agape.

"Yes, sir," the only one who could muster his voice replied.

"Very good," Anborn said flatly. "Come along."

The soldiers looked from one to another, then opened the ranks for the boys.

"All right, then," the Lord Marshal said, turning back to the lead, "let's be off."

The cohort traveled south, over the Pilgrim's Road, with the rising sun to their right. After three leagues the Lord Marshal called a halt at the edge of a small area of scrub pines and broke off from the group again.

"I need riders familiar with the following settlements for a critical mission," he announced seriously, "Southtown, Meadowfork, Hylan's

Landing, and Brindlesgate. If you know the routes to these places, present yourselves."

The ranks parted, and soldiers from each of the settlements named rode forward. In the rear came the five young boys from Brindlesgate.

"Encamp here," Anborn instructed. "You are to form the rear guard; all along the road from here to Sepulvarta I will be positioning riders in encampments to carry the evacuation order east to west and to reinforce the fields. Turn back anyone traveling this road until I come through again or you receive orders otherwise. Understood?"

The soldiers nodded and dismounted, but the boys remained atop their steeds or with their makeshift weapons, looking from one to the other.

"But, Lord Marshal," the brave one blurted as Anborn turned to leave, "we want to go with you, sir. We want to see combat."

The General looked back. "You will," he said briskly, ignoring their pleading looks and pointing at the scrub pine. "I need berms made here with pickets set against a possible cavalry charge; a thousand paces to either side of the road as well." He rode back to the head of the column and the cohort set off, leaving the rear guard behind.

"Hop to, lads," one of the soldiers said as they began unpacking their mounts. "You wanted to see what war is like? War involves a lot of waiting. But remember, preparations are crucial to victory. The entire unit strikes the killing blow, not just the arm of one man."

The young boys sighed miserably and set to work.

The ride to Sepulvarta was invigorating, Anborn observed. There was something deep within the cynical core of his being that had been planted in his youth, a devotion to the military brotherhood that had been with him all his life. Encamped at night, out in the darkness among the fires and sleeping soldiers, he thought back beyond the centuries of war and desolation, looking beyond the betrayal and the atrocity he had witnessed again and again to a time when all he wanted in the world was this, a life of selflessness and defense, of shared sacrifice with brothers-in-arms. For all that he had become acid over the years, had grown to trust very little in the world and hope for even less, there was still in his soul, black and twisted though it was, something that was moved by the camaraderie, the devotion to duty, that he was witnessing again.

He recalled how in his youth the mother who did not understand his desire to learn the ways of the sword foisted him off on Oelendra, the Lirin champion of Tyrian, a First Generation Cymrian and hero from the old world. She was the Iliachenva'ar, the bearer of the sword that Rhapsody now carried, and had trained him well, though he had never truly felt her approval, which he craved beyond that of anyone he had known. Anborn leaned back against his bedroll, looking up at a night sky scattered with bright stars, and remembered her words to him.

Fight with your strengths as they are, not as you would wish them to be.

He inhaled, taking in the acrid taste of ash from the fires, the smell of the stew and horse leather.

In those days he had been scrawny, the youngest brother with much to prove. Edwyn Griffyth would learn his father's ways of architecture and engineering and invention, and would battle with him over his responsibilities as the heir apparent; Llauron would follow his mother's teachings and go into the Filidic priesthood, serving as protector to the Great White Tree and the Invoker of the Filids, but Anborn, neither in line for the throne nor by temperament suited to the religious life, craved nothing more than to make his parents proud through prowess on the battlefield.

The Lirin champion had taught him to know better, to understand that military might must be tempered with a righteousness, to compensate for what he lacked in physical maturity as a young lad with speed and skill born of practice and intelligence. He had seen the same eagerness in the mirror that he had witnessed in the eyes of the youth of Brindlesgate, and understood what a holy thing it was, how easily lost or perverted it could become without a hero, like the Lirin champion, to nurture it in the right way.

He smiled wryly, knowing that he was just such a hero to those boys.

Oelendra had cautioned him against idolatry as well. *You may admire my skill, and seek to emulate my career,* she told him early on in his training. *But do not confuse that with* me. *I have made many missteps in my time, have done things of which I am not proud, because, in spite of my godlike longevity, I am mortal. So are you. Learn to forgive your heroes and yourself. At one time or another, you will need to do both if you are going to live this life, the life of a would-be Kinsman.*

They had both achieved that honor, he mused, so her words must have been true.

Rhapsody had said something much the same to him as they parted. *You cannot purge anything that has happened to you, as if it were an impurity of steel to be smelted away in a forge fire. All that has gone before has made you what you are, like notes in a symphony. Whole or lame, you are who you are.* Ryle hira, *as the Lirin say. Life is what it is. Forgive yourself.*

The Lord Marshal hesitated for a moment, then rolled stiffly to his side, seized his leather pack, and pulled it closer. He unwrapped the bindings and pulled forth the conch shell she had given him, fondly remembering her pale face in the reflected light of the fire.

At least try to be as whole as you can, if not for yourself, then for the men you lead. And for me.

"All right, m'lady," he said softly to himself. "I suppose there is no harm in trying, especially since you aren't around to see."

He lay back against the bedroll and put the shell to his ear. All he could make out was the crashing sound of the sea wind above ocean waves. He exhaled and drifted off to sleep, dreaming of faces he knew he would never see again.

The battle for Sepulvarta was lost before it began.

For over an hour the defenders waited in trepidation, gazing from the wall at the fifty thousand men encamped outside their city. The army had fanned out until the wall was surrounded on all sides, but then everything seemed to grind to a halt; some of the soldiers made battlefield camps around small cookfires, while the cavalry remained mounted but at ease. The wagons carrying the ballistae and catapults and other weapons of siege remained untouched, while the army itself did little or nothing to advance farther past the line of initial confrontation. If anything, the siege appeared to be one of wills alone, as no further threats were issued, no weapons trained on the gate.

"They are going to wait us out," Gregory, the sexton of Lianta'ar, said, his voice brittle. He had presided over the quartering of the itinerant faithful, pilgrims, and tourists within the walls of the beautiful basilica, and already was showing the strain of having so many people in the people's cathedral. "Thankfully food and water is plentiful, and the Lord Cymrian will surely not sit by and allow the army of Sorbold to command the deliverance of the head of the Patrician faith. So we are at an impasse. We will never concede to their demands. Sooner or later we will either be rescued or they will give up in boredom and go away."

"I hope you are right, Your Grace," said Fynn uneasily. He was watching the throngs of people milling about in the city streets, far too many to be forced indoors in spite of the orders he had issued, clogging the narrow roadways around the shops and shrines.

When a second hour had passed, the falconer of the holy See appeared.

"I am ready to send that message to Haguefort if you still wish to do so, Your Grace," he said to the sexton.

"I see no other choice," Gregory replied. "Very well, let slip the raptor."

The falconer bowed respectfully and loosed the jesses. The bird flapped its wings twice while on his arm, then took wing and rose into the air, catching a warm updraft and heading north. It ascended to a pitch that was as high as the buildings that lined the street leading to the spire.

A shadow streaked overhead, sailing above the gate and over the city streets. Larger than a horse, it shot through the air on the trail of the falcon, then, with a sickening *crack,* caught the bird in jaws that snapped audibly and swallowed it in flight, sending a shower of bloody feathers spiraling down on the soldiers below.

A collective gasp rose from the streets.

A moment later the sky darkened with similar shadows.

From all sides of the city great beasts appeared in the air above the houses and shops, sailing on wide, batlike wings. They were serpentine in their movements, with long barbed tails that thrashed as they flew; their legs and jaws, however, were insectoid, sharply jointed, like the plague locusts that had been one of their progenitors.

Atop each of them was a rider with a burning bundle of wheygrass stalks soaked in pitch or oil.

Within seconds the thatched roofs of several buildings had ignited in flame. Black smoke poured from them, followed by the shouts of witnesses on the cobbled street and screams of terror from those trapped within the buildings.

"What—what in the name of the All-God is *happening?*" Gregory demanded shakily, interposing himself in front of Fynn.

"With all due respect, Your Grace, get out of my bloody *way,*" the captain of the guard shouted back, shoving the priest to the side and hurrying to the wall. "Fire at the beasts!" he screamed at the archers, who were staring over their heads in shock.

Another round of burning bundles descended from above. More roofs caught flame, the glistening white stone buildings that Sepulvarta was famous for glowed pink in the firelight as roofs and carts ignited in the streets below, raining burning ash into the streets and onto the terrified crowds.

"To the basilica!" Fynn shouted to the soldiers in the streets, but his voice was drowned in the noise of panic. He pointed above for the benefit of the stunned archers again. "Fire at the damned *beasts*!"

One of the archers finally was able to shake off his shock and take aim as the flying lizard soared over his head and landed on a nearby roof. He drew back and let fly, a clean, hefty shot that caught the beast square in the side, just below the wing.

The arrow bounced off harmlessly with a resounding *thud,* the same noise it would make against a cobblestone or brick.

We are surely done for, Fynn thought. "All right, then," he said, struggling to keep his voice calm. "Shoot the rider." The archer, shaking, complied, another clean shot that made its mark in the split of the man's cuirass.

The rider straightened up sharply, then fell heavily from his monstrous mount into the street below.

The captain of the guard and the archer both gasped in delight. "That's it!" Fynn exclaimed. "That's how we take them—aim for the *riders*."

The beast seemed to stare at them for a moment. Then it stood and launched off the roof with a great leap on its insectoid legs, diving down to the street below, its serpentine head snapping viciously. The pilgrims, cowering in doorways of burning buildings, screamed as if in one voice as it caught a fleeing woman in its razor jaws, snapped her spine with a single bite, then took off in a great leap into the sky again, its prize in its mouth.

Madness descended upon the City of Reason.

Shremus observed the initial assault from the air with satisfaction.

He surveyed the smoke pouring into the sky from the center of the city, black and oily with the rancid odor of pitch and burning thatch. A plethora of birds had taken wing, roosting swallows, pigeons and doves that made their nests in the eaves of buildings that were now alight. From within the city, great cries of anguish and horror could be heard issuing forth over the wall.

He turned from his seat on horseback and looked up at the titan, who had been standing stock still since they had arrived at the city gate.

"Are you ready, Faron?" he asked, not certain if it was even awake or aware.

The milky blue irises in the stone orbs appeared. The giant statue nodded perfunctorily.

Fhremus swallowed, then cleared his throat. "Very well, then. Open the gate."

The gigantic statue flexed its arms and legs, then began to walk forward alone.

The commander turned to his aides-de-camp. "At my signal," he said. They saluted and rode back to the column heads.

The entire army watched as their standard bearer neared the great gate of Sepulvarta, a gate that had not been broached in the thousand years since it was hung.

ℱire! *Fire,* damn it!" Fynn screamed to the archers.

The men, reeling from the aerial attack, from the smoke and the burning ash raining down on them from the buildings around them, turned their concentration on the titan and let fly.

About half the arrows found their marks. About half of those shattered; the rest bounced off the enormous statue with the same resounding *thud* they had heard from missile contact with the flying beast.

"Dear All-God," Fynn whispered. "This must be a nightmare."

His words were echoed by the deafening sound of stone contacting wood.

The archers reloaded, shaking, and let fly again, with the same result—every arrow that impacted the stone man shattered or was repelled without apparent harm.

"Save your arrows," Fynn cautioned, looking out over the wall at the force surrounding the city. "They're preparing to storm the gate—hold your fire for those it might actually affect. Stand as long as the arrows hold out, then topple the braziers onto anyone entering the gates. Make that count—it will probably be your only chance. Godspeed, gentlemen—it's been good to serve with you."

"You as well, sir," came a weak chorus of trembling voices.

The wall nearest the gate shuddered as another blow battered the wood, sending splinters flying into the air. Fynn steeled his nerve and looked down over the wall.

The stone giant was slamming his fist into the holy gate of Sepulvarta, punching deep holes into the wood, then ripping apart the ancient timbers of trees that had been made of Living Stone with his hands. The gate screamed as if alive as he tore it asunder.

In the distance a clarion call sounded from within the Sorbold columns.

The archers raised their bows, training them on the front line.

With a hissing streak, one of the flying beasts soared over the wall and snatched an archer in its jaws, toppling a few more into the streets below.

The gate crashed open with a sound like thunder in the mountain passes.

With a roar, the attacking force surged like a tidal wave into the city of Sepulvarta as the sun began its descent below the horizon.

NORTH OF SEPULVARTA ON
THE PILGRIM'S ROAD

Fornication!"

Anborn dragged his horse to a shocked halt. The Alliance forces quickly followed suit behind him.

As they came to a stop in the center of the Pilgrim's Road, the force that had assembled with the greatest of speed and had ridden with alacrity to the rescue of the holy city could only stare from atop horses dancing in place at the sight that unfolded before them.

Black smoke billowed from the towers and rooftops of the city, clogging the sky with ash and oily grit. Flames could be seen ascending from the rooftops, dancing off the tower of the Spire and lighting the night sky for miles around.

In the shining reflection of those fires, black winged beasts circled in the hazy air above the city proper, diving occasionally with the snap of an adder striking.

And even from where they were, five miles or more off, the sound of screaming could be heard, rending the night.

"Lord Marshal—"

"Silence!" Anborn thundered, shifting atop his horse.

The Patriarch rode his side and stopped next to him. His great craggy face, hidden within a peasant's hood, was white as the ceremonial robes he often wore. "What are those figures flying above the city?" he asked, his thunderous voice strained.

"I've no idea," said Anborn, "but their presence changes everything. We are going to need a new plan of attack. I was prepared to break a simple siege, which we could do, even outnumbered. But with the enemy attacking from the *air*—"

"Contemplate it no further," the Patriarch said, his voice stronger. "The city is lost—to intervene now would be to condemn every one of these men, and us, to death."

Anborn's eyes flared in fury. "That is your assessment as a battlefield commander?" he asked icily.

The Patriarch shook his head, his eyes burning with angry fire. "That is the assessment of the Ring of Wisdom," he said. He held up his hand; the clear stone in the ring was glowing as intensely as the sky above Sepulvarta. "I am now consigned to exile; if by turning myself over to the attacking force I could spare the city, I would do so. But that is not their intent. They have just moved the border of Sorbold north by the distance of my lands."

"Indeed," murmured Anborn. "And they no doubt expect to use the city as a base to annex as much of the southern Krevensfield Plain as they can." He yanked back on the reins, ignoring the terrified whinny of his mount. "That area is too vast, too spread out to defend. All the people of those farming settlements and villages are border fodder if we don't evacuate them to Roland immediately. Take one last look at the citadel, Your Grace; I expect the next time you come through here the place will be in ashes. And if they take the Spire, who knows what they will use it for."

"I know," replied the Patriarch. "And the horror of it defies description."

Anborn was not listening; he had already turned and ridden the line, shouting orders to the troops for the mass evacuation that was to follow.

*W*hen daylight came, after a night of pillage and sacking, Fhremus called a halt to the hostilities.

"Empty the basilica and seal it," he ordered; Minus saluted and passed along the command. "Truly it is one of the wonders of the Known World; I'm sure the emperor does not wish to see it damaged any more than was necessary to subdue the city."

He looked around at the remains of Sepulvarta. The historic white buildings were smeared and marred with soot; whole sections of the city, especially the pilgrim sites, were still in flames, and in the cobbled streets, blood ran in rivers between the stones.

"Where is Faron?" he asked Trevnor.

The aide-de-camp shook his head. "I saw him last within the garden district, sir. He broke open the doors of the Patriarch's manse, as directed, but then he went off on his own; we could not follow him in the smoke."

"The Patriarch has still not been found?"

"No, sir. And the priests and acolytes in the manse swear they do not know where he is, even under pain of torture."

"Hmm. Well, keep looking for them both. There is only one gate in the city wall—and Faron did not come back to it, so he must be in here somewhere. He's rather large to overlook; I'm certain we will find him sooner rather than later."

Fhremus's certainty changed a short time later, when a massive hole was found in the wall at the northern edge of the city, torn through by what appeared to be a hand.

*W*hen finally the earth beneath his feet had cooled sufficiently, Faron stopped.

The battle had meant little to him. Destruction sometimes was a primal pleasure, but there was little of that in the sacking of Sepulvarta, though Faron had no idea why. Perhaps it had been the parsimoniousness of the commanders and the soldiers, the troops who were following him like a great pagan or animist god, not realizing that the great animist god was once a quivering pile of pale dying flesh, gelatinous and pathetic, until Talquist had sealed him within this body of Living Stone on the Scales of Jierna Tal. Faron had found the transformation ironic at best, child of the demon spirit that he was, he had come to be sealed within a Vault of Living Stone just as his father had once been.

Titan or no, soldier of incomprehensible strength or carnival atrocity, Faron missed his father deeply. In spite of the abuse he had suffered at his hands, he had been for the most part lovingly cared for by the man whose body the demon clung to, a man that had been called the Seneschal later in life, but in earlier times had been known as Michael, the Wind of Death. He had regaled a fascinated Faron with the exploits of his days as a soldier, had made him long for a body that would allow him to follow his father on such exploits, such joyful outings of murder and pillage, but nature had not been kind to him.

And ironically, now that he had the perfect housing for a soldier, he was alone, being directed by men he cared nothing for, who he could crush with a mere thought.

Somewhere on the wind there was a hint of dark fire. Faron had no idea how he was aware of this, but in the depths of his solid being something had stirred, had called to him off to the north, something he recognized from the time before everything had gone sour.

Faron reached into the huge leather belt at his waist, once the harness for a team of horses, and clumsily pulled out the blue scale.

It was his favorite, he thought, the card that allowed him to see hidden things, or objects at great distance. He loved the picture that had been drawn on it as well; one side bore the image of a clear eye, the other one an eye shrouded in clouds, much like his own milky blue ones.

He could not see anything yet, but there was enough invisible ash on the wind that the scale hummed with life when he held it in a northerly direction. Whatever was there was too far away to be seen yet, but he could follow its path.

And maybe find one of his own kind.

Faron turned his primitive head in that direction and followed the faint whisper of evil creosote, leaving the noise and chaos of the burning city behind him.

PART THREE

Ashes on the Wind

31

KURIMAH MILANI, NORTHWESTERN YARIM,
IN THE SHADOW OF THE TEETH

The dragon extended her claws in her torpor, reveling in her ease and the dimming of the pain that had been chewing on her since the turn of the moon.

With the partial healing of her body came a similarly partial revival of her memory. Deep in slumber, she was dreaming now, and in those dreams she did not inhabit the draconic form that was her current reality, but rather she was a woman, the Lady of legendary beauty and power that she had been only a short time ago.

The wyrm stretched lazily, allowing herself to enjoy the motion of her torn muscles as they mended. She was recalling her halcyon days, flashes of memories she didn't understand—the echoes of childhood laughter with two other shapes that seemed to be those of young girls, like herself, chasing after each other in a virgin forest, no adult, or in fact any other person, in sight. She did not remember her sisters, nor the dragon mother who left the three of them at the foot of the Great White Tree, save for a sour taste in her mouth that was pittance beside the hate she felt for the woman named Rhapsody. But she did recall the laughter, the sense of freedom, and of loneliness, from those times, and little else.

Her breathing grew deeper as it grew easier. The image in her mind faded from childhood revels to the day when, as a young woman alone on a bluff overlooking the same beach where her mother had first spied her father coming off of the ocean, she saw the arrival of ships, storm-tossed and broken, landing one after another on the heels of a terrible storm. The people who debarked from those ships were like none she had ever seen—some tall and fair, some broad and sturdy, some the size of children with slender hands and enormous eyes that spoke in flowers rather than words, a panoply of mankind, their skin arrayed in all different colors; one by one, the ships unloaded their living treasure, leaving her breathless, her golden face scored with tiny lines was wet with tears for the first time in her life. *My horde,* she thought, then and now, the closest she had ever come to love at first sight.

The other memories that loomed, threatening to displace those happy ones, she pushed away, shrinking from the pain they caused in much the same way as she had from the broken shards of metal still wedged within her. *No, no,* she thought hazily, banishing all other thought from her mind and returning to happier times, images of celebrations at the seaside, feasts and joyous dancing and a ceremony at the foot of the Great White Tree in which she was elevated above all and called Lady by the living treasure whose name she still could not recall. The Cymrians, the refugees of the First Fleet from the dead Island of Serendair.

I want to stay asleep, she mused, stretching again, luxuriating in the memory of a time when she was honored, not despised, celebrated and sought after, not cast out and ostracized.

She opened her mouth and, as before, the liquid gold of sunshine, sweet and healing, dripped within it. The fire in her, brewed by the firegems that all members of her race had in their bellies, cooled, leaving her dreamless and at rest.

For the moment.

𝒯he windy silence was shattered simultaneously by the sudden squeal of the infant and the ringing slap of leather glove against flesh a split second afterward.

Achmed reined his horse to a stop, the delicate nerve endings in his skin burning from the sound.

"What *now*, Rhapsody?" he demanded, glaring over his shoulder as she opened the folds of the mist cloak, a look of consternation on her wind-stung face. "You *just* fed him; this demanding brat is becoming far too much of an irritation. One more sudden shriek without cause and I'm going to skewer him on a horse spike and leave him for carrion."

"How do you know it was without cause?" Rhapsody asked, examining the baby.

Achmed glanced over at Grunthor, who was rubbing his neck. "What's the matter?"

"Somethin' stung me," the giant muttered.

"Probably a sand fly of some sort," said Achmed. "They can be brutal, though one would think you'd be fairly invulnerable to them, given your Bengard skin."

"One would think," the giant agreed, still examining his neck, "but this was no lit'le sting. Oi got right bit. *Ow.* Bloody *ow.*"

"So did Meridion,' Rhapsody said. She plucked the stinger from a large red welt on the screeching infant's leg and ran her finger over it, warming it gently with her fire lore to soothe the pain.

At that moment Achmed became aware of the hum. He signaled to Grunthor and reined his horse to a stop, following the irritation in his skin. He draped the reins over Rhapsody's arm and dismounted, letting the buzzing guide him over the sand, until he found the source.

Several small wells pocked the otherwise unbroken layer of sand, over which a few itinerant bees were hovering while others appeared to be burrowing into the ground near the wells.

"I've found your assailant, Grunthor," he said, crouching down and examining the wells, which resembled large anthills. "Do you wish me to wreak vengeance on your behalf? I could piss on them if you want. Or are we ready to move out?"

"What are bees doin' out 'ere in the desert?" the giant Bolg wondered aloud. "Nothin' for them ta eat, no flowers, vegetation. No real water. Strange."

Achmed mounted again and took the reins back. He clicked to the horse and they returned to a smooth canter, riding the rising and falling dunes and drumlins with alacrity, heading east as the distant mountains seemed to grow closer, their red and purple hues gleaming at the horizon like a promise of shelter that would not be reached before the coming of night. The light had already begun to fade as the red sun made its way down the welkin of the sky; the wind picked up, sweeping the sand across the cracked earth in great spinning devils of dust.

They had not gone very far when Achmed yanked his horse to a stop again, this time making a grab for Rhapsody to keep her from falling forward. Grunthor stopped a few seconds later, a few strides ahead of him, staring, as he did, into the east.

"Criton," the Bolg commander murmured. "Whaddaya make o' *that*?"

"Gods," Rhapsody whispered, drawing the mist cloak closer to her to calm the baby.

Achmed said nothing but stared with mismatched eyes at the sight before them.

Jutting from the seemingly endless desert was a broken tower, a minaret, tilted on its side. It seemed to appear from nowhere, emerging from the red sand in which little to no vegetation or in fact any sign of life had been seen for days.

Around it were similar ruins, remnants of domes and walls, up-rooted from the sand as if they had been pulled and tossed aside like weeds. The scale of the ruins was enormous, as if the original occupants of whatever city they had once been part of had been giants, or perhaps it was just that the city itself had been mammoth. The sun overhead beat down on the detritus, which shone eerily in the light with an almost translucent radiance.

"Did we not come through this place before, years ago, when we were returning to Ylorc with the slave children of the Raven's Guild in Yarim?" Rhapsody asked. "I don't remember seeing ruins then."

"They were not here," Achmed agreed. He continued to stare at the husks of what had once been walls, now little more than building blocks scattered in the hot sand. Somewhere nearby the hum he had heard from the ground-nesting bees had grown stronger. "These ruins appear to have been evicted from the sand. I suppose that happens from time to time, especially if there has been an earthquake or other disturbance of the strata of the earth. The ground here is riven—there are rifts and cracks in the clay." He pointed to a great fissure where the sun-baked ground had been rent apart north of them, which the wind was beginning to fill in with sand.

"I don't remember feelin' any tremors lately," Grunthor said seriously. He dragged back on his reins again and dismounted; the sand atop the red clay sprayed in all directions as he thudded to the ground. "That looks pretty recent." He knelt down and rested his hand on the ground. "Somethin's wrong 'ere; everything's all jumbled up, distressed-like. As if this place had been asleep, or dead, even before we left the ol' world, and then was suddenly shocked awake."

Rhapsody and Achmed exchanged a glance; the earth lore that Grunthor had absorbed, like the two of them, when passing through the fire at the Earth's core, was never wrong. Rhapsody rocked the baby, gentling him back into sleep again, as Achmed scanned the horizon. The wind picked up; Rhapsody pulled the hood of the mist cloak lower and Achmed raised the veil on his face over his eyes against the sting of the sand.

"Even our patrols at the northernmost edge of our borders are days from here," he said finally. "I've no idea what this is, or was, but another sandstorm appears to be brewing. Either we ride full out and see if we can find shelter over those hills, or we may be forced to take it here. Whatever this is, I am not certain I want to be trapped in this place in another dust devil."

Grunthor shrugged. "Might be as good a place as any, sir," he said, surveying the towering fragments of walls sprouting from the sand before them. "Looks pretty solid—that wreckage ain't goin' nowhere. Should provide decent cover if you think another storm's comin'. There's nowhere else we could make it to before nightfall." He looked over to where Rhapsody had been standing, then tapped Achmed's shoulder and pointed. The Bolg king turned back to look as well.

The Lady Cymrian had wandered slightly to the south, as if following a call only she could hear. She crouched down as they watched, still listening. From within the billowing folds of the mist cloak they could see her reach out her hand and pass it over the ground. Then her arm withdrew into the cloak; she looked down at the baby, then turned to meet their gaze.

"How's your neck, Grunthor?" she asked.

The giant shrugged again, then reached up and patted it. A look of surprise came over his massive features.

"Good as new," he murmured aloud.

Rhapsody rose and came back over to them. She stopped in front of Achmed and pushed aside the folds of the cloak of mist to reveal the infant's leg.

The welt was gone, healed as if it had never been there.

She turned around, taking in the sight of the vast desert behind them, the mountains in the distance to the east, listening intently.

"What is it?" Achmed asked.

"Can't you feel it?" she asked. "There's a very deep vibration here, a vibrant song, but I missed it in the hum of the bees and the howl of the wind. It is ancient in tone, the musical note *Lisele-ut,* attuned to the color red in the spectrum."

"Blood saver," said Achmed. "Healing?"

"Yes. But I can't even fathom how strong this is—it's too deep to be audible; I can only feel it. Can you as well, Grunthor?"

The Sergeant-Major nodded in assent. "We should stay 'ere tonight, sir," he said loudly, watching Rhapsody as she wandered northward, her eyes closed, following the tone. Then he leaned over and spoke quietly to Achmed.

"Look at 'er, look at 'er face."

As they had done once long ago in the light of a campfire, having just emerged from their long trek through the belly of the Earth, the two Bolg stared at Rhapsody. Then they were seeing the effects of the elemental fire she had absorbed in the Earth's core, a purging of physical flaws, a brightening of her eyes and hair until it radiated the same warmth as the element. She had become hypnotic to behold, an experience similar to gazing into roaring flames on a hearth.

Now what they saw was different, but similarly compelling. The woman who had ridden with them from Haguefort had been wan and pale, thin and listless from the difficulty of bearing a dragon's child. Even though she had remained fair, she was waiflike, a shadow of herself, her health fragile, her vitality, so much a part of her before, weak and sapped. She seemed almost *dry,* bloodless, as though color had been drained out of her in childbirth.

As she passed northward, however, guided by the tune the Earth was singing in this place of endless arid clay and merciless cold sun, she seemed to rehydrate, as if she was drinking in the color from the world around her. The flaxen hair peeking from beneath the hood of the mist cloak was growing brighter, back to the gold of the old days, her pale skin turning rosier, her flesh gaining more solidity and heft the farther along she walked. Even her gait grew stronger; there was more vigor in her step, more energy in her movements.

As she approached the fissure in the ground, the Sergeant started back to the horses.

"Whatever this place is, sir, it seems to be 'ealing the Duchess. Oi think we oughta just settle 'ere until she gets a lit'le better; she was lookin' about ready ta drop."

Achmed watched as she knelt down next to the fissure, then nodded. "All right," he called to Grunthor, "let's see if we can find a sheltered spot within the ruins where we won't be buried if another sandstorm blows through." Then he walked over to where Rhapsody was kneeling and stood silently while she listened to the music only she could hear.

At last she looked up, her face shining brightly in the light of the setting sun.

"I think I know what this place may have been," she said excitedly, her eyes shining green as the forest canopies in Tyrian. "When we were in Yarim Paar, drilling beneath Entudenin to restore water to the province, do you recall hearing a legend of a lost city named Kurimah Milani?"

Achmed chuckled wryly. "No, when the Bolg artisans were in Yarim Paar we were not being accorded fancy hospitality and having legends related to us—we were digging every hour of the day and night, sweating blood and enduring the hostile stares and jeers of the imbeciles who we should have allowed to die of thirst in the heat. You, on the other hand, were the guest of that idiot duke, Ihrman Karsrick, if I recall correctly, so I can see how you may have had a moment to indulge in the gathering of lore and legend." He stopped, seeing her face fall, and remembering that in fact she had arranged for better housing and treatment for the Bolg workers, which he had refused. "Tell me the tale."

Rhapsody stood, cradling the baby close to her.

"I don't know the tale, I only have heard snippets of the lore. In the oldest days, long before the Cymrians came to this continent, there was said to have been a marvelous city called Kurimah Milani somewhere around here, in the lee of the northern mountains. I'm not sure of the origin of the name, but the sounds it contains are all the musical notes that promote healing, much like the red spectrum of your Lightcatcher is supposed to. I heard fragments of the tales from the Shanouin priest-esses, that tribe of well-diggers who alone were able to locate water in the desert clime of Yarim. The Shanouin are said to have been descended from the inhabitants of Kurimah Milani, but the city has been lost to the ages for so long that even they do not know if that is truth or fantasy.

"I know little else about it, except that it was said to be a place of hot springs rich in minerals, runoff from the Manganese Mountains to the north of the Teeth. The legends said that the hot springs imparted heal-ing and other magical properties to those fortunate enough to bathe in or drink from them. That's all there was; the lore is too old for anyone now living to remember. It may all have been a mirage of the mind, a fantasy that desert dwellers told each other in the hot seasons when wa-ter was scarce and they were made a little insane by thirst.

"But somewhere beneath here a song of immense power is resonat-ing, emanating from the One-God only knows what. It is a melodious tune, deep and slow, faster than the heartbeat of the Earth that we heard when we were walking within it, but regular, like tides of the sea; strange, all the way out here in the desert. The power is vibrating within the ground—can you feel it?"

Achmed lowered his veil to allow his skin-web access to the open wind, then pulled the glove from his left hand. He crouched down and held his palm over the fissure.

"I can," he said after a moment.

"Then perhaps these are the ruins of that place," Rhapsody said. "In-teresting, and potentially useful. I think Meridion needs changing."

The Bolg king flinched against the wind as it roared through again, stinging his eyes. Grunthor jogged back to them, having settled the horses and the provisions in the shelter of the ruins.

"Right nice spot, out of the wind," he said cheerfully. "C'mon, Duchess, I got a place set up fer you an' the lit'le one; you should be clear of the wind, most part."

The Bolg king gestured at the ground.

"Grunthor, can you tell what is beneath here? Is it sand and clay for as far as you can sense, or are there other strata? Is there a city below?"

The Sergeant-Major walked to the edge of the fissure, then jumped down onto a clay ledge and examined the ground. "The ruins o' one, maybe," he replied. "Can't rightly tell—there's somethin' powerful in the way makin' noise, masking whatever the Earth says. There seems ta be a lot o' broken bits below, but that's all Oi can tell. O' course, we could just go see fer ourselves. There's a right big tunnel just beyond this fissure, tall and wide—we could go below; we done it before, after all."

Rhapsody shuddered. "Don't remind me, please. The nightmares will only get worse. Let's take shelter with the horses in the ruins."

"Oi'll go get the diaperin' supplies and the rest o' the provisions," Grunthor said, jogging to the ruins.

"Oi think you're right about the young prince needin' changin'. *Hrekin*."

"You don't want to see what's below the sand?" Achmed asked while they waited.

"No. I want to get to Ylorc, get out of the wind, and get started working on your bloody Lightcatcher. I don't need a reminder of our travels along the Axis Mundi, thank you very much. I'm Lirin; we don't belong underground, and you well know it."

"Oh, come now, you said you were looking forward to returning to Elysian, and that's underground," said Achmed in exasperation. "What's the difference? How can you, a Namer, pass up the chance to possibly find what sounds like it would be one of the greatest recoveries of lore in the Known World? If this *is* Kurimah Milani, do you want to leave it for someone else to find?"

"Yeah," said Grunthor, dropping her pack in front of her. "What would ol' Talquist make of this place, Oi wonder?"

"I will not deliberately take the baby into danger just to—"

"It can't be any more dangerous than being out in plain sight, especially with night coming on," Achmed said.

"It could be a good deal *less* dangerous, miss," said Grunthor seriously. "Look be'ind you."

Rhapsody and Achmed turned around simultaneously and were slapped full in the face by the sandy wind. From the west a great wall of dust was approaching, sweeping ahead of it whatever scrub vegetation had been drying in the wide expanse of red clay desert, its force growing with each second.

Grunthor leapt down into the fissure again and began clearing the sand away from in front of the rift where he had indicated a tunnel to be present.

"'urry in if you're goin'," he said. "Can't 'old the bloody sand up fer long. Give me good ol' Bolgish basalt any day."

Achmed climbed down into the fissure and crawled within the rift, emerging a moment later.

"It's all right, Rhapsody—the ceiling is high, and it appears to be a vault or cavern of some sort. We can stay in here until the sandstorm passes, then be on our way."

The Lady Cymrian exhaled, then climbed down behind him, followed by Grunthor, into a place of vast and endless darkness.

As the gathering windstorm approached, a shadow followed silently behind them.

32

"Grunthor, can you see me in the dark?"

"Yes indeed, Duchess."

"Can you give me the pack and some light, then?"

"Certainly."

A cold blue light emerged, casting a glowing radiance at the mouth of the tunnel. The three companions looked around.

They were in a smooth hallway formed of ancient clay, with semicircular walls in which long deep grooves had been carved. The light of the globe reflected off those walls and glittered in the darkness with the same eerie radiance as that of the broken walls and towers of the ruins above. A cool breeze blew in from the darkness at the end of the corridor.

"Looks like a sluice of some sort," said Achmed. Grunthor nodded assent. "Perhaps part of a sewer system."

Rhapsody removed her cloak with the baby wrapped in its folds.

"Wonderful," she muttered as she riffled through the pack. "Why is it that whenever the three of us enter a city, we always seem to come in through the sewer? If I recall, that was our first sight of the Bolglands as well."

"Seems oddly appropriate, given what you are currently engaged in doing," said Achmed acidly over the soft cooing sounds of the baby. "Gods, Rhapsody, are you certain you're not feeding him sulfur?"

"Fairly certain," she replied, smiling down at the child in the dark. In the gleam of the cold light globe his hair and skin were almost translucent, the tiny vertical pupils of his clear blue eyes twinkling. She kissed his tiny belly, then swaddled him quickly as the howl of the wind rushed past them, screaming in and around the tunnel entrance.

"Good thing you got over yer fear of the underground in time, Duchess," said Grunthor, looking outside. "That's a strong one, strong as the last. Oi 'ope the 'orses don't get buried. Glad Oi got the supplies when Oi did."

Rhapsody stepped over the grooves in the floor of the tunnel, cradling Meridion in the cloak, and sat with her back against the wall. Achmed and Grunthor turned away while she nursed the baby, watching the fury of the sandstorm outside the tunnel and listening as the harsh cry of the wind and the soft sounds of the child both faded into silence.

When the storm appeared to have passed Grunthor hoisted himself out of the tunnel and looked around. "Fissure's filled in a bit," he reported upon returning. "May 'ave ta dig out when we leave."

The Bolg king nodded, then turned and walked past where Rhapsody was sitting and followed the broken sluice down into the breezy darkness. He gestured to the others.

"There's a large opening ahead at the tunnel's end, where that wind is coming from. Bring the light, and we'll have a look around before making camp for the night."

Grunthor offered Rhapsody his enormous hand and helped her to her feet, then took out the light globe. They followed the Bolg king down the sluice to the end of the tunnel where a dark opening yawned.

As they neared the opening, both Rhapsody and Achmed flinched. A humming drone of immense volume was issuing forth from beyond it, echoing up the sluice tunnel and vibrating against their skin and eardrums. It was not the deep, slow song that Rhapsody had described, but more the noise of static, a discordant buzz that was electric.

Rhapsody's eyes glinted nervously in the cold light. "I'm not certain this is a good idea, Achmed," she whispered. "Isn't that constant droning irritating to you?"

"Your constant droning has been irritating me for fourteen hundred years," he replied. "I will survive. Better to know what is in there than to be caught unaware. Stay here. Grunthor, give me the light. Careful; the floor has some oily spots beyond here."

The blue-white ball was passed forward; the Bolg king stepped up to the opening, avoiding the thick pools on the floor, holding the light ahead of him. He leaned in and looked around.

"Well, that explains the bees," he said after a moment.

Rhapsody and Grunthor exchanged a glance, then joined him at the opening.

Beyond the hole was an immense cavern, the ruins of what may have at one time been a huge public bath. Gigantic stone columns glittering with mother-of-pearl held up the remains of the ceiling that had at one time been painted with extravagant frescoes, intricate mosaics lined the walls, formed from tiles of fired glass, the colors still brilliant though partially obscured with grit, the reds especially vibrant, even in the cold blue light. It was difficult to see much of the floor below, hidden as it was in shadow beyond the light's reach, but the remains of a system of water delivery could be made out, leading away from the sluice, where long trenches lined with colored tile fed into long-dry fountains containing what appeared to be rows of stone seats. An enormous vault reached into the darkness above, shattered at one end. The trickling sound of water could be heard, just below the droning hum that rose to the level of a roar past the opening.

Growing along the walls and columns at the extreme edge of the light were nodules of every size, thick mold spores of fungus that covered entire frescoes. Higher up, the ceiling was covered with what appeared to be massive stalactites, long hanging threads that looked like fangs in an enormous maw. Around those stalactites bees were swarming, more bees than their eyes could even take in.

The buzz of the immense hive was as loud as thunder echoing through the mountains. The stalactites were only the outermost edge of it; the remainder, cemented by sand and bee saliva over two millennia, sprawled threatening across the ceiling of the vault and out of sight in the darkness beyond the light's reach. Near the hole in the vault, the hive was shattered, with broken combs of wax and honey oozing thickly down to the floor below, around which tens of thousands of agitated insects swirled, buzzing angrily. The vibration of it traveled up Achmed's skin, leaving it burning with static. Rhapsody drew the baby closer within the folds of the mist cloak and struggled to cover her ears with one arm.

"All right, Duchess, perhaps we *were* safer outside," whispered Grunthor.

"Don't make another sound," Achmed cautioned in a low voice. "If you spook them, they'll swarm us; we can't outrun them."

Nor can you outrun me, Ysk.

The words crawled over Achmed's skin, echoing in his blood. Though no sound reached his ears, he heard them as clearly as if they had been spoken right next to him. Almost imperceptibly he started to turn to look behind him.

Do not move.

The command scratched against the insides of his eyelids. The Bolg king flinched in pain. There was a familiarity in the words, an unspoken and voiceless communication that was transmitted through his skin-web, inaudible to his or any other ears. He had been spoken to like this twice in his life before, once by his mentor in the old world, Father Halphasion, and again by the Grandmother, the ancient woman who guarded the Sleeping Child, but neither of their methods of communication had transmitted the raw power and pain that was being forced upon him now. They were spoken in no language, just transmitted in understanding.

Tell them to move within.

Achmed swallowed. With each command it seemed as if another invisible thread was cemented around him, hampering his ability to move. He inhaled into his sinuses, attempting to loose his *kirai* to see if the Seeking vibration would help him glean information about the speaker, but his breath stopped in his throat.

"Rhapsody," he said quietly in Old Cymrian, "step forward and aside, out of the sluice. You as well, Grunthor."

The Lady Cymrian, standing at his right, who was at that moment assessing the tone of the hive's vibration in the hope of generating a complementary one, looked askance at him and, seeing the serious expression on his face, complied, stepping onto the ledge and to the right of the opening.

Grunthor, on his left, obeyed as well, but as he crossed in front of the Bolg king he glanced back up the sluice behind him and slowed his gait. A shadow of a man stood directly behind Achmed, robed and hooded in the darkness, less than a breath away. Grunthor continued to cross, but subtlely reached for the throwing knife in his belt.

Suddenly, the breeze that had been blowing up the sluice, generated by the movement of millions of wings, died away, along with all the rest of the air in the sluiceway. The two Bolg gasped for breath as even the air within their lungs was dragged from them. Grunthor's hand went to his throat, but Achmed remained still, the veins in his neck and forehead distended.

Rhapsody turned and, seeing her two friends compromised, stepped hurriedly back toward the opening in alarm. A voice, this time audible, spoke in a low tone that hovered below the droning of the hive.

"Stay within, lady, unless you wish to see the same visited upon your child."

The globe of cold light fell from the Bolg king's hand and thudded on the ground. Rhapsody froze, drawing the cloak and the baby closer to her chest, as both of the Bolg sank to their knees, struggling to hang on to consciousness.

"Stop, I beg you," she whispered in the same tone as the voice had sounded.

Be silent. The command stabbed her eardrums; Rhapsody gritted her teeth and leaned back against the wall. She watched in horror as both of her friends fell forward, Achmed first, then the giant Bolg Sergeant-Major, their eyes protruding, faces purple in the remains of the cold light.

She steeled herself against tears, rather feeling hatred running like fire through her veins, as Grunthor's body finally went limp. Achmed, who had fallen with his face toward her, met her gaze with his own, then tried, and succeeded ever so slightly, in smiling encouragingly at her. Rhapsody thought she saw him wink.

Then his face went slack as well.

A shadow approached and fell over the bodies in the blue light. Rhapsody stood as still as she could as a robed hand, long-boned and thin, reached down from the opening and seized Achmed, dragging him to his feet and out of her sight.

Suddenly the breeze picked up; it had been blowing on her all along, but she saw it riffle through Grunthor's oily hair and across his cape, making it flutter on his back as he lay prone. After a moment the giant Bolg stirred slightly, then coughed.

Achmed came around after a moment, his head thudding, to find himself gazing numbly into two pinpricks of light within a dark hood. The figure that held him in its grasp stared at him for a moment longer, then dropped him to the floor and pulled down the hood of his robe.

In the diffuse light Achmed could make out features he recognized instantly, but in a form he had never seen before. The man who stood before him was thin as a whisper, taller than Achmed, with wide shoulders, sinewy hands, and skin that was scored across every inch with exposed traceries of veins in a great web that gave a dual tone to it. His head was smooth and bald, tapering in width from the crown to the angular jaw, his eyes black as ink without a visible iris, bisected by silver pupils; looking within them was like looking into a mirror in a dark room.

A Dhracian. Full-blooded.

But one very different than any he had seen before.

Get up and step within, the man ordered. This time the command did not cause pain, but rather thudded succinctly against his skin. Achmed obeyed, rising slowly, allowing his body to unfold until he was standing erect. He stumbled past the opening where Grunthor was lying and shook him until the giant shuddered with life, struggling to breathe, then helped him sit up.

"What the bloody—?"

"Shhh," the Bolg king cautioned. Grunthor's gaze focused on the figure standing before them, then swung in the direction of Rhapsody, who was still leaning against the cavern wall, the baby wrapped within the mist cloak in her arms, panting. "Can you stand?"

"O' course Oi can stand," the Sergeant-Major muttered. "It's just a matter o' how long it'll *be* before Oi can."

"Stand and step deeper within," the Dhracian said in his audible, fricative voice, the same sandy voice that Achmed spoke with. "Each moment you tarry you risk waking the beast."

"Beast?" Rhapsody whispered as the three men came closer to where she stood.

The thin, bald man picked up the light globe, handed it to her, and gestured impatiently down toward the bottom of the cavern. Achmed nodded; Rhapsody turned and led the way along an angular, descending ledge, at one time one of the feeder channels in the water system, being careful to avoid the nodules of mold and broken bits of hive on the walls down to the enormous cavern's floor.

They passed beneath thin long strings of dripping honey, trying to avoid making contact with it; the viscous liquid expanded after each heavy drop fell, then lengthened again, spilling its golden treasure across what had once been a fountainbed. All around them the air swirled with the beating of innumerable wings and the heavy sound of droning that drowned out all other noise.

They finally came to a large basin for what had once been an immense bath lined with seats of fired tile, through which a trickling stream was slowly running, meandering around obstacles of broken statuary and the wreckage of walls. The robed man stopped beside the stream and pointed to it.

"Drink," he said to Achmed and Grunthor. "It will restore you."

"Oi'll pass, thank you," muttered the giant Bolg. "Oi feel just ducky."

The Dhracian snorted, and eyed the Bolg king. "And you?"

Achmed said nothing.

The Dhracian watched him a moment longer, then crouched down by the spring and cupped a hand into it, then drank from his palm. "As you wish," he said. He turned away and walked over to a sheltered alcove with blue marble walls that had most likely been a place where bathers had disrobed before taking part in the medicinal baths. The Bolg followed him, but Rhapsody stayed beside the stream, listening to it as it trickled through the cavern floor; it was a musical sound, similar in tone to the song she had heard when they were above. She crouched down, still clutching her mist cloak close to her, and removed her pack, fumbled around in it, and finally brought forth an empty water flask, which she quickly filled one-handed, then capped again and returned to the pack. She joined the men inside the alcove, one of the few places in the entirety of the massive vault that the bees had not chosen to colonize, probably because of the slippery finish of the blue marble walls. Between the shelter of the spot, the breeze whistling through, and the hum of the bees, all noise seemed to be swallowed, occluded, she noticed.

Achmed turned to the Dhracian. "Why are you here? What do you want?"

The ancient man stared at him without rancor, as if assessing him for market. Finally he spoke, and when he did his voice was toneless in the wind of the cavern.

"I have a task for you."

The Bolg king chuckled wryly. "You have come to assign me a task? Why would you think such a thing possible? And do you really believe that strangling me is the way to assure my cooperation?"

The dark eyes narrowed.

"You are of the blood, yet you do not feel the call of the Primal Hunt?"

Achmed's eyes narrowed similarly.

"I feel it," he said sullenly. "I have answered that call more than once, and have sent more than one putrid F'dor spirit back to the Vault of the Underworld, or into the ether. But I still do not understand why you feel you can attack me and my man-at-arms, nearly choke the life from us, and then expect me to accept a task from you, as if I am your errand boy. I actually have my own thoughts about how I might spend my time, not to mention my own responsibilities—and neither of them involve accepting a task from anyone, let alone *you*." His voice rang with rancor, and the last word echoed in the alcove around them.

The ancient Dhracian said nothing, just stood in silence, watching Achmed carefully. Finally he pointed to the place in the vault where the wall and the hive around it was shattered.

"Beyond that wall is a *Wyrmril*, a beast that came here a short time ago seeking healing from a place that was nothing but a memory. She sleeps now—her fire is cooled in a surfeit of honey and sweet water—but any sound, any distraction, could stir her awareness."

"Oh, goody," Grunthor said under his breath. "Anwyn. Oi wondered where that ol' bitch had fled to."

"You may feel competent to take her on—but what of your child, lady? Can he survive a dragon's breath?" The Dhracian looked up at the expansive hive that had consumed the entire ceiling of the vast place. "That being said, you are in far greater danger from the bees, even though it is their noise that is keeping you alive, the movement of their wings allowing you to hide within the wind from the dragon," he noted, almost idly. "When Kurimah Milani stood as a haven of healing, the ancestors of those bees were captive, raised by a follower of the man who built this city for their honey, which was used in medicines and soothing emollients. They were the only creatures to survive the destruction of the city." His reflective gaze returned to the three. "Whatever their harmlessness was then, they could now kill us all with but a thought—and, like our kind, they are of a single mind, able to communicate silently among the entire hive as if it were one entity. Should they swarm and attack, our dead bodies will swell like figs soaked in wine before they burst, and the bees feed upon our carcasses."

"Please forbear from further description," Rhapsody interjected. "I think we understand."

The Dhracian smiled coldly, still addressing Achmed.

"This is the only place in all the world that bees of this species live; they were brought from the old world, a place that no longer exists, and have grown and changed over the centuries to be unlike any other. If someone were to come into this vault, with flame perhaps, he could eradicate all of the bees of this type from the face of the earth." His voice grew even more toneless and soft. "It is just so with another Vault."

"You are talking in riddles," Achmed said darkly. "I probably neglected to mention how much I hate riddles. What is it you want?"

The Dhracian met his gaze with a piercing one in return. "I have come to bring you into the Hunt, as you should have been all along. You are needed, Ysk. Time is growing short."

A sarcastic smile crawled over the Bolg king's face. "And here again you address me by the name that was bestowed on me in spittle, as reviled and disgusting a title as has ever been conferred. Why should I help you? I have my own responsibilities, my own burdens to bear. A kingdom that requires my attention."

"Yes," said the angular man, "the Assassin King; so I have heard. I called you by the only name I had for you, though you had cast it off long ago, because the one you were given after that, the Brother, made you all but impossible to find on the wind."

"That was the point."

"I have been looking for you all your life," said the Dhracian. "I knew of you before you were born; so it is with all the Brethren." His voice grew less harsh, as if the wind was softening the effects of the sand in it. "The *Zherenditck*, those who have joined the Hunt and walk the upworld in search of the F'dor, share a link, a communication, that transcends time and space; they are of one mind, and so what happens to each of them is known to all. But you are not *Zherenditck*, you are *Dhisrik*, one of the Uncounted, a Dhracian of the blood who is not tied to a Colony, and therefore outside the common mind. You do not understand the bond between us; ironic, for someone who was renamed to be Brother to all, but akin to none. You have kin, Ysk—or whatever you choose to be called now—kin that have been combing the wind for you since your birth. Your mother was one of us, one of the Gaol. We witnessed your conception, experienced it, suffered through it as she did, though not as much as she did.

"We searched in vain, across the years, across the wide world. You were not to be found. Then, when one of the other *Dhisrik*, Halphasion, sent us word that you had been taken in and renamed, trained, made aware of your Dhracian heritage and the blood pact that it commands, we waited for you to come to us, to join in the Primal Hunt. But you have not been compelled by the deepest calling in your blood, though you may have heard it, may have used its power to make a name for yourself. Instead you have listened to a lighter voice, an upworld call, that has wheedled you to the concerns of earthly men—power, comfort, friendship, security—who knows what pleasure, what commitment, could have swayed you from that which is primordial in you, allowing you to deny the undeniable? It nauseates me to know that such a thing is even possible in one of our order. I took the air from you to see if the ultimate obscenity were possible—that one of the Brethren had become the host of a F'dor. I am glad to see it was not so, that a tainted spirit feeding off of you did not beg or wheedle, or try to run to another host as your body was dying. But I confess that had it happened, it would not have surprised me, given how you have been able to deny the undeniable, to undo the inevitable, and ignore what runs in your own veins. Perhaps you were aptly named by the Firbolg. There is something inherently odious about one of the Brethren who feels the needles in his veins, knows the burning of the skin, the blood rage that is our shared burden, but does not join in the Hunt.

"So I have come to discover this, Assassin King—are you more king? Or more assassin?"

Achmed's face was a mask of stoicism, but his mismatched eyes gleamed with an intensity that frightened Rhapsody.

His answer was drowned in a sudden squeal from within the mist cloak in her arms. The sound pierced the noise of the hive, drowned out the tricking of the brook, and resounded through the ruins of the bath.

All three men started. Rhapsody's eyes widened in panic; she jostled the bundle, reaching within to try and soothe the child, but the squeal only intensified into high-pitched shrieking, louder than she had ever heard before.

"Meridion, Meridion, shhhhhh, no, no," she whispered, futilely trying to put the baby to the breast. "Gods, please, you'll wake the dragon." But the child continued to wail, his plaintive cries echoing off the cavernous chamber and shattering the low hum.

Because, unlike his mother, he knew the beast was already awake.

33

$\mathfrak{T}$he dragon had been coming to consciousness for some time before she actually heard the name.

In the lightness of her slumber the dreams she had been luxuriating in had grown less comforting; for all that there had been moments of celebration and acclaim in her long life, they had actually been few and far between when compared with the centuries of distrust and deception, rejection, plotting, war, murder, defilement, leading ultimately to even more centuries of banishment, exile, and solitude. Eventually the happy memories were used up, repeated too often to be of comfort.

She twitched in her sleep, fighting to keep the unpleasant thoughts at bay, but they were beginning to mass outside the gates of her mind, like rebel hordes eager for conquest.

The honey and wax she had devoured, believing it to be healing sunshine, was cloying in her maw, coating her throat and making her gag. The bees that had attacked her had done little to damage her hide; she felt no pain from that, but the stings that landed in her eyes had left them swollen and sore, irritating her back into low-burning anger again.

So when the name was spoken, even though it had been a great distance away in a different chamber of the bath, it went right to her ear and clanged like a cymbal against her brain.

Rhapsody, step forward and aside, out of the sluice.

The beast's sore eyes opened wide in the darkness of the broken bath, casting an eerie blue light around the gloom.

Rhapsody.

At first it was a struggle to waken; her mind, buzzing with the sound of the hated woman's name, caught fire and began to hum with eager energy, but the body that had been torn and rent from the inside by the shards that still remained within her was slow to react, in need of more rest and healing. The wyrm steeled her will and began to assert dominion over her limbs; one by one she stretched her legs and forearms, extended her claws until her muscles tensed in the sweet pain of controlled movement.

She stretched slowly, not the languid extension of muscle and bone that had felt so sinuous and delightful in torpor, but the careful, calculating reinvigoration of a dormant body into motion again. At the same time she listened carefully, hoping to catch the name again, or some sign of where the woman was. This place of ancient magic, with its low abiding song of healing and the hellacious buzzing from the hive, left her senses jumbled and unclear; there was no way to allow her inner sight to scan the ruins.

She would have to do it with her own eyes.

When finally she adjudged her body to be working as well as it could, she slithered back into the streambed and made her way to the hole she had caused in the vault, her forked tongue tasting the air, seeking to banish the last vestiges of sweet honey and replace them with an altogether more enticing sartorial experience.

Blood and bone, flavored with hate.

𝒞he three men froze only for the briefest of instants.

A second later they were in motion. The Dhracian, seemingly familiar with the ruins, ran at the lead, making his way over the broken vases and urns that had once held medicinal water and soothing oils, clearing a path as much as he could. Achmed snatched the light globe from Rhapsody's hands and followed him, illuminating the path as Grunthor grabbed her and the baby up and carried them, knowing his stride was more than twice hers.

They crossed the floor of the ancient bath with alacrity, leaping and ducking to avoid the scattered ruins of the public bath, past enormous statues of smiling robed women with hands outstretched in blessing, around the pieces of what had once been beds for basking beneath a sheltering desert sky, all the way to the channel down which they had come and began climbing back up to the sluice.

Just as they had reached the midpoint of the channel, the beast burst forth into the chamber through the hole in the shattered vault, bellowing forth a roar so filled with caustic hatred that could have melted glass.

The firmament of the vault rumbled in response, loosing a hail of sand and grit, followed by pieces of the hive that had been adhered to the ceiling.

Rhapsody ducked her head against Grunthor's chest and pulled Meridion as much under her chin as she could, hoping to spare his head from the falling debris. The thudding of the giant's massive heart as he charged up the channel was like thunder; she closed her eyes, struggling to keep the infant sheltered with her own body.

At that moment the hive shattered, sending a black storm of bees, thick as the dust wall of a sandstorm, cascading out and swirling angrily in every direction. The low drone became a ferocious scream, rising in volume, pitch, and fury.

At that moment, the Dhracian stopped where he was. He leaned forward on the channel ledge over the cavern and gestured to Achmed to pass him nearer to the wall. The Bolg king complied, holding the light aloft for Grunthor to follow, taking shelter in the sluice as a wave of angry insects swelled toward them.

Rhapsody, hearing the mounting buzz, took a corner of the mist cloak and swathed the side of Grunthor's face nearest the cavern, holding it like a tent for them both. The giant barreled up the last of the channel and into the sluice, dropping her gently to the ground.

"Take cover, Duchess," he said urgently. "Throw that thing over yerself."

Achmed was watching the cacophony of the hive. Black currents of insects swirled and raged, their mutual anger communicated in a rising scream. He turned and looked behind to see the Dhracian still standing at the channel's edge, his eyes closed, his long bony hand raised, palm out, to the cavern beyond. He was chanting, repeating a series of sounds over and over again. The words made no sense to Achmed; in his mind they sounded like a repeated series of hisses and buzzes. But in his viscera he knew what the man was saying.

Enemy. Enemy. Enemy.

He also knew in his guts that the Dhracian was directing the bees toward the dragon, the way a hill of ants or a hive communicated with a common mind.

A moment later his intuition proved correct. The cyclone of insects ceased their random fury and swarmed down as of one mind toward the beast, swamping her, covering her from maw to the spike on her tail, coating her wings until they were black.

The wyrm staggered in shock, then writhed as the stingers met her eyes again. Blindly she let out a roar of rage, then made her way, fighting the swarm, to the trickling stream.

The Dhracian opened his eyes and turned to Achmed.

"Run," he said in his low, sandy voice. "She will only be deterred a moment."

The Bolg king turned and fled through the opening and up the sluice, where Grunthor was furiously digging out a tunnel from where the sandstorm had filled in the fissure. The Dhracian was behind him a moment later, his footfalls silent in the echoing scream of the dragon, growing louder and nearer, in the cavern beyond the opening.

"Cover yerself and the baby, miss, Oi'm gonna push ya through," Grunthor said, gulping air from exertion. Rhapsody checked the child, quiet since his shriek, pulled the end of the mist cloak in which he was swathed over her head, and nodded her readiness. The giant Bolg seized her and shoved her through the last layer of sand, where she stumbled out into the dusk of the desert wind, where a thin crescent moon hung ominously in the sky above them.

"Make for the horses!" the Sergeant shouted, emerging a moment later behind her. Rhapsody obeyed, pushing back the cloak and keeping her head down, making for the ruins as quickly as she could, her heart pounding in her chest, trying to avoid dropping the baby at all costs.

The Bolg king and the Dhracian were just emerging from the fissure when the sluice exploded.

A backwash of angry bees, swirling madly, roared around the head of the beast as she lunged up and into the tunnel, cracking the walls as she smashed into them. The dragon vomited fire, though most of it came out as little more than smoke, the firegems within her belly lulled to sleep by the honey and sweet water she had been consuming. With her cruel talons extended, she swiped at the Dhracian as he exited the sluice, howling obscene sounds of threat in draconic words that even she did not understand.

Grunthor had almost caught up to Rhapsody by the time Achmed and the Dhracian cleared the fissure and followed them over the cracked clay dunes into the fading twilight. The desert wind spun devils of dust all around them, obscuring the horizon.

"You'll never make it on horseback, even if you can reach them," the Dhracian said as they ran. "She will torch us all, especially if she can fly. We can't outrun her."

Achmed stopped, breathing heavily, and nodded. He pulled forth the cwellan and loaded three rysin-steel disks on the spindle.

The Dhracian stopped as well, but turned into the windstorm and began his cant, choking as the sand swirled into his mouth and sinuses. His cloak whipped around him but where he stood the wind died down, remaining still like a column of air, the eye within a swirling hurricane.

Just then the earth was rent asunder in a horrific spray of rock and sand as the beast reared up from the fissure, her massive body shattered the ground around the sluice. She was coughing red sputum and bees along with rancid fire, slashing her great tail back and forth across the sand, striking blindly at whatever she could reach.

Then she opened her wings, her crippled one healing but still black with bees, and attempted to take to the air.

ℜhapsody came to a halt at the top of the dune overlooking the ruins.

"Where are the horses?" she gasped to Grunthor.

The Sergeant-Major put his hand to his eyes.

"Can't see 'em," he shouted back over the scream of the wind. "Might o' been buried in the sandstorm or trotted off—Oi left 'em loose-hitched in case we didn't make it back. Duck, miss."

Rhapsody slid on her heels and rolled, the squirming bundle in her arms, as a gigantic shadow passed over her head and landed, off kilter, on a ruined tower several hundred yards away. From atop the minaret, the beast looked around, scanning the horizon, the malice of its intent clear even at the distance.

"Get back in that cloak!" Achmed shouted. "She's looking for *you*." He sighted the cwellan on the beast in the distance, but the chaotic gusts of the whipping desert wind and the darkness cloaked her, making his shot uncertain and likely to go astray.

"Can't," Rhapsody gasped as she struggled to stand with the baby in her arms. "It might expose—Meridion to—being seen—"

Come. Each of the three heard the word in their ears, a scratchy command behind them.

They turned to see the Dhracian, his hand still held aloft. Before him a part of the air was motionless, still as doldrums inside the swirling currents, like a doorway in the air.

Make haste. The beast comes.

Of one mind, Grunthor and Rhapsody ran straight for the door in the wind. Achmed maintained his sight on the beast in the distance while the Dhracian held it open.

Come, Assassin King. You are nearest.

At that moment the dragon caught sight of the movement in the lee of the ruins. She loosed a thin plume of caustic fire that rolled down the parapet and into the ground, setting fire to the minimal scrub vegetation there. Horrific screaming rent the night wind as the horses caught flame, their pathetic cries echoing up through the night.

A terrible stench tore through the air, the smell of brimstone and burning flesh. The dragon reared up and bellowed in frustration, then caught sight of other movement. Hobbled still by her torn wing, she leapt and glided to a lower ruin, a broken dome with arched windows, and steeled her sights on the four human figures running into the wind in the last light of the setting sun.

"Feint right, Grunthor!" Achmed shouted, then fired the cwellan. At that instant the beast recoiled and inhaled, a deep and horrible rattle in her chest that echoed over the desert plain.

The shot caught her wing just as the Dhracian seized the Bolg king and pushed him through the door in the wind. Unbalanced, the wyrm stumbled forward on the dome and loosed her breath, this time a greater billowing wave of heat and light that scorched the ground and caused the mother-of-pearl coating of the ruins to glisten with the reflected radiance of a million candleflames.

The giant Bolg started to reach back for Rhapsody, but was himself shoved within the swirling vortex of wind, followed by the Dhracian. The Lady Cymrian, bringing up the rear, reached the door just in time to be engulfed in the flames of the dragon's breath, her golden hair took on the light of a torch in full radiance as the fire swept around her, leaving her unharmed. She lunged inside.

The wind door closed, leaving the dragon alone in the darkness of the ruins.

The only sight the three companions caught before the door in the wind opened again was being elevated high above the desert plain, wrapped in a strong, sand-ridden current of air that glided southeast, whipping the desert sand ahead of it as it gusted along. Then all sight was engulfed in the mighty roar of the desert wind, a vortex of swirling, primeval power that carried them along the waves of sound as they rose and fell, finally terminating in silence.

When the gust that had carried them died away, the four people were standing at the base of a hilly dune not unlike the ones that they had been riding before they came to the ruin. The mountains in the distance were still there, but nearer; they had reached almost to the steppes before the piedmont of the Upper Teeth.

Achmed turned to see Grunthor shaking his head as if trying to expel the screech of the wind, or sand, from his ears, then looked over to Rhapsody.

She was standing, her face white as the crescent moon, her arms filled with the ashes of the mist cloak.

And nothing more.

34

$\mathcal{W}$ell, that was a neat trick," Grunthor said to the Dhracian, still picking the sand from his ears. "Oi've traveled the wind myself, but only when—" He stopped at the sight of the look on Achmed's face, then turned around to see Rhapsody staring at the ashes in her arms.

For a moment he could say nothing; seeing the expression on Rhapsody's face was like watching the end of the world. When the words came to his bulbous lips finally, they were gentle.

"How now, Duchess—where's the lit'le prince?"

Achmed shot him an acid glance.

The Lady Cymrian stood stock-still, not breathing. Then, after the shock passed, she began looking rapidly around her, her arms twitching, causing the remains of the cloak to drift gently down to the ground like black snow. Her eyes took on a mad light, a glitter of panic that was almost too ugly to behold.

"We—we have to go back," she stammered, turning around and scanning the ground. "I must—I must have dropped him. Please—o-open the door again—please, we have to go back—"

"Rhapsody." Achmed's voice was quiet. "Come here."

But the Lady Cymrian did not hear him. The sound of her heartbeat was pounding in her ears, threatening to burst; time had become suspended for her. She numbly crouched to the ground and felt around for something solid among the ashes, but there was nothing, just burnt strands of fabric and soot.

Finally she looked up.

"Achmed," she said softly, "where is my baby?"

The Bolg king reached out his hand.

"Stand up," he said gently.

Rhapsody shook her head, feeling around on the ground in the darkness once more.

"No, no, he must be here somewhere—he—Achmed, help me find the baby."

"Rhapsody—"

"Damn you, *help* me—he has to be here somewhere—I had him tightly, Achmed, please, help me find him—"

The Bolg king crouched down in front of her while the other two men looked on. He watched her in silence as she knelt on the ground, continuing to pat the earth helplessly in all directions, until she finally turned back to him. Then, before their eyes, she seemed to collapse; Achmed caught her as she fell forward into his arms.

"No," she whispered. "Please, no."

Achmed said nothing, but ran his bony hand awkwardly over her shining hair. He held her as she began to shudder, then she abruptly stopped and slowly looked up into his face, her cheeks wet with tears, but her eyes wide again in shock.

Then she looked down at her abdomen.

Distended there, between them.

Rhapsody's hand went to her belly, now expanded and swollen. Her expression became dazed.

"It can't be," she murmured.

Achmed's brows drew together. He stood, pulling her up with him.

"Where's the light?"

Grunthor jogged over and handed him the globe. "Ya dropped it just outside the sluice."

Achmed held the cold lantern up above her; there was no mistaking the bulge in her waist. A moment later, to his utter disgust, he thought he saw it move.

Stunned relief came over Rhapsody's face. "He's kicking. I can feel him kicking."

"I'm going to be ill," said Achmed.

"Well, well, look at that," Grunthor said, sounding immensely pleased, "the lit'le nipper found a safe place in all o' that. 'Ow'd 'e do that?"

"'Born free of the bonds of Time,'" Rhapsody said. "Perhaps that means he can be in whatever time he knows of—and this is the only other time he has ever known."

Achmed exhaled, annoyance evident in the sharpness of his breath.

"It's to be expected, I suppose; history is riddled with many young men who could not resist staying inside Rhapsody as long as they could."

"Well, that was ugly, sir," Grunthor admonished reprovingly. "You're talkin' about a mother, after all. So what's the plan?" He looked around for the Dhracian in the dark, but the man was not to be seen. "And where's yer friend?"

He stands behind you, holding the door.

Why are you still here? Achmed demanded of the darkness in the silent speech of his race. *I am sorry to disappoint you, but I cannot, and will not, join your endless quest for F'dor, though when I come across one, you can be comforted in knowing that I have been trained in the Thrall ritual, and will gladly do whatever I can to destroy it. There—are you satisfied?*

No. There is much that you still do not know.

I expect that will be the case throughout time, Achmed answered. *But for now, I have a kingdom to get back to, and preparations to make. We can waste no more time here; we've lost the horses, and we are ten days' walk from the nearest outpost in the northern Teeth. So be on your way, and best of luck in your quest. I am sorry to have disappointed you after all this time.*

I will come with you, the inaudible voice said. *I will open the doors of the wind for you, that the journey will be swift. And I will tell you of the Gaol, and of the Vault. And of your mother.*

Achmed thought for a moment. *I will not be beholden to you,* the Bolg king finally replied. *I guard the Sleeping Child—and I will not be threatened, or wheedled, or coaxed into abandoning her, even for as worthy a quest as the Primal Hunt. We can travel together, and I will listen to what you have to say. But after that, you will go back to being an assassin. I will go back to being a king. If you agree, then we have a deal.*

The wind whistled around him, raising sand to his eyes. The stars twinkled brightly above as he waited for his answer. Finally, it came.

Agreed. The Dhracian opened another door in the wind, behind which swirling currents of air could be seen. *I am Rath; and so you may call me.*

PART FOUR

The Tempest Rising

35

GOLGARN

Wars of conquest all have the same father, went the saying among the desert-dwelling tribe known as the Bengard race. *He is Hunger. He and his children–Lust, Greed, Rage, Vengeance—are all formed of the same sand.*

If anyone knew the lineage of war, it was the Bengard. Tall, oily-skinned, warlike men and women of gargantuan height and mass, whose history of conquest was unparalleled in the Known World, they had a long and deeply held belief that war was not only unavoidable, it was necessary and valuable. There was something almost holy in the constant state of readiness, of willingness to fight for almost any reason, that in the minds of this culture of limited resources and harsh environment was to be cherished and admired above all else. It was not aggression for aggression's sake, but rather the readiness for a war, whether of invasion or defense, that drove the race into the gladiatorial arena during outbreaks of peace.

And the fact that they found mortal combat to be rather fun.

But one thing the Bengard never truly understood was that while the father of war might always be Hunger, occasionally the mother of it was Fear.

More than any fear that clung, when banished by his waking mind, to the depths of his unconscious soul, Beliac feared being eaten alive.

In a different situation, a different man, that fear might be considered more irrational than most. While fear itself was a hobgoblin of the black crevasses of the mind, requiring no basis in the bright sunlight of reality in order to exist, the dread of being consumed while still living was strange even among the more ordinary terrors humans harbored: the fear of darkness or enclosure, of reptiles or arachnids, of heights or being buried alive. If it were anyone other than Beliac, the fear that his flesh might be chewed off of him and swallowed before his eyes would have bordered on insanity.

But Beliac had more reason than most to fear such a possibility.

Beliac was the king of Golgarn, the seaside nation to the southeast beyond the Manteids, the mountains known as the Teeth.

And his neighbors, to the north, were the Firbolg.

Beliac had been king of Golgarn for a long time by comparison to the other monarchs on the continent. He had assumed the throne of his peaceful nation more than a quarter century before, and his reign had been a pleasant one, his twenty-fifth jubilee marked by genuine celebration on the part of the populace. The mountains that were the bane of easy trade to the north were also his greatest protection, and given the legends of the population that inhabited the other side of those mountains, he was grateful for the barrier.

Nonetheless, in the recesses of his mind were the tales of horror told to him in childhood by his nursemaids and the other children, tales of marauding and murderous monsters who scaled the mountains like goats, their hands and feet equally articulated, searching for prey in the form of human children. As he grew older and studied the history of the continent, he learned the genesis of those fishwives' tales was real—that in fact the Firbolg truly were a cannibalistic race, hardened by the conquest of every land they had ever inhabited, a conglomeration of bastard strains of every culture they had ever touched. They were demi-human rats, and like rats, they did whatever they had to in order to survive.

Including eating their enemies.

It did not matter that Beliac had never seen a Firbolg within five hundred miles of his lands. Nor did it matter that none of his counselors or allies had, either. The Firbolg had taken the mountain city of Canrif in the northern Manteids, mountains they called the Teeth, at the end of the Cymrian War three hundred years before Beliac's father's reign, and had lived there ever since, preying on itinerant mountain goats, wayward deer, and each other. No raids had ever been made, no violence ever perpetrated on the citizens of Golgarn.

But it didn't matter.

Beliac, like every other young boy in his kingdom, had been told the tales in childhood of the nighttime stealth attacks, where Bolg crept in at children's windows, stealing babies from their cradles and carrying them off into the night to the sound of crunching jaws and smacking lips. Children were gobbled up a piece at a time, the legends said; it was rumored the Bolg would cover their faces with pillows to ensure quiet while they devoured the Golgarn little ones from the feet up. Beliac, at the age of eight summers, had adopted the customs of his friends and had eschewed sleeping either with pillows or without shoes for that reason.

Upon attaining manhood, he had begun to realize that the tales were lies, legends of the same caliber as the ghost stories and tales of monsters that were imparted between children for the pleasure of frightening each other. Still, there was something planted deep enough in his mind, somewhere between irrationality and reason, down in the deepest spaces where, unlike other children, he was bred with an inborn responsibility to safeguard an entire kingdom, that he could just not shake loose. It was a meaningless terror he had never truly overcome, something he laughed nervously about, all the while attempting to banish it from his conscious mind.

It was also a personal flaw that he had made the mistake, years before, of mentioning in the course of a supper well lubricated with the fine spirits of Argaut, to a friend of his.

A merchant named Talquist.

The Raven's Guild of Yarim had always had a guildmistress.

No one knew exactly why that was; most guilds in the underworld system of organized thieves and assassins were led by a guildmaster, a man whose reputation for strength and ruthlessness had been tested over and over again until he could reign undisputed, aided by a cohort of similarly strong henchmen and lackeys. It was the same politics that played out in palaces, barracks, and mercantiles the world over, but often with less backstabbing. Thieves and assassins, unlike kings, soldiers, and merchants, knew when to leave well enough alone where power was concerned.

But the Raven's Guild of Yarim was different. Unlike its brother guilds across the Known World, it had been led and held in the steely grasp of a series of women from its inception. As a result, it not only was the best organized of any known guild, holding all of the power of the province's capital city, Yarim Paar, in its tight control, but it was the most merciless and vengeful.

The mothers of the guild had established from the very beginning the need to own or have a major interest in all the industry of the city—in Yarim Paar's case, a massive tile foundry—so that the more nefarious aspects of the guild's business were only sidelines and methods of maintaining supremacy, rather than the main enterprise. The guild operated openly, and even the duke of the province knew better than to attempt to restrict their activities; one of his ancestors had been foolish enough to attempt it, and the dynastic line had almost not survived because of it.

The members of the Raven's Guild, therefore, had an almost religious devotion to their guildmistresses. The most recent of these women, Esten, was revered as a goddess, from the moment that Dranth, the guild scion, had spotted her eviscerating a soldier in a back alley at the age of eight summers. She had grown quickly to womanhood and dominance, holding the guild, the city, and much of the province of Yarim in her merciless grasp for her entire adult life, propagating the Raven's Guild's undisputed reign in black market trafficking, murder, thievery, assassination, and a host of even more brutal crimes, raising their skulduggery to the level of pure artistry.

Until her recent unfortunate, and wholly unexpected, death at the hands of the Bolg king's general.

The guild was still in shock from the delivery of her head, ripped from her shoulders and stuffed into a leather crate wrapped perfunctorily in parchment. The blood oath that the entire membership had taken against the man who was her enemy, Achmed the Snake, king of Ylorc, and his military commander who had been her assassin was the darkest and most eternal of any promise of revenge ever sworn. If the guild had been aware that even as they met in secret discussion and nefarious planning, that king, his Sergeant, and the Lady Cymrian were silently making their way across the red clay-sand of the province's open desert, the guild-hall would have emptied like a bursting heart, and blood would have flowed into that sand until it ran black.

But the guild was unaware of the passage of the Three across their region.

And the leaders of that guild were not in Yarim. They were in Gol-garn, a nation to which neither of them had ever traveled, in search of their brother guild within the port city's darker streets.

$\mathcal{D}$ranth, the Raven's Guild's scion, paused in disgust outside a filthy tavern in a back alley of the sailors' district, and turned to Yabrith, one of his lead guildmen, a petty thief, assassin, and general thug, the expression of annoyance making his already hollow features even more frightening.

"What sort of operation *is* this Spider's Clutch?" he asked disdainfully. "This is the third location, each one abandoned. Proletarians! This guild doesn't even have a permanent hall. I cannot believe Esten even entertained commerce with them. They're nothing more than street rats, scurrying from rathole to rathole each time they are flushed out. It embarrasses me to think that even distantly we are of the same profession."

Yabrith glanced about the alley nervously. "Never can be sure, sir. P'haps we best just check the last of the places we've been given, eh?"

"We have little enough choice," Dranth agreed. He pulled the hood of his cloak closer about his head and made his way back up the alley to the wharf, looking for signs of a smithy with a red-banded barrel out front.

The wind off the sea was fresh and salty, so unlike the hot breezes heavy with sand and the smoke of the tile foundry fires from whence they had come. The two men braced against it as they came around the street corner; the smell of the wind there changed to one of putrid barrels and fish, rotting wood and pitch.

The port of Golgarn was impressive in its size for a small nation, with seven hundred quays and slips in full operation at all times of the year. Golgarn's navy had its own outer harbor through which merchant ships and military vessels of other nations had to pass, protecting the docks from becoming a haven of illegal commerce, for the most part. Shipping was the nation's main industry, due to its sheltered nature as one of easternmost ports of the Known World, and its location far enough away from the Skeleton Coast of Sorbold to prevent competition. The secondmost industry was hospitality in support of that shipping trade; inns, hostels, and taverns of every stripe lined the streets leading away from the waterfront, catering to whatever proclivities their seafaring clientele might have.

The easternmost side of the city, known as the Jeweled Streets, was the most elegant, with beautiful inns, expensive eateries, and well-stocked shops that dealt in wares from all around the Known World, as well as the work of Golgarn's renowned weavers and jewelers, artisans who made exceptional use of the soft wools of the native stock of mountain sheep and the sapphires, rubies, and tourmalines mined from the face of her mountains.

The farther one went away from the Jeweled Streets the plainer and more homespun the offerings became. The central district, built around an immense dormitory known as the Sailors' Arms, was a clean, serviceable area with plentiful food and goods available to the working men and women of the town, and those who plied the seas for a living, seeking a peaceful night's rest before shipping out again.

The shops and alehouses became poorer farther west, near the less-traveled piers and the fishing villages, where Golgarn's poorer sons dragged their living out of the waters that had been the livelihood of their families for time uncounted. The trade in those parts was rougher, the constabulary less in evidence, but still the presence of the maritime soldiers and armed Coast Watch troops was never too far out of sight. Shipping trade invited unsavory sorts, and so Golgarn had one of the best equipped naval forces in the Known World, not to wage war upon the sea, or form armadas to threaten other ports, but to fend off the pirates and other scum of the ocean that preyed upon coastal nations.

As Dranth and Yabrith traveled the wharf in the fading afternoon light, they looked to the skies for a clue to help them find the smithy. Within a short while it became clear that the air about the smokehouses where fish were being cured was different in color from the fumes above businesses dealing in more durable goods, so they moved away from the streets closest to the harbor and deeper in the western district where blackened stone buildings stood with only narrow alleyways between, their shutters and stairways largely broken or rotting from the salt air.

In front of one such building, its storefront open like a yawning maw, was a red banded barrel. Acrid black smoke poured from the wide chimney and out the front of the small building, causing the opening to look even more like a demonic mouth. A harsh, deep clanging issued forth from inside the shop.

"This is the last 'un," Yabrith whispered.

Dranth strode to the doorway, waving aside the smoke, and looked inside.

A heavyset man with muscular arms and a bulging belly was hammering with an enormous sledge against an anvil, banging a red-hot iron brace into shape. His almost hairless head was crowned with a snowy fringe, the only part of him that appeared the least bit white, so covered was he in soot. His face was red in the heat of the smelting fire, and he grunted with each blow of the sledge. Three scrawny boys were taking turns working an old, shoddy bellows.

Dranth choked back his displeasure and stepped through the smoke. "John Burgett?"

The man at the anvil looked up; he took two more short whacks at the brace, then put down the sledge beside the anvil.

"Who's askin'?"

"I bring you greetings on behalf of my cousin in the hills," replied Dranth. It was a countersign used only by those familiar with the darkest of guild workings.

The heavyset man inhaled deeply, then damped the fire. He turned and yelled over his shoulder.

"Taffy! Get out here an' tend the anvil! You 'prentices, keep pumpin' them bellows."

A thick, black-haired man with a weasel-like countenance appeared from the back. The heavyset man took off his leather apron and tossed it to him, then wiped his hands on his trousers and came over to where Dranth and Yabrith were standing.

"Does this cousin of yours have a name?" he asked.

"Yes," replied Dranth. "Her name is Esten."

"Hmmm," said the man. "Then I suppose I'm John Burgett. What do you gents want?"

"I have a business proposition for you," Dranth said.

The man smiled broadly. "Your horse throw a shoe?"

"Yes," said Dranth acidly. "That's it."

The broad man chuckled, nodded to Taffy, then gestured for the two men to follow him.

He led them out of the smoke-filled smithy and along the narrow alleyways back toward the wharf without speaking; Dranth and Yabrith were accustomed to such silence.

They followed him past ramshackle houses and bait shops, taverns and pubs, until they finally came to the waterfront. The man who had called himself John Burgett whistled merrily as they approached the wharf, heading straight for a long dock at the western end of town, deep within the fishing village.

Night was falling, and no one paid any attention to them; scores of fishermen were heading in, unloading their second catches of the day, emptying the spoils of their clam traps and lobster pots into wagons and horse-drawn carts poised along the docks, then dousing the shellfish with seawater, paying little mind to anything else taking place around them. The flurry of evening activity was electric and covered their passage perfectly.

Dranth and Yabrith exchanged a glance as the blacksmith stepped out onto the long pier and began heading for the end of it. Neither man had ever been on the water before; neither had even seen the sea, but Dranth had ice in his veins and Yabrith was afraid enough of Dranth not to be able to refuse him anything, so after a second's hesitation they both stepped gingerly onto the shaky pier and followed the heavyset man to the end.

As they were walking, they watched in alarm as he turned and stepped off into the water, or so it appeared. When they reached the end of the dock they saw he was standing in a small dingy, tossing a coil of rope out of the way of the rough boards that served as seats. The man looked up at them and grinned.

"Come aboard, gents," he said, then went back to his work.

"Where are we going?" Dranth demanded, his dark eyes nervously scanning the pier and the water.

The blacksmith shrugged. "I thought you wanted to meet John Burgett," he said cheerily. "My mistake—never mind. Good day to you both."

Dranth exhaled sharply and looked farther offshore. In the distance he could make out a cluster of medium-sized boats, moored many yards out but still within the inner harbor. He silently acknowledged that such a place would be a formidable haven for an enterprise such as the Spider's Clutch, a movable hideout surrounded on all sides by water, where the chance of being overheard was minuscule.

The two desert dwellers steeled their nerves and stepped down into the rowboat; Yabrith stumbled and fell to his knees as the dingy rocked beneath him, to the great amusement of the blacksmith. He offered Dranth his hand, but the guild scion shook his head and stepped down carefully, only eliciting minor rocking. He took a seat on a slimy board, choking back his disgust and trying not to be overwhelmed by the smell.

The blacksmith sat down heavily in the other end of the small boat, fitted the oars into the oarlocks, and began rowing for the cluster of boats.

All during the passage Dranth and Yabrith struggled to hold on to the contents of their stomachs. Water was a precious and rare commodity in Yarim, so the sight of the endless sea and its accompanying odor and motion was overwhelming. By the time the little dingy reached the encampment of boats, both men were green, to the obvious amusement of the blacksmith. The man merely continued to row in silence until they reached the outer edge of the cluster, where cabin boats and barnacle-encrusted fishing trawlers bounced gracefully on the waves.

As they grew closer, the blacksmith began to whistle, a cheerful melody that cut through the sound of the splashing waves slapping against the hulls of the boats as the sun began to sink below the rim of the world, splashing the sea with red light that resembled a rippling pool of blood.

After a moment, a small round man with a dark blue cap and jacket appeared on the closest boat's deck and stood, his hands in his pockets, looking down at the dingy as it approached.

When the rowboat was finally alongside the outer cluster, the blacksmith secured the oars and stood up. He grabbed hold of the rope mooring and tossed it to the round man, who caught it with a movement so quick that Dranth didn't even see him take his hands from his pockets. The two men of Golgarn tied the dingy to the mooring irons of the boat, then the blacksmith stepped easily out of it and onto the deck. He turned and beckoned to Dranth and Yabrith to follow.

The two Yarimese assassins looked at each other.

"Ya coming?" the blacksmith asked patiently.

Dranth stood up slowly and stepped carefully over the gunwales, trying not to look down at the green sea looming between the boats. He stepped onto the deck and slid on the salt spray, but managed to right himself before falling. He turned quickly and pulled Yabrith over, then gestured impatiently at the blacksmith, who chuckled and disappeared around the bow of the boat.

The two men of Yarim followed him quickly, only to discover when they rounded the bow themselves that they were staring at a corridor of boat bows, all aligned nose to nose with one another, bobbing gently in the tide. While a few of the boats were open skiffs, most of them were trawlers and houseboats, with dark cabins in which flickering lights beckoned ominously.

The blacksmith reappeared, six boats away.

"You gents coming in?" he asked solicitously. "Or are ya planning to swim back?" He laughed aloud, then vanished into the black hold of the houseboat.

Dranth and Yabrith inhaled collectively, then slowly began to pick their way between the moorings, balancing carefully, as the red light on the sea faded to gray with the coming of night.

36

*W*ithin the dark hold ahead a candle was flickering.

Dranth peered within.

"Do come in. It's impolite to linger in doorways."

The voice was rich and deep, but with a knife's edge to it. It issued forth from the blackness of the ship's hold, disembodied. Dranth looked for the source, but the shadows were too heavy, and kept shifting as the boat rocked. He steadied himself and stepped through the opening.

Around the small open room other candles began to spark into light. Dranth, no stranger to such meeting tactics, remained still, waiting for the illumination to drive some of the shadows out. He could see shapes in the corners, far enough away from the candleflames to avoid clear sight, but near enough to present a show of numbers. At least one of them was the blacksmith, from his outline. By his estimate there were eight people in the room in addition to himself and Yabrith, who was still lurking outside the opening. He snapped his fingers, and his henchman stepped into the room.

The flickering candle that had been alight the whole time began to glow brighter as other wicks in it were lit. Dranth saw that this was being done by a slight man with red hair and thin, sharp features, all except for his eyes, which were enormous and owlish; they glowed like beacons in the dark. As the radiance in the room expanded, he could see the man was wiry and not particularly tall, with fair skin mottled by the sun and vaguely pocked with age, and perhaps drink.

"And who is calling this fine evening?" the red-haired man asked.

"Dranth, from the Raven's Guild," the guild scion said. "I come under the auspices of the Golden Measure."

Some of the dark figures around the room exchanged glances, but the red-haired man merely nodded. The countersign was one known only to guild hierarchs of all types, and would only be recognized by the leaders of such organizations, whether they were tradesmen, craftsmen, merchants, or thieves. Dranth had used it to confirm what he already suspected; the man at the table was the leader of the Spider's Clutch.

"Do you now, Dranth from the Raven's Guild?" the red-haired man said idly. "And what is it you want?"

"I'm looking for John Burgett."

"Aye, you've found him," said the man. "And to what do I owe the pleasure of your visit? This is the first time one of your guild has come in person; generally we have just communicated with your mistress by bird."

Dranth's dark eyes took on an impatient gleam in the half-light.

"I have a proposition for you that was too important to trust to any messenger."

"Really now?" said the man who called himself John Burgett, amused. "We're honored, of course. What is this weighty proposition? And why didn't your mistress come herself if it's so important?" He pointed at two stools near the table. "Please, sit. You're looking a little green around the gills."

Dranth did not know if the guildmaster was testing him, or if word had just not reached the distant shores of Golgarn, but he decided the risk of revealing the truth was minimal, given the geography.

And given the poison gourds he had stashed about his person, a toxin to which he and Yabrith were both immune, but that would be released upon any attack against him.

He sat, nodding to Yabrith to do the same.

"Esten is dead—murdered," he said flatly. The words cost him dear; he still had a gnawing pain in his gut at the very thought. "I speak for the guild now."

The shadows in the room exchanged glances again. There was even an intake of breath from one corner, Dranth noted with some satisfaction. His mistress's reputation had been well known.

And well deserved.

Only the red-haired man appeared unmoved.

"I'm sorry to hear that," said Burgett. "What is your proposition?"

Dranth crossed his hands on the table board in front of him. "I seek your help in the planting of some information valuable to a friend of mine," he said directly. "A simple task, really, and easy to accomplish, especially given the Spider's Clutch's proclivity for moving headquarters."

Burgett smiled broadly, revealing remarkably white teeth.

"Aye, we do that indeed," he said. "Like our namesake. I assume you've seen dock spiders, or perhaps their desert-dwelling cousins, who spin webs of singular artistry in eaves or between fence posts or on pylons? Someone comes along with a broom or a cloth and destroys this beautiful creation with a single sweep, and yet the next morning there it is again, in the same place or another, equally magnificent?"

"I suppose," said Dranth dryly.

"Well, such is the need of our guild. Unlike your own, which I hear is able to operate in plain sight, due to the weakness of the leaders of your province, we are a poor band, struggling under the oppression of the crown. With all the trade in the port of Golgarn, every other blasted person on the street is a soldier or military sailor, skilled at fending off piracy and other sea crimes. In short, Dranth, Golgarn is crawling with the law. Not much for a self-respecting guild to do but operate in the shadows and learn to be adaptable."

"Understood," Dranth said. "And if you agree to help me, I may be able to assist in changing that situation."

The shadowy figures exchanged glances again.

"Is that so?" said John Burgett. "That's a tall order. Let's hear the details of your proposition."

Dranth sat back. He reached into his cloak and pulled forth a packet wrapped in leather.

"You will begin meeting again in one of your former eaves, fence posts, or pylons—some place that has been raided before and was known to have been a hideout of yours, where your proverbial web was swept clean. It doesn't matter where, as long as the crown has known of it. Then you will arrange for them to know of it again—and they will raid it again. When they do, you will have scattered, naturally—but they will find various booty, perhaps weapons, perhaps contraband, but most especially, they will find these documents."

"And if I could read these documents, what would they say?"

The boat shifted, and Dranth's stomach lurched. The men from the Spider's Clutch didn't seem to notice.

"They are maps," he said, "maps of tunnels five miles beyond Golgarn's northwest border, where the Firbolg are encamped, massing for an attack."

The only sound in the room was the creaking of the ship and the slapping of the waves.

Then, to a one, the shadows began to laugh.

"Firbolg?" said John Burgett in disbelief. "Are you certain they are not also in league with hobgoblins and trolls?"

Dranth did not laugh in return.

"I assure you, Mr. Burgett, that when your king sends scouts to investigate these documents, and he will, he will find such an encampment in those mountains."

"He will?"

"Yes, he will. Bad sanitation, bones strewn at cave entrances, the entire nightmarish scenario—however ludicrous you and I know it to be. It's cost me quite a bit to set up, but it's impressively realistic."

The red-haired man smiled even as his brow furrowed. He interlaced his fingers and brought his hands to rest on his belly.

"All right, I'm intrigued. What possible gain is there for you—and me—in persuading Beliac that the Bolg are massing in the hills outside Longsworth?"

"It's a diversion," said Dranth. "Beliac will panic at the prospect of Golgarn being a feeding ground for the Firbolg. And since he does not have the land military power to do anything to stop it, he will turn to an ally who does—and commit his naval forces, as well as whatever pathetic army he has—to the service of that ally in return for being saved from the big, bad Firbolg—who could care less that he, or any of you, exist. For you, it means that the omnipresence of the military will be over; once the men of Golgarn have been conscripted into the war that is to come, you can emerge from the shadows into the light, where you will discover many unguarded citizens and visitors to your fair land who are without the protection they once enjoyed. Not to mention ships. You can raise the practice of your profession from shadow thuggery to, well, whatever you wish it to be. And my aforementioned friend, who coincidentally happens to be the ally to whom Beliac will turn, will get the support he craves for his war."

Burgett exhaled. "And for you?"

A tight smile finally cracked Dranth's features.

"The Raven's Guild will obtain what it most dearly desires—vengeance on the one whose actions put me in charge."

The owlish eyes glistened with interest.

"Very well," the red-haired man said after a moment, his deep voice smooth and resonant. "I will accept your proposition, Dranth from the Raven's Guild. Go back to the wharf—follow the man you came here with—and proceed on alone by night to an inn just to the lee of the north gate of the city. You'll know the place by its firebrands outside, and the white straw of its roof. Go in the side door and ask the woman at the bar to send out her husband to speak to you. Tell him you are looking to buy a dray mare, and give him your papers. You can be assured they will be found as you hoped."

"And what is the name of the man I am seeking?" Dranth asked, rising from the table and steadying himself on his feet. "Just in case there is more than one woman in the bar in the inn with a husband."

The pearly teeth gleamed white in the darkness of the boat's hold.

"Why, his name's John Burgett, of course."

When the raid on the inn was accomplished, the papers took almost no time in making their way to Beliac's table.

The king was in the middle of his breakfast at the time, sweetening the whey in his porringer with molasses, when the messenger arrived from the very efficient commander of the city's police brigade.

Upon opening the commander's packet and reading the contents, the king spat his breakfast the entire length of the table. The Queen of Golgarn, seated across from him, rose from her chair in disgust, even as his adult children choked back laughter.

Scouts were dispatched forthwith, as Dranth had predicted. Upon entering the mountain passes to the northwest of the prefecture of Longsworth, they came upon a sight that had been relegated to the stuff of nightmares a thousand or more years old.

From the bases of the first mountain pass to the summit of the hills that led up into the mountainous reaches, a pathway of human bones had been carefully bordered with a series of fencelike posts.

Each crowned with a human head in varying stages of decay.

The stench of the encampment, issuing forth from a variety of repulsive sources, was so overwhelming that two of the four scouts immediately turned from the scene and retched. The more intrepid two, possessing somewhat stronger stomachs, ventured up alongside the path in tree cover until they were in position to observe through a spyglass the encampment itself.

A series of caves, hidden from view from below, were being loosely guarded by tall, broad manlike creatures, hirsute and covered in filth, who sat sharpening cruel-looking weapons and setting up catapults with arms that could easily lift burdens of two hundred stone or more. They appeared to be training their weapons defensively on the mountain passes, but had shown evidence of positioning similar encampments farther up the hillside, from which the town would be not only visible, but within range.

$\mathcal{D}$ranth and Yabrith remained in Golgarn, taking rooms at the beautiful Sea Duchess inn in the heart of the Jeweled Streets and enjoying the fine cuisine of the port city, including the new experience of seafood, which Dranth found to be quite to his liking. Yabrith, still suffering queasiness from the smell of the sea, was unable to stomach anything more gastronomically challenging than fish stew.

It was only a matter of days before the word came back to the palace. While neither of the men were privy to the conversations of the king and his scouts, there was no mistaking the outcome.

They were sitting out on the terrace of the Sea Duchess one fine morning when a royal mail coach came clattering through the finely cobbled streets, the driver urging the horses mercilessly in order to meet the outgoing tide.

"What do you suppose the message he's carrying says?" asked Yabrith idly, picking the sausage out of his teeth with an ivory shard as they watched the carriage driver delivering a package under seal to the yeoman at the docks.

"Can't imagine," said Dranth, folding his napkin. "But something tells me it may be time for us to head home—I have had as much as I can tolerate of the hospitality of John Burgett."

37

KRALDURGE, YLORC, THE BOLGLANDS

$\mathcal{D}$eep within the old Cymrian lands, past the wide heath beyond the canyon and sheltered by a high inner ring of rock formations was Kraldurge, the Realm of Ghosts. It was the only place the Bolg, without exception, did not go, a desolate, forbidding place from the look of its exterior structures.

What heinous tragedy had occurred here was unclear in the legends, but it had been devastating enough to permanently scar the psyche of the Firbolg who lived in the mountains. They spoke in reluctant whispers of fields of bones and wandering demons that consumed any creature unfortunate enough to cross their paths, of blood that seeped up from the ground and winds that ignited anyone caught on the plain.

It also was the place that marked the beginning of the lands of their king's First Woman, as the Firbolg called Rhapsody. For them this was an even better reason not to go anywhere near the place.

Within a range of guardian rocks that reached high into the peaks around them stood an uncovered meadow, overgrown in meadow flowers that Rhapsody planted upon coming to this place, now untended in her absence. A hill-like mound rose in the center of the meadow, a place she had paid special attention at the time, due to the unsettling nature of the vibration she found there. There was something innately sad and overwhelmingly unsettling all throughout the hidden canyon-dell, but most especially at this place on top of the mound. For that reason she covered it in heartsease, flowers that in the old world the Lirin planted in cemeteries and on battlefields as a sign of mourning and reconciliation, and most particularly of condolence. She did not know at the time, nor did she know now, what she was trying to apologize for, what had happened deep within the history of the sad, windswept place that caused the very ground to cry out in pain, but she knew that whatever it had been was so traumatic, so ultimately wrong, that nothing could be done save for the gentle offering of flowers and a song of comfort in the hope of reclaiming the earth at least a little there.

Some of the reputation Kraldurge had as a playground for demons and other harbingers of evil came from its geology. Anyone walking through the circle of guardian rocks found themselves in a hollow canyon, surrounded by a circle of towering cliff sides. It was impossible to walk there without one's footfalls sounding up the canyon walls, echoing at an enormous amplification, so that anything that might have been waiting would have had ample warning, something always dangerous in the Bolglands, which for years had been roved by hungry demi-humans in search of any prey they could find.

The canyon that hid the grassy field was so tall that the wind rarely reached down into it; it howled around the top of the surrounding crags, creating a mournful wail. Even the bravest Bolg or most educated human could mistake the noise for demonic shrieking. Despite the natural explanation for the sound, there was still the sense of an innate sadness to the place, a feeling of overwhelming grief and anger.

In her time as putative duchess of these lands, Rhapsody had begun to wonder if Kraldurge was a forgotten burial ground from the earliest conflicts of the Cymrian War. There was no mention of it in the manuscripts of Gwylliam's vast and spectacular library, a collection of manuscripts and scrolls containing much of the wisdom of the world that they had located upon discovering this place four years before. The offering of peace flowers had seemed to work; now, though the wind continued to shriek and howl around the top of the rocks, filling the canyon with the same eerie, unsettling noise, the ground seemed to sleep, peacefully if not really in peace.

Or at least it had before the dragon came.

The wind moaned high above the canyon, still laden with the last ice crystals of winter, as the final door of their journey opened. Rath stepped out into the dell, then moved aside to allow the other three travelers to come off the breeze.

Rhapsody was the last to come forth. The return of the baby to her womb had caused many of the symptoms she had experienced in the course of her pregnancy to return; the nausea and light-headedness and, more particularly, the blurring of vision made her feel more unsteady than the the two Firbolg in the course of traveling the wind. As a result, she sensed a sudden silence from the three men, a silence unusual in that none of them was given to talk much in the first place. But she could not see why.

"What's the matter?" she asked. "Is everything all right?"

"That would depend upon how you define 'all right,'" Achmed replied, turning slowly around and surveying the damage before him.

The towering walls of rock were scorched in places rising up almost to the summit. The ground that at one time Rhapsody had believed might contain the bones of soldiers who fought and died in the Cymrian War or, perhaps even before that, the bodies of those souls, starving or sickly, who had not survived very long after the stragglers of the Third Fleet had arrived in Canrif was sundered from one side of the meadow to the other.

"Don't look quite the way it did when you were 'ere, Duchess," Grunthor said. "The new tenant is a bit less tidy than you were."

"New tenant?" Rhapsody said humorously, struggling to focus her eyes. "What new tenant? Who did you rent my lands out to, Achmed? I thought you were going to keep them for me in perpetuity; I earned them, after all."

"Well, this is more a squatter than a tenant I would say," Achmed answered, searching for the passage down to the hidden grotto known as Elysian. He found it a moment later in a pile of overturned rocks and sod that had been riven by the wyrm's passage. Originally the passage had been hidden in an alcove that always seemed touched by shadow, so carefully obscured that it had taken Achmed quite some time to find it the first time. "I don't know if you're going to be able to go down to the grotto or not, Rhapsody. Perhaps it would be best if you just come into the city itself, and take rooms inside the mountain."

Rhapsody recognized the tone in his voice. "What are you not telling me, Achmed?" she asked sharply, turning again and struggling to see.

"As always, you are listening for what I am not telling you, rather than to what I am."

"That's because you always say much more in what you are *not* saying. Tell me; what has happened here?"

The Bolg king sighed. "Before she came to find us in the forest at her mother's lair, Anwyn came here looking for you," he said. "Whether she remembered this place from the battle at the Moot, or whether there was something about it that called to her from the Past, Grunthor and I have no idea. I did not know until after we had set forth on our journey that she had come to the Bolglands first. Apparently she did not like the fact that your scent now was clinging to her cottage, or maybe she hated the way you redecorated it. In any event, it's my understanding that she's destroyed the grotto, or at least the house on the island in the middle of the lake. There's no sense in going down there now, Rhapsody; the firmament that holds up the cave is probably unstable. It's not safe, and I promised your infernal husband that I would do everything in my power to keep you safe, so while this was a good choice of destination because of the strength of the wind here, there's really no reason to stay."

The men watched as the Lady Cymrian turned around again, still struggling to see the place they first came when they arrived in the Bolglands. She extended her arms out in front of her and made her way to where the passage had been, then felt about on the rock wall. She turned back to them, her face contorted with grief.

"The opening is still here, Achmed," she said. "Please; I want to see the grotto. I need to know what has happened to my house."

"Oi don' think that's a good idea, Duchess," said Grunthor gently.

"Are you telling me that the structure of the cave is unsafe?"

"No," said the Sergeant-Major, unwilling to lie to her. "Nuthin' but an earthquake will take down that dome. That cave's right solid, and the lake is there still. But there's nothing left of your house; nothing worth mentioning, anyway."

"Are you certain?" Rhapsody pressed, numbly feeling the wall face again. "My instruments, my clothing? Did nothing survive?"

"Nothing Oi saw," said the giant Bolg. "I didn't row out to the island itself, o' course, but that was partly because Oi could see pieces o' the house floating all about the lake. If ya want to come back at some point and see if there's anything we can salvage, Oi'd be glad to come with you. But for right now Oi think we should get you settled inside the complex. It'll be good to have you in there again, miss."

"What are you looking for specifically?" Achmed asked impatiently. "Whatever need you have, it can be met within the walls of Canrif."

Rhapsody sighed and began to walk back to them, her hand on her swollen belly.

"I doubt it," she said. "But we can go if you wish. There was a Naming garment there, one that no doubt had been worn by the three brothers, Meridion's grandfather and great-uncles. It was a family heirloom, and I thought perhaps it would've been nice for him to be able to wear it when we have time for a proper Naming ceremony."

Achmed snorted and started out of the meadow.

"Perhaps you ought to wait and see when and if he decides to be born again," he said, following the pathway out of Kraldurge. "If I heard the prophecy correctly, he's not subject to the whim of Time. For all you know you could be carting him around in there until his eighteenth birthday or beyond."

"All right," Rhapsody said briskly, ignoring him. "Let's get to Canrif; now that I'm pregnant again, I'm in desperate need of a privy."

Rath had not expected to find what he did in Canrif.

He had not had occasion to walk within the mountain for centuries, a reasonably long period of time, even for one of his advanced age. At that time he had been tracking the demon known as Vrrinax, a F'dor with an inordinate amount of patience that had taken refuge on the last of the ships of the Cymrian Third Fleet, too weak to subsume any host but a sickly cabin boy. The demon had bided its time, slowly growing stronger, passing to more and more powerful hosts as it could, until it had learned to hide so successfully that Rath had been asked to take it on.

For all that he was modest, and had not shared the information with Achmed, Rath was the most accomplished of all the Gaol, the single greatest hunter of the Brethren.

In short, an Assassin King himself.

He could still smell its essence as he silently traversed the hallways of the underground city that the Cymrians had called Canrif, the word meaning *Century* in their now-dead language. It had been a very long time, but some traces of evil remained in stone, in water, in wood where great wrongs had been perpetrated, or great deeds of maliciousness formulated.

Something of that ilk must have happened here, he reasoned. And in particular, he believed it had begun on the floor of the throne room.

Still, the Three were inured to it. Even the Firbolg king did not notice as he trod the floors of the place, an action that made Rath almost sick with disgust. Only the Lady Cymrian avoided the place where the taint was emanating from, as if she had seen a vision there, or was made uncomfortable by the traces of memory.

What troubled Rath about that was the lack of racial memory. While the Lady Cymrian and the Sergeant could hardly be expected to do so, those of Dhracian blood carried within them forever the scent of the blood of every beast they slew.

And Achmed had killed two of them in relatively short time.

It did not bode well that the Assassin King could even sleep within the walls of such a place, the place where the blood of a F'dor that had died at his hands still vibrated in the walls, the very floor of the place.

He followed his hosts silently around as they went about their business, to the corridor where his quarters were, to the hallway outside the mountain peak of Gurgus, where the Lightcatcher was being rebuilt, and even to the overlook of the underground city itself, still in the process of being restored. Everywhere he looked, he saw Firbolg artisans and soldiers, archons, educators, and masons, all working to restore what had been one king's vision. It was clear to Rath that the Bolg were another king's vision, a king who saw himself as building a people, not a mountain stronghold, a noble cause in the eyes of men, but a distraction for one who could be an even greater hunter than Rath.

He would watch closely.

When the two Bolg, Rhapsody, and Rath entered the room at the base of Gurgus Peak, a tall young man with a full beard and head of dark hair came up to the Lady Cyrmian immediately, smiling broadly.

"Hello, Rhapsody," he said. "Welcome back; it's wonderful to see you."

Rhapsody stared at him, befuddled. "I'm sorry," she said, "do I know you?"

The two Bolg and the bearded young man laughed.

"You don't remember Omet?" Achmed asked mockingly. "And you were the one that insisted on saving him in the kilns of the Raven's Guild."

Rhapsody's bright green eyes opened wide in shock. "Omet?" she asked in amazement. "You are twice as tall as you were the last time I saw you—and were you not bald?"

"I was," said the young man agreeably. "But it was hot in Esten's kilns, and it is cold here in the mountain."

"Omet has taken the lead in the annealing of the glass and building the Lightcatcher," Achmed said. "He's one of the few artisans I allow alone in the room." His voice fell away awkwardly; Omet had been gravely injured in the explosion that rocked Gurgus Peak, and it was the red spectrum of the Lightcatcher itself that had saved his life.

Rhapsody hugged the young man warmly. "I'm so very glad to see you," she said.

"Well, you're the one that told me to go carve my name in the mountains for history to see," Omet said, smiling. "I'm only doing what you told me to do."

Rhapsody looked around. Any evidence of destruction from the explosion was no longer present; the room had been restored as if nothing had ever happened. A wooden dome covered the ceiling of the tower, beneath which she could see colored glass of all hues.

"I look forward to you showing me what you've done," she said.

She looked behind her to see Rath standing beneath the dome of the ceiling, staring up into the circle of glass. "Are you all right?"

The Dhracian nodded. "I have seen this before," he said, still staring up into the tower. "It was in such a place I first learned the Prophecy of the Decks."

The Bolg king inclined his head.

"Care to elaborate?"

The Dhracian finally broke his black gaze away and stared at Achmed.

"You have not been told the Prophecy of the Decks?"

"No."

"It is this," Rath said. "'That which was Stolen will be given freely. That which was freely Given will be stolen.'"

"It means nothing to me," said Achmed crossly.

Rath inhaled deeply.

"I will tell you the tale. And then you will know what you are up against."

38

"On the Before-Time, a great battle was waged against the F'dor by the four remaining primordial races born of the elements," Rath began. "Our race, the Brethren known to man as the Kith, banded together with the Serenel, the Mythlinus, and the Wyrmril, that which men call dragons. It was determined that unless these four races, separate and distrustful of one another, worked together and sacrificed some of what was most precious to them, the unbridled destructiveness of the F'dor would shatter the world.

"Before this battle began, the F'dor managed to steal one of the first six eggs produced by the Progenitor Wyrm, the being that was mother and father to the race, and secreted the egg away in the bowels of the Earth beyond the fiery core, where it could never be found. The wyrmling from this egg was known to the dragon race as the First Child. The F'dor removed the heat from this wyrmling, allowing it to grow, unborn, perverting it, feeding it on the earth itself, until its mass began to become part of the heft of the world."

"We have seen it," Achmed said. "It still sleeps—Rhapsody wove a song of endless change around it, a pattern of confusion that she hoped would prevent any speaking of its name to be heard."

Rath's eyes of liquid black gleamed. "Let us hope you are right. From this Sleeping Child the F'dor harvested seven precious scales, and took the two more that served to protect its blind eyes. Because dragons have lore from each of the other elements, there was power in these scales that encompassed the entire color spectrum, the vibrations of light and musical tones that make up the magic of the universe. Each of the colors in the seven scales has a specific power attuned to its wave length, as well as a note in the scale, which are the visible and audible manifestations of those vibrations. As your Namer can tell you, there are many more manifestations that are neither visual nor audible. You know this yourself as well, Bolg king—you can feel them in your skin-web as each moment of the day passes.

"The F'dor, therefore, were able to make use of these dragon scales to affect the material world which they otherwise could not be part of, because they were without form and noncorporeal. Thus, they had control of a complete color spectrum of seven, plus the two most powerful opposites, one black, representing Void, and one white, representing Life, from its eyes. They used these powers destructively, to scry, ignite volcanoes, shed blood, steal heat, and otherwise wreak havoc on the material world.

"It was for this reason the other primordial races joined together in the battle against the F'dor. For all that history relates this as if it were an obvious conflict, I can assure you that was not the case. While it may seem to you that the elements of starlight, earth, water, and wind are in opposition to that of fire, in fact they were all like siblings, more similar than they were disparate. This decision was undertaken in agony, not in triumph, nor in conquest; the pact to remove that which brought warmth and light to the world, and condemn those races to be less than they could have been in the mind of the Creator. For all that it was the only thing that can be done, we were all poorer as a result of it. This is lost lore, something that history, and even some who lived it, have forgotten.

"When the decision was finally made, it was determined that terrible sacrifice would be required from each of the four remaining races in order for it to come to pass. You know what it is that our race sacrificed, Bolg king—the sons of the wind had a unique ability to track and trace the movements of that which was noncorporeal, and so it was decided the tribe of Kith known as the Dhracians would serve as jailers, would give up their tie to the wind and their ability to walk the upworld, for the purpose of guarding the Vault. The Dhracians abandoned the wind that was their father, and moved forever to the black and airless quadrant of the Earth, a soulless, lifeless sector of the world to guard against that which would see the world in flames.

"The dragons contributed most of the remaining Living Stone of the earth, their most prized possession, for the construction of the Vault to contain the F'dor. In the course of the battle, and the confinement of the F'dor, the scales were taken back from the demons. The Progenitor Wyrm, horrified at the desecration of his child, ripped seven similar scales from his own hide, for the purpose of being melded to the first set, to balance out their destructive power with the positive aspects of the same vibrations, the sharps to the flats of each note. The Progenitor sacrificed his life in the course of the battle, surrounding the fragile prison and Ending, becoming effectively a lead casing for the Vault, inert and totally devoid of any lore the demons could use. The seven colored scales were melded to the ones given by the Progenitor in the fiery core by the Seren who led the campaign. This group of scales, plus the white and black, became known as the Stolen Deck.

"The remaining eggs hatched, producing the Five Daughters, known to the Wyrmril as the Guardians, the matriarchal wyrms who each protected one of the World Trees that grew at the sites where each of the five elements first appeared in the world. In order for the power of the Stolen Deck to be broken, each of these dragons was given one of the scales that had once been part of both their sibling and their father. The other four scales were given into the care of other beings in different parts of the world, to keep them as far apart as possible. This is referred to in the Prophecy of the Decks: *That which was Stolen will be given freely.*"

The Three exchanged a glance.

"Do you think that Elynsynos was still in possession of such a scale when she—up until now?" Rhapsody asked nervously.

"I would hope so," Rath said. "Elsewise it is in other hands, and one of the Stolen Deck in the control of an evil entity could bring about the end of the world all by itself."

"Ducky," Grunthor muttered. "Just ducky."

"All went well throughout the end of the Before-Time and into the First Age," Rath continued, "until the day when a falling star crashed to Earth and shattered open the Vault. Some of the F'dor escaped and went upworld, chased by their Dhracian jailers, while others of the four primordial races sought to contain the F'dor and mend the Vault. Many of the race of dragons each contributed a scale to serve as a patch of sorts while the Vault was being resealed. These scales had powers in the color spectrum as well, and while they were not as powerful as the embryonic scales of the First Child, they were strong enough to hold the remaining F'dor at bay while their prison was restored. While I do not know exactly how many dragons contributed, there were at least forty-three identified scales that survived the rebuilding intact. These scales were gathered, and the dragons left them in the care of the Seren leader who led the undertaking, in case the Vault ever needed to be patched again.

"The F'dor that escaped to the upworld sought the Stolen Deck, hoping to retrieve all of it, because the series of tones it produced was the True Name of the First Child, and would call the beast to life if it could be 'spoken' aloud. In addition, they desperately sought the black scale also, as it was a key that could open the Vault and free their imprisoned comrades. In the ensuing pursuit of the Dhracians, however, only one scale was ever recovered by a F'dor who had taken on a human host.

"I caught a whisper of your old name, Ysk, in the course of my searching for one of the Younger Pantheon. I was on the hunt for a demon named Krisaar, a brash and arrogant F'dor who had an even greater need for control than the members of his race were known for having. He survived the destruction of the Island of Serendair by making a pact with a soldier of similar ilk, exchanging eternal life of a sort for an agreed-upon parasitic arrangement. To my knowledge, this is the only time in the entire history of the Known World where a human being has voluntarily taken on a F'dor as its host."

"The Waste o' Breath," Grunthor said.

"Michael," Rhapsody whispered, as if the name itself caused a bad taste in her mouth.

"The other scales, the ones donated by the dragons to seal the Vault, became known as the Given Deck. It was kept in the safekeeping of the Seren lineage for many generations, and the powers of the scales were recorded by the Seren Seers and Namers who could read them. Unfortunately, sometime in the Second Age they came into the possession of a Seren Namer who was cataloging them. This woman, Ave, fell victim to the solitary silver scale, the Fallen Moon, which was a mirror of endless reflection that distorted her view of the world. She then took it upon herself to mark the cards in a way that made them into a deck of prediction and power granting, and secreted them away among her tribe, where they remained in the hands of one Reader at a time. The same prophecy notes this action thus: *That which was freely Given will be stolen.*"

"I remember this vaguely from the old world," Achmed said. "In the Gated City of Kingston, a market of thieves the likes of which I've never seen again, there was such a Seren woman. She was almost impossible to find if you were looking for her, but if you were not, you might perchance come upon her in a booth or behind a tent. She would offer you a reading from her deck in exchange for gold."

"Did you ever take her up on it?" Rhapsody asked.

Achmed gestured impatiently at Rath. "Go on," he said, ignoring her.

"After many centuries a Nain explorer and historian met up with the last of the great Readers, Sharra, who taught him about the deck. It became an obsession of his to reclaim the deck and return each of the scales to the dragon who donated it, in return for which he received a story for a book he was writing. Other scales remained scattered across the world, where they were hidden, used, destroyed, or fell into the hands of people who would eventually come to bring them together—to terrible ends. One such person was the demon's host I told you of, the one you called Michael. The Faorina child he had fathered of a Seren woman was believed to have inherited the power of her tribe to read the scales; if that child survived, those parts of the Decks are still out in the world, where they might be put to unimaginable purposes."

"More likely they are at the bottom of the sea," Achmed said.

"It's always pretty to think so," said Rath darkly. "In my experience, those scales never quietly go away. They seem to have remarkable power to stay where they will do the most damage, will cause the most destruction, as if the taint of the F'dor is on them still."

"What do they look like?" Grunthor asked. "So's we know 'em if we see 'em."

"The scales are of irregular size," said Rath. "All of them are oval and most are tattered finely at the edges. They appear gray or colorless until tilted or exposed to light, where their color can be discerned, and often appear prismatic, signifying all the lore that is within each of them.

"I have never actually seen any of the scales of the Stolen Deck. It was considered far too sacred and terrible to be viewed by any other than the entities who were asked to guard it. I was told of the symbology of each of the scales, however, as were the other Gaol, so we would know how to identify them should we come across them in our travels. The white scale, one of the two most powerful and awful of the Stolen Deck, was said to have no image inscribed upon it at all. It symbolized Life or

Creation, and was thought by many to be a picture of the very face of God. Its counterpart, the black scale, had inscribed upon it a picture of a key, a terrible harbinger of its power to open the Vault itself. It symbolized Void or destruction; as you can surmise, it had the power to bring about both of those things to an unimaginable magnitude.

"The rest of the scales followed the pattern of the color palette, attuned to the lore you already know. The red scale was inscribed with a drop of blood, the orange scale flames, the yellow had an image of the sun rising or setting, depending upon whether it was the concave aspect, the original scale torn from the First Child, or the convex aspect, donated to the world from the hide of its parent. Likewise, the green scale showed an image of the earth, either clear or obscured, as did the blue scale, inscribed with the image of an eye surrounded by clouds or covered with them. The indigo scale, about which the least is known, was said to have been inscribed with a picture of a comet, in the old lore signifying change of great magnitude; hence the appellation Night Stayer or Night Bringer, indicating its power to bring about tremendous change, or to prevent it."

"Makes me wish we had that one right now," said Rhapsody.

"Hardly," said Rath dryly. "The power that exists in those scales could cause even those who seek to save the Earth to bring about harm, intentionally or otherwise. History is littered with accounts of those of good intent and purpose who were dragged to stray by the power of those scales.

"Finally, there was the violet scale. It was said to have been inscribed with the image of the throne, and it was the only scale that had but one side. Although the Progenitor Wyrm donated seven scales, for whatever reason that final note in the spectrum only had one tone, not a flat nor sharp. It was known as The New Beginning. I do not know for certain, but I suspect that any being who comes into power unexpectedly or inexplicably might have control of this scale, or at least had its power utilized on his behalf."

The three exhaled simultaneously.

"Talquist, perhaps," Achmed said.

"Let's hope not," Rath said.

"And the Given Deck?" Rhapsody asked. "Did you ever come upon any of those?"

The Dhracian shook his head. "I have seen some of them," he said, "but that was before the Seren Reader defiled them. The sole silver one was the Fallen Moon, the one whose misdirection allowed Ave to desecrate them in the first place. I believe there was one scale for each of the five trees that grow at the birthplaces of Time: Sagia, the tree of the stars which now is gone from the world; Ashra, the tree of pure elemental fire; Eucos, known as the Cloud Catcher, the tree of living air; Frothta, the tree of water which grows beneath the sea; and, of course, the Great White Tree. There may even be one for Bloodthorn, the evil vinelike tree of thorns that has its roots in the Vault itself. There are others—I only know of a few: the Forgotten City, the Endless Mountains, the Golden Measure, the Molten River, the Broken Plate, the Thief Queen, the Infant, Breath, Missive, the Time Scissors. I only know of any of these because I once read pieces of The Book of All Human Knowledge, the tome written by that Nain historian. I believe it was lost at sea centuries ago, brought to the shores of this world by the Third Cymrian Fleet, where it drowned in their shipwreck.

"This new entity, the one you call Michael," Rath went on, "both man and demon, rose in worldly political power as the centuries progressed, finally becoming the Baron of Argault, one of the most powerful magnates in the shipping world on the other side of the Wide Central Sea. It was he whom I was following when I came to this place. He'd always managed to elude me by hiding near water, which any Dhracian will tell you is the bane of our existence when we are on the Hunt. His strategy was successful; while he operated in broad daylight, in the plain sight of the eyes of the world, his constant presence proximate to the sea kept him from my *kirai*.

"What is significant about this particular member of the Younger Pantheon was that his weakness was his need for control, coupled with his inability to maintain it over himself. Whether this was his human aspect or the demonic one is hard to say, because the man he chose as his host had a similar weakness." Rhapsody shuddered, having been the recipient of that weakness.

"His shortcomings occasionally took the form of desires of the flesh, culminating in the worst of all of his conquests: a Seren woman, born of ancient blood, who had refugeed from the island to the shores of Argaut to avoid the Cataclysm. While most F'dor will never procreate, because it saps their power, breaks open their souls, or whatever passes for a soul, when they do, the host of this demon could not resist the opportunity to defile the woman, to impregnate her, which he did, gaining, I suppose, an ill-considered thrill at the tarnishing of the one lore, ether, that was older and more powerful than his own lore of black fire. The result was an unbelievable freak of nature, an entity known as a Faorina, a denatured F'dor. There are very few examples of them in the world, not only because the demons themselves are jealous of their own power, but because those that are actually born usually do not survive. Most worrisome, the woman who bore this child and died because of it was a Reader, one of the tribe of Seren priestesses that is charged with the protection of and the ability to read the scales. If she brought any of them with her from the old world, from the Lost Island before it sank into the waves, those scales fell into the hands of the man who ravaged her. And her child was thought to have inherited her ability to read them.

"I believe that man made use of a blue scale, perhaps even the blue scale of the Stolen Deck, to hide from the hunters of the wind. For a moment I tasted his signal, his vibration, coming from this place, as if he had lost the scale for a moment, but now it is gone again. One thing you should know, Bolg king, is that when I was making my way to this place in search of him, I had to slip between an armada of ships of all types, pirate vessels, merchant carriers, even warships, all massing in a great blockade far out of sight of the coastline off the western shore of your continent. I crossed the damnable sea in little more than a rowboat to escape their notice. But they gather; the Baron of Argaut had an impressive fleet of shipping vessels, which he maintained by being in league with a far-flung band of pirate ships." He stopped, brought to silence by the look of horror on Rhapsody's face.

"So if in fact the one you called Michael, the Wind of Death, brought any of those scales with him to the shores of this land, and if they survived the wave that took him from the upworld and into the depths of the sea, and if by some freakish twist of fate they are the hands of your enemies now, you are fighting not only the greed and lust for power that has been in existence since the dawn of Time in all men, but a far deeper, far more malicious, avaricious, and deadly hatred, a destructive primal power born at the beginning of Time for which there is no antidote, nothing to allay it.

"And if this is so, I would say you have your work cut out for you."

39

Trug was the Archon known as the Voice.

The Bolg were an emergent race, demi-humans that were both primitive and instinctually resilient. In the time that Achmed had been king, they had gone from being scavengers and cannibals who scratched out whatever meager living they could from the rocky and jagged peaks that were their home to an up-and-coming nation of weapons builders, agriculturalists, carpenters, craftsmen, and weavers of tensile nautical ropes and fine women's undergarments. It was a strange and comical medley of trade that sensibly exploited the resources of their kingdom of mountains, canyons, and forests of unique bluish wood and ancient vineyards planted in the Cymrian era that had been revitalized into producing fine grapes for wine.

Achmed's vision required more of a support network of leadership than could be provided by just he and Grunthor alone, especially now that Rhapsody had moved on, claiming a protective responsibility for the Bolg as well as for the sleeping Earthchild, but spending the majority of her time tending to the needs of the Lirin kingdom and her duties as the Lady Cymrian. To that end the Three had selected Bolg children who had been identified as especially intelligent or gifted, most of them orphans, to train in specified areas that would assist in the growing of the kingdom.

Trug was one such child. Like most of his race, he did not give voice to his inner thoughts but rarely. Unlike most of his fellow subjects, it was part of Trug's training to be able to speak; what he was speaking, however, were the thoughts of the Bolg king, both within the mountain and outside it. It was his path to be trained as the Voice, the Archon that King Achmed expected to handle all of the communications, both official and secret, on behalf of the Bolglands, including the management of the miles of speaking tubes that ran throughout the mountains, left over from the Cymrian Age. In that capacity he had been trained from childhood for the last seven years, selected at an early age by Rhapsody as having the potential for the task at hand, and systematically familiarized with language, cryptography, anatomy, and a thousand other studies of communications, verbal and otherwise. More than a year ago he had been deemed worthy to supervise the aviary, with its extensive fleet of messenger birds, as well as the mounted messengers who rode with the mail caravans. Shortly thereafter he had assumed responsibility for King Achmed's network of ambassadors as well as his spies.

Now he served as one of Achmed's most trusted archons. And so when his voice came resounding up the speaking tube into the Firbolg king's planning chamber within the throne room of Canrif, it was almost always answered immediately in the raspy tone the Bolg had come to know and fear.

"Your Majesty?"

Achmed, Grunthor, and Rhapsody looked up at each other in surprise. Trug had chosen a formal address, generally indicating that someone from outside the mountain had arrived.

"What is it?" Achmed demanded.

"There is a visitor to see you, sire," the thin, uncomfortable voice answered in return.

"Whoever he is, tell him to go away," Achmed retorted. They had been poring over schematics in the back chamber in secret since returning to Canrif, and his mood was already sour.

"He has been here for quite some time, sire." Trug's voice echoed back up the tube, followed a moment later by another sound.

"Tell the bastard I must see him at once," came a familiar voice that was not immediately recognizable. "I have been waiting more than a fortnight in this godforsaken place, and I will not wait a moment longer."

Achmed closed the speaking tube. "Who do you suppose that is?" he asked.

Rhapsody was listening, her forehead furrowed. "It sounds a little bit like Faedryth, the Nain king," she said uncertainly. "But what would he be doing here?"

Achmed opened the tube again. "Tell the misbegotten warthog he can wait another fortnight as far as I care," he said in a surly tone. "Or for the rest of his unnaturally long life. I'm busy."

A string of ugly words uttered in a guttural tone and an unknown language rumbled up the tube in return.

Rhapsody nodded. "Yes, those are Nain curses," she said. "It's probably Faedryth."

"What is he doing here?" Grunthor asked. "'Is kingdom is more than two weeks away, and unreachable by normal methods of land travel. Oi don't remember any event that would give 'im cause to be in this area."

"I'm not at all enamored of the Nain," said Achmed, studying the parchment scroll before him. "When they were here for the council at the Moot they consumed more than four times the victuals of any other race. I have finally returned home, and I am not in the mood to entertain a slugworthy lout like Faedryth at this moment."

"What on earth are you thinking?" Rhapsody demanded. "Faedryth is your ally, and mine. Now is not the time to be inhospitable to members of the Alliance, especially those who have done you no harm and offered you no real offense. Besides, if common courtesy is a requirement for visits of state within our realms, no one would ever have received *you*." She pushed him away from the speaking tube. "Send His Majesty up forthwith, Trug."

Achmed glared at her and returned to the schematic of the Lightcatcher Rhapsody had been graphing.

After a surprisingly long period of time, the Voice archon appeared, the Nain king in tow. The two Bolg ignored him, but Rhapsody rose immediately and made her way across the floor of the throne room that had been built more than a thousand years before during the height of the artisanship of Gwylliam's reign. It was richly inlaid with mosaics and fashioned from some of the most beautiful marble mined in the Manteids.

"Your Majesty," she said warmly, "what a pleasure to see you. To what do we owe the honor of this visit?"

The expression of thunderous annoyance knitted into the Nain king's brow softened a bit at the side of her.

"I hardly expected to see you here, m'lady," Faedryth said. He was attired in leather garments and boots of fine workmanship, but without the standard trappings of royalty. His glorious beard showed signs of inattention and travel, and he carried in his hands a velvet sack that he was clutching tightly. "I'd have thought you would most certainly be at the new home your husband has written to me of; he sought my advice in some of the fortifications, you know."

"Yes, indeed. He was most insistent that Nain traps and defenses would make it most secure."

"No doubt," Faedryth agreed. "And yet I find you here, in the lands of a man of questionable wisdom, instead of the safety of your husband's home." He glanced at her bulging belly. "I offer both congratulations and the rebuke of being a father myself, m'lady; I had not heard that you were with child."

Rhapsody cleared her throat. "Yes," she said.

"Well then, I suggest you take yourself at once to Highmeadow. No child, and no one of any value, is safe here at this time."

"What are you blithering about?" Achmed said in annoyance. "I did not invite you; you're not welcome in this place without a legitimate reason to be here, and yet here you are, insulting me. What do you want?"

Faedryth eyed the Voice. "Send your servant away," he said quietly.

Achmed did not even look up, but gestured to Trug with his head to comply. Trug coughed politely and left the room, looking relieved.

"All right, now, what do you want?" the Bolg king asked again. "Or perhaps you need a hot bath and some biscuits first?"

Faedryth's nostrils flared, and his brow blackened again.

"Your arrogance is precisely why I am here," he said. "Once again, you are meddling with forces you do not understand, and yet it does not stay your hand, or make you even reconsider your actions. I have to say this does not surprise me, at least in your case." He turned and looked at Rhapsody. "On the other hand, given your training and your profession, m'lady, I have to say that I'm shocked to find you participating in such a dangerous and inadvisable activity."

Achmed rolled his eyes. "Oh, this again," he said. "Did I not throw out your ambassador several months ago when he came to bring me this very same demand of yours? I believe that I was quite specific in my response to him. I directed him to give it to you in no uncertain terms, and if I recall it was rather to the point. And yet here you are, in my lands, without an invitation. Go away, Faedryth. I find your concern to be insincere at the very best, and hypocritical at the very worst, given that you yourself have built the same instrumentality that you would see me not reconstruct."

"You arrogant horse's arse," Faedryth retorted angrily. "I built the original instrumentality of which you speak, I did. It was designed by a man who had more genius in the clippings of his toenails than is present in your entire kingdom, even with the presence of the Lady Cymrian. And it was an unwise thing to do. You do not understand the risks that you are undertaking; if it were only your wretched kingdom that was in the balance, you could blow yourself to smithereens for all I care, along with your entire miserable population. But alas, your ineptitude and indiscretion may spell disaster and doom for all of us—all of us. And I do not intend to see that happen."

"Well, hooray for thee," replied the Bolg king. "Contrary to what you may believe, Faedryth, I do not intend to see that happen, either."

"It is precisely that you believe that you know what you're doing that makes you so dangerous, Achmed," said Faedryth. "That really does not surprise me." He turned to Rhapsody. "As for you, m'lady, I am disappointed to discover that you are part of this. I would've thought you had better sense."

"I am here precisely to lend my knowledge of lore to this project, in the hopes of ensuring its success," Rhapsody said flatly. "And, quite frankly, Your Majesty, I am insulted by your assumptions about both the Bolg king and me. Rude as we all may be to one another, we are still allies."

Faedryth exhaled, and looked suddenly older.

"Please reconsider," he said less stridently this time. "You do not know what you are risking."

Achmed finally looked up. He threw the quill he had been using to scribble notes on Rhapsody's drawings onto the table, and walked over to the much shorter man. He looked down into the Nain king's broad face, studying it for a moment, then took down the veils that shielded his own nose and mouth from the stings of the world's vibration.

"Hear me," he said quietly. "You would not even be aware of my rebuilding of the Lightcatcher if you did not now have one of your own, which you use to spy on my lands. I know two things very much better than you do, Faedryth. First, unlike you, I understand how this magic works, or at least Rhapsody does. I know that the incarnation of it that *you* possess threatens to wake a sleeping child that dwells within the Earth." He smiled slightly at the look of surprise on the Nain king's face. "Yes, *Your Majesty,* in spite of what you believe, there are others in this world who understand its lore as well if not better than you do. If I did not feel the need to have its power available to me in order to prevent something irreversible from happening, I would not be wasting my time; there are, after all, so many innocent villages of humans to raid, so many fat, adorable youngsters to feed upon.

"Second, and far more significant, is this—I have actually *seen* what it is you fear to waken, Faedryth; *with my eyes I have seen it.* And if you fear that your puny ministrations with powers you don't understand are justified, allow me to set you straight; the Nain would be the first to be consumed should that Sleeping Child be awakened. It will come up from the depths of the earth beneath the mountains, following the heat of the river of fire, and swallow everyone in your kingdom whole before it consumes the rest of the world. So trust me when I say that I'm not listening to your wisdom, but to my own on this matter. Now get out of my mountains and go back to your own. We are not in need of your counsel here."

The Nain king stared at him with undisguised astonishment that melted a moment later into black fury. He walked over to Rhapsody and placed the velvet pouch in her hands.

"I have to say, m'lady, that while your friend's abominable rudeness does not shock me in the least, I'm appalled at you. If anyone should know the dangers of toying with elemental lore, I would think it would be a Lirin Namer."

"Again, no one is toying with anything here, Your Majesty," Rhapsody said. "And I do apologize for Achmed's impoliteness. But what is unfolding is beyond the bounds of normal discretion now; we need every tool at our disposal to safeguard the mountains and those that live within them, as well as all the other members of the Alliance. Sorbold is gearing for war, and the holy city of Sepulvarta appears to be in its sights. I hope that when the time arrives, if you are needed you will come."

"I suspect this is the last time you'll ever see me, m'lady," said the Nain king bitterly. "We retreated once to our lands because of the greed and selfishness and stupidity of a male and female ruler in this place. I had hoped to never see such a situation again, but alas, history appears to be repeating itself. May you not bring about the destruction you seek to avoid in the very process of doing so."

He turned on his heel and strode from the throne room, slamming the great gold doors behind him.

The sound waves reverberated through the room, showering dust from the columns that held up the ceiling.

"What's in the bag?" Grunthor asked after the noise had died away.

Rhapsody loosed the string and opened the bag. Within it was a small hinged box of solid gold. She lifted the lid to find it was lined in black ivory, a dead rock formation that was said to be implacable to all methods of scrying.

Lying within it was a single scrap of brittle material, filmy and translucent. She picked it up gingerly, and suddenly felt as if the world had ended around her.

"I've no idea," she said.

40

The last place that Achmed took the Dhracian was down to the ruins of the Loritorium, an unfinished repository that Gwylliam had intended to use to house the artifacts of ancient lore in his collection. It had been built deep in the belly of the mountains, at the base of a tunnel whose only entrance was in the Bolg king's chambers.

This was because on an altar of Living Stone in the center of that unfinished repository slept the Child of Earth, the middle child of the prophecy.

He and Rath stood over her catafalque, staring down at her. The child was as tall as a full-grown human, her face that of a child, her skin cold and polished gray, as if she were sculpted from stone. She would have, in fact, appeared to be a statue but for the measured tides of her breath.

Below the surface of filmy skin her flesh was darker, in muted hues of brown and green, purple and dark red, twisted together like thin strands of colored clay. Her features were at once coarse and smooth, as if her face had been carved with blunt tools, then polished carefully over a lifetime. Beneath her indelicate forehead were eyebrows and lashes that appeared formed from blades of dry grass, matching her long, grainy hair. In the dim light the tresses resembled wheat or bleached highgrass cut to even lengths and bound in delicate sheaves. At her scalp the roots of her hair grew green like the grass of early spring.

Achmed recalled his first sight of her, and what the woman who had tended to her, the last surviving member of a nearby Dhracian colony called the Grandmother, had said about her.

She is a Child of Earth, formed of its own Living Stone. In day and night, through all the passing seasons, she sleeps. She has been here since before my birth. I am sworn to guard her until after Death comes for me. So must you be.

He had taken the words to heart, probably more than he had ever done in his life before.

"She is much smaller and more sickly than when last I beheld her," said Rath.

"The bastard emperor who is gearing up for war has been harvesting the last remaining Living Stone from a basilica in Sorbold called Terre-anfor." Rath nodded; he knew the place well. "Perhaps that is what is taking its toll on her."

Rath nodded again silently, and followed the Bolg king back into the upper mountain to a causeway tunnel overlooking the vast canyon that separated the main part of Canrif from the Blasted Heath beyond.

The wind echoed down and through the tunnel, singing a mournful song. The Bolg king and Rath took seats on the ground at the opening of the tunnel, staring west, and watched the sun spill its light like blood over the piedmont, the steppes, and the wide Krevensfield Plain beyond.

They sat in silence, awaiting the sundown, until finally Achmed spoke.

"Tell me of the F'dor, and of those who guard them," he said. "I only know what little I was taught by Father Halphasion. Being disconnected from the Hunt, he could tell me very little, so I have carried the bloodlust in my veins with no understanding all my life."

Rath looked down into the rocky canyon, where great fissures had caught the last of the daylight in their crags.

"There are two pantheons of the beasts—the Older Pantheon, and the Younger. They are not faceless, but each a unique personality, each with strengths one must guard against, and weaknesses that can be exploited. We know each one, for they have all been alive since the very dawn of Creation—and they have not reproduced, at least for the most part.

"The demons of the Older Pantheon were born of the fire that burned on the surface of the Earth at Creation. Those of the Younger Pantheon were born of the flames that sank into the Earth's core shortly thereafter. The Younger are more innately evil, because tainted fire is all they have ever known, the element that destroys and consumes. But the Older had access to another way, a way they did not choose. Formed as they were, they were witnesses to the sky, to the stars, to the universe and its infinity—and they chose to disregard the life they saw abounding, to embrace the Void instead of the Creation they knew was out there. They knew of fire's creative and positive uses—warmth, heat, light, the smelting of steel, the cooking of food for sustenance, the purging of illness—but they disregarded it, choosing instead only to torture and destroy with it. That choice of path is why the Older Pantheon is considered so much worse.

"The Older Pantheon stole the egg of the Progenitor Wyrm. Those of the Younger Pantheon stole its scales. Both are evil, avaricious, and seek destruction at all costs; so it is with those that worship Void. It does not matter that their actions will spell the end of their own race; our outlook is merely to help them achieve that end without taking us, and the rest of the world, with them."

Achmed nodded, then was silent for a long time. Finally he spoke, and when he did his voice was devoid of its usual arrogance, its customary edge.

"In the ruins of Kurimah Milani, you said something about the bees, how a man could destroy every living specimen of their kind should he come into their vault with flame. Then you alluded that it was such with another Vault as well. I told you, I abhor riddles. Speak to me plainly—tell me what you want of me."

Rath stared at him, then looked out over the deep canyon to the place where the light from the setting sun was bathing the Blasted Heath in colors of fire.

"It is a great irony that to the Bolg you were polluted, unclean, a half-breed among mongrels that somehow made you less in their sight. Somewhere deep in the scars of your past you have assumed that the blood of your unknown father somehow tainted you in the estimation of the Kin as well—but I tell you, with the wind as my witness—that nothing is further from the truth. To the Gaol, and all the Brethren who have been seeking you since your conception, you are a special entity, a rare gift to our race, the one who might finally tip the scales in our favor. We have not been searching for you to torture or abuse you, to cleanse the race of your blood—but because we need you. You, in a very real way, are our last hope." Rath smiled at the look of rancid disbelief on Achmed's face.

"You alone among us are born of wind and earth, Bolg king," he went on. "While we tread the tunnels and canyons of the Underworld in our endless guardianship, we are strangers there—and the demons know it. They understand how deeply our sacrifice costs us, how much the wind in our blood resents being trapped within the ground, away from the element of air for all time. And even within their prison they laugh at us, because in every way that matters, we are as much prisoners as they.

"But the earth is in your blood as much as the wind is. You have a primordial tie to it that neither the Kin nor the Unspoken have. You have power there, a corporeal form that would be protected by the element of earth bequeathed to you by your father, protected by the very Living Stone of the Vault, should you choose to walk within it."

Achmed felt his throat tighten. Deep in his blood the words appealed to him, fed the dark racial hatred that he harbored within him. Still uncertainty held sway.

"I am not of the Gaol," he said. "I am but half of the blood of the Brethren—and that which was of the other half raised me, if such words can be applied to my upbringing. I know none of your lore, your prophecies—your history. My skills are limited, my talents pale in this area. While I was given a blood gift that allowed me to unerringly track the heartbeats of any of those born on the same soil as I had been, that was an upworld gift. Each time I have faced one of the Pantheon, I have needed help to complete the task. Without that assistance, I would be dead or possessed myself."

The silver pupils of Rath's eyes expanded as the light faded over the steppes. He fixed his gaze on Achmed, as if to add measure to his words.

"What you do not know is this—you could walk the Vault alone, and when you were done the silence would ring with nothing but the whisper of your name."

"I think you overestimate me as an assassin," Achmed replied. "The answer to the question you asked me in the cavern is this—though it was not always so, I am more king than assassin now. My primal calling is to protect the Earthchild, and the Earth, but not for the sake of old racial enmity, but rather for her own sake, and the sake of those who live upon that earth. And for my own selfish ends as well. It is, as you said before, an upworld calling. So I am a king, though if you knew me better, you'd judge me not much of one."

The Dhracian hunter shook his head.

"I do not have to judge you. You guard the Sleeping Child. A king with foresight, but no courage, no mercy, would have shattered her, broken the ribs, smashed all possible keys. The doorway would be just as safe. No, whatever reputation you wish to have, I know what kind of king you are."

"Tell me of the Older Pantheon," Achmed said, his curiosity finally getting the better of him. "What do you know of the eldest of the F'-dor? What are the names of those that you hunt?"

Rath pulled the small dagger from his calf sheath and ran it idly over the wall of the tunnel. "To say the entire name is rarely possible. It would be like identifying a waterfall by imitating its rhythm until it could be distinguished from every other waterfall. How long would that take? A year, all spring? This is a race not bound by the motion of tongue, nor, at first, by the notion of time. They were all born whole, so to speak. Their growth is a measure of fuel, not years; their experiences and strength counted in souls, not centuries.

"Nevertheless, we must name them, to catch them, to call them, to count them. There are few enough now to begin to master the list. I shall give you enough of a name to hold in your ear, but too little for the wind. Hrarfa is one that I seek; she, a whispering flame, like incense, sometimes smoldering, more scent than fire, like a beacon, or flickering bog light at other times, beckoning with false promises. The Liar of liars.

"Then there is Hnaf, sputtering, almost wet, at home near water, hiding by it, pretending to be nearly extinguished. In the small lore we have of the Vault, he was mistrusted by his own kind, possessed of a cheap malice. The Outcast of outcasts.

"Some we track by the human shells they leave behind. The greedy Ficken lays in wait for unsuspecting small folk, both of stature and spirit, at the forest edge. It—we know not its gender—prefers to consume many, farmers, goodwives, half-wit laborers, rather than take prize victims and grow fat on ambition and fear. The Glutton.

"Some are bold, even brave, have fought and survived the Thrall ritual. The hunters of the Gaol do not always win. Like Bolg or men, the F'dor speak at the hour of their doom. Some snarl, some beg, some bargain, some weep. Do not mistake me. You are a fool if you treat them as if they think as we do, feel as we do. Each one is different, like a village of candles, or a hillside of armed fires. This is all they have in common with us. They beg, they bargain, they weep because they have been hunting us so long, and have seen us, *been* us. They know these keys to the human soul, and manipulate them, though they themselves are immune to such pleas for pity. And sometimes their deception has worked, even on the Gaol.

"Few other than the Gaol have the gift to see them, and then their nature is hidden, just like ours. The Nain king has been making lenses to scry for that which is hidden, but none has proven reliable either to detect or predict. I do not think it will be long before he wishes to attempt to capture one, so he can study it. The Nain king is great, and learned, and ancient, but he will gaze upon this thing which is not really a thing, but only a being, and he will not realize that it gazes also at him."

"He is a fool," Achmed said. "And is far more likely to bring about the wakening of the wyrm than I am."

Rath shook his head. "He was an ally—and in this battle, you will need every upworld ally you can muster. It was a mistake to rebuff him, Bolg king. Far better that you should have to suffer him as your foolish ally than as your wise enemy."

"He would never aid the Bolg in a time of need; it is more like the Nain to retreat to their mountains and make a stand there, even when the rest of the world is falling apart. It is how it was at the end of the Cymrian War, and how it will be now. So whether he is my enemy or my ally matters not—he will behave in the same selfish, isolationist manner either way. That's what kind of king *he* is. And if that is how he has judged best to protect his people, I cannot fault him for it—but I don't have to tolerate his stupid demands, either."

Rath shrugged. "Either you are an assassin, or you are a king," he said, closing his eyes and letting the night wind pour over his face. "A king must tolerate such things. An assassin cares not." Achmed fell silent.

As the breeze kicked up, the Dhracian opened his mouth out of habit and began to cant his list.

Hrarfa, Fraax, Sistha, Hnaf, Ficken.

The wind shifted, blowing from the north.

Rath sat up as if struck.

His mouth was filled with fire, the back of his throat burning with caustic blood.

He had caught a trace of one of the Older Pantheon.

Hrarfa, he whispered. The word sank down into his heart and anchored itself through his vessels.

Beating in time now with another heart, far off.

Rath scrambled to his feet, his face twisted in pain and excitement. Achmed stood quickly with him.

"You have caught a trail?"

The Dhracian nodded.

"I will go with you."

Rath shook his head. "Stay here," he said with great effort. "Guard the—Earthchild. It may be a diversion. It is my lot to follow this now."

The needles had begun to pulse through Achmed's veins, whispering words of hate as they ran hot through him. Reluctantly he nodded in assent.

"Good fortune be with you," he said as Rath made his way down the causeway.

Rath stopped and looked over his shoulder.

"I will bring you the tale, if I am alive to tell it," he said.

Then he vanished into the wind.

41

BEYOND THE WALLS OF HIGHMEADOW,
NORTHERN NAVARNE NEAR THE PROVINCE
OF BETHANY

Che day had been a long and fruitless one. Ashe's head was pounding, from the reports of damage to Sepulvarta and the clashing of soldiers in the course of the evacuation of the Krevensfield Plain, to the arguments of the dukes about the allocation of resources for defense of the various provinces. The reconvening of the Council of Dukes in this new fortress had done nothing to ease the contentiousness of their discourse, as Ashe had hoped it would. He had been as patient as he could for as long as he could, until finally the hollow ache inside him threatened to cause his head to split.

"We will reconvene in the morning," he had told the Council of Dukes from behind an enormous pile of papers on the desk before him. All had withdrawn quickly at the tone in his voice save for Tristan Steward, who had remained behind in the grand library.

"You could do with a glass of brandy, my friend," he said, "and something to eat; if an army travels on its stomach, he who is commanding the army should not neglect his own. I will have something sent up for you."

He went to the sideboard and retrieved a heavy crystal glass into which he poured three fingers of clear amber liquid, a honey brandy from the province of Canderre, known the world over for its excellent libations and other luxurious goods. He poured a glass for himself as well, and handed the first one to the Lord Cymrian.

Ashe waved him away.

"Thank you, no," he said. "I'm not hungry."

"But you must be thirsty," Tristan Steward pressed. "You've been answering inane questions for the better part of the day, Gwydion. Even the Lord Cymrian deserves a cessation of the constant barrage of war preparation." He set the glass down on the table in front of Ashe, whose head was resting on his forearm. "I'll leave you to your thoughts. Be certain to get some sleep. Good night."

"Thank you," Ashe murmured as the door closed behind him, staring at the firelight dancing within the bowl of the glass. There was something fascinating about the way the gold liquid caught the light, refracting it into the warm colors of flame. As always, anything to do with fire reminded him painfully of Rhapsody.

Against his better judgment, he took the glass in hand and allowed the alcohol fumes to seep into his nose, stinging his sinuses and warming them a split second later. He took a sip; the liquid was as smooth as silk, and warm, filling his mouth with the delightful taste and his nose with a rich vapor. He had to credit Tristan Steward for knowing his drink.

The door opened quietly again. Ashe turned and glanced over his shoulder.

Rhapsody was there again, this time clothed not in traveling garb but in a filmy gown of thin white silk. Backlit by the fire, he could see the slender lines of her legs, the appealing curves of her torso shadowed through the flimsy material, tapering up to the swell of her breasts, above which the naked skin of her throat gleamed.

I miss you, she said, her voice at once soft and smoky.

Ashe took another swallow of the burning liquid.

"Go away," he muttered. "You are a phantasm, a figment of my pathetic imagination. Or a sign of my pending insanity; go away."

She smiled and came to him, the silken gown whispering around her bare feet.

I am no phantasm, she said, bending down beside him and filling his nostrils with the warmth of her scent. *Not as long as I am within your heart.*

Exhausted from keeping the dragon at bay, lonely and overwrought, Ashe reached out his hand, a soldier's hand, calloused and worn from battle and the heft of a sword hilt, and brought it, trembling, to rest on the smooth hollow of her neck. Her skin was warm and smooth; her breath quickened beneath his touch.

"You are not real," he said softly. "Though the All-God knows I want you to be."

I can be, she whispered in return.

Ashe looked away. He closed his eyes and brought his forehead to rest on his forearm again. He lay there, allowing the fumes of the brandy to seep into his brain, his dragon sense registering the shape of the dream that stood beside him, waiting.

He felt the warmth of lips on his neck, the tickle and sweet scent of freshly washed hair, the aching availability, the willingness, the need.

And then he brought his head around quickly, and opened his eyes.

The chambermaid was there again, looking down at him with the same smile that had been on his wife's face a moment before.

"Why are you here, Portia?" he asked brokenly. "What do you want of me?"

"Whatever you want of me." The tone of her voice was almost magically inviting, stirring all of the nerves in his body to life.

Ashe slammed the chair back and brought his hands down on the table before him.

"What are you doing?" he shouted. "Why do you always manage to be around me when my mind is fragmented—or is it that my mind is fragmented because you're around me?" The Lord Cymrian seized the hair of his own head and clawed at it. "What sort of insidious game are you playing with me, Portia?"

The young woman's eyes brimmed with tears.

"M'lord, I—"

The dragon within his blood exploded in rage.

"Enough! *Enough!*" Ashe shouted. He swept the papers before him off the desk angrily, splattering the contents of the ink well across the thick carpet. "Leave this place; go back to Bethany or wherever it is that you came from. Go work your evil wiles on Tristan Steward; climb into his bed. Perhaps he will succumb to your seduction, but I never will. Do you not think I would know you from my own wife? Did you think you could seduce me in my misery, cause me to betray all that I hold holy? You damnable beast." Even as the dragon in his blood rampaged, his words and the voice that spoke them sounded mad to his own ears.

The chambermaid broke into tears and shuddering sobs.

"M'lord, I never—"

But the dragon in Ashe's soul was raging, rampaging through his blood, leaving it burning in his veins.

"Silence!" he snarled, his voice more the roar of an animal than the words of a man. "*Silence!* Get out of my house. I want you out of here tonight; this moment! Take whatever you have and get out of here; leave my presence and do not return. I do not wish to ever see you or behold you in any way again. I do not know what trickery of the mind you are employing, but if you do not leave at once I cannot guarantee your safety here. Take whatever you brought with you; I want this entire keep purged of your presence, your essence, and anything to do with you. Go. Get out of my sight. Get out of here!" He stumbled blindly to the speaking tubes and shouted for the chamberlain.

"Gerald! Gerald Owen! Come at once and rid me of this monster!"

The chambermaid stared wildly at him for a moment longer, then buried her face in her hands and ran from the room, weeping loudly.

As she departed, something in the air of the room around Ashe seemed to shatter; the Lord Cymrian could not be certain it was a spell of some sort, a twisted snare like an invisible spider's web that have been woven from evil power to deprive him of his sanity.

Or if it was the shattering of his sanity itself.

Ashe felt every clattering step as she bounded down the stairs, absorbed the slamming of every door in the course of her exit in the nerves of his skin. He was oddly grateful that her mourning appeared to cease very quickly; her calm returned almost immediately, judging by the beating of her heart in a normal rhythm, the slowing tides of her breath, and the deliberation with which she hurriedly packed her belongings and dashed out into the night by the back door, not even waiting to be shown out by the chamberlain. He closed his eyes, hoping for the same return to calm himself, and monitored her leaving until he could no longer feel her presence within his lands, no longer smelled the scent of vanilla and sweet soap, wood smoke and meadow flowers in the upper reaches of his sinuses. He did not realize how badly his hands were shaking, or how rapidly his heart was thundering against his chest, or how, when the chamberlain came to him in a calmer moment, he would reconsider his tantrum, be swallowed by remorse, and need to rectify his actions.

He did realize, however, how close he had come to a mistake that would have cost him more than the whole world.

*P*ortia ran out into the night, her heart pounding, but with the calm of one who had survived many such evictions.

She wandered the cold paths of the forest under the moon until she came to a shady glen, where the budding leaves cast black lacy shadows on the ground in the ghostly radiance all around her.

She shivered from the cold; her body had never been well padded, and the chill of the night air sank into her skin, leaving her trembling.

He will come for me, she thought. *Already he regrets what he has done, and when the remorse takes over, he will come out into the night for me.*

And bring me home with him again.

Tonight it will finally be consummated, she thought in delight, rubbing her hands quickly up and down her arms to warm them with the friction of it. *Tonight he will finally take me in his arms, and to his bed. I will have all of him; I will ride him to the ends of the cliffs of pleasure, and as he drives himself into me, I will drive myself into his soul as well. I may not be able to evict the shadow of his wife, but she will find mine within him when she returns.*

And then it will all begin.

*I*t only took a few moments for the remorse to set in and take hold. Ashe stood up from the table and went to the speaking tube again.

"Come, Owen," he said, summoning the chamberlain. "I've been an ass. I didn't mean to drive her out into the night, alone and without protection. Saddle up; we have to find her and bring her back. And then Tristan can make certain to take her with him when he returns to Bethany tomorrow."

42

THE HALLS OF CANRIF, YLORC

$\mathcal{A}$s Ashe had predicted, the nightmares did return.

All the while they were traveling, Rhapsody had not really noticed them. There was too much occupying her mind as she, Achmed, and Grunthor made their way in haste out of the west and into the desert. When she had left the security of her husband's arms with the baby in tow, the fear she felt at the thought of eyes above and below the earth searching for her child was nightmarish enough. Bad dreams were hardly noticeable in that time; reality was worse.

When they were encamped, she and Meridion had slept on Grunthor's massive chest, much as she had when traveling along the Root through the belly of the earth itself. The bad dreams had been especially strong then, and while Grunthor had not been able to chase them completely away in the manner that Ashe and Elynsynos had, he had provided a large, gruff, and wide surface on which to sleep that proved to be surprisingly warm and comforting. He had also gotten good at jostling her from her dreams, talking her through the night terrors, and providing distracting conversation should he decide what she actually needed was to waken. He had not lost the knack, and especially had enjoyed cradling the tiny baby, curling up with the infant near his neck.

But the baby was gone, and now they were back in Ylorc among the Firbolg, who looked at her suspiciously as someone who had gone away and left them, the king's harlot, or just a source of food.

Rhapsody was alone again.

She shifted in the linen sheets that dressed her large bed in her quiet chamber within the inner hallways of Canrif. She'd never particularly liked staying within the cold mountains, and in her time in the Bolg-lands, she had always chosen to remain in Elysian, alone, in the tiny cottage Gwylliam had once built for Anwyn in the days when they were in love, or at least pretending to be.

Rhapsody rolled over in her sleep and sighed brokenly. She missed the little house on the island in the center of the grotto's lake, a place of hidden magic where she had first felt safe upon coming to the new world. She and Ashe had fallen in love there, or at least had admitted that they had for the first time. They had spent a short but sweet spring there, exploring the purple crystalline caves, swimming in the dark water where filaments of stone formations and underwater stalagmites formed lazy cathedrals of beautiful muted colors beneath the surface. The firmament of the cave had been carefully bored through with dozens of holes, allowing spots of sunlight to shine down upon it, making gardens possible. Rhapsody had passed many happy hours tending to the baby trees, planting flowers and herbs, and generally reliving her childhood, in a simpler time on a farm in the middle of the Wide Meadows of Serendair.

Now, alone and frightened in the darkness of Ylorc once more, she was defenseless against the demons of the night that lived in her own mind. As long as she could remember she had been prescient, had seen the future and sometimes the past in her dreams, and so she did not drug herself into a deeper stupor or consume the herbs that might have made her slumber so intense that her mind could not process what it had seen, for fear that she should miss something that was important, the need to be known in order for those she loved to remain safe.

And so she submitted to the dreams, to the horrid sights of burning ships in a harbor alight with flames; the images of terrified villagers running from soldiers with swords, attacking from horseback as they passed through, riding down anyone they saw; of great winged shapes that streaked through the night sky, raining fiery death down on the thatched roofs of houses below.

But mostly she dreamt of Ashe.

Except for the times when she employed her skills as a Singer, reaching out to him over the waves of time with the musical lore she had studied, most of her dreams of her husband were terrifying. Night after night she saw him in her sleep, cold and wandering, sometimes adrift in the waves of the sea, lost without the family that the man treasured, that the dragon considered its own. She could feel, even hundreds of miles away, the unraveling of her husband's mind, of the ascendancy of the dragon in his soul as the broken-hearted man receded back into the shadows.

Each night she wept, often losing sleep and lying in exhausted numbness throughout all the hours of the long night until the morning finally came, when it was time to return to her work on the Lightcatcher.

One particularly brutal night, she dreamt of her old home in Merryfield, of the Patchworks in the Wide Meadow where she and the boy she had called Sam had fallen in love beneath a starry sky, beneath the willow tree, alongside a meadow stream. The pasture, the stream, and the tree were all still there, all burned black to ashes in the aftermath of the Seren war. The bones of those she loved lay strewn in the field around her, and at her feet a tiny skeleton lay, its skull graced with the traces of flaxen curls.

Rhapsody began to weep as if she was seeking to empty herself of every tear.

And then, just as her mind began to fill with scenes of terror and destruction, she felt a soft musical vibration surround her, fill her ears with gentle music, chasing her dreams into the darkest corners of her mind again, as if it were opening a window in her soul, allowing sunshine in. She recognized the vibration.

It was the one emitted by both of the dragons she loved in her life, her husband and Elynsynos.

Though exhausted, Rhapsody struggled to awaken. *It can't be Ashe,* she thought drowsily, fighting the dark cobwebs of sleep. *I know he is not here, but I can feel the song which he used to chase my dreams away, settling me down to dreamless, restorative sleep again. It must be Elynsynos; she's here somewhere, not dead.*

Fighting the heaviness of her eyelids, Rhapsody struggled to find the vibration and opened her eyes, looking for the dragon that had chased her nightmares away.

There, on the coverlet beside her, she was greeted with the sight of tiny, twinkling blue eyes, scored with vertical pupils expanding in the dark, taking in the sight of her. Porcelain hands and feet moved about in the air amid soft cooing sounds, coming from a head crowned with flaxen curls.

Her baby.

Rhapsody's hands immediately went to her abdomen, once again flat beneath her palms. Then, tears of joy pouring down her cheeks, she reached out gently and caressed the smooth skin of his face, sliding her hands carefully beneath him and bringing her lips to the hollow of his neck, kissing him over and over again gratefully.

Meridion just lay on the coverlet, staring up at her in the dark, his eyes twinkling.

"I should have known," Rhapsody murmured, smiling down at her son. "I knew you would come back; I just didn't know that you already have the power of dragons to chase away dreams. My, aren't you a special boy."

The infant gurgled.

43

IN THE NORTHERN FOREST OF GWYNWOOD,
PAST THE TAR'AFEL RIVER

$\mathcal{I}$f Melisande had not seen two hundred foresters mount up and ride into the woods around her, followed immediately by another five hundred on foot who disappeared into the great forest behind them, she never would have known that she and Gavin were anything but utterly alone on their journey.

The mounted men who had accompanied them from the Circle for the last several weeks had taken off in two cardinal directions upon crossing the Tar'afel River, riding north and west with the rising sun behind them to the outermost edges of the lands of the dragon. The Invoker had explained to her that only the scouts assigned to the farthest reaches would continue to ride; foresters could move far more quickly and quietly on foot than on horseback when traveling through the heavy glades of virgin wood such as those that comprised the lands of Elynsynos. His face had no hint of a smile as he further explained that foresters would not wish to tempt a dragon with horse meat unless the distance made it necessary. The young Lady Navarne had listened to his explanation from atop her own mount, a thick-bodied forest mare with gray dappling.

"Why are we mounted, then, if it is more easily done on foot?" she had asked.

The bearded Filidic leader had smiled. "Do you fancy yourself a forester, then, Lady Melisande Navarne, as well as all your other accomplishments?" He turned away quickly as her face changed color, but the gentleness of his tone left her vanity intact even as she choked on her own foolishness.

As soon as Gavin's contingent was out of sight, the Invoker mounted his own horse, a Lirin roan that had been given to him by the border guards of Tyrian in tribute, took hold of her mare's reins, and rode smoothly into the greenwood. Melisande clung to the mare's bridle at first, but soon discovered that the Invoker's quiet vocal cues led the horses easily around deadfall and the deeper pits in the mossy floor of the forest, ensuring a reasonably stable ride.

They traveled northwest in silence, following the path of the sun that gleamed through the budding leaves of the ancient forest, casting lacy shadows on the ground before them. Melisande struggled to stay awake in the saddle; the exhaustion of her ordeal was compounded by a dreamy lulling sensation that surrounded her thickly the deeper they traveled into the greenwood. Her eyelids grew heavier as the sun made its way down the vault of the sky, and by dusk she had drifted off to sleep, jostled awake only for a few seconds at a time, and only by the most egregious of bumps. She surrendered to the sensation of riding the spinning world, helpless in the force of its turning, and let her chin come to rest on her chest. For the most part she was able to doze, led by Gavin's skilled hand and the horse's gentle canter.

She was dreaming of her mother, or at least a woman who looked like the painting of her mother over the fireplace in her father's library, when she felt the world stop spinning around her. Melisande was startled awake; the light was gone from the sky, leaving nothing but the faintest hint of aquamarine peeking through the trees to the west, while clouds sped through the darkening canopy above her.

She looked around for the Invoker, and spied his horse a few feet beyond her own, but the saddle of the roan was empty.

"Gavin?" she called softly, her voice trembling a little.

A gentle birdcall that blended in with the night sounds of the forest answered her. Melisande knew immediately it was the response of the Invoker, and was reassured, but still she leaned forward in the saddle and peered into the growing forest shadows, trying to find him.

The Invoker stepped out of the darkness behind the horse,

"You really have a terrible sense of direction, Lady Melisande Navarne," he said pleasantly. He extended his hand to help her down from her mount.

"Are we stopping here for the night?" Melisande asked.

"A little farther north, about a hundred paces. There's a spring-fed fairy pond there where the horses can drink."

Melisande nodded and took hold of her horse's lead, preparing to follow Gavin.

In the distance, a mournful howl rose on the wind, a high, dark whine that held steady for a moment, then undulated down the scale into silence.

The hair on the back of the little girl's neck was suddenly damp as cold chills ran through her body. She stiffened, just as the horse she was leading did.

Gavin did not turn around. "Don't panic," he said quietly. "Keep walking, and stay behind me."

A chorus like animal voices took flight on the wind, whining in discordant unison in reply. They seemed closer than the first, or at least louder.

"Wolves?" Melisande whispered. She had heard dark tales of the beasts from her nanny, and from listening to the servants talking among themselves in the buttery in hushed tones, long after she was supposed to have been to bed.

In front of her, she could hear the Invoker chuckle.

"Nothing so dramatic," he replied, his voice still soft, but stronger now. "Coyotes. Perhaps wild dogs, or half-breeds."

"Aren't they the same thing?"

"Hardly. A wolf alone will seldom bother a human, but in packs they are fierce, because they have a strong hierarchy and a sense of community. Alone, surrounded by wolves, you would be in great peril. Coyotes are cowards for the most part, carrion feeders with no real organization, smaller and weaker, preying on rabbits and moles and eating that which larger predators leave behind. With a walking stick, and an adult who has one, you will be fine. Fear not, Lady Melisande Navarne." The Invoker came to a stop beside a small forest pond, black and deep with the beginnings of water lilies fringing its edges.

"Take down your bedroll while I start the fire," he directed as the horses stepped forward and bent to drink. Melisande, suddenly thirsty, followed their lead and dipped her hand in the water, raising it to her lips, but Gavin shook his head. "I'd advise against that if you don't want to swallow a mouthful of frog eggs or, even better, tadpoles." He snorted in amusement as the little girl leapt away in revulsion, spitting and wringing her hand.

"Why do they call this a fairy pond?" she asked, curiosity replacing disgust, as she unrolled the thick blanket on the mossy ground.

The Invoker was bent over, assembling their campfire.

"I don't know," he said. "That's just what a small, spring-fed pond is called, I guess. I never really asked."

Melisande sat down on her outstretched bedroll.

"*You* don't know? You're the Invoker of the Filids, the head nature priest in all the world, and the guardian of all the holy forests, aren't you? I thought you were supposed to know about fairies and nature spirits and all those magical things. If you don't know, who on earth would you have asked?"

"*Vingka*," the Invoker said to the small bundle of sticks and dry grass. The wood ignited, snapping into flame. Gavin turned back to the girl, whose eyes were wide, and regarded her thoughtfully. "Now, that's a good question," he admitted. "I don't really know. I suppose I could have asked Llauron if I had thought of it, but alas, there was not time. I didn't serve as his Tanist, so I did not have much time to learn the lore of the Invoker from him."

Melisande uncapped her waterskin. "Have you ever seen fairies at a fairy pond?" she asked before she took a drink.

The Invoker shook his head. "I'm not certain they exist anymore, though I am told by ancient Cymrians who I respect that they once were real, long ago, before the death of magic in the world."

Melisande took another sip, then dried off her lips and recapped the skin. "I'd hardly say that magic is dead, given that you and Rhapsody can say a single word and make wood burst into flame."

Gavin shook his head again. "Some people might call that magic, I suppose, but really it's elemental lore, power left over from the creation of the world," he said seriously. "Magic was more complex. It was formed from elemental lore, but it needed a certain atmosphere in which to survive. When the sister of the Great White Tree, the ancient oak known as Sagia, was destroyed along with the Island of Serendair, where both our ancestors came from, it took a good deal of the magic out of the world, Lady Melisande Navarne. The world's a darker place than it used to be, and growing dimmer all the time." He regarded the child in the shadows of the flames. "But after what you've been through in your life, I don't suppose I have to tell you that."

Melisande inhaled, then let her breath out slowly, considering. "My father didn't believe that," she said finally. "He believed in fairies, and magic, and honor and chivalry, and that you could hang on to the ideals of better times in history, and if you did, they would one day come back. I think that's why he kept the Cymrian Museum so carefully. I used to help him polish the statues and clean the exhibits, and he would tell me of the grand times of the Luminaria, the age of Enlightenment, when the Cymrians were building great cities and cathedrals, and making advances in science and music and literature. He felt that if we maintained the memory of those times, we could recapture them someday."

Gavin leaned back against a tree as the horses moved away from the pond.

"Your father was a great man, Lady Melisande Navarne," he said quietly, without a hint of sarcasm. "May he rest peacefully beyond the Veil."

Another chorus of primal howls broke the stillness, much closer than before.

Melisande skittered away from the fire as the Invoker rose, in one smooth, quick movement, to a stand.

"Mount your horse," Gavin said, taking the mare's lead and holding her steady. Melisande complied, fumbling for the horn of the saddle, with a quick boost from the Invoker. He handed her his staff. "Hold on to this—you won't need it, but it will make you feel better."

Then he turned and walked away from the fire. The shadows seemed to open and swallow him.

Melisande waited atop the mare, nervously gripping the staff. *Well,* she thought ruefully, *you wanted responsibility and adventure, stupid. How do you like it?* She glanced around the forest glen where Gavin had made camp, at what appeared to be glittering eyes watching her from the dark recesses beyond the edge of the firelight.

Another brief howl was suddenly cut short, and in the distance she could hear the muffled sounds of cracking branches and the rustle of leaves, louder than what the wind was making. The moon broke through the clouds above the forest canopy, spilling silver light over the dark trees, making them shine eerily, their still-bare arms twisting menacingly in the dark.

Melisande swallowed the impetus to call out for the Invoker again, and waited.

The wind whispered across the glen, fluttering the grass and the newborn leaves, making the fire crackle and wink.

The Invoker appeared at last at the far edge of the glade. As always, he had made no sound in passing, but his face was grim and his body tenser than it had been when he left.

"What's wrong?" Melisande asked; her voice came out in a choked whisper. "Where did the coyotes go?"

The Invoker came back into the circle of firelight.

"I drove them off," he said. "But I think we will move on from this place just the same."

"Why? If they're gone, why don't we just wait until morning?"

Gavin exhaled. "The second set of howls you heard was the pack warning each other of our presence," he said seriously. "The first was a call to food. They were feasting on the remains of what appears to be a woman; it's hard to tell. She's unrecognizable."

The backs of Melisande's ears tingled numbly.

"I thought you said coyotes don't generally harm people, especially full-grown ones."

"They don't," said the Invoker. "I do not believe they killed her. Strange—even the foresters who travel the holy forest of Gwynwood south of here would never broach these lands. I wonder what a woman was doing here, in this place that has been sacrosanct from the beginning of history."

"Oh, no," Melisande whispered. "Oh, no." The Invoker lowered his chin and stared at her. "I—I forgot something Rhapsody told me to convey to you."

"What is that?"

Melisande fought back tears. "She said I was to tell you that the foresters should comb the woods for a lost Firbolg midwife named Krinsel, and should they come upon her, they were to accord her both respect and safe passage back to the guarded caravan to Ylorc. But I—I forgot, in all the commotion." She began to tremble so violently that Gavin reached quickly up and pulled her down from the mare, who was starting to dance impatiently in place.

"It's all right," he said soothingly, or at least an approximation of an attempt at comfort. "You've told me now. We'll keep watch for her on the way to the dragon's lair."

"But what if the foresters who set out first came upon Krinsel and killed her, not knowing she was supposed to be left unharmed?" Melisande persisted.

"Foresters are trained to accompany and guard wanderers, not kill them, unless they are threatened," the Invoker said. "Had they found a Bolg woman, lost in the woods, they would have reported it to me, and taken her back to the Circle. And they would not have left a body for carrion in any case; it's against Filidic practice. She would have been burned. I don't know what happened to this woman, if she in fact is your lost Bolg midwife, but I do know that whether you had told me at the outset or not, it would not have dissuaded Fate if she was to meet it. Stop looking for reasons to be worried, Lady Melisande Navarne. You will have more than enough of them when we get within a few miles of the dragon's cave. Now come; there's a thicket up ahead where we can pass the night in safety and a semblance of calm, if not peace."

The little girl nodded, and allowed the forester to lead her away from the fairy pond, the dark waters of which reflected back the racing clouds passing in front of the shimmering moon.

44

By the time Rath reached the glen the back of his throat was burning with the caustic taste of acidic blood.

Cautiously he slipped through the shadows, following the buzzing in his throat and sinuses, the sensation of needles running through his veins. Rath fought down the racial hatred that was causing his teeth to clench and his heart to pound furiously, concentrating instead on the demonic whisper of the name, hovering on the wind just beyond his sight. Each step, measured against ten of his heartbeats, brought him closer. Rath focused on being quiet. After such a long journey, so many centuries of pursuit, it would be cataclysmic to lose the beast at this moment, when it was almost within his grasp.

His night-sensitive eyes could see something now, at the outskirts of his vision, something tethered to the end of the gossamer thread of sound that glittered evilly in the moonlight, hanging amid the branches like a strand of spider silk, evanescent and deadly. Even the threat of what it led to could not prevent Rath from hesitating for a moment, enraptured by the beguiling beauty of it, the visualization of *kirai,* this fiber of undying connection between the wind of his heritage and the black fire of the F'dor.

A few more steps, he thought. *Slowly.*

Millennium of experience had trained him to never anticipate the host of the demon he was seeking. He had found F'dor clinging to any number of different types of men, women, and children. Rath had no fear of whatever form the monster took; he had watched dispassionately as the heads of toddlers in which the beasts had hidden exploded at the end of the Thrall ritual, because Rath understood the consequences of being swayed. Still, his curiosity got the better of him. He closed his eyes and tasted the wind on his tongue.

Hrarfa.

The name resounded in his sinuses, clear as a bell. His heart, and that of the demon's host, beat in perfect synchronicity.

Assured again that he had found his quarry, Rath opened his eyes and moved silently closer to the glen.

In the moonlight a woman was standing, her back to him, her long hair glistening in rivers of dark silver. She was stretching lazily in the moonglow, her hands running over her shoulders and through her hair in a slow, sensual dance, as if to gather the power of the heavenly light into herself. Rath inhaled; in what few tales were known about the hosts this demon had chosen, Hrarfa had rarely allowed herself to be seen in female form, the one closest to her formless spirit's own.

He took it as a fortuitous sign that she was about to die appropriately.

Portia smiled. She had heard nothing, seen nothing, in the pale light of the waxing moon. Nothing but shadows moved in the dark glade, but still she sensed a presence. The wind was high, and it caressed her human form like a lover, whispering over her skin with evanescent kisses, then moved on to tousle her hair.

The nascent fire in her poisonous spirit crackled with delight, both in the erotic sensation of wind on her skin and in the knowledge that her trap had been successfully sprung. Unlike her kin, many of whom saw the human form as a distasteful necessity for survival in the upworld, she had found the carnal delights of being encased in flesh to be a wonder that she both enjoyed and craved. There was a joy in the domination of a host, the pursuit and eventual capture of a new body, a pleasure in the eviction of its original owner through an exquisite painful devouring that left her aroused, alive in a way like no other. And there was solidity, a comforting sense of being still and real, so unlike the natural insecurity of being that was each F'dor's bane.

She had always been a bit of a risk taker, more daring than her fellow escapees of the Vault. Many of the Unspoken, as the dragons had called her kind, had discovered patience, a trait not naturally occurring in the children of dark fire, when they made their way upworld and away from their eternal prison. They had been able to build up empires slowly over the ages, trading hosts as cautiously as humans traded pieces in chess, biding their time, growing stronger in the material world, in the hope that the power they were gaining would enable them to at last find the rib of an Earthchild or some other way to free their fellows.

But she was different. She had found an intoxicating excitement in the lure, the switch, the deception of drawing unsuspecting humans to her, studying their ways, their traits, the very patterns in which they drew breath, then catching them unawares and ravaging their souls, taking their bodies for her own.

She had taken the form of a young Liringlas Skysinger once, several millennia ago and half a world away, and had learned some of the science of names, had made good use of what she had gleaned from him before she discarded his useless corpse in favor of one more interesting. She knew, as a result, how to bend her vibrations, alter the signature that her human form conveyed, until it could be almost anything that she wanted it to be.

She also learned the intricacies of male lust, something she had used to her advantage on both sides of the bed.

Eventually that led to her conquest of a First Generation Cymrian girl in Manosse, whose body was not subject to the ravages of time or age-related illness, seemingly immortal like the rest of the refugees from the Island of Serendair. She had liked the girl's name—Portia—because it was very close in sound to her own, and the additional power the young woman's lithe form and beauty gave her in enchanting foolish men through wanton sexuality. Finally, there was an irony in subsuming a Cymrian—like the F'dor, they were a race of exiles with endless time to brood about being driven from their homeland.

It was a perfect fit.

Thus, trading hosts was almost never necessary anymore.

But occasionally one came along that proved irresistible.

The Lord Cymrian had been one such temptation. Portia licked her lips, suddenly dry from the heat of anticipation and the kissing breath of the wind on them. Though she was in female form she had none of the physiological longings of a woman, did not feel the burning desire, the attraction of the flesh the way a human woman did. Rather, her desire was for the connection to power she gained in the fornication of powerful men. Her partners' surrender in the heat of passion had fed the very essence of her being, their vulnerability and openness to her dominion was an orgiastic feeling. When a man was knobbing her body, his very soul lay open and exposed.

And not only did she then have access to it, to drink in the essence of it, absorbing whatever primal, elemental power was within him, but she was able to tie that vulnerable soul to a twisting vine of Bloodthorn, the perverted sapling of Ashra, the tree of elemental fire, that grew deep within the Vault.

As any member of the Older Pantheon of demons could.

Slowly she ran her hands through her hair, raising her breasts to the wind that caressed her nipples through the thin cloth of her shirt, and sighed happily. She could hear her name on the wind; she knew it was only a matter of time before the Lord Cymrian found her. And now her quarry had arrived; she could feel his presence, even if she did not yet see him.

The tree of blood had tasted the soul of Gwydion of Manosse once before. Another of her kind, one of the Younger Pantheon, had managed to tear a piece of it free some decades ago, had experimented with it, formed a body of ice and the desecrated blood of children around it, and had used it to procreate without tapping its own soul, something a few other F'dor had tried but had failed to do. Bloodthorn had reveled in the taste of Gwydion's essence, had almost been able to find and obtain the Sleeping Child with it.

Once she had taken his body as her new host, the Unholy Tree would feed again.

The wind picked up slightly, tickling the back of her neck and arms, and tousling her long dark locks.

Portia's smile grew brighter in the light of the moon. She couldn't resist a chuckle at her own insatiability, one of the traits that the pathetic Tristan Steward had loved about her. Most F'dor of her power would have considered Gwydion of Manosse to be the ultimate prize, but she wanted more, as she always did.

She wanted his wife.

There was something bewitching about the Lady Cymrian that both disturbed and fascinated Portia. She knew immediately what it was—the sublime beauty that the common folk who swore allegiance to Rhapsody were enchanted by was nothing more than an inner core of elemental fire burning within her, something she must have absorbed from a primal source. Unlike the dark fire of the Vault from which the F'dor drew their power, the element within the Lady Cymrian was pure, untouched by the taint of evil.

And thus, a challenge.

The flesh between Portia's legs quivered at the thought. Like the corruption of a child, or the rape of a virgin, certain acts of defilement were profound in their glory, a sensation of destruction of innocence that defied description, surpassing all other acts. The chance to take a source of pure fire and twist it, damage it, pollute it until it, too, served the same mission of Void that all F'dor did, was almost too thrilling to contain. She inhaled deeply, trying to do so, and failing utterly.

I will have you, lady, she thought excitedly. *In your very husband's body, I will have you. I will feed off your passion, your surrender. And when you are open to him, vulnerable in the throes of sickening love, I will take your soul and have your body for my own as well. And right before I do, I will tell you, in his voice, what is happening, so I can pleasure myself with your horror—at least for a moment.*

And as I eat your soul, I will take your fire. But first, I will take your husband.

Her excitement was reaching a fever pitch. She could leave her next conquest waiting no longer.

The woman in the dark glen turned slowly around, her eyes glittering in the moonlight.

"I knew you would come after me," she said softly. "I knew you could not let me go."

The breeze picked up around her, caressing her hair. At first there was silence in the glade. Then a voice spoke, not the warm baritone she had come to recognize, but a flat, toneless one that vibrated against her eardrums, inaudible to the wind.

All of your kind should know the same, Hrarfa. So it has been since the beginning of history, and so it shall remain until each of you is extinguished and buried in ash, like candleflame.

Deep within her, Portia felt the words echo.

Terror, old and consuming, rose up inside her and spread through her like fire on pine. She turned to run, or tried to, but ahead of her, almost as close as her own shadow, the darkness of the glade moved.

A figure in shadow held up his hand, palm forward.

Zhvet, it said. Halt.

All around Portia the wind died suddenly. All sound, all air, seemed to vanish from the glen, leaving her breathless and gasping. Panic swelled and overran her defenses; each of her kind knew this moment, feared it almost from the beginning of Time. She, like many of the escapees of the Vault, had come to disbelieve the possibility of it, especially after the racial pogroms and campaigns against the Dhracians that all but extinguished the hunters from the face of the Earth.

Yet the time had come, and she was trapped by one that had her name.

ℜath inhaled again, allowing his skin-web to relax, and gave a tug on the first net of wind he had woven from the invisible silk of his *kirai*. The demon's body flinched, then shuddered to a frozen stance, he noted with satisfaction.

Slowly he spread his fingers and began to chant.

Bien, he canted in the inaudible buzzing voice of his first throat. It was the name of the north wind, the strongest of the four and the most easily found. The wind responded immediately, as it always did for him, wrapping itself snugly around his index finger, anchored in the first chamber of his heart.

"No," the woman whispered, rigid in place. Rath could see her eyes darting wildly even from where he stood. "No."

He hadn't expected a F'dor of the Older Pantheon to beg. In his experience, the older, more powerful demons were stoic, furious, but generally silent or threatening rather than supplicant when facing destruction. He remembered her penchant for deception and cleared his mind, returning to his state of inner calm.

Jahne, he whispered over the aperture of his second throat. This was a call to the south wind, the most constant and enduring of the winds. Rath felt the answer in both his finger and his chest, where the wind had knotted in the second chamber of his heart.

The woman screamed, not the harsh, atonal scratching of an angry F'dor, but a heartrending wail of human despair that had no impact on Rath whatsoever.

"Please," she begged, her eyes growing wide from fear and the pressure that was building up in her skull. "Have—have mercy. I know much that would be—valuable—"

Rath did not even hear her words. His focus was his entire existence now, and all sound, all fury, faded into the shadowy twilight at the edge of his consciousness, leaving nothing but the pure, ringing tones of the winds responding to his call. Satisfied with the clarity of the first two, he summoned the third wind, the wind of justice, that blew from the west.

Leuk.

"I—I know where—others are," the woman whispered now, the effort of forming words causing the veins in her neck to distend grotesquely. "I—will—tell—you—"

In the darkness of his ritual, Rath called for the last, the east wind, and waited patiently for the tentative breeze to appear in the glen, hesitantly wrapping itself around his fourth finger, entwining itself in the last chamber of his heart that was now beating erratically with the changeable breezes.

Thas. The wind of morning, the wind of death.

Like strands of spider-silk, the currents of air hung on his fingertips, waiting, tethered through the valves of his heart. Once he cast the second net and began the ending of the Ritual, he would be vulnerable; he could not stop until the body of the host and spirit of the F'dor were dead, even if he desired to, lest his own heart be sundered in his chest.

Rath opened his eyes and met the terrified gaze of the beast. The woman who had been Hrarfa's last host had been beautiful in life, with large, dark eyes that gleamed in reflected light. Those eyes brimmed with tears that he almost could believe were tied to actual emotion.

Almost.

Rath closed his hand into a fist.

The woman twitched again, still frozen in place.

With a fluid motion, he cast the net of tangled winds around the demon, anchored in his palm, cemented in his heart, and pulled with all his might.

The demon screamed again, this time in a primal voice that scratched Rath's inner ears like nails on flesh. The lovely face began to contort into something dark and hideous, with black eyes flashing hatred that was palpable. Smoke rose around her as the winds encircled her in an unbreakable cage and began to close in, pressing against her with the force of a cyclone.

Rath inhaled deeply. The Thrall ritual had reached its climax.

It was time to cut the net.

He opened his mouth slightly wider, inhaling the air over all four of his throat openings, each holding a single, unwavering note. With a skill born of uncounted hunts, Rath clicked the glottis in the back of his throat.

A harsh fifth note sliced through the monotone of the other four.

The winds screamed discordantly with the beast, tearing through the glade and causing the trees to shiver violently.

Rath felt the threads of wind attached to his fingers go slack. Quickly he clicked his tongue, tying off the ends of the wind-cage and allowing his first net to dissipate. Then he clenched his thumb to snap the wind-thread taut against the flailing spirit.

His heart thudded against his chest. Now that the beast was stationary, unable to escape, he began the final chant, the note that would build to a crescendo of such intense sound, aligned with the vibrations of their interlocked heartbeats, that the host body's blood would reverse in its path and flood the brain until it exploded.

All the air in the glen was sucked into the vortex of knotted wind swirling around the ancient monster.

The rictus of fury twisted the woman's face into a mask of even more hate. She grimaced in agony and tried to scream curses back, but her pupils were beginning to expand almost to the size of her irises, her forehead scored in deep furrows of pain.

Rath matched the intensity of her gaze. He could hear in the rising sound of imminent death the age-old calls of his Brethren, living and dead, joining him, unlimited by time and space, adding their voices to the chant. For all that the climax of the Thrall ritual left the hunter vulnerable, his heart in synchronicity with the essence of pure evil, there was a comfort in the solidarity of the cause that his race had sworn fealty to thousands of years ago.

He was too in thrall himself to hear the cracking of the branches under the feet of someone entering the glade.

45

The moon gleamed silver on the open fields, lighting a path.

"Are you all right, Owen?" Ashe called to the elderly chamberlain as they left the horses at the roadway and made their way through the grass at the glade's edge.

"Yes, m'lord," Gerald Owen replied between grunts. "I—still say that the wench is—probably hiding out in the—garrison, servicing the—"

"Desist." The Lord Cymrian stopped long enough to examine a beech tree that had sustained a snapped branch, the sap still running fresh from the break. "She did nothing, Owen, nothing save remind me of things beyond my grasp. It was wrong to send her away in such a state; there will be blood enough on my hands in due course. I don't wish to inaugurate this war with that of an innocent servant."

"Her blood's—on Tristan Steward's—hands," replied Owen, struggling to keep up. "He should have taken her—back when we moved to—Highmeadow. She wasn't—needed—"

"With any luck, her blood will remain in her veins, if we can find her soon enough," Ashe said. "Hurry, Owen—I have to return forthwith."

"I know, m'lord, I know." Owen doubled his pace and kept sight of the Lord Cymrian as he traveled through the glen by the metallic gleam of his hair, silvery red in the light of the bloody moon.

Ashe stopped in his tracks, the dragon in his blood enflamed.

In the near distance they could hear the sounds of strife, a hissing whine that thudded and scratched against the eardrums like nails. Each man put a hand to his temple as the pressure inside his head began to rise, throbbing in a sudden sharp headache. A vortex of power, ancient and deadly, was sucking all the energy, all the lore, from the air in the vicinity.

The Lord Cymrian drew his sword, flooding the woods with pulsing blue light, and ran for the glen.

Rath did not see the shadow that loomed behind him until it had already blotted out the light of the moon pooling in the glen at his feet.

He was barely aware of the sound of the chanting now. From all corners of the Earth, the voices of the Gaol were whispering in primal melodies, the fricative buzz of the common mind, adding their power to the ancient ritual. The world stopped spinning for a moment, it seemed to him, as it always did when one of the denizens of the Vault was about to be extinguished, leaving behind nothing to taint the earth.

The beast before him was in its death throes; he could see the devouring darkness of its spirit locked in the struggle to escape the woman's body it had been inhabiting for years before that body died. Even as it grappled with its looming demise, its hatred was as caustic as acid, hissing and gurgling in fury as it writhed on the ground, blood pouring from eyes locked on him in malicious fury.

Smoke, acrid and sulfurous as the stench of the Vault, began to issue forth from the demon's chest. Her eyes bulged as the blood swelled in her brain, her back arched rigidly as the pathways to it burst.

The air went suddenly dry on the verge of cracking, rent with the heat of evil being violently torn from its earthly connection. The smoke that had emerged from Portia's sundered chest swirled angrily, then dissipated, as the beast was returned to its vulnerable noncorporeal form, choking and shuddering in the grip of the Dhracian's net of wind.

The body fell to the ground, limp and without life.

Rath felt the woman fall, felt the strangling and twitching in his hand and heart as the invisible threads that bound its heart to his tugged, growing weaker with each breath, like a fish fighting on a line. The beast would continue to struggle for a few moments longer, he knew; being from the Older Pantheon, Hrarfa had a good deal more strength than the demons he had most recently destroyed.

Each twist, each attempt to sustain itself, caused Rath's heart to cramp. The unbreakable bonds of wind that tied them together were threaded through his arteries; every tug was like a knife in the chest. But Rath had sustained worse, and oddly, the pain cheered him, did his heart good. Each contraction was weaker than the one before, a sure sign that the spirit would shortly follow the body in death and into oblivion.

And so he was far too submerged in the thrall of the moment, in the import of the event, in the revel of a thousand years of searching finally coming to fruition to be aware that the glen had been entered.

Until the blow that caught him in the back with the force of a lance at full charge, snapping half of his ribs, flinging him across the glen and headfirst into a beech tree.

The shock kept him conscious, at least at first.

Faron stood still for a moment, watching the man in the robe he had just slapped away crumple to the ground like a pile of cloth.

There was a smell in this place that had brought him to it, a dry burning of the air that reminded him on an innate level of the father he had lost in the sea. He had followed that odor to the glen and had come up on a sight he didn't understand, except that whatever was being wrought was bringing back that loss in his mind.

A loss he had not been able to fathom, let alone accept.

The heft of the man was nothing; he had been flung with little more than a glancing blow. Faron looked around the glen, but saw nothing.

Aid me! Please.

The voice scratched against his ears; the stone titan slowly shook his head from side to side, recognizing the tenor of it. It was the same desperate wheedle that sometimes could be felt, if not heard, in the air around the Baron of Argaut, the man the world had once known as Michael, the Wind of Death.

Except that it was decidedly feminine.

Faron's mind was too primitive, too malformed by birth, rebirth, and circumstance, to grasp what was happening. Something primal in him warned him to run, some long-ago sense of self-preservation and horror bequeathed to him by his long-dead mother, yet at the same time there was also something familiar, something entrancing about the voice that also rang in the core of his being.

Please—shelter me. I am dying.

Faron turned to leave the glen.

Please. The voice was fading, though its tone was more desperate. *We are kin, you and I—there is dark fire in you. You and I are kin. I will nurture you, teach you. Don't let me die—please. Shelter me; take me on.*

Faron stopped. For all that the words were frantic, there was a truth in them that could not be denied. The concept of kin was one he had long since abandoned, but now, the possibility of belonging, of being related, connected, of not being alone in the world, made him hesitate, like a child longing to touch the fire that he knew could burn him.

Please.

He had seen his father battle the demon that long ago he had taken on; that demon was as much his sire as his father had been, though one had created his body and the other his spirit.

It was an ugly arrangement.

And yet it had kept the man he loved, alone among all the people in the world, alive throughout time.

And given him power beyond imagination.

Together, we would be invincible, the voice whispered, light as air now in its last moments. *I know so many corners of the world, so many secrets. Please, please—trust me. Shelter me.*

Had Faron been a man of flesh, and not of stone, he might have recognized the seduction in the voice. It was husky, even as the demon was slipping away into the ether, enticing in a way that spoke to the most primal urges in him, the longing for connection, for power.

For identity beyond that of being Michael's child and tool, and Talquist's seer and toy.

Slowly the titan nodded acceptance, answering the request with an inner surrender, knowing fully that the creature he was about to accept into the shell of his body would control him without a second thought.

Yes, he assented. *Come unto me.*

The glade suddenly became warmer, the air gaining heat and power at the same moment.

For only the second time in known history, the act of voluntary surrender to one of the Unspoken was accomplished.

The air in the glade sharpened to cracking as the lore of primordial earth blended with the demon's dark fire and the ether that was extant in the blood of Faron's Seren mother, all now fused within the statue of Living Stone.

The demon shrieked joyfully within Faron's ears as it recognized its own, the seed of tainted fire that had been bequeathed from his father. *With your lore and mine together, we are truly godlike,* it whispered, reveling in the solidity of stone flesh and the spark of ethereal magic. *We alone have the power to find and take the Sleeping Child—and then the Vault will be opened.*

The voice dropped to an almost maternal croon.

And all the world will burn beneath your feet—my child.

The demon's mutability, its innate power to change form and aspect, coursed through the titanic body, refining its features. The milky eyes that had at one time been out of place in the rough-hewn stone sharpened, became more lifelike and clear, growing lids that allowed him to blink and close them against the grit of dust. The hands stretched and extended, the rough edges resolving, the place in the palm from which the stone sword had been torn smoothed into the image of calloused skin. Each finger appeared to grow knuckles, each knuckle defined by a series of tiny grooves in the smooth earthen skin. The swirls of clay that had at one time suggested hair lengthened and became heavier, with each individual strand visible. The muscles of the shoulders, torso, genitals, and legs lengthened and striated until they appeared as human tissue, pulsing as if they were alive.

Faron raised his head to the moon, basking in the light, reveling in the sensation of wind passing over the tiny earthen hairs in the smooth skin of his stone arms.

A rasping gasp on the other side of the glen caught his attention.

The titan turned to where the man he had struck had been flung. He was lying on his side, clutching his chest, his sinewy hand held shakily aloft in the breeze that rustled the newborn leaves on the trees and scrub bushes all around him.

Behind him he could hear someone approaching.

Someone comes, the demon's voice cautioned. *Kill the Dhracian, and let us be gone from here.*

Faron lunged across the glen.

Rath lay still, struggling to breathe, feeling the hiss of air in the back of his throat from his punctured lung. He willed himself to keep from losing consciousness, softly canting into the wind a report to the Gaol of what he was witnessing, knowing that no more dire news had been sent in all the time of their upworld history.

A favorable breeze caught the words and carried them aloft, into the sky, where they would circle the wide world, bearing their dread tidings to those who could hear them.

The titan's volcanic blue eyes came to rest on him. A light of malice entered them, causing them to gleam in the reflected light of the moon, the edges tinged with the red rim of blood that occasionally betrayed demonic possession.

And then it was coming for him.

Rath reached up with a shaking hand.

For all that the currents of air had been confounding him since his arrival in the Wyrmlands, a beneficent wind was blowing through the glade, a strong, warm updraft with a heavier gust behind it. *Thank you,* he thought as the titan bore down upon him.

Just as it arrived, Rath disappeared into the wind.

𝒯he sound of cracking branches and pulsing waves of blue light flooded the small glen in the woods beneath the moon.

Ashe froze. The dryness of the air was unmistakable, the thin charge that hung, like static energy, from every current of air. Great power had been expended here, power that was primordial, elemental. The wyrm within his blood could feel it, and shrank away at the intensity of it.

And yet there was nothing to be seen, no scorched ground or trees, no violent upheaval or signs of destruction. The breeze blew gently through the glade, rustling the infant leaves that had just grown large enough to flutter on their stems in these early days of spring.

Ashe slowed his steps. It seemed to him that this innocent setting had a taint to it, an odor of malice, of deadly intent, but then the whole world was beginning to taste that way to him.

A prickling ran down his neck and over his skin; his dragon sense urged him forward, warning him of what he would find.

Deeper in the glade the woman's body was lying, curled as if she were sleeping.

The Lord Cymrian exhaled dismally, then came to her side.

"Portia," he said brokenly. He crouched down and put his hand against her neck, but it was merely an attempt to deny what he already knew. There was no breath, no warmth, no heartbeat, no sign of life—in fact, all sense that life had ever resided within her was missing. Her skin was as cold as marble, her body frozen in the rictus of death.

On her cheek a bloody tear had frozen.

"M'lord—"

"Stop, Owen. Spare me your consolation; I don't deserve it. My family's bane has always been its temper, its lack of control, and I am just the most recent one to stain our collective soul with the destruction of innocent life." Ashe took off his cloak and gently laid it over her as if it were a blanket. "My father would find this ironic, I have no doubt. All the years I walked the world unseen, hidden from the eyes of men, with no power or authority of my own, I condemned him for the decisions he made, for the suffering he willingly visited upon others in the accomplishment of his goals, all of which were intended to serve the greater good. And now that I am the one who holds the responsibility for the Alliance in my hands, I have inaugurated the prosecution of what will no doubt be a grim and devastating war with the blood of an innocent peasant."

"Innocent peasants die in war all the time, m'lord," said Gerald Owen flatly. "If you'll forgive my impertinence, you've been in enough conflicts to know this, have fought in enough battles to be inured to it. You were the one who told us that what is to come will change us all. Did you think that you were above it happening to you?"

Ashe just continued to watch the dead woman's face as clouds passed before the moon, sending shadows across it.

Gerald Owen bent to the ground. "Come, we must return to High-meadow. I'll carry the girl."

"No," said Ashe. "I'll do it." He gathered the body in his arms and carried it back to the horses, keeping it before him in the saddle as they made their way home.

Deep in his mind, mixed with the grief and guilt that was threatening to consume him, was the unmistakable and undeniable sensation of relief.

46

The Teeth
(Manteids)

★
● Night Mountain
Earth Basilica

Desert

PALACE OF JIERNA TAL

The wild ringing of bells from the distant garrison, caught and picked up by the carillon towers of Jierna Tal, dragged Talquist from his repose.

The bells of the garrisons along the border had been ringing regularly day and night each changing of duty shift since the invasion, or to signal comings and goings of troops and divisions. Until now he had barely noticed them. But this pealing was different; there was an urgency, an insistency that rang with portent and caused dread in the Emperor Presumptive's heart.

Talquist rose from his thickly besilked bed and robed himself. Then he went to the balcony and looked out over the dark streets of Jierna'sid glowing in the lanternlight and the radiance of a hundred duty fires burning at the patrol centers. The smoke of the foundries belched into the night sky, on the other side of the city, hovering in the air like a thousand ghosts before the wind carried it into the desert.

"Why are the bells ringing?" he demanded of one of the guards stationed there. "Go and discover this." The soldier bowed and hurried away down the inner steps.

He was back several agonizing minutes later.

"The titan returns, m'lord," he said.

The emperor's brows arched, then knit in consternation. He looked down over the balcony railing to the main street far below, where noise was beginning to issue forth the way it had not long ago, when Faron had first returned to the site of his animation, his birth upon the great weighing plate of the Scales. Then, it had been the noise of panic and terror, as the titanic statue had lumbered down the street, smashing ox-carts and destroying anything in its way, most especially any troops that tried to interdict it before it reached Jierna Tal.

This time, however, the sounds were muted, confused, but orderly.

The commanders had apparently ordered more light, for the signal fire braziers atop each street post roared suddenly aflame at the far end of the street, casting illuminated pools on the cobblestones below.

The titan was, indeed, approaching, casting an enormous shadow that twisted against the buildings in the dark as it neared.

The gait was somehow different. Unlike the lumbering statue that had violently lurched down the street, this time Faron's stride was measured, even; he walked slowly, standing erect, with a control that Talquist had not seen before. Walking down the center of the thorough-fare, ignoring troops and carts, he approached Jierna Tal with a manner that in a being with less innate power and musculature would not even be seen as threatening.

Talquist's eyes narrowed. The merchant in his blood was suspicious; he had many times seen men with daggers behind their backs ambling as if they had not a care in the world, and so was always suspicious when situations that should be worrisome appeared innocuous. But the shadow of the titan continued to approach in the dark, leaping in the light of the fires, while the soldiers of the city garrisons stood in the gutters and muttered under their breath.

When it finally reached the main gate in the wall surrounding the palace, the living statue stopped and raised its eyes to the balcony on which Talquist stood.

The Emperor Presumptive held his breath.

Then, with all the humility of a kitchen wench, its arms at its sides, the statue bowed.

Talquist exhaled again. He signaled to the guard on the balcony of the library below his chambers.

"Tell them to let him in directly," he said.

He turned away from the window, listening to the sounds of murmuring reduce to silence as the portcullis was lifted, the wood screaming, the chains clanking, then lowered again.

Talquist willed himself to be calm as the minutes ticked by. He sat in his great walnut chair, one of the first things he had imported from Manosse when he first took over the Mercantile, and watched himself in the mirror at the end of the room.

I look regal, he decided. *And nervous.*

The heavy footsteps thudded against the stone of the inner staircase. Talquist swallowed.

He clutched the arms of the chair as the resounding steps grew closer, forcing himself to breathe.

Finally Faron appeared in the entranceway at the top of the stairs. He cast a glance at the guards on the balcony, then pointed down the stairs.

The Emperor Presumptive considered their usefulness for a moment and, deciding that it was minimal, nodded.

"Leave us," he said.

The guards complied rapidly.

"I am glad to see you have returned," he said smoothly, years of negotiating in tenuous situations aiding him in his attempt to sound calm. "I was worried that you had become lost, or misdirected, even captured."

The muscles of the stone titan's face curled into what, in a living man, would have been a wry smile.

Please, it said. The word dripped with irony.

The emperor's black brows shot up into his hairline. He stood quickly and looked more closely at the titan, noting the appearance of details that had not been present in the rough-hewn statue of the ancient soldier he had harvested to make it. Eyebrows, lids and lashes, articulated joints and opposable digits; the formerly primitive effigy of an anonymous indigenous warrior had evolved into a giant man, a soldier of titanic proportions, an animist god of a sort.

And though its mouth did not move, it could speak.

The voice it spoke with belied its appearance. Not the deep bass or thundering roar that might have served as a complement to its appearance,

Faron's voice was instead harsh and high-pitched, with a crackling edge to it. In that voice the echo of other voices could be heard, some low and soft, others shrieking, all brimming with a nascent and ominous power that made the skin on Talquist's neck prickle in fear.

"What—what is your intention now, then, Faron?" he asked. "When I heard that you had left the battle at Sepulvarta, I thought perhaps you had tired of leading the army."

I had.

"Then why are you back?" Talquist set his teeth, knowing that there was nowhere to run.

I wish to continue our association for now, the statue said in its harsh voice. *But on my terms.*

Suddenly Talquist relaxed. He had been in the Mercantile long enough to recognize when a deal was about to be laid on the table that would be beneficial to both sides.

"All right," he said. "What are your terms?"

The statue's eyes met his directly, sizing him up.

I will lead your army. We will take the Middle Continent, even unto the northern reaches of the Teeth. The land will be yours—but I want a particular prize.

"Certainly," Talquist said quickly. "What sort of prize?"

Like you, I seek a Child as well—a child that sleeps in the mountains. I want that child—and the scales. All of them.

The emperor's throat tightened.

"I've—I've never denied you access to your scales, Faron," he said quickly. "Or to mine."

The titan's blue eyes gleamed more brightly.

They will all *be mine, Emperor. One way or the other.*

Talquist inhaled. The threat in the sharp voice was unmistakable.

The thought of relinquishing the violet scale that had given him his throne, and his power, was a loss almost too painful to contemplate. Even the knowledge that the titan was offering to fulfill one of the crucial elements in his greatest plan was scarce comfort; the ancient piece of a dragon's carapace had taken root in his soul, had appeared in his dreams almost every night from the moment he had found it in the sand and fog of the Skeleton Coast buried beneath the bones of ships of the Cymrian Third Fleet. He had spent a good deal of his life trying to discover what it was, and what it could do, apprenticing himself to ships' captains and miners, merchants and priests. All that servitude was finally beginning to reap a benefit.

But, he reminded himself, should he try to withhold it now, Faron would grind him into pulp where he stood.

It seemed little enough to pay for getting everything he desired.

The merchant met the titan's eyes, then went to the secret chamber, returning a moment later with the scale swathed in its velvet wrapping. He walked directly to Faron and extended his hand.

"Done," he said.

The titan smiled.

In that moment Talquist thought he could hear the rumblings of the gears of the world turning.

47

GURGUS PEAK

"Consider this," Rhapsody said as she unrolled a sheet of parchment on the worktable in front of Achmed, Grunthor, and Omet. "The lower-mid spectrum, the blue and green sections, *Kurh-fa* and *Brige-sol*, are more innocuous in their powers; they alter less of the reality of the world as it is. Part of this is because of the length of the waves of light, the song that they emit is the longest in duration. This is because so much of the blue spectrum is present in the reflection of the sky, which is why the Liringlas are so attuned to this lore, revering the sky as they do. Knowing the blue is key to the rest of the spectrum. So since their primary powers in the Lightcatcher are scrying and obscuration, perhaps these would be the safest to test first. The risks are not as great as some of the others, at least of the primary powers."

"Indeed," said Achmed. "Though the secondary powers may be even more risky."

"I'm not in any way prepared to begin experimenting with the secondary or tertiary scales," Rhapsody said seriously. "The consequences of misuse are far too great. But if you want to try and see if the blue spectrum will add further cover to the realm, and keep prying eyes even farther at bay than they are at the moment, I suppose I am ready to attempt it. It's not without risk—nothing with this instrumentality is. But it's the safest of the ones we have, a little like only leaving your hand unarmored upon entering the lion's den instead of your head."

Bolg king.

Achmed went rigid. The voice in his ear was light and strained.

I am in the causeway. The wind went silent for a moment, then rustled in his ear again, this time the voice weaker. *Come.*

Achmed was on his feet before Rhapsody could blink. She and Grunthor followed him out of the mountain peak and down to the outer battlements of Canrif overlooking the canyon that separated the city from the Blasted Heath.

In the tunnel Rath was waiting, crouched on the floor, his arms around his middle, struggling to breathe. His head was shiny with sweat, his skin sallow in the dim light from the torches beyond the causeway.

"The—news I bring—could not be—worse," the Dhracian said, gasping between breaths. "The Gaol—know of this—but—you could not—hear me—"

"Tell me," Achmed ordered as Rhapsody knelt beside Rath, loosening his shirt.

The Dhracian attempted to wave her away. "I found—the—beast's host and—had her in—Thrall, but I was—interrupted—"

"By what?" the Bolg king demanded. "What could even have entered the area with all that power in the air?"

"A—man of Living—Stone," Rath whispered as the Lady Cymrian began to softly sing a chant of sustenance, the healing reserved for those on the battlefield at the point of death. "Titanic—and able—to walk under his—own—power. The demon—escaped—and has found—a new—host—in him.

"And it is—invulnerable."

The two Bolg looked at each other as Rhapsody continued her ministrations.

"We are going to need to take risks earlier than we planned," Achmed said finally. "While it's imperative to test the blue spectrum, tomorrow the first rays of the sun should be aimed at the Blood Saver panel—I assume you agree, Rhapsody."

She looked up at them, then somberly nodded.

"Grunthor, carry him to the Lightcatcher," Achmed instructed. He turned to go, but Rath seized the edge of his robe and dragged him back a step.

"Hear me," the Dhracian whispered, his eyes alight with fire. "You—now no longer—have a—choice. Someone has to—kill—this titan. It is beyond—the skills of—the Gaol. No—more can you remain—a king—"

Achmed snatched the hem of his garment from the Dhracian's failing hand.

"That is where you are wrong, Rath," he said flatly. "I will remain a king for as long as it suits me. One of the few things Ashe has ever said that I agree with is that a king must stay and hold the land, until there is no choice but for him to leave. For now, no matter what goes on in the world outside, I will remain here. I have a Child to guard, and if nothing else, I am the last bastion in that fight.

"But," he continued as the Sergeant-Major lifted Rath from the ground, "now that the F'dor has chosen a host who is formed of Living Stone, elemental *earth,* I happen to have an assassin who is just perfect for the job."

Grunthor broke into a gigantic grin.

"Oh, goody! An' it ain't even my birthday! Thank you, sir."

He proceeded back up the tunnel, whistling a merry tune.